DUST AND STEEL

Patrick Mercer joined the army from university. He completed tours of Northern Ireland and commanded his battalion in Bosnia. He left the army as a colonel and became the defence correspondent for the *Today* programme before becoming an MP.

Also by Patrick Mercer

To Do and Die

PATRICK MERCER

Dust and Steel

HARPER

Harper
An imprint of HarperCollins*Publishers*
77–85 Fulham Palace Road,
Hammersmith, London W6 8JB

www.harpercollins.co.uk

This paperback edition 2011
2

First published in Great Britain by
HarperCollins 2010

Copyright © Patrick Mercer 2010

Patrick Mercer asserts the moral right to
be identified as the author of this work

A catalogue record for this book is
available from the British Library

ISBN: 978-0-00-730274-1

Set in Sabon by Palimpsest Book Production Limited,
Falkirk, Stirlingshire

Printed and bound in Great Britain by
Clays Ltd, St Ives plc

Mixed Sources
Product group from well-managed
forests and other controlled sources
www.fsc.org Cert no. SW-COC-001806
© 1996 Forest Stewardship Council

FSC

To my wife, Cait

Acknowledgements

A second book requires those who have to tolerate the author to be even more forbearing than the first book, as everything needs to be tested against earlier efforts. Accordingly, I must thank my family, the real Richard Kemp, Sue Gray, Heather Millican and a host of others who have read and read these pages. I must also thank my agent, Natasha Fairweather of APWatt and my indefatigable editor, Susan Watt.

Skegby
February, 2010

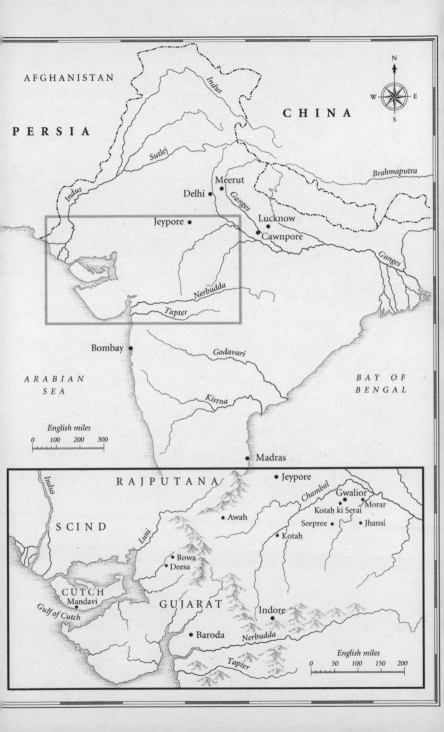

ONE

Bombay

'Get into four ranks, yous.' Six foot tall and completely poised, McGucken pushed and shoved the first couple of dozen men onto the jetty into a semblance of order. At thirty-two, the Glasgow man looked ten years older. A life spent outdoors had left a wind-tan and myriad wrinkles on his face that his whiskers couldn't hide, whilst his Crimea medals – both British and Turkish – and the red-and-blue-ribboned Distinguished Conduct Medal spoke of his achievements and depth of experience.

'They look quite grumpy, don't they, Colour-Sar'nt?' Captain Tony Morgan tried to make light of the situation. He, too, looked old for his years. He was shorter and slimmer than McGucken: school, much time in the saddle or chasing game, and Victoria's enemies had left him with no spare flesh, whilst a Russian blade at Inkermann had given him the slightest of limps. He was twenty-seven and by girls in his native Ireland would be described as a 'well-made man', dark blond hair and moustaches bestowing a rakish air that he wished he deserved. On his chest bobbed just the two Crimea campaign medals but a brevet-majority – his reward for the capture of The Quarries outside Sevastopol two years before – was worth almost fifty pounds a year in additional pay.

1

'Better load before they push those sailors out the way, don't you think, Colour-Sar'nt?' Morgan watched as the mob surged forward. 'Must be three hundred or more now.'

'No, sir, them skinny lot'll do us no harm. They've not got a firelock amongst 'em; they're just piss an' wind.' McGucken had been at Morgan's side through all the torments of the Crimea, watching his officer develop from callow boy from the bogs of Cork into as fine a leader as any he'd served under. Muscovite shells, and endless nights together on windswept hillsides or in water-logged trenches had forged a friendship that would be hard to dent, yet there remained a respectful distance between them. 'Let's save our lead for the mutineers. We'll push this lot aside with butts and the toe of our boots, if needs be.'

Morgan knew McGucken was right, and as the next boat-load of men shuffled their way into disciplined ranks, he reached down the ladder towards his commanding officer, Lieutenant-Colonel Henry Hume. He was another old Crimea hand whose promotion and Companion of the Bath had come on the back of the efforts of some of the boys who now jostled in front of him in the heat of the Indian sun.

'Right, Morgan, as soon as your men are ready, let's get moving to the fort. The other companies will follow as soon as they're ashore, but gather these sailors in as we go. They may be useful.' Hume stood no more than five-foot seven and wore his hair and whiskers long. At thirty-eight, he was young to be in command of an infantry battalion.

Morgan looked quizzically towards the angry crowd.

'Come on, we've got the Honourable East India Company to save. Then you'll be wanting your dinner, won't you, Corporal Pegg?' chaffed Hume.

'Nice quart o' beer would suit me, sir,' replied the chubby corporal. Pegg was twenty, a veteran who had been with the Grenadier Company for his entire service, first as a drummer and now with a chevron on his sleeve.

The piece of sang-froid worked. It was as if the crowd simply wasn't there. Morgan had seen Hume do this before – he would defuse a crisis with a banality, speaking with an easy confidence that was infectious. Now all uncertainty vanished from the men and at McGucken's word of command, the ninety-strong scarlet phalanx strode down the jetty and fanned out into column of platoons as they reached the road. As the dust rose from their boots, the crowd melted away in front of them, the cat-calling and jeers dying in the Indians' throats as the muscle of a battle-ready company of British troops bore down upon them.

'Morgan, this fellow, Jameson, here, knows the town and the way to the fort.' Hume had grabbed one of the sailors who, along with the rest of his and two other civilian crews, had been the only armed and disciplined force available to help the slender British garrison of Bombay when the talk of mutiny had started.

'I do, sir. Commanding officer of the Tenth is waiting for you there.' Jameson had seen Colonel Brewill of the 10th Bombay Native Infantry just a couple of hours before, when he was sent to guide the new arrivals over the mile and a half from the docks up to the fort. 'Mr Forgett as well, sir.'

'Who's he, Jameson?' asked Hume.

'Oh, sorry, sir, he's the chief o' police. Rare plucked, he is. Been scuttling about dressed like a native ever since we got 'ere, 'e as, spyin' on the Pandies at their meetings an' their secret oath ceremonies.' The squat sailor's eyes shone out of his tanned, bearded face. 'Things was fairly calm till yesterday when he arrested three of the rogues, 'e did, an' took 'em off to the fort. Then the crowds came out an' the whole town's got dead ugly.'

The company tramped on towards the fort, red dust rising in a cloud behind them, their rifles sloped on their right shoulders, left arms swinging across their bodies in an easy rhythm. They were an impressive sight. The Grenadier

Company still had the biggest men of the Regiment in their ranks, and at least a third of them had seen fierce fighting before. At the very sight of such men even the parrots fled squawking on green and yellow wings from the thick brush that lined the road into the centre of Bombay.

'Bugger off, you mangy get.' Only a pye-dog with a patchy coat had chosen to stay and investigate the marching column, but with a shriek, and its tail curled tightly over its balls, the cur ran off towards a drainage ditch as the toe of Lance-Corporal Pegg's boot met its rump.

'Fuckin' 'orrible, sir. Did you see all them sores on its back?' Pegg was adept at casual violence, particularly when the recipient posed little threat to himself.

'I did, Corporal Pegg, but I should save your energies for the mutineers, if I were you.' Reluctantly, Morgan had grown to value Pegg, for whilst the young non-commissioned officer lacked initiative, he was always to hand in a crisis.

''Ave this lot of sepoys gone rotten then, sir, like that lot up by Delhi?'

On board ship news had been scarce. The first mutinies in the Bengal Presidency in Meerut, Delhi, Cawnpore and Lucknow had started in May, rumours of terrible battles and massacres filtering down to the British. Now, a month later, no one was sure whether the native troops across Madras and especially the three sepoy battalions here in Bombay were fully trustworthy or not. So news that the *Polmaise* had been diverted from her journey to the Cape, with half a battalion of experienced British troops aboard, had been extremely welcome.

'I don't know, Corporal Pegg, but we shall find out soon enough, if we can get past those things,' replied Morgan, as the company approached the arched timber doors of the City Fort, where four camels and their loads of hay were jammed tightly together.

'Com . . . paneee, halt!' McGucken brought the men to a

stamping stop that sent two great brown and black scavengers squawking out of the nearby peepul trees. 'It'll take a while to get this lot clear, sir.' There was no sign that the camel drivers, despite liberal application of their sticks, were clearing the snorting creatures from the gateway. 'Think this is deliberate, sir?'

'What, to stop us getting into the fort, Colour-Sar'nt?' The idea hadn't occurred to Morgan, who had been too busy watching the strange swaying animals to think of any subterfuge.

Now he looked up above the gate to the crenellated sentry points where two sepoys gazed down at the new arrivals. Both had their rifles pointing over the walls over the heads of the British.

McGucken had noticed them as well. 'Don't like the look of that pair either, sir. Shall we load?'

But before Morgan could make a decision, pushing low beneath the bellies of the camels came a young Englishman in scarlet shell jacket and the white trousers, which instantly marked him out as an officer of one of the Bombay regiments. His shoulders brushed the camels' underbellies, and as he straightened up he subjected the drivers to a stream of what sounded to the 95th, at least, as remarkably fluent Hindi. His comments were met with redoubled efforts with stick and slaps, followed by renewed complaints from the animals.

'Where's your company commander, you?' the officer asked the nearest soldier. Unfortunately for him, it was Corporal Pegg, who studiously ignored him, preferring to stand at the regulation position of 'at ease', weapon tucked comfortably at his shoulder, left foot forward, hands clasped over his belly.

'You, are you deaf? Where's your company commander?' the Bombay officer repeated in a impatient growl.

'Oh, sorry, sir.' Pegg suddenly came to life, his left thumb casually stroking the pair of Crimea medals on his chest.

'Thought you must have been talking to some native. My name's not "you". I'm *Corporal* Pegg of *Her Majesty's* Ninety-Fifth. Captain Morgan's yonder, sir, with *Colonel* Hume . . .' Pegg pointed over his shoulder to where both officers stood, before adding, very quietly, '. . . you cunt.'

With a sidelong glance the young officer passed down the ranks, before seeing Morgan and Hume and stamping to attention, his hand flying to the peak of his white-covered cap.

'Sir, I'm Lieutenant Forbes McGowan, adjutant, Tenth Bombay Native Infantry. My commanding officer, Commandant Brewill, has asked me to bring you into the fort, but to keep the men outside.'

'If that's what your colonel wants, McGowan, of course I will.' Hume immediately took charge, 'But would it not be better to get my boys within the fort?'

'The commandant doesn't want anything too unusual at the moment, sir. Things are pretty tense, what with the arrests last night; the slightest little thing might set the sepoys off.' As if to illustrate the young officer's fears, a ripple of sharp cracks sounded from within the fort. The sentries on the walls whirled round, eyes wide with alarm, rifles brought to the aim in an instant. The British troops, too, started and tensed at the noise.

'It's all right, sir. It's just the bloody workmen that are stripping planks off the old barrack roofs and chucking them to the ground. But you see what I mean . . . everyone's as tight as whips at the moment. Can you just get your men to wait here, sir, brew tea or anything that looks normal? Please don't do anything that might unsettle our people further; just act as if everything's harmony and bloody light, please, sir.'

Leaving the men under McGucken's charge, Hume and Morgan followed McGowan back under the bellies of the still wedged camels, just as one let go a great stream of steaming, yellow liquid, much to the delight of the waiting men,

'Better to be pissed off than pissed on, ain't it, sir?' yelled Corporal Pegg as the officers crouched and scrambled into the fort's interior.

Inside the high stone walls, the sun beat down on a deserted parade ground of packed, dusty soil. At the far side, some two hundred paces away, were two flagpoles, one naked whilst at the head of the other, motionless, hung the colours of the Honourable East India Company. Just beyond, were the main buildings of the fort, white-washed offices on two storeys set behind porched verandas. Two sentries mechanic-ally paced their beats, slowly marching towards each other before facing about, perfectly in time, and strutting back to their grey-painted, wooden watch-boxes.

As the three officers approached, the sepoys halted and faced their fronts before bringing their rifles to a smart present.

'They look trim enough, McGowan,' Colonel Hume said quietly as he, as senior officer, returned their salute. 'Why d'you think they might be wobbly?'

Certainly, there was nothing in the men's bearing that suggested unrest. Both were clean and smart in white trousers and cross-belts over old-fashioned scarlet, swallow-tailed coatees. Their peakless shakos and sandals looked odd to the Western military eye, but the new Enfield rifles were well oiled, their fixed bayonets glittered in the sun, and both men – smaller than their typical British counterparts – looked alert and intelligent.

'Aye, sir, they probably are . . .' McGowan broke off, telling the sentries to order arms, '. . . the problem seems to be just amongst a few hotheads, but I'll let Commandant Brewill tell you everything before the court martial starts.'

'No, it's not been like that here in Bombay.' Colonel Brewill, commanding officer of the 10th, had been defensive with

7

Hume and Morgan from the moment they had been ushered into his office.

On the upper floor of the fort, the room was spacious enough, though darkened by the slatted blinds at the windows, shut against the midday sun. Above their heads a four-by three-foot rush screen, or punkah, swung on hinges, flapping gently backwards and forwards on a string pulled by a boy who crouched on the veranda outside.

'Our men are very different from those up in Bengal. I've always said that you mustn't keep all your high-caste men together in one company or battalion. The Bengal officers have always had a wholly misplaced conceit – in my eyes at least – in the fact that all their people come from the higher castes and classes. That's all very well, but some of those buggers are touchy as hell. Why, I'm told that some of the Brahmins regard their food as being defiled if one of us walks past and lets his shadow fall upon it whilst it's being prepared. No, we recruit from across all castes, and whilst our fellows might not be as big and well set up as those northerners, they're the better soldiers for it,' Brewill continued.

'Ain't you got any high-caste men in your regiment, then, Brewill?' Hume asked, genuinely trying to grasp the size of the problem.

'Yes, but not as many as the Bengal regiments tend to have, and there's always been a tradition of slackness and mollycoddling of the jawans up there that would never be tolerated in this Presidency,' Brewill replied sniffily.

Despite a lack of solid news during the voyage, Hume had done his best to explain to the officers the situation that they were likely to face when dealing with the mutiny. They were fully aware that there were three Presidencies, through which 'John' Company ruled and administered British India. So far, the outbreak of trouble had been confined to only one of them – Bengal.

'At the same time that the first mutinies started last month, we issued the latest Enfields and I expected drama when the troops had to draw new cartridges. The rumour in Bengal was that they were greased with pork or beef fat – both degrading to Musselmen and Hindus when the paper cartridge is torn open with the teeth – in a deliberate attempt to break the men's caste before forcing them to adopt Christianity. That shave spread like wildfire with mysterious bloody chapattis being hawked around the place as some sort of mystical sign that British rule would come to an end one hundred years after it started.

'The dates were right – it was the anniversary of Clive's victory at Plassey in 1757, but the rest was complete balls, of course, but in the light of all the trouble, we allowed our men to wax their own rounds with whatever they chose, and there were no difficulties. Then, a couple of weeks ago we got orders to start warlike preparations for operations against the mutineers around Delhi, and that's when the boys got a bit moody. It was one thing for the men to be outraged by the news of the fighting, but quite another to be told that they were going to have to fight against their own people, no matter what their caste or background.' Brewill was doing his best to present his own regiment's conduct in the most benign light.

'But we'll need every armed and disciplined man in India, won't we, sir, if we're going to crush the mutinies?' Morgan asked. He was trying to keep up with Brewill's account, but was struggling to understand the niceties of caste and religion, of what was taboo and what was not. He thought they had difficulties with some of the papists in his own regiment, but clearly it was nothing compared to this. 'So are all the native regiments here in Bombay suspect, sir?'

'Well, the Tenth seem sound enough, but we're less sure about the Marine battalion, and the Sappers and Miners . . .' Brewill obviously hated to malign his command, but he knew friends of his and their families who had been murdered and hurt by their own men, apparently loyal and trusted sepoys alongside whom they had fought and campaigned for many years. Reluctantly he recognised that the same could happen in Bombay.

'. . . but let Forgett here explain in more detail.'

A short, slight, sun-browned man in his early thirties, wearing dun native pyjamas had come quietly into the room. His black hair was slicked back, his moustache and beard worn a little too long in the native fashion, whilst around his waist was a broad, leather belt with a tulwar on his left hip and an Adams revolver clipped on his right. His bright, intelligent eyes flicked across all of them.

'Gentlemen, allow me . . . I'm Forgett, thanadar of Bombay police. I've a little over three hundred native constables and sergeants at my hand, but they're as good as useless whilst there's unrest amongst the troops – they're mostly low caste and in thrall to the sepoys.' Forgett looked at Hume and Morgan to see if they were taking in what he was telling them. 'But what they are good at is tittle-tattle. They let me know that a series of badmashes, from way up country around Cawnpore, were at work amongst our troops and by dint of good intelligence—'

'What he means by that, gentlemen, is some of the most valorous work I've ever seen,' Brewill cut in. 'He disguised himself so that I would have taken him for a *bishti* an' went poking around amongst the bloody Pandies—'

'Forgive my ignorance, sir, but who or what is a Pandy?' Morgan asked. 'Everyone uses it about the mutineers, but no one can explain it.'

'Oh, Sepoy Mangal Pandy of the 34th led the first uprising in Barrackpore in May; he was hanged in short order, but he's become a hero to the mutineers, and they go into action yelling his name, I'm told.' Forgett took up where he'd left off: 'Anyway, we got to hear that our troops would reject the new cartridges the day after tomorrow when the first drafts are due to march from Bombay for Delhi, and refuse to serve against their "brothers" in Bengal.'

'Aye, you could cut the atmosphere here with a rusty razor for the past couple of weeks,' Brewill continued. 'The men seemed detached enough from the mayhem of the last months in Bengal, but when we were told to prepare for operations, the lads got sulky. We knew you were on your way, but Forgett had to act yesterday and arrest the three ringleaders before you got here. Since then we've had mobs out on the streets, and if it hadn't been for the merchant sailors, I suspect that there might have been outrages committed against some of the European wives and families already.'

'How many Europeans are there here, Brewill?' asked Hume.

'There's about three hundred women, nippers and some Eurasians in the cantonment below the fort; couple o' hundred sailors, and Bolton's troop of Bombay Horse Artillery – we'll use them for the executions after the court martial.'

Hume and Morgan exchanged glances.

'Yes, Hume, I know it's a nasty business, but I'll have to ask you to try the scum that we've caught and also to oversee the executions. Queen's Regulations specify that trials and punishment should, as far as possible, be carried out by officers and men from other corps, as you know. The gunners will blow the rascals from the muzzles of their guns, but I shall have to ask your men to be ready to open fire, along with Bolton's guns, if any of our men get ticklish.'

Both 95th officers were more than familiar with this grisly but traditional method of execution for disaffected, native troops. It had been used since Clive's time a century before, borrowed from the Indians themselves by the British as a way of further defiling the victim in death.

'Again, sir, please don't think I'm trying to interfere, but if you're preparing execution parties already, doesn't that suggest that a decision on the men's guilt has been arrived at even before they've stood trial?' Morgan knew he was speaking for Hume.

Caustic smiles spread over the faces of Colonel Brewill and the policeman. 'Fine words, young Morgan, but you've no idea what those brutes have done around Lucknow.' So far, Brewill had been measured. Now his voice sank to a flat whisper. 'Don't you know what they did to General Handscome and half the European and Eurasian civilians up there, or their depravity in Bareilly? Why, Commandant Peters of the Third Light Cavalry had to watch whilst his wife and children were butchered in front of him before they roasted him to death over a fire – his own men, mark you. No, there's no place for mercy here.'

'Or justice, sir?' Morgan couldn't stop himself.

'Justice, goddamn you?' Brewill's voice rose as all attempts to control himself disappeared. 'What fucking justice did those poor souls get from the animals in Delhi last month? Have you read Mrs Aldwell's account – how twenty or more European ladies and children were roped together like beasts of the field and then chopped to pieces by servants they thought they could trust? Don't come the nob with me just because you chased a few Muscovites around the Crimea. No, heed my words: unless we show our people just who's in charge, we'll have the same problems here, and if you think that you can do without the help of the Bombay regiments to put those whoresons in Bengal back in their place then you're very much mistaken. The only answer is to give them a sharp lesson, and if that means getting blood on your lilywhite Queen's commission hands, then you'd best get used to it!'

The room was suddenly silent. The punkah squeaked and an insect chirruped from the rafters whilst Hume, Forgett and Morgan looked at Brewill in shocked embarrassment.

'Right, Morgan, Mr Forgett, leave us, please.' Hume spoke quietly, soothingly, as Brewill mopped at his great red face with a silk square. 'Wait outside, please. I will issue orders once the commandant and I have decided how to proceed.'

Morgan stood on the veranda with Forgett outside the commandant's office, the two colonels' voices just audible within.

'Dear God, Forgett, I didn't mean to twist Colonel Brewill's tail like that.' Morgan ducked his head to accept the light for the cheroot that the policeman had given him, before blowing a cloud of blue smoke up into the air, outlining the dozen hawk buzzards that wheeled on the thermals above the barracks, waiting to swoop on any carrion.

'Indeed, Morgan, but you did.' Forgett paused and picked a piece of loose tobacco off his tongue. 'You must understand that the unthinkable has happened here. There have been mutinies and trouble from time to time – you'll have heard tell of the affair at Vellore in the year Six, and General Paget's execution of a hundred lads from the Forty-Seventh back in Twenty-Four . . .'

Morgan was loosely aware of troubles in the past in India, but tribulations in John Company's forces hardly caused a ripple in the ordered world of British garrison life and he had never bothered to learn the details.

'. . . but nothing on this scale. Our whole lives have been turned upside down, even here in Bombay where, DV, nothing will happen – so long as we act quickly.'

Morgan thought back to all those discussion that he had had at home, Glassdrumman in County Cork. Finn, the family groom, had ridden knee to knee with Indian cavalry regiments against the Sikhs, whilst Dick Kemp, his father's best friend, had not only led sepoys in war, he was even now in command of the 12th Bengal Native Infantry up in Jhansi. Morgan remembered the fondness and respect that both men had shown for the Bengali soldiers and how Kemp's life was interwoven with the whole subcontinent, its culture and mystique. Now he had no idea if the great burly, cheerful man's regiment had turned or not; whether Kemp was even alive.

'And you've got to remember what sort of people we are, what sort of backgrounds we come from.' Morgan shifted uncomfortably, recognising Forgett as one of those people who didn't shy away from saying the unsayable, and made to interrupt. 'No, hear me; most of us don't come from money like most of you. Why, I wanted a commission in a sepoy regiment – it would have cost a fraction of what your people have to fork out – but still my family couldn't afford it. So, I came into the police service; this post's cost me not a penny and I have to live off my pay. My poor wife – when we met and she agreed to marry me, she thought that her life would just be England transposed, a dusty version of Knaresborough and how difficult she found the first couple of years – didn't I catch it! Anyway, once the children began to arrive she took to it more and, I think it's fair to say, we've made a go of it in our modest way. Now all that's in peril, any chance to live like a gentleman and bring my children up respectably may just go up in smoke, so please be careful how you treat the things we hold dear.'

Morgan thought of Glassdrumman and its acres. His family were certainly not especially rich, nor well connected, but they lived in a different sphere from those who would be referred to, he supposed, as the 'ordinary' classes. It made him ponder Brewill's earlier comments.

'But tell me, Forgett, how does this caste business really work? It seems mighty tricky for soldiers who are expected to act under one form of discipline to have another, unspoken, code that they've got to obey.' Morgan suspected that Forgett's explanation would be rather more incisive than Brewill's earlier one.

The policeman gave a short laugh. 'Tricky . . . yes, that's an understatement. You'll mainly come across Hindus serving with the Bengal Army up north where you're going, but don't be surprised when you meet Musselmen and Sikhs. You won't be able to tell the difference, but the Hindu troops will treat them as untouchables – *Mleccha* – just as they regard us so, despite our rank or influence.'

'But you're talking just about classes, aren't you? What about this caste business?' asked Morgan.

'There are four classes in Hinduism . . .' Forgett paused before continuing, '. . . they are a fundamental part of the religion, and grafted on top of them are a terribly complicated series of castes, or jati. The caste is based on a mixture of where a man comes from, his race and occupation, and is governed by local committees of elders. No good Hindu wants to offend them or be chucked out for mixing with those of a lower class or generally breaking the rules. That might result not just in his being expelled from his caste – his place in society – but also losing his peg in the cosmic order of things – his class.

'Whilst all this might sound like mumbo jumbo to us, try to explain our social classes, or the difference between Methodism and Baptism to a native. And the whole damn thing has got to be made to work alongside the needs of the army or the police – as you rightly observe, Morgan. It's not too bad down here in Bombay where the people are much more mixed, but in the Bengal Presidency, where most of the sepoys are of the higher classes cack-handed attempts to introduce the men to Christianity, or new regulations that troublemakers can interpret as attempts to defile the caste of a man, have been at the heart of the trouble. So, we may struggle with the differences in what sort of commission we hold or whether we're Eton or Winchester types, but out here there's a whole bucketload of further complications,' said Forgett with a slight smile.

Morgan was prevented from seeking further knowledge by the door of the office opening with a bang. Hume sauntered

15

out onto the veranda, his eyes narrowed against the glare.

'Ah, cheroots, what a grand idea.'

Morgan had seen this act from Hume before – and each time it worked like a charm. As Forgett offered his leather case to Hume, then lit the cigar he'd chosen, Morgan remembered just such coolness as the bullets sang around Hume at the Alma and the splinters hummed at Inkermann. Whilst Brewill fussed over documents at the desk inside the office, Hume gave his orders.

'Right, Morgan, be so kind as to send me an escort of a sergeant and ten. They'll bring any sepoys whom I find guilty and condemn down to the Azad *maidan*, where the three Bombay regiments are, apparently, already.' Hume took a long pull on his cheroot. 'By now the other three companies of ours should be waiting outside the fort where we left your lot, and the troop of Horse Gunners should be there as well.'

Morgan looked from the raised veranda towards the gate of the fort. The camels had now been cleared and knelt in an untidy row whilst the fodder was unloaded from their backs. He thought he could just see movement and hear the noise of horses outside the gates.

'I want you to take command of the other companies until I get to you. Yes, I know,' Hume waved Morgan's embarrassment aside before he could even utter his objection. '*Captain* Carmichael will just have to take orders from a brevet major until I'm available.'

Richard Carmichael was the senior captain in the Regiment, but he would have to bow to Morgan's brevet rank and the imprimatur of the commanding officer.

'The gunners will know what to do with any prisoners that have been condemned, but I'm much more worried about the native battalions. You'll be guided down to the *maidan* by one of Brewill's officers where you should find the Tenth, the Marines and the Sappers waiting for you – about eighteen hundred native troops all told. They'll be carrying their weapons, but they've got no ammunition, so confidence and bottom will be everything. Make a judgement and load the guns with canister, and our men with ball if the sepoys look ugly, but whilst you have my complete authority to open fire if necessary, do be aware that it will be the sign not only for the sepoys to rise up – those that live – but also the mob that Brewill tells me are already gathering.'

Morgan looked into Hume's cool, blue eyes. He'd had plenty of responsibility thrust onto his young shoulders before and it was said by many that, had he been in a more fashionable regiment, his achievements before Sevastopol would have been recognised with a Companion of the Bath or, failing that, one of the new Victoria Crosses, rather than a brevet, but this was a different sort of problem. Now he would be heavily outnumbered in a situation that he had barely grasped, where a misjudgement would be catastrophic. Barely four hundred British infantry and gunners would have to cow several thousand angry Indians and, if they failed, the mutiny would almost certainly spread right across the Bombay Presidency.

'What in God's name is going on, Morgan?' As Morgan emerged from the now clear gate of the fort, he was hailed by Richard Carmichael, commander of Number One Company.

As usual, Carmichael was perfectly turned out. He'd been the very definition of irritation on the voyage out from Kingstown with an inflatable mattress, waxed-cotton waterproofs and all manner of gutta-percha luggage and opinions to match. Now he stood before Morgan in his scarlet shell jacket and snowy cap, pulling gently at a slim cigar whilst his company and the other two of this wing of the 95th trooped up to join Morgan's own men.

'What are the commanding officer's orders; what does he want me to do?'

There was almost six foot of the dapper Harrovian, and whilst he wore the Crimea medals with aplomb, there wasn't a man present who hadn't heard the rumours of his ducking from the fight at Inkermann. 'I'll tell you as soon as the other companies are complete, Carmichael,' Morgan replied as calmly as possible. 'Bugler, blow "company commanders", please.'

This was going to be difficult, thought Morgan. That prig Carmichael was senior to him by a long chalk; indeed, he'd served under him for three months in the Crimea until he was wounded – and he'd hated every minute of it. But his brevet rank of major now meant that he was the senior captain present in the field and, especially as Colonel Hume had given him his authority, he would take command of the four companies present – and Carmichael could go hang.

Now the bugle notes floated over the hot midday air, signalling the other captains commanding companies to gather together to receive orders. Carmichael's company had arrived at the head of the marching dusty, sweating column, but as the bugle brayed its command, so Captains Bazalgette and Massey came trotting past their men, swords and haversacks bouncing, to be told what to do.

'So, Morgan, tell me exactly what Hume wants, if you please, so that I can tell the other two.' Carmichael stared hard at Morgan, who made no reply. 'Come on, man. We've just passed three battalions of natives, who seem to be heading off to some parade yonder.' Carmichael flicked a well-manicured hand towards the *maidan*, half a mile down a gentle slope below the fort. 'This could turn damned sticky, so don't waste time.'

When Carmichael wasn't physically present, Morgan was fine. He knew how badly he'd behaved in the Crimea, how the men hated him and the other officers resented his arrogance and snobbery, yet in the flesh his supreme confidence and belief in his own rectitude was hard to overcome.

'No . . .' Morgan had to clear his throat, '. . . no, Carmichael, the commanding officer has asked me to take command whilst he's conducting a court martial in the fort. I'll just wait until Bazalgette and Massey join us.'

Carmichael was about to object when Colour-Sergeant McGucken came striding up to join them. With a stamp that raised a puff of dust, the Scot banged his boots together and slapped the sling of his rifle in a salute straight from the drill manual.

'Well, sir, grand to see you.' The irony in McGucken's voice was hardly noticeable. He'd been Carmichael's Colour-Sergeant until he was wounded at Inkermann – not that the cowardly bastard had dared to come to help him amongst the death, screams and yells that still haunted McGucken's dreams. 'Quite like old times, ain't it, sir?' With a hawk, the Glaswegian sent a green oyster of phlegm spinning into the dust.

'You'll be wanting the other companies to move off straight away, will you, sir?' McGucken had read the situation perfectly. He wasn't going to let the wretched Carmichael, senior captain or not, ruin *his* company commander's chance to command a whole wing, particularly when it looked as though there was a sniff of trouble in the wind. 'I'll keep 'em in the same order of march, sir, whilst you brief the officers, with your leave. Is there time to loosen belts and light a pipe, sir?' McGucken's steady stream of common sense overwhelmed Carmichael.

'Yes, Colour-Sar'nt, same order of march, but I'll be no time at all with the captains, so just stand them easy, please,' Morgan said, making no room for argument from Carmichael. 'Then send a sergeant and ten up to the commanding officer in the fort. They'll be used to escort any prisoners down to the execution site.'

'Sir, I'll send Sar'nt Ormond with Corporal Pegg an' a peck o' lads.' Then, with a bellowed, 'Colour-Sar'nts on me,'

McGucken took charge of the other companies whilst the three captains formed a knot round Morgan.

'Gentlemen, Colonel Hume has asked me to move the wing down to the *maidan* for a slightly unpleasant task.' Morgan kept his voice deliberately low so that the other captains had to give him every bit of their attention.

Commanding Number Three Company, Captain the Honourable Edward Massey, with a recently bought captaincy in the 95th from the 7th Fusiliers, had kept a friendly, if slightly aloof distance from his brother officers since he'd joined six months before. Bazalgette, commanding Number Two, was as different as possible – adored by his men and a great favourite in the mess. Below a thatch of hair his coarse features were split by a grin that was as open as a book; not even his sun-peeled nose, which stuck blotchily out from beneath the peak of his white-covered cap, could spoil the obvious pleasure that he had in being there amongst friends. Typically, he'd let his company smoke on the march up from the docks and now, out of respect for Morgan's temporary authority, he held his own pipe discreetly out of sight behind his back.

As he pulled the bit of clay from his mouth, Morgan noticed the claw that held it. Two canister shot had passed through that hand as Bazalgette led the advance on the bullet-swept slopes of the Alma almost three years ago; now it was permanently clenched into a pink, scaly comma that Bazalgette never bothered to hide.

'You saw the three native battalions on the march, I gather. They're armed but have no ammunition, just in case they decide to turn on us. Three men, one from each battalion, are currently being court-martialled by the colonel for attempted mutiny and it seems likely that some or all of them will be condemned to death.' Morgan looked at the three faces that were gathered around him; he had their complete attention.

20

'A troop of Bombay gunners should meet us at the Azad *maidan*. I'm sending an escort to the commanding officer to bring anyone that he condemns down to the execution site, and we'll then have to blow the poor wretches from the muzzles of the guns whilst their comrades watch.' Morgan looked at his brother officers. All of them had seen death before, but never an execution.

'It's crucial that we don't give an inch in front of these people. Any hesitation, any sign of uncertainty, could be enough for them to rise, so we'll put one gun between each of the companies, let the gunners load and allow the sepoys to chew on that for a while. Then, as the prisoners are tied to the muzzles by the gunners, I'll give the order for us to load . . .' Morgan paused to let this instruction sink in, '. . . and I want that good and clean, no dropping of cartridges or ramrods. Then, at my word, the front rank will kneel. Any sign of unrest and we'll volley into the lot of 'em, but that will only happen on my or the commanding officer's order, is that clear?' Morgan looked hard and deliberately into Carmichael's eyes.

'Yes, sir,' Bazalgette and Massey replied formally, whilst Carmichael just nodded.

Morgan produced his watch from the breast of his shell jacket. 'We'll march at five-and-twenty past, at attention. No smoking, if you please. Any questions? None . . . right, carry on.'

Only Carmichael failed to acknowledge Morgan's new authority with a salute. He turned stiffly away from the group, striding off to his own command as quickly as he could, his whole beautifully tailored frame stiff with indignation, little puffs of dust spurting up from his boots where his angry heels met the ground.

Belts were settled, haversacks pulled down on the men's sweat-damp thighs and water bottles hung carefully in a vain attempt to cool the small of the back before rifles were sloped over the right shoulder and the whole wing, at Morgan's word, turned to the right and swung off down the gently sloping packed-earth road towards their unwelcome task.

'Goin' to blow some poor bastards to kingdom come, ain't they, Clem?' Private Peter Sharrock, twenty-one and at five-foot nine an average height in the Grenadier Company, was the product of a Peterborough slum. Bored with milling powder for the Crimea, he'd enlisted, but too late for any fighting.

Next to him marched Private Clem James, an old man at twenty-five, no stranger to hard knocks. 'No, Peter, that's the 'ole bleedin' point.' There was an almost theatrical impatience in James's voice. 'There'll be no kingdom come for this lot if we blow 'em to bits. Buggers up their caste system, 'avin' to 'ave all the little bits picked up by the sweepers – an' they're the lowest of the low – an' means that they'll never go to their 'eathen 'eaven. Punishes 'em twice, it does, first by killin' them, then by condemnin' 'em to eternal damnation or some such . . .'

'Sharrock, James: shut yer grids!' McGucken's bellow silenced both men instantly. 'Report to me for water detail once we stand down.' Each night parties would be formed to find and collect water, a back-breaking task.

The column tramped on with the sun beating on their backs. Morgan had been aware of a steady trickle of people loping down the road beside them, mainly men young and old, but a handful of women as well. As they came round a slight bend that was screened by low trees, he heard the same, discordant hum that had greeted them when their boats first touched Bombay's quay. This time, though, it was lower, more of a subdued growl than the pulsating shriek that he'd heard before.

About a quarter of a mile away, where the ground flattened out into a great featureless parched meadow, a multicoloured slab of humanity eddied and wobbled, hemmed in

22

by a deep drainage ditch on one side and the road on the other. Opposite the crowd stood three long blocks of scarlet and white – the sepoy regiments waiting in the heat for whatever fate their British masters would hand down.

'Jesus, Mary and Joseph, Colour-Sar'nt, how many people d'you reckon are in that crowd?' Morgan knew that the sepoys would outnumber them, but he had not expected a crowd of this size.

'Ye sound like a bloody papist sometimes, you do, sir.' McGucken always mocked his officer when he used one of the Catholic men's expressions. 'Dunno, but let's have a look.' Now he sectioned the crowd off into eight imaginary blocks, just as he had been taught to do as a recruit and, as they drew nearer, tried to count the bare heads and turbans in one of them. ''Bout three-thousand, I'd say, what d'yous think, sir?'

'Yes, that's about right.' Morgan tried not to let his concern show, but three sepoy battalions was quite enough for less than four hundred men of the 95th to deal with, let alone thousands of angry natives. What should he do? The colonel had told him that confidence was everything, but they would be swallowed up in an instant if the crowd turned. Should he halt and wait for orders? He found his pace getting involuntarily shorter and his bottom tightening with fear and indecision – but he was spared. Above the rhythmic thump of his men's boots came the clatter of hoofs and wheels.

'Not before time, sir . . .' McGucken caught sight of the troop of horse gunners before Morgan could see them above their own, scarlet phalanx, '. . . just like when the guns came up at Balaklava, sir, d'ye ken?'

Morgan did, indeed, ken. He remembered how nine-pounders like these had hammered at the Russian cavalry in that grape-laden valley three years before. Now the covered brass helmets and ruddy faces of the Bombay Horse Artillery bobbed above their cantering animals, the 95th biting off a

23

ragged cheer as the horses, limbers and guns enveloped them in dust as they swept by.

'Troop, halt!' Three horses led the way: Bolton, the captain commanding, his troop staff-sergeant, and the trumpeter, who now repeated his officer's order with a series of brazen notes. As the guns pulled up behind him, Bolton trotted forward to the still marching Morgan and McGucken.

'Who's in charge here?' Bolton was thirty-five, short, chubby and clean shaven. Unlike his men, he wore a light, cork *solar-topee* to protect his head from the sun, but it appeared to have done little for his temper. Before either could answer Bolton repeated, 'I said, who's in charge here?'

'*Major* Morgan of HM Ninety-Fifth, sir,' McGucken snapped a salute whilst invoking Morgan's brevet, before muttering, 'Why are these damned nabobs always in such a pother, Sir?'

'Dunno, Colour-Sar'nt; don't suppose they've seen much action before.' Morgan's answer belied the relief he felt at the sight of the guns.

As Bolton dismounted, both officer and colour-sergeant searched his chest for medals – but there was none.

'Good day . . . sir.' There was a slight question in Bolton's voice for on Morgan's collar there were only the star and crown of a captain. 'Colonel Brewill has asked me to execute some rogue sepoys of his whilst you kindly protect my troop. Is that what you understand?'

As the column of 95th continued to swing by, the trio stood in the shade of a leafy tree inhabited by a knot of silent monkeys, which looked quizzically down at them. Seeing that a conference was taking place, Captain Carmichael detached himself from the head of his company and strolled over towards them.

'Something wrong, sir?' asked McGucken breezily, turning and placing himself carefully between Carmichael and the other two officers.

'No, Colour-Sar'nt, but I assumed that Captain Morgan would need to speak to me.' Carmichael was thoroughly out of sorts and McGucken's reply only added to his agitation.

'Aye, sir, I'm sure he will in his own good time. Please listen for the bugle, sir.'

Seething, Carmichael turned away quickly whilst Bolton and Morgan completed their plans.

'So, swing one gun between each of my companies, please, then I'll halt the whole column in front of the crowd and opposite the sepoys yonder . . .' Morgan looked towards the nearer flank of the 10th BNI, now only a few hundred paces away, '. . . and load with charges only. Have a canister round very obviously to hand by each of your six barrels, please, then make ready any guns that are spare when we know how many executions are to take place. Meanwhile, my men will load and take aim; if there's trouble, prime as fast as you can, but fire only on my orders. I'll leave all the execution side to you; I imagine that you've done it before?'

'Well, no . . . actually this is the first time I've done anything like this.' All Bolton's initial bluster had gone. He'd taken a good look at the two infantrymen's decorations and now he seemed glad to have someone else in charge.

'Aye, sir, well dinna fret, there's a first time for all of us, but the Old Nails'll look after ye.' McGucken used the nickname given to the 95th in the Crimea and it was hard to imagine that there had ever been a first time for a man like this. His lean frame and combed whiskers burst with confidence, yet his words were sensitive and immediately reassuring.

With a cautious smile and a salute, Bolton turned back to give orders to his own men.

'How does that work exactly, sir?' McGucken asked Morgan. 'Them gunners ain't Queen's troops, yet they're mainly Europeans: how's that?'

'Well, John Company started to recruit some all-white

regiments of its own after trouble with the sepoys years ago,'
Morgan explained. 'All the artillery out in India is manned
by European crews – and just at the moment I'm damn glad
it is. I'm told they're pretty sharp lads – not that it's going
to take any great skill to blow the lights out of some poor
wretch strapped to the end of your barrel.'

The sepoys stood taut and erect as the 95th marched along
the road in front of them. As the British troops approached,
the crowd's murmur had turned to heckles and catcalls, even
a few sods had been thrown and some rotten fruit, but as
the pacing red column had neither checked nor hesitated,
so the crowd drew back. Now the mob fidgeted and swayed
as the two bodies of troops scanned each other. As the sepoys
stiffened and stood more rigidly, more fixedly than any line-
drawing from the drill manual, so the arms and legs of the
95th swung more regularly, more perfectly than they had
ever done on an English barrack yard.

'Right Wing, Ninety-Fifth Regiment, halt!' The non-
commissioned officers were waiting for Morgan's word of
command; once it came it was passed down the sweating
ranks, bringing the scarlet and white-belted lines to a dusty
stop.

'The wing will advance . . .' Morgan paused whilst the
ranks tensed, '. . . left face.' The British troops pivoted,
backs now to the crowd, and stared at the native regiments, no more than thirty yards away from them across
the road.

Under Bolton's words of command the guns wheeled into
position between the slabs of infantry, the sparkling brass
barrels being unhooked and thrown about to stare at the sepoys,
bombardiers' yells sending gunners scurrying to the ammunition limbers, ramrods whirling and thrusting as the charges
were pushed home, the black, menacing muzzles silently
challenging the native troops. The whole, slick process ended

when by each gun a lance-bombardier stood hefting a linen bag of canister shot.

'Wait a moment, sir, let the fuckers see what's in store for 'em,' McGucken growled quietly. 'D'you want to untie ten now, sir?'

'Yes, do that, please, Colour-Sar'nt.' Morgan knew that the sepoys were studying their every move, and as the men fiddled to take the string and greased paper from one little parcel of ten paper cartridges that sat in their pouches, he looked across at his targets.

The sepoys swayed slightly in the heat, the odd tongue quickly licking dry lips, fingers flexing nervously on the stocks of the rifles that they all held by their sides, expressions fixed but difficult to read under the sweeping, exaggerated moustaches that all the jawans wore. Morgan saw the native officers, swords drawn, standing just behind the trembling ranks. They were all older men, most grey-haired, some wearing campaign medals. The subadar-majors waited at the centre of each battalion's line, where the colour-parties would normally have been with long strings of 'joys', the religious beads that looked, to the British at least, so odd around the neck of a uniform coatee. To their rear were a handful of white faces, the European officers.

'Right y'are, sir, let 'em see we mean business.' Quietly, McGucken guided Morgan.

'Right Wing, Ninety-Fifth Regiment . . .' Morgan's mind flew back to the first time that he had spoken the order that he was about to give, '. . . with ball cartridge . . . load', it had been at the Alma. Despite the heat, Morgan shivered.

Rifles were canted forward before each man reached to the black, leather pouch on the front of his belt and pulled out a single, paper tube. After a regulation pause, the tops were bitten off the cartridges before the powder was poured down the muzzle of every Enfield, then the steel ramrods were pulled from below the barrel of each weapon before the charge and lead bullet were rammed home. Another pause, then the rifles were lifted obliquely across the men's bodies, left hands catching the stocks at the point of balance before each right hand thumbed back the steel hammers to half cock.

Right down the line the sergeants craned their heads, making sure that all the troops were ready for the fiddly operation of fitting their percussion caps. The sergeants nodded to McGucken, now standing at the centre of the four companies beside Morgan.

He quietly prompted, 'Right, sir.'

'Caps!' Morgan's word of command was repeated and four hundred right hands groped in the little leather pouches that sat just beside the brass buckles on their waist belts for the pea-sized, hollow copper percussion caps to fit over the nipples at each rifle's breech. One or two men fluffed it, dropping the caps, the tense silence being broken with the customary sergeants' cries of: 'You wouldn't drop it if it was wet and slippery, would you? Pick the fucker up!' And the offenders, embarrassed at their own clumsiness, scrabbled in the dust.

Then again came sergeants' nods and McGucken's, 'Right, sir,' before Morgan's command, 'Front rank . . . kneel.' Half the men pushed their right feet back and then sank to their knees, the rank behind bringing their rifles level with their waists, pointing over the heads of those in front.

'Ready.' At Morgan's order, each hammer was clicked to full cock, making every weapon ready to fire.

'Right Wing . . . targets front, preee . . . sent!' Morgan's final word of command from the centre of the line brought all the rifles into the aim. As damp white faces squinted down the Enfields' sights at the bellies of the sepoys no more than a handful of paces away, a gasp and an involuntary flinch swept down the Indian ranks. The native troops blinked, hardly believing their eyes. They were only too aware of the devastation that a rifle volley would cause at that range;

they'd been shown when the Enfields were issued to them that the bullet would scythe down not just one man, but any who stood packed closely behind him as well.

The crowd at the rear of the 95th had gone still and quiet, and Morgan believed that he could read the thoughts of the men in front of him. Their great brown eyes stared at his own men's muzzles and it was if an unspoken belief in their innocence loomed over them. Morgan hoped he was right, for the time of reckoning was almost upon them.

'Left, right, left, right . . . get 'ere, can't you?' A flat, Sheffield twang was clear on the hot air.

''Ere's Sar'nt Ormond and the commanding officer, sir,' said McGucken. ''Bout time, too.'

The detachment of the Grenadier Company had formed a hollow, marching square around the prisoners – Morgan couldn't yet see how many – as they tramped down the slope towards the rest of the troops. Sergeant Ormond's face was as expressionless now as it had been when he slashed Russians down at Sebastapol, thought Morgan, all stumpy, five-foot six of him, as dependable at issuing the bread ration as he would certainly prove to be at eviscerating Hindus.

The detachment had their bayonets fixed and just beyond the bobbing points came a gaggle of horsemen, the commanding officers of the native battalions, a cloud of adjutants, and Colonel Hume, who'd been lent a cob of dubious age and wind that hardly did him justice. It was difficult to see exactly what was going on in the centre of the square, but Morgan could hear shouts in what he guessed was Hindi and, quite distinctly, in best Wirksworth, 'Coom on, yer *barnshoot*, keep up with the sergeant.' Predictably, Corporal Pegg had landed the job of escorting the prisoners. As they came closer, Morgan could see Pegg's stubby arm thrusting first one and then the other of the two leading prisoners hard in the small of the back. Each time the yellow cuff shot forward,

29

so the sepoys staggered and shouted; each time they shouted, so the piston-like wrist administered another shove.

'Stow all that bollocks, you two; you can try to persuade Joe Gunner not to jerk 'is lanyard, if you like, but you're wastin' yer breath.' Pegg was as sympathetic as Morgan had come to expect. 'Stop draggin' them chains in the dust, won't you?'

Morgan and McGucken marched forward to meet Hume and the party. They could see that the two prisoners who stumbled side by side were shackled ankle and wrist, they were barefoot and had exchanged their uniform trousers for shabby dhotis. Their swallow-tailed coatees hung open where the buttons had been cut away – on sentencing by the court martial, Morgan supposed. Despite Pegg's attentions, both continued to yell, whilst the third man, who was bound only by rope at the wrists, was utterly silent.

There were a few hisses and hoots from within the crowd and Morgan thought he could make out the words 'Mungal Pandy' being chanted by a handful, but for the most part the advancing party was surrounded by an awed silence.

'Sir, the right wing and Captain Bolton's troop deployed as you ordered.' Morgan braced to attention and saluted with a graceful sweep of his drawn sword as Hume clattered up on his borrowed mount.

'Stop, you damn screw, can't you?' Hume hauled on the reins of the scruffy cob, whilst the other mounted officers came to a more elegant halt. 'Mouth like bloody iron,' he muttered as the horse jerked its head round bad-temperedly. 'Good, thank you, Morgan. I see you've got the men ready to fire. Any sign of trouble?'

'No, sir, the poor lambs look quite wretched, but the crowd might give us a problem.' Morgan looked round at the rabble, who were beginning to get a little bolder, advancing step by step closer to the backs of the 95th and Bolton's men.

Hume quickly walked his horse to the centre of the 95th's

line, McGucken and Morgan scrambling to keep up. With hardly a pause, Hume pulled a sheet of paper from the breast of his jacket, cleared his throat and, in a high, clear voice, started to read, 'Verdicts and sentences of a court martial convened at Fort George, Bombay on the second of June Eighteen Fifty-Seven under the presidency of Lieutenant-Colonel Henry Hume, Companion of the Bath, Her Majesty's Ninety-Fifth Regiment.' Hume paused; every man, even those who didn't understand a single syllable of what he was saying, were straining to hear him. 'The three prisoners are charged with: having at a meeting made use of highly mutinous and seditious language, evincing a traitorous disposition towards the Government, tending to promote a rebellion against the State and to subvert the authority of the British Government. Private Shahgunge Singh, Bombay Sappers and Miners: guilty. Sentence: transportation for life.'

Morgan looked at the third prisoner, who was only lightly bound; he hung his head and trembled slightly, but he made no other outward sign of relief.

'Drill-Havildar Din Syed Hussain, Bombay Marine Battalion: guilty. Private Mungal Guddrea, Tenth Bombay Native Infantry: guilty.' Hume looked at the native troops who faced him. 'Sentence: death by gunfire, to be carried out forthwith.'

The 95th, who could hear the details of what their commanding officer had said, shifted a little as they continued to point their weapons at the sepoys; there was a murmur of quiet satisfaction as they cuddled the butts of their rifles even closer.

No sooner had Hume pronounced sentence than Commandant Brewill spurred his horse slightly forward of the 95th and in slow, distinct Hindi repeated what Hume had said. A sigh swept up and down the waiting ranks of the sepoys, and a ripple of movement, almost as if the under-standing of the news had slapped the Indian troops across the face. The drill-havildar tried to yell a desultory slogan or two, whilst his companion stood silent, his face lifted up towards the sun, his adam's apple bobbing in his throat. The crowd had been listening intently too, one or two voices protested but most stood in awed silence.

'I'll have Bolton's outer guns loaded, with your leave, sir?' Morgan knew that two of the four guns would have to be used to execute the prisoners, but the pair pointing at either end of the sepoys' ranks could do great damage, sweeping the lines of troops with an iron storm of canister, if things got out of hand.

'Aye, do that, please, Morgan. Cant 'em in a bit so that they catch the rascals in enfilade, if needs be . . .' Hume's words sent Morgan off to speak to Bolton. Then, in a parade bellow the colonel added, 'Sar'nt Ormond, carry on, please.'

'Sir!' Ormond, as calmly as if he were checking the men's oil bottles, gave a few, quiet instructions that saw a pair of brawny, red-coated lads grab each prisoner by the elbows and hustle them towards the waiting guns.

'Numbers One and Four guns, with case shot . . . load,' Bolton, on Morgan's instructions, gave the word of command to his outer guns, and the lance-bombardiers, who had been toying with the linen bags for the best part of an hour, slid the deadly projectiles into the barrels of the guns, followed by a well-practised push with a rammer from each waiting gun-numbers. Again, Morgan saw how the Indian line flinched as the yawning black muzzles were turned ready to rake them.

'Don't bloody struggle, Havildar; it won't make a blind bit of difference.' Lance-Corporal Pegg showed scant sympathy for his sweating prisoner. The non-commissioned officer seemed to have shrunk in his clothes – now his mana-cled wrists and ankles were as thin and bony as a famished child's – as Pegg and Private Beeston dragged and pushed the prisoner towards the gun.

Any cockiness had quite gone from the native NCO. Morgan had thought how confident he'd looked as the party had approached down the hill, the havildar keeping up a stream of defiant yells, hoping, he supposed, that his friends would come to his rescue. But now the moment of reckoning was here and there was no sign of any action from the sepoys. Even the crowd had fallen quiet.

'Excuse me, sir.' McGucken stood to attention beside his commanding officer's stirrup leather. 'It's no' right to let this mutinous filth die in British red, is it, sir?'

Hume looked down from his saddle at the colour-sergeant, taken aback by the intensity of his words. McGucken, like most of the other long-serving NCOs who had seen more blood and killing than they cared to remember, was usually taciturn, passionless in circumstances that would have more callow men at fever pitch.

'Aye, Colour-Sar'nt, you have a point. I don't see why this scum should dishonour our uniforms.' Hume paused for a second before adding, 'Get those coatees off their backs if you'd be so kind, Sar'nt Ormond.'

Sepoy Guddrea already had both feet and one hand tied to the struts of the wheels of Number Two gun by stout, leather thongs. Lance-Corporal Abbott and Private Scriven were pulling his right arm back for the waiting gunner to complete the last set of bonds when they heard the order. So the coatee was dragged off Guddrea, the lining of one sleeve showing a greyish white as it was turned inside out. Rather than loosen the tethers on the prisoner's other wrist, though, Scriven produced a clasp knife fron his haversack and the sleeve was briskly cut away.

'Right, Havildar,' sneered Pegg, 'you won't be needing this where you're a-going,' and he pulled the coatee roughly off the second, condemned man.

At the Indian's feet two gunners kneeled, tying his ankles hard back against the gun's wheels. As Pegg and Private

Grimes held his arms for the gunners to complete the job, Morgan noticed his toes digging into the dust and the gun's brass muzzle pushing the flesh at the base of the prisoner's spine into a bulging, coffee-coloured collar.

'Prime!' At Bolton's word of command, the bombardiers at both guns slid copper initiators the size of a pencil into the touchholes, before attaching lanyards to the twists of wire that emerged from their tops. Once the strings were jerked, the rough wire would rasp against the detonating compound in the tubes, producing a spark that would fire the charge.

The pair of sepoys were stretched like bows over the ends of the barrels, their limbs strained tight against the wheels of the guns by the leather straps, their chests – with the skin pulled tightly over their ribs – directly facing their comrades. They would have seen guns being loaded many times and now they must know exactly what was about to happen, thought Morgan, as he watched the havildar arch his head slowly back, eyes closed, the knot of hair on the top of his skull hanging loose, his mouth open below the drooping moustache, waiting for the last word that he would hear.

Both lanyards were drawn tight, the bombardiers looking towards Bolton, whose horse skittered and pawed the dust. The crowd remained quiet; even the crows in the trees seemed to be keeping a respectful silence, thought Morgan.

'Ready, sir,' Bolton reported.

'Fire by single guns, if you please, Captain Bolton,' said Hume, with exaggerated courtesy.

'Sir.' Bolton looked towards the crew to his left, making sure that they were quite ready before shouting, 'Number Two gun . . . fire!'

The concussion thumped Morgan's ears. The crows and scavengers rose from the trees in a black bruise, tattered wings beating in alarm, cawing and squawking, whilst the crowd gasped and the horses gibbed and pecked. Morgan expected the gun to recoil until he realised that, with only a blank charge, there was nothing to hurl it back on its wheels. Then, as the smoke hung around the muzzle in the still air, he saw the crew clawing at their faces.

Naked arms and legs were still attached to the nine-pounder's wheels by their leather straps, raw chopped meat at the end of each buckled limb. But when the piece had fired, the vacuum created by the explosion had sucked a fine stew of blood and tissue back over the gunners. Their white, leather breeches were now pink with matter, their helmet covers a bloody smear, whilst their faces were flecked with the same gore. Each man wiped frantically at his eyes and cheeks in disgust.

But there was worse to come. As Morgan and all the others gawped, so a tousled football fell from the heavens and bounced towards the 10th Bengal Native Infantry, their ranks swerving and breaking to avoid Sepoy Gudderea's bounding, blistered head. Ripped from its shoulders, the man's skull had shot straight up into the sky before falling like a bloody stone to deliver the starkest, possible message to his living comrades.

'Number Three gun . . . fire!' Then Bolton's command turned Drill-Havildar Din Hussain into carrion. Each face on the *maidan* turned upwards like a crowd at a firework party as, rising from the smoke, the black disc turned over and over, its mane of hair flailing around its scorched flesh, unseeing eyes staring wide in death. It rose to its zenith, every eye watching its plunge to earth then, with a thump and a couple of dusty bounces, Din Hussain's head rolled towards his last tormentor.

'Now that'll teach you not to be a naughty little mutineer, won't it?' grinned Pegg at the lump of bone and blackened skin.

Morgan gagged as the hideous ball came to a halt in the dust.

TWO

Bombay Brothers

'Christ, I never want to see anything like that again.' Morgan and Bazalgette were sitting in the shady anteroom of the officers' mess in the fort, chota-pegs in hand, icecubes clinking, still dusty from the *maidan*.

'Aye, I thought I'd seen some sights at Sevastopol, but nothing like that.' Bazalgette's forehead was cut across by sunburn, stark white above his peeling nose where the peak of his cap had kept the rays at bay. He pulled hard at his brandy. 'It hardly made the right impression on the sepoys when Mabutt from my lot and that other lad from Carmichael's company fainted dead away. *We're* supposed to be the hand of a vengeful God, not a bunch of swooning tarts. I didn't see a single sepoy drop out, did you, Morgan?'

'No, I didn't, and I agree that our men droopin' around the place ain't good, but the jawans did have Bolton's guns to help 'em on their way, didn't they?'

As the Bengal officers had bellowed the orders to the three native battalions that sent them marching back to their own cantonments, the Horse Gunners had hand-wheeled the two loaded guns behind them just to make sure that there were no second thoughts. It was as well they did, Morgan had thought, because the sepoys had missed the sight of the sweepers, the lowest of the professions, picking up the remnants of their comrades and untying their limbs from the wheels of the guns, so defiling their caste and punishing the victims after death.

Then, with a muted curse, brushing dust from the knees of his overalls, Captain Richard Carmichael came stamping into the mess.

'Hey, chota-peg, *jildi*, boy.'

It hadn't taken the big Harrovian long to pick up the arrogances of the worst type of white officers, thought Morgan. In their own mess in England or Ireland, the soldier servants would have been called by the discreet ringing of a bell, but here in India, the mess staff hovered just out of sight, instantly gliding to obey their officers' wishes.

'Can't you keep the noise down, Carmichael? Haven't you had enough din for one day?' Morgan asked peevishly, tired of Carmichael's boorishness.

'Enough Din . . . I've just seen more than enough of Din, spread all over the *maidan*, poor bugger . . . ha!' chortled Carmichael. Morgan immediately regretted feeding him the line. 'And I don't know who you think you are to be telling me what to do . . . you've let that brevet quite go to your head, ain't you?'

The mess waiter had slid into the room, proffering a tiny silver tray to Carmichael on which sat a beaker of brandy and soda: it was snatched without a word or gesture of thanks.

Morgan said nothing, fearing that Carmichael had recognised his indecision as the wing had marched down to the execution site. Bazalgette, sensing the tension, leapt into the breach. 'The lad of yours who measured his length, is he all right?' Typically, Bazalgette asked an innocent question, not seeking to tease or mock; equally typically, Carmichael saw a barb where none existed.

'What, that bloody fool Jervis? Aye, about as all right as

that greenhorn o' yours. Nothing that a dozen strokes with the cat wouldn't put right. Not that Colonel-go-lightly bloody Hume would let us touch the men's lilywhite skins, would he?'

Morgan wondered at this outburst. Carmichael was normally much more subtle in his disloyalty.

'Aye, those two made us look right fools in front of that Bombay rubbish – and the bloody natives, come to that. No, you have to wonder what dross the Depot's sending us these days and – mark my words – today was just a flea bite compared with what we'll come up against later, see if it ain't,' Carmichael continued at full volume.

'Please, Carmichael, I'd thank you to remember that we're guests in the "Bombay rubbish's" mess at the moment,' Morgan tried to hush him, 'and we're going to have to learn to trust them, and them us, if we're going into action shoulder to shoulder in Bengal. So it makes no sense to upset our hosts, does it?'

'Aye, Carmichael, the white officers are going to have quite enough on their plates making sure that their own men stay loyal, without us sticking a burr under their saddle as well,' Bazalgette added.

Morgan watched Carmichael's reaction. Full of bluster with just one opponent, when the pendulum swung against him, he instantly backed down – and what a damn nerve he had to talk about the quality of the soldiers: Carmichael, the officer who was always in an indecent rush to find himself a safe job on the staff, leaving the men and his regiment without a second thought.

'Aye, well, we'll soon see if we can trust the rascals or not, won't we?' Carmichael continued more quietly. 'Now that you're in the colonel's pocket, Morgan, did he give you any idea where they might be sending us?'

'No. There's some talk amongst the Bombay officers that we'll be sent up towards Delhi, but I think that's just speculation.'

'Oh, so nowhere near your old countryman Ensign James Keenan, and his peachy little wife, then?' said Carmichael with a curl of his lip.

'No . . . no, why should we?' Morgan was instantly uncomfortable when Keenan's name was mentioned. 'The Keenans are up at Jhansi near Agra with the Twelfth BNI. Safe as houses, no hint of trouble – and there won't be, if I know anything about the commandant, Colonel Kemp. He'll keep 'em well and truly in line, so he will,' he continued, keen to steer the talk away from his former sergeant and his wife.

'Aye, just as well now that the Keenans have got a son and heir to look after.' There was a troublesome note in Carmichael's voice. 'You remember Keenan, don't you, Bazalgette?'

'Of course I do; wounded at the Alma, wasn't he, did a wonderful job at The Quarries and got commissioned in the field, sold out and then went off to an Indian regiment? Didn't know you were still in touch with him, Morgan,' Bazalgette answered.

'Oh, I doubt if he is,' Carmichael cut in before Morgan could answer, 'but I guess he still corresponds with Mrs Keenan – much to discuss about life back in Cork, eh, Morgan?'

'Haven't had anything to do with either of 'em since they left Dublin last year,' answered Morgan, a little too quickly,

'No? Well, who knows when we'll knock into them again.' Carmichael drained his glass noisily and stood up. 'That would be an interesting meeting for you, wouldn't it? Right, must go – there's any number of delightful loyal sepoys to re-train whom "we must learn to trust" – wasn't that your phrase, Morgan?' And he strode from the cool of the mess out into the heat of the early afternoon.

'Christ, you've really got under his skin this time, ain't you, Morgan?' Bazalgette held his glass in both hands, sipping at the brandy. 'Why's he prosing on about Keenan, though?

He'll never be coming back to the Ninety-Fifth now that he's taken John Company's salt, and what's the chance of seeing him again out here in India?' Bazalgette watched Morgan carefully, much more interested in his friend's impending answer than he was pretending to be.

Morgan hesitated; James Keenan had been his batman before winning laurels and a commission in the face of the enemy, whilst Mary, his wife, had been a chamber maid in Glassdrumman, the Morgan family home in Cork. The close relationship between the Protestant officer and the Catholic girl in the Crimea had caused rumour to swirl, particularly when Keenan, with a new and valuable commission in a Queen's regiment and a heavily pregnant wife, had sold that same commission and scuttled off to India no sooner than the 95th had returned to Dublin eighteen months ago.

'D'you really not know?' Morgan asked quietly.

'I'd sooner hear the truth from you, old lad,' Bazalgette answered sympathetically.

'Lord knows, it's been a strain. The child – Samuel – is mine; he was conceived when Keenan was on trench duty and I was visiting the wounded just before we attacked The Quarries . . . I know, please don't look at me like that.' Bazalgette had heard the rumours, but it didn't make the truth any less shocking. 'So when the Keenans decamped to India I thought that that would be an end to the whole chapter.'

'How much of this does Maude know?' Bazalgette thought back to the Cork society wedding last year where the gallant Tony Morgan, hero and heir to a fair spread of pasture and farms on the Atlantic coast, had married Maude Hawtrey, judge's daughter, so cementing the two families into one of the most influential Protestant enclaves in the county.

'Nothing . . . nothing at all,' Morgan answered, 'and now *she's* pregnant, so there's to be another Morgan coming into the world, only this one shall be able to carry my name.'

'Well, it's a fine pickle, but as long as Keenan's not hounding you, then I reckon that your usual streak of luck has seen you right.' Bazalgette knew Morgan better than most of his friends, yet the subject had never even been hinted at before. 'Why, there's no reason to think that we'll come across the twelfth BNI, nor that we'll be sent up Jhansi way. I suspect that this is the last you've heard of it and, frankly, it's not in Keenan's interests to go blethering about his boy's real father, is it?'

'But that's the whole goddamn point, Bazalgette,' Morgan blurted, holding the bridge of his nose between finger and thumb. 'He's my son – mine and Mary's – not bloody Keenan's. Jesus, the girl only married Keenan because she wanted to follow me, and now I've a son that I shall never see whilst I'm stuck with the driest, coldest creature in the whole of Cork, who can't hold a candle to Mary. What a bloody pother.'

'Come on, old feller, it may seem a mess to you, but it'll have to wait until we've settled the Pandies' hash.' Bazalgette reached across and gripped his friend's shoulder. 'Now, there's the bugle, the men will be waiting for us.'

'Grenadier Company formed up and ready for demonstration, sir.' Colour-Sergeant McGucken's hand came down smartly from the salute.

On the parched parade ground of the fort, the left wing of the 10th Bengal Native Infantry stood at ease in their cotton shirtsleeves, white trousers and round forage caps – almost four hundred of them – waiting for the skirmishing demonstration that Morgan's company had been told to organise for them. The butts of their rifles rested in the dust, the weapons comfortably in the crooks of their elbows, their faces alert and apparently keen to learn.

Kneeling opposite them were Morgan's men. Like the sepoys, they had been allowed to strip down to their shirts and now they kneeled in two, staggered ranks.

'How are our boys, Colour-Sar'nt?' asked Morgan quietly as his hand flicked casually to the peak of his cap, returning the salute.

'They'll do as they're told, sir,' McGucken replied equally quietly.

'No, Colour-Sar'nt, that's not what I'm asking,' said Morgan. 'How are they about it?'

'They're no' very pleased, sir. They don't understand why they've been detailed off to teach the sepoys how to be better soldiers when they might turn on us at any moment. That scunner Corporal Pegg asked if we shouldn't be loaded with ball, "just in case", but I told him to button his fuckin' lip. They'll do what you want them to, sir – and bloody like it.'

The 95th, with their recent battle experience, had learnt the value of skirmishing – the fire and manoeuvre by independent pairs – that was utterly unlike the formal old-fashioned drill movements by which the Indian regiments still moved in battle. Now the colonel had decided to teach the sepoys this tactic, not just as a battle-winning skill, but also as a device for his men to show their trust in their new comrades – a pair of whom they had just blown to infinity.

As Morgan arrived, the three British company commanders and their subadars came marching towards him and halted as one man, throwing up the dust of the barrack yard, before the senior captain took a pace forward and saluted.

'Sir, Numbers Five, Six and Seven Companies paraded ready for training, sir.' The captain remained at the salute, his right hand at the peak of his covered cap.

'Right, Captain Mellish, I'm obliged to you,' Morgan returned the salute, 'but please drop all that parade-ground stuff. We're here to learn to fight, not to play at guardsmen. How d'you suggest we tackle this?'

Morgan looked at the trio of Indian officers. Again, he was struck by their age – they were all at least forty – and their smartness. Even in shirtsleeves they were beautifully pressed and brushed, whilst their moustaches swept down and over their lips, a stark, dyed black compared with their greying hair. But it was their eyes that held his attention most. Did he detect humility there, a supplication that seemed to beg him not to compare them with their faithless comrades? It wasn't yet possible to know – but the next couple of hours of running and crouching in the heat would soon tell.

'Well, sir,' all the British and native officers of the 10th had relaxed at Morgan's word, 'if you would be good enough to pause in your demonstration every few minutes so that we can translate the instructions for the boys, they'll soon cotton on. Then it's up to us to drive home what you've taught us.'

'Good. Form the companies in three sides of a square around my men, please, and we'll try to show you what little we've picked up.'

Captain Mellish and the others smiled politely at Morgan's self-deprecation, saluted and doubled off to the waiting sepoys.

'They don't look half bad, sir.' McGucken cast an appreciative eye along the long, smart, lean ranks of the 10th.

'Aye, Colour-Sar'nt, as long as they're on our side I reckon they'll do rightly,' Morgan replied quietly, 'but I can see why Pegg and the others have their doubts.'

The three companies of the 10th were quickly wheeled around the waiting ranks of the Grenadiers.

''Eathen sods . . .' Lance-Corporal Pegg knelt in the dust at the far right of the company, rifle at his knee, with his skirmishing partner, Private Beeston, one pace to his left and rear in the same pose, '. . . bit too close for comfort, sez I.'

'You're right, Corp'l. If the bastards rush us now we'll be fuckin' lost,' came the reply in dourest Nottingham.

'Right: falling back. On sighting the enemy the even numbers fire without challenging on their own initiative,' McGucken bellowed to the assembled multitude, slow and clear, before pausing and glancing at the subadar who stood alongside him.

'Ee-nish-a-tif, sahib?' The Indian looked puzzled.

'Aye . . .' McGucken was stumped for a moment, '. . . without needin' no bloody orders.'

'Ah . . . yes.' The subadar grasped what was meant quickly enough before turning it into rapid Hindi.

'Whilst the odd numbers prepare to cover them,' the big Scot continued, 'shouting, "Moving now" the evens fall back fifteen paces, turn to face the enemy and immediately reload.' The subadar repeated everything he said. 'Once they've reloaded, provided the enemy's not pressing too hard, the evens shout, "Ready" allowing the odds to fire and fall back in exactly the same manner. Got it, Mister . . . er, Lal?'

Subadar Lal had indeed got it, translating fast and accurately.

'Right, look in and you'll receive a complete demonstration.' There was no need to repeat these words. 'Grenadier Company, skirmishing by numbers, falling back . . . one!'

On McGucken's word of command, thirty or so weapons rose to the men's shoulders, 'Bang!' was shouted the same number of times as the rifles' hammers fell dully against leather-rimmed nipple guards, then, 'Moving now' was yelled as half the men darted back through the dust, a regulation fifteen paces.

To Morgan and McGucken's bemusement, the three sepoy companies suddenly cawed with delight, hands clapping in appreciation, feet stamping in the dust in noisy admiration for the precision of the British troops.

'What are those cunts laughing at?' Pegg, already sweating hard and slightly out of breath after even a modest dash in the afternoon heat, went through the dry drill of reloading his rifle, steel ramrod rasping on the rifling of the barrel.

'Ready,' he and half the company bellowed.

'Bang!' boomed the other half before, 'Moving now,' to

be greeted by more ecstatic applause and cries of admiration from the 10th.

'Boggered if I know, Corp'l,' panted Beeston as he sped past Pegg who, in time with the rest of the leading rank, was just bringing his rifle to the present. 'Must think we're fuckin' off back to England,' he added drily.

'An' so on until contact is broken with the enemy . . .' McGucken's voice brought the precisely regulated, darting ranks to a halt, all of them puffing with exertion as their equipment banged on their hips and the dust roiled around them in the heat of the day.

'Now, the advance to the enemy . . .' the colour-sergeant paused for translation, '. . . is exactly the same but the other way round.' The subadar looked confused by that phrase. 'Och, just watch,' and with a few simple commands the skirmish line advanced back to the point from which it had started, as precisely as it had fallen back, to the intense and noisy pleasure of the audience.

'Well, Mellish, I'm not quite sure why we've caused such a stir with your lads,' Morgan said to the 10th's senior captain, 'but d'you think they've grasped the principle?'

'Yes, of course. You don't understand them yet, Morgan: they delight in anything new; they're impressed by organisation and regulation. It's what makes them such a pleasure to command but also leaves them so vulnerable to big-mouthed badmashes who can exploit their religious beliefs better than we can. Let's see if they've hoisted the idea aboard, shall we?'

With remarkably little fuss, the British officers gathered the sepoys around them, talking to them in quiet Hindi almost as a schoolmaster might speak to his most promising pupils. The jemadars and subadars spoke rapidly to the havildars and naiks and in no time the ranks were numbered off, kneeling attentively and waiting for orders. There were a few hesitations and some mistakes, but very quickly the sepoys were trotting and crouching, loading almost as smoothly as the well-practised 95th.

'Looks like this lot picks things up dead quick, don't it, sir?' Corporal Pegg and the rest of the company were standing on the edge of the yard in the shadow thrown by the white-washed buildings, sucking greedily at their big, blue-painted water bottles once the order had been given. All of their grey flannel shirts were stained wet at the armpits and down the spine, and they pulled at the damp crotches of their blue serge trousers.

'They seem to have got the hang of things remarkably well, Corp'l Pegg. I imagine we'll be glad of their help when we meet Pandy,' Morgan replied.

'Aye, an' they've 'ardly broke into a sweat, 'ave they?' Beeston said. 'But what's that noise they're mekin', Corp'l?'

'It's just the sound that these wallahs mek rather than "bang" like a good Christian would,' Pegg explained as the sepoys smacked their lips to simulate the firing of their rifles. 'All sorts of strange 'abits, these foreigners, you know, Jono.'

'Aye, but the officer's right: they'll be 'andy to 'ave along-side when we get to Delhi,' Beeston added, a note of grudging respect in his voice.

'P'raps, but pound to pinch o' shit they'll be no bloody use at all when the lead begins to fly, you mark my words,' added Pegg, his twenty years and single chevron weighing heavily.

'So, who's your man, Mellish?' asked Morgan.

The afternoon's exertions had left the sepoys excited and delighted by their new-found skills, and the 95th utterly exhausted. Now, as the next stage of bringing the two battalions together before they had to face the trials of battle, the 10th BNI had decided to entertain the British soldiers with some roasted goat and mutton, and a wrestling challenge. Colonel Hume, knowing the reputation of Private Lawler, a vast, Lincolnshire bruiser from Carmichael's company, much loved and admired by the men, had accepted Commandant Brewill's suggestion with alacrity, knowing that he was on a safe wicket.

'Oh, Sepoy Ranjiv Nirav from our Light Bobs,' Mellish answered casually. 'There's not much of the lad, but you'd be surprised at the speed and strength of some of the Brahmins who are bred to this sort of thing.'

'Indeed I would,' replied Morgan as the two antagonists strode to their respective corners of the ring, which had been marked by a rope pegged in the dirt.

'Now, don't sneer at our boy, Morgan.' Forgett, the policeman, had come to watch the spectacle as well. 'Just because he's half the weight of your great monster, don't underestimate him. Those who choose to wrestle spend hours perfecting their skills and I've got the marks to prove it. Soon after I arrived here in Bombay I decided to impress my command with my martial skills . . .' Morgan saw how Mellish chortled at the memory of Forgett's story, '. . . and that was a mistake, I can tell you. One of my lads – another of these full-time wrestlers – had me in the dirt in seconds; chucked me about like a child's doll; had me begging for mercy and then stood over me and made the lowest *namasti* you've ever seen. I promoted him the next day – best thing I ever did. So, I'd be a bit cautious about putting too much money on Private Swede-basher over there.'

Private Lawler was broad and squat; wearing a pair of cotton drawers and canvas shoes, his milky white torso stood in almost painful contrast to his tanned face and lower arms where his uniform had left him exposed to the sun. Now he stretched his limbs, massaged his shoulders and rotated his head to ease the pressure in his neck, whilst another soldier stood ready with a bucket and towel.

Opposite was Sepoy Nirav. Barefoot and thin, Nirav was easily a stone and a half lighter than Lawler, narrow where the Englishman was broad, nimble where he was stolid. The sepoy, in nothing more than a loincloth, had coiled his long hair up into a knot on top of his head and now he stood on one leg, pulling at the toe of his other foot in a gesture that reminded Morgan more of Sadler's Wells than the Fancy. Like his opponent, Nirav was attended by another soldier, an even shorter man, very dark-skinned, with drooping moustaches.

'Ah don't give much for that Pandy's chances once Terry Lawler gets a grip on 'im, d'you, Corp'l?' Beeston was sitting on a mat, cross-legged as he'd seen the natives do, nursing a china mug of rum and water in both hands.

'Naw, our Terry'll bloody murder 'im,' Pegg replied. ''E won't see the end of one round, 'e won't.'

The officers were of much the same opinion. As Morgan, Forgett and Mellish studied the form, Carmichael sauntered up. 'My feller was runner-up in Dublin last year.' He was suddenly proprietarily interested in a soldier who might reflect well on him. 'Saw off Shand from the Dragoon Guards. You'll remember him – quite a celebrity in his day.'

'Shand . . . yes, I do recall him; beat the Navy's top boy in 'fifty-two, if I'm not wrong. But watch Nirav: he's as fast as a snake,' replied Mellish, sticking to his man.

It was all too much for Morgan's sporting blood. 'Twenty rupees says Lawler'll best yours inside a round.'

Carmichael glanced disapprovingly at his vulgar brother officer, whilst Mellish pulled his hand from his pocket to shake Morgan's with no hesitation at all. 'Aye, make it forty, if you like,' he said.

'Forty rupees! Why, that would keep my family in clover for a month, that would,' exclaimed Forgett.

'Forty it is.' Morgan shook Mellish's hand as the two wrestlers moved to their corners.

One of the younger naiks was the referee. In excellent English, followed by Hindi, he explained the rudimentary rules to both contestants before, at a single blast from a bugle, he signalled the contestants forward.

Lawler dominated the centre of the ring, gently turning to keep his face towards Nirav who, crab-like, circled slowly round him.

'Fuckin' easy meat, this is,' jeered Beeston from his ringside seat.

'Aye, no bleedin' contest. Just watch how Terry'll—' But Pegg didn't finish his words, for Sepoy Nirav darted at Lawler's vast, pale form, threw his wiry arms around his waist and drove him right back to the rope by sheer force of momentum.

Lawler scrabbled, almost lost his footing as he tried to stay upright, and caught hold of Nirav's sweat-sheened shoulders more to steady himself than as a countermove. But as he was pushed further and further back, Lawler came to his senses and, with a series of crude double-handed blows to the back of Nirav's neck, swatted his assailant away from him.

This one sally, though, had allowed Nirav to gauge Lawler's lack of speed as well as his strength. As the sepoy massaged his neck but continued to circle, the crowd became increasingly vocal, the Indians cheering and stamping their feet in applause, just as they had done during the skirmishing demonstration earlier, the British whistling and catcalling.

'Your boy doesn't want to get in the way of another of Lawler's roundhouses, does he, Mellish?' Morgan was transfixed by the speed of the sepoy and suddenly worried about his stake.

'True, but Nirav's got the measure of Lawler now that—'

'Oh, come now, Mellish,' Carmichael butted in. 'Your fellow's just skin and bone, more used to snake-charming and rope tricks than wrestling, just watch how—' Then it was Carmichael's turn to be interrupted, for a great cry went up from the 10th as Nirav skimmed through the dust feet first at Lawler, striking the Englishman with both heels just below the left knee.

The bigger man crashed on his chest, whilst Nirav rolled skilfully to one side and leapt to his feet. A gasp came from the 95th.

'Bloody hell, that'll 'ave broke our Terry's shinbone, that will.' Beeston said what everyone was thinking, but whilst Nirav floated around the downed giant, Lawler dragged himself onto all fours, squatted momentarily whilst he pulled a paw across his eyes and then launched himself at Nirav with a low roar.

As Lawler charged like Goliath, the 10th's David saw his chance. Falling almost flat on his face before scrabbling quickly forward through the grit, Nirav shot between Lawler's pumping legs and whirled round behind him in a crouch; he seized the wrestler's trailing ankle, then stood and lifted the flailing leg high in the air, all in one easy, fluid movement. Lawler's weight and speed were skilfully used against him and for the second time in a few moments, the champion of the 95th thumped into the ground. This time, though, Lawler's forehead was the first part of his body to meet the sun-hardened earth.

As Morgan heard the crunching impact, he knew that Lawler wouldn't make the count. The referee counted down the seconds and the Scunthorpe champion lay in the dust, as cold as the setting sun was hot.

'You see what I mean, gentlemen? Never underestimate these people. They'll always surprise you,' Forgett observed, as Sepoy Nirav grinned mightily, making *namasti* to all four corners.

'There now, I said 'e was an 'andy little bugger, didn't I?' Pegg, by the side of the ring, pulled his clay pipe from his mouth and spat. 'But let's see how they take to powder an' shot, shall we?'

*   *   *

50

As the troops of both regiments – the 10th noisy in victory, the 95th sullen in defeat – wandered off towards the smell of cooking, Commandant Brewill bore down on the knot of officers. 'Well, gentlemen that was a treat, even if it was rather brief. Thought you said Lawler had done a bit of this sort of thing before, Hume?'

It was the first time since the arrival of the British troops, three days before, that the sepoys had done anything to restore their honour; now Brewill was going to make the most of it.

'Aye, he's been tidy in all the bouts that he's had in the Regiment,' Hume replied modestly. 'There's no question, though, that Nirav beat him squarely.'

'But he's hardly got used to the heat or the water yet, Colonel.' Carmichael sprang to Lawler's defence. 'Once he's into his swing I'll back him against anyone. Why, you remember him at Aldershot, don't you, Colonel?'

'I do, Carmichael, and he did well then, but the commandant's feller showed him a trick or two this time and he won handsomely.' Hume's tone brooked no further intrusion from Carmichael, his humility causing Brewill to beam with pleasure.

'Well, let's get some drinks and toast our partnership against the bloody Pandies, shall we?' Brewill led the way up the steps of the officers' mess, the great wooden doors of which were opened silently by waiters as the officers approached.

Caps and swords were passed to servants, Hume pointedly unhooking his pistol from his belt as well. Carmichael was the only officer not to follow Hume's lead and remove his revolver.

'Don't forget to leave your splendid pistol, Captain Carmichael. You won't need it in this mess any more than you would in ours.'

'But, Colonel, in Meerut . . .' Carmichael's voice trailed off as Hume stared hard at him.

'We've got some more guests, ain't we, McGowan?' Brewill appeared not to notice this little scene, hesitating before leading the party into the anteroom.

'Yes, Commandant,' Brewill's adjutant replied. 'A Captain Skene, the political officer from Jhansi, and an escorting officer from the Twelfth Bengalis.'

Morgan's ears pricked up; guests from Jhansi – the station not only where his father's friend Colonel Kemp commanded the 12th but, much more importantly, the godforsaken place where Mary Keenan was.

'No matter, but you have told Forgett that they're here, haven't you? Our policeman is bound to want a discreet word with the political, won't he?'

Morgan noticed how much more relaxed Brewill was once he was back in control of events.

'I have sent word to his bungalow, sir,' McGowan replied. 'I'm sure he'll be with us directly.'

After the court martial in which the police officer had been the principal witness for the fatal prosecution, it had been thought wise to move Forgett, his wife and daughter into the fort until tempers had cooled.

The officers strode into the anteroom, where the curtains had been pulled against the night that would suddenly rush upon them. Where it had been cool and shaded earlier, it was now stuffy, the tables alive with candles, their light flickering off crystal bowls of punch and glasses that lined the sideboards, ready for the press of thirsty guests. There were some modest pieces of silver in the corners of the long, low room, but the décor relied mainly on countless heads of stuffed animals, skins of tigers and leopards, and a vast pair of elephant tusks from which hung a brass gong.

'Christ, I hadn't noticed earlier – the place looks more like a bloody zoo than officers' quarters.'

Hume frowned to silence Carmichael but it was true, Morgan thought: there was little of the grace or taste of a

British regiment's mess, but then wasn't that exactly the point that Forgett had made to him a couple of days ago? What had he said – something about 'most of us don't come from money like most of you'?

As the waiters fussed around the guests, Morgan noticed two figures at the far end of the room; they rose respectfully as the senior officers came in. One was small and dark, his well-tanned face set with heavy whiskers below carefully combed, wavy black hair. He was dressed in a simple blue frock coat, and his long riding boots were still dusty. On the table beside him was a thin leather document wallet.

'Hello, sir . . . gentlemen . . . I'm Skene, Political Officer from up-country in Jhansi.' Five foot seven of nervous energy pushed into the gaggle of new arrivals, all of whom were trying to get at the drink, returning Skene's greeting only perfunctorily.

At first, Morgan scarcely noticed the other figure, hovering in the background; he was concentrating too hard on the servant's brimming punch ladle and his own empty glass. But there was something about the way that Hume looked up, his face breaking into the widest grin, his drink forgotten, that caused Morgan to pause.

'Well, I'll be damned, this gouger needs no introduction, Brewill!' Hume pushed his outstretched palm out to the other man, who practically ran down the room to shake it.

Almost six foot of handsome, hay-rick-headed, scarlet-coated ensign of Bengal infantry pumped the hands of the 95th officers with glee.

'You know all this lot, don't you?' Hume continued delightedly. 'Bazalgette, Massey, Carmichael . . .'

'I do, Colonel Hume, I do,' said the ensign, greeting them ecstatically.

'And your old friend Morgan, of course,' Hume added.

'Indeed, sir.' The ensign's grin suddenly faded. 'Brevet Major Anthony Morgan; how could I ever forget?'

Morgan shook the hand of his old sergeant, the husband of his lover, the man he'd never expected to see again, James Keenan.

Christ, this is ghastly, thought Morgan as he shifted on the horsehair-covered mess chair. How, in the name of all that's holy, in a country the size of India, have I knocked up against James bloody Keenan again?

Keenan sat opposite Morgan, looking fixedly at Skene as he explained the situation in Jhansi to the assembled officers.

'You all know what's happened in the north and around Delhi, and the telegraph reports this morning that General Wheeler and a small force of mixed white and native troops have been besieged in Cawnpore which – as I am sure you all know – is about seven hundred miles north-east of us here in Bombay.' Skene pulled at his drink whilst the audience – most of them, at least – listened intently to his assessment.

'There'll be Queen's troops from Malta and elsewhere along shortly to swell our forces, and I believe that so long as the mutinies don't spread to the Madras and Bombay Presidencies – and may I congratulate you, Commandant, on the way that things have been handled here in the city – the main centres of rebellion, including Delhi, should soon be under control. But, there's a lot of countryside and difficult terrain that's less easy to dominate, and it's crucial that we must keep the native princes and lesser rulers loyal.'

Brewill was genuinely pleased to be praised by a 'political', but he hissed to his adjutant, 'Where's bloody Forgett? He ought to be here.'

'I don't know, sir. I'll go and find him, shall I?' McGowan replied.

'No,' the commandant muttered. 'You need to hear this as well; sit still.'

'And around the Gwalior area in southern Bengal, ten days' hard riding up-country from here, things are particularly difficult to gauge. Now, gentlemen, I need your complete discretion concerning what I'm about to say . . .' Skene looked around the dozen or so officers in his audience, Brewill and Hume, the company commanders of the 10th and the 95th and a clutch of subalterns. 'The whole area is dominated by a series of princelings and maharajahs who are overseen to varying extents by British agents and political officers like me, and referred to as the Central India Agency. Now, I know that sounds untidy and unsatisfactory to the military mind – and it is – but it works, or it has done so far. Despite persistent rumours, there have been no uprisings amongst these states. But much hangs on how the Rhani of Jhansi now reacts to changing events. Her little fiefdom is wealthy and well organised and she pulls the strings at the centre of the spider's web. She may be a woman, but her intelligence, family connections and strength of character make her damned influential. The others will probably follow her lead, and between them they have about twenty thousand irregulars and household troops – pretty mixed quality, mark you, but fine horsemen and a fair amount of artillery – who'll be worth their weight in gold against the mutineers, not due so much to their fighting quality but because of the powerful influence that they'll send to their rebellious "brothers".'

Again Skene paused. Even Morgan was concentrating now, and one or two of the subalterns' jaws hung slack with suspense.

'And talking of gold, India ain't England: the Rhani runs on graft and geld, so Keenan and I are here to collect enough guineas to buy her loyalty. I'm confident, gentlemen, that if she and her upright supporters – and, gentlemen, if you'd met the lovely Rhani you'd be upright as well . . .' Skene had woven his spell so well that this little joke was met with a positive storm of laughter, '. . . will fight alongside us and help to tumble the Pandies to ruin. I look forward to being at your elbow when the prize money for Delhi is decided upon.'

Aye, thought Morgan, spoken like a real tyro, my lad, those of us that are still alive. And you can bet your best hunter that it'll be A Morgan and the rest of the Old Nails that'll be sent in first whilst you and the other nabobs hang back, leaving bloody Keenan with the last laugh.

As Skene finished speaking and the officers rose to talk and drink before dinner, Morgan saw a servant quietly approach the group of officers he was with, bow slightly to McGowan to attract his attention and then whisper urgently in his ear. The adjutant's face contorted, he said something in Hindi to the servant, who shook his head and pointed outside before moving back to the edge of the room, clearly agitated.

'That's bloody odd,' McGowan said to the group in general. 'Bin Lal has been to the bungalow where we've put Forgett and his family but the doors are locked, all the shutters are down and barred, and there are no lights showing.'

'Well, didn't your man just bang the door down, then?' Carmichael, slightly belligerent with too much brandy and hopes of bloodless glory on an empty stomach, asked.

'No, a sepoy wouldn't do that,' the adjutant replied. 'They've too much respect for a sahib.'

'What, like they had in Sitapur?' muttered Carmichael acidly – the news had just reached them of wholesale massacres in the garrison north of Lucknow just days before.

'Well, we'd better go and see what's detained him, hadn't we?' said Morgan, seeing the perfect way of avoiding a deeply awkward conversation with James Keenan.

'Yes, I'd be delighted to have you with me, Morgan,' said McGowan, as the pair moved towards the entrance to the mess. 'Better take our revolvers, don't you think?'

'Oh, aye, quite so,' said Morgan, taking the proffered Tranter and clipping its reassuring weight to his belt.

'I'll come too, if I may,' Carmichael interrupted. 'Too much toad-eating that bloody political for my liking.'

Yes, you too want to avoid Keenan, don't you? thought Morgan. Keenan had seen Carmichael at his cowardly worst in the Crimea, and a meeting between the two of them would be almost as difficult as the one he was trying to dodge.

'Do: get your weapons,' said McGowan as the three of them set off to Skene's bungalow, which lay with a series of others some quarter of a mile from the mess, just within the walls of the sprawling fort.

'You're a bit jumpy, ain't you, McGowan?' The night air had cooled Carmichael's brandy-warmed head. 'Thought we had to act as normal as possible; sahib bristling with iron-mongery ain't exactly calming for John Sepoy, is it?'

'P'raps not,' McGowan answered, 'but you never quite know with Forgett. He discovered the whole of the mutin-eers' plot, you know, by skulking around dressed up like one of them, skin stained, sucking betel-nut – the complete damn charade – all by himself. Slings the bat like a bloody native, he does, and has now made more enemies than you can count. That's why we've dragooned him and his family into the fort.'

'Think this is it . . . should be number eight.' It was trop-ically dark. McGowan lit a lucifer and searched round the front door frame until he found a small, brass plate engraved 'Sobroan House', below a figure eight painted in the 10th's regimental green. 'Aye, we're here.'

He rapped on the door. 'Forgett . . . Mrs Forgett, are you in?'

'Does it look as though they're bloody in?' Carmichael asked quietly. 'Here, let's see if we can't . . .' and he pushed at the front door, which gave as he shoved, but refused to open. 'There's something jammed against the door from the inside. Here, Morgan, lend a hand.'

The two captains applied their shoulders to the door, and

each time they crashed home against the woodwork, it opened a little more, inching something heavy and awkward away into the darkened room until there was just enough space for one man to squeeze in.

Morgan drew his pistol, cocked it and thrust his shoulder and chest into the gap, squirming between the door and the jamb.

'Can you get a lucifer lit, one of you? I can't see a blind thing.' Morgan had pushed inside but his eyes were unaccustomed to the dark, and as McGowan scrabbled with another match, he stumbled hard over something on the ground, crashing onto the wooden floor, sending his pistol flying.

'Goddamn . . . what filthy mess is this?' As Morgan pulled himself to his feet he was aware of something wet and gluey that had stuck to the palms when he'd broken his fall. The feel was horrid yet familiar, and as he held his hands up to his unseeing eyes, a match flared behind him, showing him that his fingers, forearms and knees were covered in blood. Indeed, he was standing in a puddle of it, which spread as far as the pool of match-light reached, blackly red.

'Christ alive!' Morgan was appalled. 'Come in quick, you two.' But as the others barged through the half-opened door, Morgan looked at the bundle on the floor over which he fallen. 'Careful, there's a body there . . . there, just where you're standing.' Carmichael had hung back and as McGowan pushed in, he almost tripped over the corpse, as Morgan had.

'I'll get the lights going.' All the bungalows were designed in the same way, and on the wall McGowan quickly found an oil lamp, which he tried to fire. It guttered briefly, shrank from the match and then caught, revealing everything in the room. 'There, that's done.'

Other than the heavy *chaise-longue* that had been used to bar the door, and the lake of blood, things were remarkably orderly. There was no sign of a struggle, but lying just inside the entrance was the body of a young woman. Both arms were pierced with bone-handled carving knives, which pinned her to the floor, whilst a brown satin dress was pulled up around her waist, showing her underwear and a bush of pubic hair between the separate legs of muslin drawers. There was blood on her thighs whilst round her mouth and neck a towel had been wound. Her auburn hair was thrown into chaos, both blue eyes wide open but seeing nothing.

'God, that's Kathy Forgett.' McGowan instantly leant down and pulled her dress back over her bloody knees and ankles, returning a little modesty to her in death.

'Oh, no . . .' Morgan had seen dead women before during the famines back in Skibberean – but those corpses were different – and more dead men killed on the field of battle than he wanted to remember, but nothing like this. He, like the other two, pulled his handkerchief from his pocket and pushed it against his nose and mouth, for there was the most ghastly, foetid stench of blood and abused femininity all about them.

'If this is what they've done to Mrs Forgett, where's the Thanadar?' McGowan dreaded the answer to his question, but as the three officers moved from the tiny hall of the bungalow to the sitting room and lit the oil lamp there, the answer was apparent.

'What the hell's that in his mouth?' asked Carmichael.

'It's a pig's tail,' answered McGowan matter-of-factly.

There was very little blood, for Forgett had been executed with a butcher's axe. The policeman lay sprawled on the floor. One blow had fallen obliquely across his neck, severing, Morgan guessed, the spinal column and causing almost instant death, and then the horrid little iron spike that backed the axe's blade had been buried deep in Forgett's sternum. Lying on his back with his legs folded under him, the chief of police could almost have been laid out ceremonially, and the impression was only underlined by the pink, curly gristle that emerged from his mouth.

'Aye, that's what it is.' Between finger and thumb Morgan delicately pulled the distasteful bit of pork from Forgett's lolling lips. 'What does that mean?'

'Well, at a guess, it's an allusion to the biting of pig-fat-greased cartridges,' McGowan volunteered. 'I told you that Forgett had enemies.'

'Yes, and we need to get after them.' Carmichael led the others back to the hall and gestured towards the open kitchen door and the yawning back door beyond, which showed as a black oblong of night air. 'Look at the trail – that's the way they've gone.' He indicated some smears of blood on the floor, drew his revolver and led the others back to the hall and towards the open kitchen door.

'Wait. What on earth's this . . . oh!' McGowan exclaimed, noticing a rolled bundle of curtain cloth close to the woman's cadaver.

The mainly buff, floral-patterned cotton curtain had been pulled from the pole above the window, that much was obvious, and something wrapped within it had bled into the material, staining it a rusty red.

McGowan pulled the tight-wrapped fabric to one side, revealing a crushed baby's head, blue and deep purple with bruises and contusions. 'It's baby Gwen. They've beaten the poor little mite to death.'

Morgan had seen plenty of starvation-dead babies back in Ireland, and one of the servants' still-born children at Glassdrumman, but nothing like this. The toddler had been deliberately wrapped in the curtain to drown any noise, then, from the look of things, heels had stamped hard on the delicate bones of her head, thumping the skull almost flat, making the grey matter of the infant's brain ooze from her nostrils and ears.

'Dear Lord.' Carmichael was genuinely appalled. 'Come on, there's not a second to lose.'

'Yes, but they're almost cold.' McGowan was too

squeamish to touch Gwen, but reached down to Kathy Forgett. 'They've been dead for at least a couple of hours.'

But Carmichael wasn't having any of it and went charging through the house, out of the back door and into the night, towards the sallyport of the fort.

'Right, I've got you, you murderin' Pandy, you.' The officer commanding Number One Company had run two hundred yards down the cinder path that led from the married officers' quarters to the back gate of the fort, and there seized a sentry from the 10th, thrusting his pistol against the forehead of a terrified sepoy.

One minute Sepoy Puran Gee had been quietly standing at ease, belching curried goat, guarding the least used gate of the fort and expecting an agreeably undemanding couple of hours, and the next an angry sahib had come running at him, thrown his rifle to the ground and pushed a steely-cold revolver hard against his head whilst yelling a stream of incomprehensible *Angrezi* at him. It was bad enough having the Feringees blow his friend Mungal Guddrea to dog meat, without this sort of indignity.

'For heaven's sake, Carmichael,' McGowan exclaimed, running across after him. 'He's not your man!'

Carmichael had forced the sepoy to his knees, one hand twisting the soldier's collar, the other ramming the barrel of the revolver into his temple, a series of jerks causing the man's cap to fall off and his face to twist in a combination of fright and pain, whilst his hands shot out sideways to steady himself against the officer's assault.

'Forgett and his family must have been dead for hours.' McGowan grabbed Carmichael's wrist and pistol. 'Puran came on guard, what . . . about an hour ago?' He looked to the soldier for confirmation, but the man was too scared to follow the question in English. 'Besides, that wasn't the work of soldiers – not from the Tenth, anyway.'

Carmichael allowed McGowan to push the pistol away

from the sentry's head, and released the hold on Puran's collar. 'How can you be sure?'

'It stands to reason: the Forgetts have been dead since this afternoon, when the whole battalion was being trained by you lot, every man jack accounted for. All ranks are under curfew, either here in the fort or down in the cantonment, and believe me, all the officers and NCOs are on a hair trigger. And anyway, those executions have put the fear of the Almighty into the lads; the mood's not right for this sort of thing now. I've never seen the troops so obedient and keen to please,' McGowan answered. 'No, this has been done by bazaar wallahs or perhaps soldiers from another battalion, though I doubt that.'

'Oh, I see, you're probably right.' Now the aggression had gone out of Carmichael, who lowered the pistol and even stooped to pick up Puran's cap.

'May I suggest an apology to the man, Carmichael?' Morgan asked. He could see how this story would spread like plague back to the ranks of the 10th, the very men whose trust they were trying to restore.

'Apologise to some damned . . .' Carmichael blurted, whilst the Indian brushed the grit off his rifle and rubbed his bruised forehead with offended gusto.

'Yes, Carmichael, apologise to a man you've wronged, even if he is a private soldier and a *mere native*.' Morgan thought the apology just as important for McGowan to hear as for Puran.

Carmichael looked hard into Morgan's steel-blue eyes, opened his mouth to object, but then changed his mind. 'Er . . . I'm very sorry, my man.' He was still holding Puran's cap; now Carmichael brushed the dust off it before handing it back. 'Hasty of me and needlessly rough.' He thrust his hand out to the soldier whilst McGowan translated.

Puran looked perplexed at the big, pink mitt. McGowan uttered something more before the sepoy awkwardly put his rifle between his knees and made *namasti*, cocking his head to one side and grinning so widely that his teeth flashed below his moustache.

Carmichael was equally confused. Not to be outdone, he grasped both of Puran's hands that were now pressed, palms together, in front of his face and gave them a vigorous waggle. 'No hard feelings then, old boy,' he said, just as he might have done after accidentally tripping a fellow team player at Harrow.

'Right, thank you, Carmichael. I'm sure that's soothed the poor fellow,' McGowan said with a note of sarcasm. 'I doubt that these troops have been involved in this outrage, but they may well have turned a blind eye to those who did. After all, whilst *we* accepted Forgett, he was a policeman; the executions were pretty well all his own work. The colonel will want this investigated.'

Women and babies getting torn to bits; what sort of a war is this? It's going to be a nasty bloody bitter fight that's not really any of our business. We should have left it to the John Company boys to sort out. After all, they got themselves into it . . . thought Morgan as the little group of officers trudged back to the mess, skirting the horror of the bungalow.

All eight hundred men of the 10th Bengal Native Infantry stood in two ranks arranged in three sides of a square whilst Commandant Brewill, the British officers and McGowan, the adjutant, stood in the middle of the fort's parade ground in the early morning cool. The sun had hardly risen, the dust lay still, whilst the monkeys blinked sleepily from the branches of the trees that peeped from just beyond the high stone walls.

The men had breakfasted on dates and chapattis before parading by companies and filing down to the square under the voice of the subadar-major; now they waited for the word of their commanding officer.

'Boys . . .' Brewill's Hindi was clear and firm, if not especially grammatical, for he had learnt it from the lips of the men with whom he'd served over the past thirty years rather than from any babu, '. . . yesterday Forgett sahib was murdered in his bungalow here inside the fort. Some baboon slew him with a butcher's meat cleaver and left a pig's tail in the dead man's mouth.' There was complete silence from the troops, not a flicker of emotion. 'As if that's not bad enough, memsahib Forgett was dishonoured and murdered as well; and there's worse: their baby daughter was beaten to death by these same criminals.'

Where the chief of police's death had caused no reaction, a quiet ripple of disgust and dismay came now from the throats of the 10th.

'Men, you know how bad things are in this country and how many sins have already been committed, but the death of women and babes-in-arms is unforgivable, and I pray you to tell any details that you know,' Brewill continued.

'What the fuck's 'e on about, Corp'l?' Private Beeston and Lance-Corporal Pegg had made it their business to collect Captain Skene's and Ensign Keenan's chargers as well as the little bat-horse from the syce in the stables when the urgent message had come down to the Grenadier Company's lines. The visitors were in a sudden hurry to return to Jhansi; their mounts needed full saddlebags and their pony had to be carrying enough fodder for three days' march, whilst Pegg and Beeston wanted to see their old pal and boon companion – now a grand officer – James Keenan before he disappeared. Now they waited outside the officers' mess, reins in hand, watching the 10th.

'Dunno, Jono.' Pegg could hear the passion in Brewill's speech without understanding a word. 'But 'e's layin' into 'em. It's about that peeler's murder, ain't it?'

'So they say. Them sods did it – revenge for the executions – but the wife and nipper as well . . .' John Beeston could understand the desire to murder any officer of the law, but the death of white women and children was too much.

'Aye, it's out of order an'—' Pegg was about to produce

64

some solemn judgement when voices and clattering spurs came from within the dark entrance of the mess. 'Stand up!'

Pegg brought Beeston to attention and saluted as Skene and Keenan came hurrying out.

'Well, Charlie Pegg, ye fat wee sod, as I live an' breathe; what about ye?' Ensign James Keenan recognised his old friend instantly.

'Doin' rightly . . .' Pegg did his best to imitate Keenan's brogue, '. . . your honour!' Pegg swept down from the salute and the two men clasped each other's hands and slapped shoulders as if no chasm of rank now existed between them.

'An' Jono Beeston, heard you was both out here with the Old Nails.' There was more delight from Beeston and Keenan. 'Ain't it just the devil's own luck that I've not time for even a swally with ye?'

'No, lads, I know how much you'd like to keep Mr Keenan here with you . . .' Captain Skene was obviously eager to get moving, pushing one foot into the nearside stirrup of the horse that Beeston held and reaching up to the saddle's pommel, '. . . and talk about old times, but the Twelfth have turned in Jhansi and it's going to take us twelve days or more to get back; I knew we shouldn't have left the garrison when things were so bloody touchy.'

'What's happened, sir?' Pegg asked.

'We don't know, exactly, but the news came over the telegraph in the early hours and some clown of an operator didn't want to disturb us too early, damn him,' Skene continued. 'A fire had been started near the royal palace. Most of the Europeans – and that's not many – turned out to fight it, and whilst the officers were away, the sepoys stormed the armouries and marched on the Rhani's quarters and the officers' cantonment.'

'Ain't your missus there, Mr Keenan, sir?' asked Beeston without an ounce of tact.

'No, t'ank the Lord. She an' the wee boy are up-country

with some of the other ladies an' a horde of the Rhani's officers to look after them,' Keenan replied calmly. 'They'll be fine. And anyway, with Commandant Kemp in charge, it'll all be sorted out. He'll cool any hotheads sooner than you can say *jildi-rao*, so he will.'

Keenan, too, swung up into the saddle. So intent had they all been in the conversation that the quiet arrival of two more figures on the veranda of the mess had gone unnoticed. Still buckling on their sword belts and settling their caps came Bazalgette and Morgan, on their way to the 95th's lines for morning inspection. Both officers hesitated when they saw the group before them.

'We got all that, Skene. Keenan, you'll need every ounce of that gold to smooth things over, won't you?' said Bazalgette, full of earnest concern.

'Aye, it should come in useful, provided we can get there fast enough,' replied Skene.

But as the two officers spoke, Morgan's eyes met Keenan's. They both knew that they'd deliberately avoided conversing the night before in the mess, but now there was no choice. Morgan started towards Keenan, his mouth open, but no words coming, and as he did so the ensign walked his charger a few paces away from the mess, putting a little distance between himself and the others.

'Hello, Keenan.' Morgan stretched his hand up and gently laid hold of the horse's bridle. 'So Jhansi's risen?'

'It has, Captain Morgan, sir.' Though Keenan's voice was low and cool, it seemed to Morgan that the pair of them had never been parted. 'It'll be nothing that Commandant Kemp an' us can't cope wit', though.'

'No . . . no, I'm sure you're right,' Morgan stammered. 'Have you heard of any casualties?' He thought of dead, ripped Kathy Forgett.

'No, sir, not yet,' Keenan answered levelly. 'But you can

be sure of one t'ing: Mary. Keenan will always come through, just like she did with them Muscovites.'

Morgan blinked up at Keenan sitting high above him in the saddle, the sun turning him into a black sillhouette.

'An' there's another t'ing you can be equally certain of.' Keenan's voice now held an edge of menace. 'With the greatest of respect, sir, if ever you come near my Mary or our boy again, I'll kill ye dead.'

THREE

Bombay to Deesa

'Stop yer fuckin' swayin' about, can't you, Beeston?' barked Colour-Sergeant McGucken, cheeks glowing with the salt air, his dun sea-smock such as all the troops wore to protect their scarlet shell jackets from the tar and omnipresent stains on board ship, as smart and soldierly as if it had been fitted in Savile Row. 'Ye get more like a lassie with every tape ye get, ye bloody puddin"!'

The whole of the Grenadier Company had been paraded on the starboard deck of the Honourable East India Company's steamer, *Berenice*, as much out of the sun as possible to be addressed by their company commander, Captain Anthony Morgan. As they'd left Bombay the swell had increased a little, reducing a good third of the company to mewling, puking hollows of themselves, fit only for sympathy – and that was in short supply. Now, four days into their six-day voyage north to the Gulf of Cutch and Mandavie, where the whole of the three hundred men of the left wing of the 95th were to disembark, most of the troops had recovered as the seas became more moderate.

Most of them, but not all. To his intense embarrassment, Private Beeston, veteran of more scrapes and skirmishes than he cared to remember, and the wearer of two good-conduct stripes, was amongst the worst affected, and only now was he beginning to stagger about, so pale that he made the ship's canvas look positively ruddy.

'Keep still, can't you, Jono?' Lance-Corporal Pegg muttered to his wobbly pal as the company, now drawn up in four ranks, obediently standing at ease on the rolling decks, waited for their officer. 'Else Jock McGucken'll bloody 'ave you.'

'Aye, Corp'l,' Beeston whispered back through the side of his mouth. 'I'll be fine.' Drops of sweat were forming at the edges of his nostrils. 'Where are they tekin' us now, Corp'l?'

After four months' enforced idleness in Bombay, alleviated only by swirling rumours and counterrumours that they were off to deal with first one hot spot and then another, which resulted in nothing more than early rises, kit inspections and then numbing waits in the heat, they had all been glad to embark on the *Berenice* – glad, that was, until the seasickness struck. Then the electric excitement of the news that they were going to crush the mutineers, of new adventures and, above all else, the prospect of loot, had been dampened under a blanket of vomit.

'Dunno. That shave about Delhi was all bollocks,' Corporal Pegg opined. 'That's safe back in our hands now, an' you heard that Sir Colin took Looknow, couple o' weeks back?'

'Oh, aye.' Beeston brightened a little. 'That's that Scottish bogger, Sir Colin Campbell, in't it? Last saw 'im at Ballyklava, din't we, with them Jocks 'oo couldn't shoot.'

They both sniggered at the memory of the 93rd Highlanders' appalling musketry all that time ago.

'Aye, that's the bloke,' smiled Pegg. 'Stuck it to the bleedin' Pandies this time, though; killed thousands. No, I reckon it's Cawnpore for us. Needs to be. I'm bored to the fuckin' death of 'anging about whilst all the others get the loot an' quim, not to mention—'

'Listen in, yous.' McGucken's bass Scots halted Pegg's philosophising. 'Grenadier Company . . . Company, 'shun.'

At the word of command every man stiffened, pushing his clasped hands straight down in front of his bellybutton, hollowing the back and bracing his thighs before snapping the left heel back against the right, thumping his boot hard on the teak decks of the ship.

'Sir, one officer and seventy-eight men on parade . . .' McGucken made the little ritual a spectacle, 'two detached on duty, one sick.' His hand quivered at the salute as the company commander came on deck, the colour-sergeant's great legs like some satyr, straining at the cloth of his blue-black trousers. 'May I have your leave to stand the men at ease, sir, please?' The crescendo of his words made two muscular lascars in the waist of the ship look up in startled admiration.

'Please do, Colour-Sar'nt.' Morgan returned the salute with a relaxed grace, standing out clear and sharp in his scarlet coat, for Colonel Hume had forbidden the officers to wear smocks. 'An' gather the lads in around me, please; I can't be doing with any shouting.'

A few, good-humoured insults about the men's parentage from McGucken soon had the Grenadiers shuffling into a crescent around Morgan, straining to hear what news he had to tell them.

'You've put up with a great deal of boredom, lads, over the past few months, and behaved pretty well,' Morgan started. 'Fairly well, anyway.'

There was a great storm of laughter as Morgan looked pointedly at eighteen-year-old Private Pierce from Crewe, one of the new draft, who had been found wandering drunk and stark naked on the fort's yard two weeks before, making the natives, according to Private O'Keefe, '. . . t 'ank God that it wasn't a proper man from Lifford there in the nip – that would o' caused another mutiny – but amidst the wimmin this time!'

'But now we know where we're bound.' Morgan paused for effect. 'It's Cawnpore, lads, to right the wrongs that were done to General Wheeler and his people back in June.'

'See, I told you so,' crowed Pegg as a general mutter of satisfaction swept around the company.

'Now, you'll all have heard what happened there, how the general was gammoned by Tantya Tope into putting his people into boats on the Ganges, then torn to ribbons by the Pandies as they floated in the shallows.' Morgan paused again, looking at the serious faces of his men. 'And how the white women and children, not to mention the native Christians, were hacked into pieces with axes and thrown down the wells . . . and worse.'

None of the troops could have failed to know what had happened in Cawnpore. The newspapers that reached them from England had been outraged by the rapes and massacres, but long before they arrived rumour had swept from the bazaar to the barrack block, from the stables to the officers' mess: tales of treachery and black betrayal, blood and mindless cruelty. Morgan remembered it as a particularly difficult time. The news of the massacres had come hard on the heels of the murder of the Forgetts, and it had been all that the officers and NCOs could do to stop the men from visiting a little rough justice on their new 'comrades' in the 10th BNI.

'Well, it's our chance now, lads, to take Cawnpore back and to even the score a bit.' Morgan watched the men. About half of them had yet to see either their twentieth birthdays or any fighting, but the others knew what such glib phrases meant. They knew that 'evening the score' meant blood and wounds, danger and death for them as well as their enemies, but wherever Morgan looked he could see nothing but plain determination, men whose simple values had been rocked by the death of innocents.

'We're to disembark at Mandavie.' The troops looked at Morgan, utterly blank. 'Only another day on board and then we've a long march up-country to Deesa that'll take us the best part of four weeks. We'll rest there – it's the depot of our

Eighty-Sixth, and we should be there for Christmas Day – before another flog of about five hundred miles to Cawnpore.' This was greeted by a little cheer. 'But it's the march that I need to tell you about. For the first time we'll be in hostile country, but not so hostile that we can afford to treat every native the same. It's hard to understand, lads, and it's going to take every bit of wit and patience you've got to deal with the mutineers that we meet as the murdering, godless thugs that they are, yet handle the civilian population with respect – unless they betray us.' Morgan looked at seventy-odd wrinkled brows, not at all convinced that one word that he said was being understood, but he pressed on. 'Now you'll have all heard of Lord Canning's declaration back in June . . .'

'Oo's 'e, then?' Beeston asked quietly.

'You know, Jono, that cunt from London 'oo wants us to pray for the Pandies' salvation.' The Governor-General of India would probably not have been flattered by Pegg's description of him.

'He's made it quite clear that British rule is under no serious threat and that once this little pother in Bengal's been put down,' Morgan let none of his reservations about the depth and severity of the uprising show, 'Her Majesty's power will be wider and stronger than ever before. And that means that we've got to leave the country in the best shape we can. It's no good putting every man, woman and child to the sword one minute and then having to rebuild the place an' pretend that it never happened. Now, you'll come across all sorts of horrors an' meet folk who've been outraged and seen things that they should never have had to see; there's all sorts of irregulars roamin' about the country – English an' native, soldiers and civilians – who've taken the law into their own hands an' are stringing people up from every tree.' Morgan paused again to look at the men, every one of whom was listening intently to him. 'And that's fine for mutineers, but not every native is disloyal. Just look at the Tenth . . .'

'You look at the murderin' bastards if you want,' whispered Beeston to whoever cared to listen.

'. . . and we need the help of the civilian population, especially for the intelligence that they will give us about who is and who isn't a mutineer, where the enemy is located, what his plans are, and a host of other details. Now, most of you have seen harder knocks than anything that this bunch of ragamuffins will be able to throw at us, and you always behaved yourselves.' There was just a slight question mark in Morgan's voice. 'I expect the highest of standards from you: an' Christ help anyone who steps out of line. Any questions?' Morgan scanned the crowd of sun-burned faces. 'No, right, Colour-Sar'nt.'

But before Morgan could hand over to McGucken, a boot stamped on the deck and a hand shot out, seeking permission to speak. 'Sir,' Pegg's Wirksworth accent cut the sea air, ''ow d'we know 'oo is and isn't a bleedin' Pandy? The papers say they tek their uniforms off if it suits 'em an' just bugger off into the villages and pretend to be ordinary folk.'

There was a hint of nodding heads from the other men at their self-appointed spokesman's words.

'That's exactly what I'm saying, Corporal Pegg. These ain't Muscovites fighting fair and even, but we can't assume that everyone's an enemy – it's going to be difficult,' Morgan answered firmly.

'Aye, sir, but these bastards 'ave murdered women an' nippers, an' stabbed us in the back.' Pegg wouldn't be silenced. 'It's all right for some windbag politician to tell us to be Christian kind to the Pandies, sir, but they won't 'ave to do the fighting, sir, will they?'

McGucken stepped forward to shut Pegg up, but Morgan stopped him as he saw a ripple of support and concern spread throughout the troops.

'You're right, Corporal Pegg.' Pegg's face relaxed at his officer's tolerant reply. 'But that's our job; we've got to do the dirty work whilst shiny-arsed politicos blow words into the wind. So, we'll just have to get on with it, won't we; an' if you find a bit of grog an' gold in the process, the colour-sar'nt and me won't be asking too many questions.'

It wasn't much of a quip, but it worked well enough for Morgan as the men greeted it with a laugh until McGucken brought them to attention as he strode off.

As he groped for the rail that led him below decks, Morgan paused for a moment and stared at the shore, which was now quite distinct. White surf marked a strip of sand topped with dusty-green jungle, and he wondered just what danger and peril lay in front of them all.

'No 'eathen mut'neers 'ere then, Corp'l?' Beeston, footsore and bored after three hot, uneventful nights on the march said what everyone had been thinking.

'No, not so far, Jono. Just these buggers an' a stink o' shit,' Pegg replied disappointedly.

They had all got used to a cloud of Indian servants and bearers who had done the men's every bidding for a daily pittance back in Bombay, but only a handful had greeted them at the desolate quayside at Mandavie, due, they all assumed, to the imminence of battle. But there had been no sign of the mutineers; indeed, there was little to be seen of anything as they marched in the cool of the night on the muddy tracks beside ditches and drains bordered by scrubby jungle.

'We'll be in Bhuj in a couple o' hours, won't we, Corp'l?' Beeston asked, his voice flat with the tedium of marching and the lack of sleep snatched in the midday heat between double sentry duties as they waited for the attack that hadn't materialised.

'An' d'you think they'll let us put us smocks back on – this jacket's so bloody 'ot,' Beeston continued. The men had not been allowed to shed their red coats in favour of the much lighter canvas smocks for no good reason that the troops could see.

'Naw, they'll keep us dressed up like they did out East till someone saw some sense . . . Aye, we should be there soon,' Pegg replied dully. 'Hark at that lot. You'd think they were on bleedin' furlough, you would.'

It was true: the four companies of the 10th Bengal Native Infantry, who had disembarked alongside the left wing of the 95th, had sung and chanted rhythmically from the first pace they'd taken. Whilst the 95th had started in fine form bellowing 'Cheer, Boys, Cheer', their own especially ribald versions of 'The Derby Ram' and countless, sentimental Irish ballads, they had soon lapsed into moody silence as the miles dragged slowly by in the dark nights. The sepoys, meanwhile, had maintained a simple enthusiasm, great gusts of laughter occasionally reaching the ears of the tramping British as some witticism was passed up and down their scarlet columns.

'In fact, I reckon those are probably the lights of the town yonder.' But no sooner had Pegg spotted a line of guttering lanterns in the distance than the cry went up from behind them that was repeated by McGucken and the other non-commissioned officers.

'Get off the road, Grenadiers. Horse coming through!'

And as the foot soldiers took to the thorny banks of the road and leant on their rifles, easing the weight of their knapsacks, columns of bearded men in dark, loose-fitting kurtahs, brown leather belts and bandoliers, curved tulwars at their sides, carbines bouncing behind their saddles and deep red turbans on their heads, came trotting past.

''Oo's that lot, Colour-Sar'nt?' Pegg asked McGucken as they both stood and watched the horsemen jingling past.

'Scinde 'Orse, Corp'l Pegg.' McGucken pulled the short clay pipe from his mouth and rootled in the bowl with the tip of his little finger.

'Right little tatts they're on, ain't they?' Pegg ventured, stuffing a fresh quid of tobacco into his cheek.

'Well, they're not like our 'Eavies; more like scouts and reconnaissance troops on sort o' polo ponies,' McGucken answered, 'but there's two squadrons of 'em an' they'll be right 'andy against any rebel cavalry that we meet.'

As the last of the Indians clattered by, the NCOs had the men on the road again, plodding forward towards the lights of Bhuj, the vinegary smell of fresh horse dung now sharp in their nostrils.

'I didn't get a wink of sleep, did you, Morgan?'

When fatigue took some of the edge off him, Carmichael could be almost pleasant, thought Morgan.

'A wee bit, but those Sappers made a God-awful din when they arrived, didn't they?' Morgan replied.

As the wing of the 95th had arrived at the little town of Bhuj some three hours before dawn and been shown to a mixture of reed-shelters and *dak* bungalows by staff officers, where they had sunk gratefully onto mats and charpoys, other troops had streamed in. The wing of the 10th BNI had been hard behind them, more than two hundred sabres of the Scinde Horse were already milling around in the dark, and then, just before dawn, Captain Cumberland's Royal Engineers had come rumbling into camp on the squealing, solid wooden wheels of innumerable bullock carts.

'They did,' Bazalgette wiped at his plate of curried goat with a piece of rubbery chapatti, 'but this has the makings of quite a formidable little column, don't you think?'

'No, gentlemen, don't stand up, please.' Colonel Hume was just too late to stop the group of captains and subalterns, all working hungrily at a tiffin of rice and meat, from dragging themselves to their feet. 'Good to see a bit of civilisation again, ain't it?'

Morgan marvelled at the man. It was all he himself could

do to cast a rudimentary eye over the crude shelters allotted to his company when they'd arrived a few hours ago before a quick, '. . . Carry on, Colour-Sar'nt,' as he scuttled off to the officers' bungalow and stretched himself out to sleep. Not Hume, though. His red-rimmed eyes showed that he'd been far too conscientious for slumber whilst all the other units in the column had been arriving, and now he even had time to play down the wretchedness of the camp and its amenities.

'You'll all be pleased to hear – ah, thank you, *shukria*,' Hume passed his sword belt, pistol and cap to a native servant – 'that the artillery is on its way. Once the Second Field Battery of our friends the Bombay Artillery is with us, then we'll be complete and Johnny bloody Sepoy will have to look to his laurels.'

There was a general mutter of agreement from the officers, although the younger subalterns, Morgan noticed, were much too engrossed in their food to give the Colonel the attention that the older officers thought he merited.

'And on that subject . . .' Hume gratefully accepted the quart pot of ale that a servant pressed into his hand as he settled into one of the cane chairs, '. . . how have the men accepted your pep talks on "Clemency Canning's" dictat?'

'Fine, sir,' said Bazalgette, as the colonel's gaze fell upon him, though he was far more interested in the contents of a tureen of fish soup.

'And your lot, Massey?'

'It took a bit of getting through to them at first that we can't go around behaving like the mutineers themselves, but I think they took the point,' Massey answered thoughtfully.

'And Number One Company?' Hume turned to Carmichael, who having been first to get at the food, was replete; now he was rubbing an oily cloth over his revolver, having first made a great show of drawing the six charges from the chambers.

'They're all right with things, Colonel, but I explained how we'd got to be careful not to cause more trouble than we solve, and how we mustn't go around assuming everyone's a bloody Pandy.' Carmichael held the big pistol up to the light and nonchalantly squinted down the barrel.

'And they understood that?'

Hume was checking more that his officers knew what was expected rather than just the soldiers, thought Morgan, listening intently.

'Oh, yes, they seemed to,' Carmichael answered rather too easily. 'Anyway, sir, I told them that if all else failed, Mr Enfield and Mr Adams here would be able to provide the answers.'

'Oh, so that's one of the Adams revolvers, is it?' Hume asked innocently, to Morgan's delight.

Carmichael never ceased to brag about his expensive pistol and how it had saved his life in the Crimea more times than he could recall, but his casual answer had needled Hume, though Carmichael didn't seem to have noticed.

'I've noticed it before; may I have a look?' the colonel continued.

Carmichael passed the big blued-steel weapon across to the commanding officer, presenting the handsome ivory grips first. He never lost an opportunity to show the weapon off; its smooth double action and the precision of its rifling served as an excuse for everyone to admire the inscriptions in the ivory – the monogrammed 'R. L. M. C.', as well as the battles at which its owner had been present.

'Hmm . . . that balances well.' Hume handled the weapon appreciatively. 'And a craftsman's been at work here.' He studied the butt. 'Alma, Balakava, Inkermann, Sevastopol. My word, you must have cared for this, Carmichael – it looks as if it's never been out of its holster.'

Hume's barb was lost on Carmichael, but not on Bazalgette and Morgan, who looked at each other and smiled.

'I feel like bloody Noah, sir. Look at these rascals, will you?'

McGucken was rarely so voluble, but Morgan had to admit there was something biblical about the bullocks, camels, donkeys and even six vast grey elephants that swayed about the gun lines of Number Two Field Battery.

'They give us some queer jobs, they do, but the commanding officer was most particular about the safety of the guns and the gunners, and I suppose it's a compliment of sorts . . . oh, goddamit,' Morgan cursed as he stepped in a giant dollop of what looked like horse manure.

'Dunno whether standing in pachyderm shite's lucky or not, sir, but I guess you'll find out now,' McGucken grinned as Morgan scraped the welt of his boot with a handful of coarse grass, 'though I'd prefer to be with the rest of the column rather than hanging around wiping gunners' arses. The fightin'll probably be done by the time this menagerie catches up with 'em.'

'I hear what you say, Colour-Sar'nt, but there'll be no attempt at towns or cities without the guns, and if there are rebels about on the route to Deesa, they'll want to knock out the artillery first,' answered Morgan, almost convinced by his own line of reasoning.

'An' look at this lot, sir – what'll we do wi' them in the middle of a fight?' asked McGucken as he stared at the crowd of civilan bearers, grass cutters, grooms, cooks, washerwomen and general servants whom the battery had brought with them.

'D'you know, Colour-Sar'nt, I haven't the least idea.' The same thought had occurred to Morgan as swarms of civilians had appeared from nowhere once the troops had reached the relative civilisation of Bhuj and attached themselves to the company before they started the long march up-country. 'I suppose they'll make themselves scarce if the lead begins to fly. Anyway, are we ready to march once the sun's down?'

'Aye, sir, as ready as we'll ever be, but I have me doots about yon cows.' McGucken looked at the great, lazy-eyed oxen. One scratched its chin with a rear hoof, narrowly missing Private Swann as its horns flailed about, whilst its partner, shackled to it by a clumsy wooden yoke, flapped its ears incessantly at a cloud of flies.

'Yes, not to mention the rest of God's creatures that we seem to have inherited.' Morgan looked with dismay as two camels wandered past, swamped by bundles of fodder almost as large as themselves. 'Still, with such a lack of draught horses, I'd prefer to have this lot than try to pull the hardware ourselves.'

As the march started after sundown that night, Morgan regretted his words. The guns and their limbers behaved well enough – the Indian drivers keeping the horses well in hand – and the camels were aloof but quiescent, whilst their vast loads meant that no traffic could pass in the other direction. Then, after a great deal of trumpeting and general skittishness, the elephants that were pulling the extra ammunition caissons settled to their duty, plodding stolidly in the dark under the direction of their mahouts. But the bullocks: how right McGucken had been not to trust 'yon cows'.

'Get up, won't you, you lazy son of a drab,' one of the Bombay gunners, a grizzled Englishman wearing the Sutlej medal, kicked and slapped one such creature that had lain down directly in the centre of the narrow, muddy track, anchoring its yoked partner securely and blocking all the traffic that came behind it. 'Get your fuckin' arse movin' before I take the steel to ye.'

To the 95th's Grenadiers, who marched beside the column of nine-pounders, howitzers and their attendant traffic, ready to protect them from any interference by the enemy, such sights were a wonder.

'Come on, you useless sod,' the gunner continued, pulling his hanger from its scabbard and giving the animal such a poke that it leapt to its feet, bellowing forlornly and pulling its partner violently forward.

'You'll need to tend the wound you've given that beast,'

Morgan said, concerned not with any pain that the gunner had inflicted, but merely the continued efficiency of the ox, 'or it'll mortify in this climate, won't it?'

'Mortify, sir – I hope it bloody dies.' The gunner had, quite clearly, reached the end of his patience with this particular animal. 'But I doubt it; they've got hides thicker than a docker's dick-skin, these bastards 'ave, sir.'

And after a brace of night marches and sleep-short days, Morgan came to agree with the gunner, for the tiresome cattle seemed to ignore hunger, thirst, threats or reason, suiting themselves entirely whether they wished to obey orders or not, and apparently impervious to all stimuli other than those that they imposed upon themselves.

The hours of darkness were hells of delay and infuriating petty problems – slipped saddles, shed shoes, broken spokes and binding axles – whilst the days provided little sleep at all as the sun beat down.

After almost two weeks of stuttering progress, McGucken was tramping alongside Morgan one night, reliving some story of his time with the 36th in Gibraltar when vivid flashes lit up the road at the front of the column.

'What in God's name's that?' asked Morgan, though he knew well enough as the flat bangs of musket-fire and the sweeping whistle of lead shook him from his reverie.

'Bloody ambush, sir,' yelled McGucken, already sprinting hard towards the trouble. 'Come on, Captain Morgan, sir, you don't want to miss the fun.'

Morgan's belly was tight with fear, but he scrabbled after McGucken when more flashes reflected off the bushes and trees as a couple of British rifles returned fire.

The track was narrow and greasy, blocked by animals and drivers, shrieking women and cowering grooms. Worse still, as the pair ran forward, grabbing their own men as they went, so a stream of panic-filled bearers came bowling down the verges towards them, shouting, eyes wide with fright, barging and pushing their way to the rear. As the mob skittered past Morgan in the dark, one man fell under the feet of the others, pulling at something in his shoulder whilst a nearby camel suddenly sank to its knees, its breath soughing coarsely from its lips. As he jostled his way forward, Morgan was aware of something fast and menacing whispering through the night: flights of arrows were thumping into flesh and saddles and tack, or quivering in the mud around his ankles.

'Jaysus, this is like the bloody crusades, sir,' McGucken puffed as they ran up to the head of the column. 'What else will the fuckers use, boiling oil?'

But before Morgan could reply, McGucken spotted two figures stumbling hard down the track on the other side of the camels and the frightened oxen, away from the noise of battle in front.

'Corporal Pegg . . .' even though the arrows continued to fly, McGucken's barrack-yard yell brought the fugitive and his companion to a sudden halt, '. . . where d'ye think yer going?'

Despite the darkness, Morgan could see the guilt on Pegg's face.

'Er . . . nowhere, Colour Sar'nt,' Pegg stammered. 'I were just mekin' sure that—'

'Put that bint down, Corporal, and get back to your men.'

Even in this chaos, McGucken's strength of character could galvanise others. It was what made him so indispensable, thought Morgan.

Pegg objected no further: the native girl whom he had been sheltering shrieked off into the night, clutching her sari about her, whilst he skulked his way back to the front of the column, trying to look as though he'd never been away.

'What's going on, Sarn't Ormond?' Morgan found the non-commissioned officer kneeling in the grass surrounded by a handful of his men. They stared hard at the fringe of jungly forest that loomed darkly fifty yards away from them, weapons ready, peering down the barrels, looking for a target.

'Got shot at from over yonder, sir.' Ormond pointed at the trees with a nod of his forehead, never taking his eyes off the source of danger nor his finger off his rifle's trigger. 'Couple of the lads fired back.'

But before Ormond could finish, another volley boomed out from the trees, the rounds whipping high overhead in the darkness. Though they were wide of their mark, Morgan found himself flat on his belly, pressing his body into the grit and mud of the track whilst a camel danced about him, the creature's decorative bells jingling madly, more frightened of the human's strange behaviour round his feet than the noise and uproar.

Christ, that was a mile off, thought Morgan. What am I doing down here on my belt buckle? What'll the boys make of me? They're not scrubbing around in the dirt, are they?

The crackle of shots from his own men helped to restore Morgan's senses as Ormond turned to him, his face damp with sweat in the moonlight, and yelled, 'What d'you want us to do, sir?'

'He'll be leading us out to clear them.' Happily, McGucken was there at Morgan's elbow, as calm as if it were all a blank-firing exercise. 'Won't you, sir? Get yer spikes on, lads.'

And whilst the clutch of men around them pulled the slender, eighteen-inch-long bayonets from their scabbards and slipped the sockets firmly over the end of their barrels, Morgan collected himself, dragging his blade from his belt and pushing his hand through the sword knot whilst his arse shrivelled tight in an all-too-familiar way. He licked his lips, held the gently curved steel out in front of him and stumbled forward over the greasy verge at the edge of the road and into the long grass beyond.

'Come on, Grenadiers, follow me!' Morgan's words seemed to come from a stranger as the little crowd of men surged after him, weapons levelled, half cheering as they crashed over the broken ground.

His mind raced back to the last time he'd been ambushed at night outside Sevastopol. Then it had been screaming Russians, banging rifles and popping flares. But the enemy was nowhere to be seen now, just the ominous, black tree line that got closer with each clumsy stride.

'There's the bastards . . . there. Fire, lads.' Ormond's breathless voice came from somewhere behind Morgan, as drab spectral figures paused, snatched at bowstrings and scrambled away into the depths of the forest before the troops could close with them.

A covey of arrows flickered harmlessly around as a handful of rifles crashed, the yellow flashes instantly lighting up the night, giving just a glimpse of lithe, running shadows, one of which was flung onto its face as if by the swipe of a giant's hand.

'Got 'im,' McGucken growled with satisfaction, the cloud of powder smoke hanging heavily amongst the leaves and branches. 'Stop here, lads. Don't chase 'em, they're not for catching, now.'

Morgan reached for a tree trunk for support as he sucked for breath, his sword suddenly leaden. 'Get the men reloaded, please, Colour-Sar'nt.' Experience had taught him that, at least.

'Aye, sir,' McGucken replied. 'You heard the officer,' even as he pushed around looking for his quarry in the undergrowth as a sportsman might search for a downed woodcock.

''Ere 'e is, Jock . . . bus.' Sergeant Ormond had been in more bloody scrimmages with the colour-sergeant than either could count and was allowed such familiarity. Now he kneeled, parting the grass so that the moonlight might let him see just what the enemy looked like.

'Skinny little runt,' said Ormond as Morgan and McGucken clustered round. 'Nice shot, though, right through the neck.'

It was difficult for Morgan to see much in the dark; all he could make out was a man not much bigger than a child wearing a dirty grey dhoti from which stuck stick-thin legs and bare muddy feet. Stained teeth were visible under a wispy moustache, lank hair covered much of his face, whilst blood, black by the light of the moon, still pumped from a long gash that ran from under his left ear across to his windpipe.

'Yon's no sepoy, is 'e, sir?' McGucken held up a slender curved bow that he'd pulled from the dead man's hand.

'Certainly doesn't look like it, Colour-Sar'nt. He's no uniform or belts on him. More like a common badmash, I'd say,' replied Morgan.

But before the professional debate began over exactly what sort of man it was that McGucken had reduced to cold meat, a gale of shouting and frightened trumpeting from the elephants that towed the heavy ammunition carts broke out from the column waiting on the road behind them.

Morgan began to run through the brush, back towards the road, the noise of the elephants being joined by a strange, feral squealing.

'Come on, then, get after the company commander.' McGucken chivvied the troops into a stumbling run, away from the dead man at whom they had all been gawping. 'Watch out for any of these rogues hidin' in the grass.'

But the danger came from quite a different source. When the column stopped, the elephants had jammed themselves tightly together at the rear of the line behind the guns and just in front of the spare oxen and some *dhoolies* carrying the sick. Here the track was deeply sunken, its banks reaching up five feet or more, effectively penning in the animals and their burdens.

'Get out of the way!' Morgan, at the head of his panting men, had been able to make out the forms of the six elephants wildly swaying about, trunks outstretched, trumpeting deafeningly in the night, stamping and stomping at something that shrieked beneath their feet. Now, one of the huge beasts came lumbering over the bank straight towards the group of soldiers, mighty ears flapping wildly, tusks thrashing left and right, its mahout clutching helplessly to its neck as its ammunition cart floundered after it. As the monstrous thing cut a swathe through the running troops so a wheel came off the caisson, which slewed round, spilling great, black, 24-pound howitzer rounds, which bounced through the grass.

'Oh, ow . . .' yelled Private James. 'It's broke me leg!' as he was bowled over like a skittle by one of the iron shot, which knocked his feet from under him.

'They're pigs, sir.' McGucken had dodged the blundering grey form and now stood on the edge of the bank just feet from the other plunging elephants, looking down at a dozen shrieking, darting forms, ghostly pale in the night. 'The elephants are terrified of 'em – so's the natives. Where the fuck have they come from?'

He was right. Morgan saw how the squeals of the pigs were tormenting the elephants, who were trying to rid themselves of their attackers with tusks and vast stamping feet, which, in turn were making the pigs even more petrified and noisy. Meanwhile, the Hindu civilians and military drivers had gathered in an appalled huddle on the opposite side of the road, aghast and helpless as the unclean creatures ran amok.

'God knows. Kill the bloody things, lads.' Morgan leaped down amongst the huge, stamping, grey, leathery feet, immediately regretting his decision. 'But don't shoot, stab the sods.'

This is no way to die, he thought as an enormous pad with nails the size of trowels thumped into the earth just inches from him, and just look at those nuts – as a scrotum the size of a bag of flour swung past his face. It'll look just grand on the Court and Social page: . . . 'gallant fate at the head of his men; bashed to death by an elephant's bollocks whilst trying to sabre a swine.'

Eventually they finished the job. Private Saint had his foot run over by the wheel of the battery's forge wagon, Sergeant Ormond was brushed sideways by an elephantine knee, but the pigs were finally subdued by the blades of the men and order restored to the terrified leviathans.

'What d'you suppose that was about, Colour-Sar'nt?' Morgan sat on the bank by the track, as the first light of dawn turned the black sky to turtle-dove grey.

'Oldest trick in the book, apparently, sir. One of the gunner naiks was tellin' me that everyone knows that elephants and pigs are shit-scared of each other an' if yous want to stampede the big buggers you just release a few wee porkers around their feet,' answered McGucken.

'Well, there we are; they didn't teach us that back at the depot, did they, Colour-Sar'nt? Still, it shows the Pandies have got a deal of sense. If they could have knocked the guns out, or just destroyed the ammunition, we'd be in queer street,' Morgan reasoned. 'What damage is done?'

'Not much, sir. A fodder camel's down, some oxen have bolted an' can't be found yet, one bearer's been wounded, Sar'nt Ormond an' Saint are a bit knocked about, an' the artillery lads are just getting a spare wheel back on that limber.' McGucken checked a pencilled list on a scrap of paper. 'Oh, aye, one of the Bombay gunners is unaccounted for; they think he might have gone off wi' the Pandies. An' the natives reckon that judging by the archer we got, the whole thing was probably the work o' rebels from one of the maharajah's armies up north, not reg'lar sepoys.'

'So, irregular rebels, not regular rebels . . . Hmm, this is going to be even more confusing than I thought. Anyway, let's get moving once that wheel's fixed. We'll find some water up ahead, get everything square and bed down for the day.' Morgan tapped his pipe out on the heel of his muddy boot. 'But we'll have to be more alert in close country if we don't want to get caught like that again.'

* * *

'You all right, Pete, Jono?' Lance-Corporal Pegg pushed through the brush into the small clearing where Privates Sharrock and Beeston were sitting behind a modest ant hill as sentries for the column that rested in the midday heat behind them.

'Aye, we're sound as a bell, Corp'l. Too much bloody staggin', though,' Beeston replied dolefully.

Since the ambush the day before, Morgan had ordered that the sentries should be doubled, so cutting by half the small amount of sleep that the men were getting during the day.

'Well, I've got Jimmy here to replace you, Jono, so you'll soon be rolled up snug; mek the most on it.' The men were posted for two-hour shifts, a fresh sentry being brought forward by a junior NCO every hour to replace one of them, so minimising the likelihood, at least in theory, that a pair of sentries would fall asleep at the same time. The burden, though, fell heavily upon the lance-corporals and corporals, who got little rest.

'If I'm on me chin-strap, I bet you're half dead, ain't you, Corp'l?' The new sentry posted, Beeston and Pegg were walking back to the column down a narrow track.

'Well, I've 'ad more restful times, but double sentries is always a pain in the ring, ain't it?' Pegg replied.

'Wasn't the sentries I were thinking about, Corp'l.' Beeston's darkly tanned face lit into a smile. 'It was that dhobi bint that you're a-poking.'

'Less o' that, you cheeky sod.' Though only twenty, Pegg was more than capable of pulling rank with older, more experienced men when it suited him. 'Anyway, she's not just a bint, she's—'

'Hush, Corp'l, what's that noise?' Beeston cut across Pegg's retort, freezing in his steps and pulling the hammer back on his rifle, raising the butt to the shoulder.

Pegg must have missed the low gurgling snuffle amongst the hum and click of insects as he'd walked up the track with the new sentry a few minutes before. But now, as both men listened intently, the noise came again.

'What d'you reckon it is, Jono?' asked Pegg, as he too brought his weapon up to the shoulder.

'Dunno. Sounds like a man, though, Corp'l,' answered Beeston. 'There, it's coming from over there.'

Slowly, hesitantly, the two soldiers crept forward off the track and into the thicket as the rasping moan came again.

'Bloody hell, they've made a job on him, ain't they?' Jono Beeston murmured as they both looked at the torn form of a man who was tied to a tree trunk. His naked feet stuck out below his crumpled knees; the only clothes he now wore were the blood-stained overalls of the Bombay Horse Artillery, whilst from his shoulders great strips of flesh had been flayed away from the purply muscle and fatty tissue that lie below the skin. His head lolled on his slashed chest, his topknot was now undone and the hair hung down in a curtain around his face.

''E's not long for this world, poor owd lad.' Pegg gently lifted the Indian gunner's chin and pulled one eyelid open. 'Let's get 'im cut down an' carried back.'

The pair of them slung their rifles and lifted the man by armpits and knees, the way they'd carried a hundred casualties in the past, trudging back down the uneven path.

'Bring him here, lads.' McGucken had been about to visit the sentries himself when he saw Pegg and Beeston with their load. 'Who is he?'

'One of the artillery drivers, Colour-Sar'nt,' Pegg puffed as they lay him on the ground as gently as possible. 'Found 'im tied to a tree over yonder.'

'Aye, he must be the boy who disappeared yesterday.' McGucken bent down, pulled a tiny round shaving mirror from his haversack and held it against the man's lips. 'No, he's *bus*. Well done for bringing him in though, lads. Nip over an' tell the gunners, will you, Beeston.' McGucken was matter-of-fact; he'd seen too many dead men to be affected by another. 'They'll want to get 'im burnt before we move on; poor sod.'

'Mek's you wonder though, Colour-Sar'nt, what this is all about, don't it?' Pegg and McGucken stared down at the grisly sight; the blood on the man's shoulders where the flesh had been stripped away had started to congeal as death arrived, whilst flies crawled thickly over his eyes, lips and nostrils.

'All that stuff about God's mercy from Mr Canning that the officers lectured us about on the ship – 'as anyone told the fuckin' Pandies to behave like Christians?' Pegg asked.

'Doesn't seem like Christmas, does it, Colour-Sar'nt?' Morgan tramped alongside McGucken, the whining of the bullock-cart wheels deadened only by the incessant buzz of flies.

'No, sir, it doesna,' replied McGucken, routinely swiping at the insects. 'They'll be punishin' the grog back home, just gettin' the measure o' things for Hogmanay. What'll be happenin' back in Cork?'

What indeed? wondered Morgan. He remembered his mother's excitement when he was a boy whilst they covered Glassdrumman – the 'big house', as the servants would have it – in holly and pine cones; how she'd insisted on following the latest fashion from London by bringing an eight-foot fir tree into the hall and covering it with glass balls (to be greeted by, 'Balls, indeed', from his scowling father) bought at vast expense from Dublin. What would Maude (how pregnant would she be now?) be doing tonight, and how would Mary be spending the season of goodwill up in Jhansi – assuming she and Sam (what did the lad look like, was he sturdy, like him, or willowy like his mother?) were as safe as Keenan had assured him they would be?

'Will you listen to that, sir!' McGucken interrupted his thoughts with a delighted laugh.

Just in sight, a mile away, rose the mud and brick fort of Deesa, the only European station for miles around, which it had taken them over four weeks of blistering, tedious marching to reach. Their only excitement had been the botched ambush two weeks before; now, as the heat started to make the dawn light wobble and the horizon to dip and rise, as the kites wheeled above them and the camels hawked and farted, the sound of a brass band came wafting down the breeze.

'Ha . . . damn me, it's "Good King Wenceslas", ain't it?' Morgan smiled.

'Aye, sir, ". . . where the snow lay round about, Deep an' crisp an' even," – some bugger's got a sense o' humour.'

And so they had. The artillery and its escort of the 95th was the last part of the column to reach Deesa, and as they approached they could see the white-jacketed musicians of the 86th under their German bandmaster, and a neat quarter guard in scarlet presenting arms whilst the guns, carts and limbers rumbled and groaned through the gates.

'Makes you realise just how bloody scruffy we've become, Colour-Sar'nt, don't it?' Morgan returned the guard's salute as they passed. The young subaltern in command, just shaved and freshly pressed, stood with his sword held gracefully akimbo.

'Aye, sir, an' here's the commanding officer.' McGucken had spotted some horsemen trotting slowly towards them. 'March to attention, Grenadiers.'

The troops brought their rifles smartly to the shoulder, trying to make up for their dust-ingrained, sun-bleached appearance.

Several mounted figures pushed their horses through the thronging interior of Deesa fort where cavalry, infantry, sappers and all manner of native servants busied themselves around what the army chose to describe as 'warlike stores': fodder by the ton, shot and powder being issued to the men from grey-painted deal boxes, dry rations, and soft leather *chaggles*, to be filled with water and slung across mules' backs. Every language under Queen Victoria's hand was there: Hindi and Pashtun, even Farsi, whilst accents from every corner of Britain abounded, from the soft lilt of Skye, through harsh Brummagen to the brogue of Kilrush.

'Happy Christmas, Morgan, Colour-Sar'nt.' Lieutenant-Colonel Hume, his adjutant, a captain commanding a squadron of the Scinde Horse, and another, half-familiar figure reined in as the ill-assorted artillery column waddled and tramped past. 'Lost anyone or anything?'

'Hap . . . happy Christmas, sir,' Morgan stammered as he and McGucken pulled their hands down from the salute. 'All our men present, three sick, one native gunner killed but all weapons and ammunition safe and serviceable, sir.' But Morgan's attention was fixed not on Hume, but upon a stout, sunburnt figure dressed in riding boots and khaki pyjamas, a puggaree-wrapped cork helmet on his head, and a belt from which hung an infantry-pattern sword and a heavy revolver, who had dismounted and now stumped towards him, both arms outstretched.

'Tony Morgan, my boy, glad you're safe.' The horseman's face was split in a grin below his greying whiskers as he wrapped Morgan in a bear hug, thumping him on the back.

'You obviously know Commandant Kemp, Morgan.' Hume looked down from his horse, slightly surprised by such an public display of friendship.

'I do, sir,' wheezed Morgan in the big man's embrace.

But he smells worse, he thought as he remembered his last encounter with his father's closest friend. It was at home in Glassdrumman when Kemp was on furlough and Morgan himself was fresh back from Sevastopol, still limping slightly from his wound. Then Kemp had been firmly in command of the 12th Bengal Native Infantry in Jhansi: he'd talked fondly – indeed, lecherously – of the lovely Rhani, the hunting, and the pleasures of peace and plenty in the Punjab.

'I'm as sure as I can be that Mary's alive, Morgan, but quite what her position is with the damned Rhani I cannot say.'

When they'd met at the entrance to the fort earlier that day, Kemp had given Morgan the briefest of outlines of events in Jhansi almost six months before, but it had taken Morgan another couple of unbearable hours whilst he settled the company and reported to Hume in detail before he could get some time alone with the commandant. Now they sat in the poky, improvised mess of the 86th, Kemp drinking lime juice and soda, Morgan slaking a big thirst with small beer.

'The Regiment just turned on a threepenny bit, lad. One minute they were all *"Ram-ram, sahib"* and kiss yer hand, damning the eyes of their so-called brothers in Meerut and Delhi, next minute it was wholesale murder. My family's all gone, Tony . . .' Kemp dropped his eyes to the floor, '. . . and the Rhani, the harlot, played us false. There were just a handful of us left when Skene and Keenan got back from Bombay – you saw them there, didn't you?'

Morgan nodded, silently urging the big, sad man to get on with his account of the tragedy.

'Aye, well, we were besieged in the tower of the Lesser Fort, the bloody Pandies all around, my own boys from the Twelfth and a whole mob of the Rhani's irregulars firing at us with the very rifles we'd only just issued to the ungrateful sods, as well as all manner of artillery. Funnily enough, there weren't many casualties, but those there were were nursed by Mary – God, she's some girl, she is. The real problem was grub and water. Anyway, things were getting pretty tight when, after we'd been there ten days or so, Skene and Keenan suddenly turn up having – and I believe every word of it – bribed their way into the place with the mohurs they'd brought to buy the bitch's loyalty.' Kemp pulled at his drink.

'Skene told us that he'd managed to get an audience with the Rhani; that she claimed to have no part in the mutiny and, as a token of her good faith, would allow the remaining Europeans to go free under escort of her men so long as Mary remained behind as her physician-cum-hostage. There was some arguing about that, I can tell you, with Mary saying she would stay so long as her boy could be by her side . . .' Kemp paused at that point and lifted an eyebrow at Morgan, who replied with nothing more than a blank look. '. . . and Keenan shouting the odds and wanting to stay with them, but Skene saying that his duty lay with the protection of the main party. Anyway, after all manner of argy-bargy I had to step in and say that we'd accept the Rhani's terms. We hadn't heard a thing at that stage of the way they butchered poor Wheeler's people at Cawnpore, but after what had happened to my family I knew not to trust the devils further than I could spit 'em.'

'So, Colonel, you think Mary and her son are all right still in Jhansi?' Morgan was doing his best to be interested in the fortunes of the others, but he had to have Kemp's reassurance about his lover.

'Well, boy, as far as I know she is. I had word about two weeks ago that Mary had been seen – Rissaldar Batuk turned up here after flogging the whole four hundred miles from Jhansi on foot and told me all sorts of horrors – white folk hunted down remorselessly, children speared like pigs whilst their parents watched – any amount of ghastliness. The only good news being that the lass still seems to be drawing breath and can be seen in close company with the Rhani whenever that duplicitous whore shows her face in public, but whether that's at pistol point is hard to say.' Kemp took another draught of lime juice.

'But I knew the bastards would betray us – and so did Skene. We weren't allowed to carry any rifles, just swords for self-protection, so we primed every pistol and revolver we had, most of the women had knives about themselves, bade *au revoir* to Mary and one or two of the native Christians who fancied their chances better if they stayed in Jhansi, and set off to meet the Rhani's troops. Bloody uncomfortable that was, I can tell you. We were jeered and mocked by my men – my own men, mark you. Why, I even saw Havildar Preet, whom I'd pulled from under the Sikhs' hoofs at Aliwal, snarling and spitting at me as we crept away. That's gratitude for you, God rot 'em.' Kemp paused for a moment, his thoughts, Morgan guessed, straying back to happier times.

'And no sooner had we got through the bazaar than I saw one of the rissaldars signal the column to halt and start to draw his tulwar. That was good enough for me: I shot one fucker just as he turned, took his *tatt* and was away as if *shaitan* was on my tail – which he was.'

Morgan was enthralled by Kemp's account. 'You must have been damn quick off the mark, Commandant.'

'Well, I was, but I'd had more experience of this sort of treachery in the weeks before these events than I cared for. I'll tell you about that in a moment, but what I'm about to say must remain between the two of us for ever. I've told no one else and if it gets out, Skene's name and memory will be picked over by the bible-bashers till kingdom come.' Kemp looked intently at Morgan.

'I'll say not a thing, you know I won't, Colonel,' replied Morgan, utterly gripped.

'Well, I drew the first blood and I suspect that it made Skene and the others realise what they dreaded most. The next shot was Skene's; as the natives closed in, I saw him cock that big Adams of his, push it straight against poor Margaret, his wife's, temple and blow her brains out – I swear it. Every word I say is true.'

'I can't believe what you're saying, Colonel. I met Skene only briefly but he seemed like one of us, and Mrs Skene had the reputation of being a God-fearing woman, didn't she? How could such a thing happen?' Morgan was genuinely shocked; the idea of a husband killing his wife was quite outside his experience.

'I'm telling you precisely what happened, Morgan. I've seen some damned odd things out here, and the few days leading up to this mayhem were the craziest I've ever lived through. But no, Skene said nothing, he just lifted the pistol up to the side of the poor woman's head and fired without a second's hesitation. Margaret looked as surprised as could be – her expression will stay with me to the grave – but she was with her Maker before the filthy heathens could lay a finger on her. I guess that was her husband's design. Then, God help us, he fired a few more rounds before putting a piece of lead straight through his own head. I know you think I'm a liar but it's true. It took no more than the blink of an eye – the time it took me to sling my leg over that cavalry mount – whilst the rest of the party were still standing around quaking.'

'And the others . . . ?' Morgan could quite see the opprobrium that Skene's acts would attract from many quarters, but was far more interested in how Keenan had fared.

'Well, you're probably wondering why I didn't make some effort to save the rest of 'em?'

'No, Colonel, I—' But Morgan wasn't allowed to continue.

'Don't forget, these aren't civilised folk – despite all our efforts. I'd seen what they could do and knew that I stood no chance if I stayed. And I was right. Batuk saw some of it and heard the rest. He told me that the men were pinioned and made to watch whilst the women and the handful of kids were butchered. Apparently, your man Keenan asked the mutineers to allow him to be sacrificed and the women and children to be spared, but to no avail. They chopped the men to bits immediately afterwards, starting with their limbs and only dealing fatal blows at the very end before the remains were slung down a well *à la* Cawnpore. Decent folk, ain't they?' Kemp seemed remarkably composed.

'So, James Keenan's dead, is he, sir?' Morgan was appalled

with himself for even asking the question. He hated to think that James Keenan – alongside whom he'd endured so much – was dead, yet he couldn't regret the death of his lover's husband, nor the death of a man who had threatened to kill him.

'Aye, boy, I know how much you went through with that brave man in Russia and, without putting too fine a point upon it, I know what a favour he did you by taking Mary off your hands.' Kemp's interpretation of events intrigued Morgan, but he didn't correct him. 'And I know you'll want to avenge your comrade's murder every chance you get.'

'You can be sure of that, Commandant,' Morgan replied. 'But I hardly dare ask about Mrs Kemp and your family.'

Nothing very much had ever been said about Kemp's personal circumstances when he came to stay in Ireland. Morgan knew that early in his career he'd married Neeta, the daughter of a well-to-do Eurasian doctor, but she'd never come back to his native Cork with him, even for the longer periods of leave that came round every couple of years. There was always a ghost of a suggestion that Kemp's family would not be welcomed in Cork's Protestant society, but whatever the reason, it was enough to ensure that little was known and nothing seen of his brood.

'Well, it's good of you to ask, and I guess that everything I'm about to tell you will sound normal in these times of madness but, as God sits in His heaven, I shall never trust one of these people again.' Kemp slowly lit a cheroot, blew the smoke into the blind-darkened roof of the room and settled back in his chair, more sombre than Morgan had ever seen him.

'I'd been angling to get command of the Twelfth for years. All sorts of things suited me about them – good record on the Sutlej, high proportion of Brahmins, but, most of all, they were based in Jhansi where Neeta's papa was the Rhani's quack. I don't mind telling you – seems demented now – but

I'd hoped to be offered the command of all the Rhani's troops once my time was up with the Twelfth – brigadier-general's pay on top of my John Company pension and a comfortable billet for both my girls if they didn't choose white society.' Kemp looked directly at Morgan as he produced the last phrase.

'Anyway, it was early June, there had been some murmurings amongst the boys after the mutinies up north and the business in Delhi, but the subadar-major and I had held a durbar with the men and I was content that all looked well. There was a bit of moaning about the low caste of some new draft, but nothing serious, and not a whisper about whether we'd be expected to serve against mutinous regiments – that I had expected. Now, mark you, I've served all my life with Bengal troops, speak Hindustani better than I do English and I had no idea that anything was in the wind with my lot, not the least idea.'

Kemp furrowed his brow, eased the band of his cotton breeches and continued, 'That night Neeta had insisted that my damned parents-in-law should come to dinner, just the four of us. I usually insisted that we had other company when they were coming in order to try and take some of the humbug out of her bore of a father.'

Morgan realised just how little he understood about day-to-day life in India, for Kemp was talking about his Eurasian relatives in just the same way that he might discuss a dinner party in Dublin. Kemp had made a brave decision when he chose to straddle both British and Indian society.

'We'd just finished our savouries and the servants were clearing the china when I heard something odd outside the bungalow. I got up and wandered out into the garden, to be met with the sight of flames licking up from the direction of the troops' lines. It was the luckiest thing I ever did. I'd just turned back towards the house – I knew the fire meant something was very wrong – when I heard Neeta giving someone such a tongue-lashing that I hung back for a minute – I've had some of those scoldings and I trembled for the poor man – until I heard her scream like I've never heard before. Then there was fucking bedlam: shouting, crashing of crockery and crystal, and two or three shots . . .'

Kemp's fists were clenched, his face misshapen with unhappiness as he relived the memory.

'What in God's name could I do? There I was on the veranda just in an evening kurta, no weapons, looking in through a window as my servants were shot down and clubbed by half a dozen of my own soldiers. Why, I knew each of the scum by name. I'd even enlisted the leader of the mob up near Datia two years back, name of Lolemun Dunniah. I'd been as close to him as you can get with a sepoy. He'd helped my father-in-law with that bloody boat of his and acted as my orderly more than once. They'd got Neeta and her mother by the throat, threatening them with knives off the table, trying to get them to tell them where I was, but they were too bloody terrified to be able to say. Then, whilst her parents watched, Dunniah . . . well, he defiled Neeta, laughing like a bloody hyena whilst he did so.'

Kemp paused and gulped, and Morgan could see that the colonel needed to unburden himself of the full horror of that night six months ago. He'd probably spoken to no one about it in any detail.

'I don't know what I should have done, Morgan. I couldn't leave my girls as orphans, could I? But all I did was stand there like Lot's wife, gaping, instead of chucking myself at them. But would it have done any good?'

'Of course it wouldn't, Commandant. You'd have just thrown your life away needlessly,' Morgan reassured him quickly.

'I know you're right, but it's hard to accept . . . and once Dunniah had finished his vileness, the heathen brutes drew one of my razors, first across Neeta's throat and then across her mother's: Jesus, the blood, it sprayed all across the white linen tablecloth. They were dead before they hit the floor, poor blessed souls, and I console myself with the thought that at least they couldn't have known much about their final moments.'

Morgan nodded in silent sympathy.

'There was worse to come. Whilst they were murdering the two women, the rogues had stretched Neeta's father out across the dining table, ripped his drawers down and then – Christ, I can hardly tell you this – thrust a bayonet right up his . . . his fundament.'

Such a proper word sounded so odd from Kemp's lips, thought Morgan.

'Well, the wretched fellow was blind already from having his eye-glasses broken in his face, but they kept thrusting the steel harder and harder up him. Each time he screamed worse and – to my eternal shame – I used the noise the poor devil was making to get clear. And you know, Morgan, what the whoresons were chanting – in English, mark you – every time they jabbed at him?'

Morgan shook his head, horrified.

'That line from the Bible, "Physician heal thyself". I know none of this will surprise you; you'll have seen much the same in Russia.'

But Morgan had seen nothing remotely like the things that Kemp described. Certainly there had been brutality, and sometimes cruelty, but nothing, thank God, to compare with this.

'That's the most horrible thing I've ever heard, Commandant.' Morgan hesitated before asking the next question in case it brought further hideous revelations. 'And what of the girls?'

'What indeed? That day they'd been out with a party of other children and their ayahs; none of them has been seen again.' Kemp whispered the last words. 'But I tell you this,

Morgan, since that night my party of irregulars and I have given more of these Pandies the opportunity to meet their heathen gods than I care to think – all the way from Jhansi right back down here to Deesa – and there's a lot more work to be done yet. But I won't rest until I find that black-hearted git Lolemun Dunniah and roast the flesh off his back.'

'Welcome, sirs . . . welcome to us mess.' Lance-Corporal Pegg stood in the corner of one of the long, low bungalows that the 86th had made available to the 95th, ushering in his guests.

'Thank you, Corporal Pegg. I've a wee present for you, just to remind you that it's Christmas Day after all.' Morgan passed one of his precious bottles of carefully hoarded Irish whiskey to Pegg; selfishly, he regretted having to part with it, but the hospitality was a generous gesture from the men and he had nothing else suitable with which to reciprocate. 'May I introduce Mr Fawcett, lads? He and another young gentleman have been waiting for us here for days, fresh out from England.'

Morgan had no subaltern in his company since young Budgen had remained in Gibraltar, sick with fever. Now Ensign Alexander Fawcett had arrived, broad and fully grown at eighteen, with surprisingly lush whiskers and a deep tan already. He'd obviously been working on his cap to make it look more used than it was, but the newness of his scarlet jacket and his virgin half-boots betrayed him. Still, thought Morgan, he was a friendly boy, son of a vicar in Oxfordshire, and he'd handled himself steadily enough at the disaster of a parade that afternoon.

'This, Fawcett, as you've gathered, is Corporal Pegg from Wirksworth. The other cutthroats are Beeston, Cooper, Sharrock, James and Coughlin, all good hands . . . when they're sober.' The men had all jumped to their feet, taken the pipes from their mouths and now they were laughing at

Morgan's quip, appreciating it all the more after his earlier embarrassment.

'Anyway, sirs, sit yersen down. Got some traditional Christmas fare for you, curried green parrot – just like me mam used to mek.' Another ripple of laughter greeted Pegg's riposte. 'Actually, we're lucky it's not me mam's cooking; it's our little jewel, Cissy, 'oo looks after us, ain't it, boys?'

Each corner of the bungalow was filled by similar groups of men from the Grenadiers – Morgan would take Fawcett to meet them later – sitting around storm lanterns that shed pools of gentle light in which they sat, smoked and yarned. Then, gliding from the shadows came their cook, Cissy, a great iron pot of curry in both hands, a flatter dish of rice balanced effortlessly on her head. This mess had chosen well, for the girl's sari hugged her curves most becomingly, whilst her wide sloe eyes sat above a perfectly tilted nose, which was pierced by a delicate gold band. She smiled openly, warmly at the men, the candlelight catching an unusually flawless skin as she took the rice from her head with practised grace.

'Aye, yer a good lass, Cissy, *bono, shukria*.'

Morgan couldn't help but notice how Pegg's hand strayed down the girl's buttocks and thighs as she slid away into the dark – and that, of course, was where Morgan had seen her before: she'd been shrieking and running away from the ambush a couple of weeks ago with Lance-Corporal Pegg in close attendance – also making his way to the rear. He'd have to speak to the colour-sergeant about this.

'Enjoy the parade, sir?' Beeston, cross-legged on the floor in his shirtsleeves and ridiculous bright puce native slippers, a fashion all the rage amongst the men, took his pipe from his lips and grinned at Ensign Fawcett whilst the others sniggered expectantly.

'Well, it was quite an introduction to the company and to the general.' Fawcett was being as diplomatic as he could. 'He's a bit of a tartar, ain't he?'

'Tartar, sir – 'e's a right cunt, 'e is,' Beeston replied flatly, removing, with consummate distaste, a piece of tobacco from his lip.

'No, cunts is useful,' muttered someone else.

'What 'ad poor old Jimmy Pierce done anyway?' Beeston asked in mock outrage.

Pierce was making something of a name for himself. After his naked antics in Bombay, he'd been first at the native arrack whilst all the other men were eating their dinners, exhausted from the march and pestered by the NCOs' checks on weapons, ammunition and all sorts of other 'arsewipe' – as the troops styled such irritants. Then, when the whole column had been paraded to be told that they were now part of the grandly titled 'Central India Field Force' by their new commander, Brigadier-General Smith, Pierce had disgraced them all again by falling flat on his face in a drunken swoon. Morgan had never heard a rifle make such a clatter. The general had just finished speaking and, naturally, Pierce had been in the front rank of the company, the whole incident being impossible to disguise.

'Well, he *was* howling drunk on parade,' Fawcett answered.

'Naw, sir, touch o' the sun is all. 'E's just a kid – bit of a thirsty one, but just a kid.'

The others laughed out loud at Beeston's reply, Morgan noticing how he'd hung his jacket with his two good-conduct stripes prominently on display.

'You goin' to flog Jimmy, sir?' asked Coughlin in his deep Dublin brogue.

'Well, that's what The Man ordered; you heard him as well as I did,' Morgan equivocated.

Pierce had collapsed just paces from General Smith, and Morgan had never seen such immediate, apoplectic anger. Sitting high on his horse, Smith's face had mottled scarlet in an instant, his mouth – to which they had all had to listen for too long already – turned to a snarl.

'Hoo is thet man? Has he drink tay-ken, Colour-Saar-gent?' Private James imitated the general's plummy syllables.

McGucken had raced over to Pierce. His collapse might, indeed, have been sun or illness-induced but, unfortunately, as his head was raised he let out a curse that could only have come from the bottle.

'He's beastly drunk, he's to be flogged; I won't hev it, do . . . you . . . hear?' James continued the theatre, to be rewarded by the chuckles of the others.

'Well, if Pierce was indeed drunk . . .' Fawcett ventured.

Morgan was pleased to see the young man being accepted by the troops like this. It was the only high point in the otherwise dismal start to the company's service under General Smith.

'Aye, sir, but that's up to our officers to decide, not some red-arse cavalryman with bugger all on his chest 'cept Turkish tinsel.' Beeston wasn't letting up. 'An' as for talking to Captain Morgan like that, 'oo does 'e think 'e is? An' on Christmas Day, would 'ave bin Christian to overlook it, wun't it?'

'All right, lads, the commanding officer and I will decide what happens to young Pierce.' Morgan had taken his first mouthful of parrot curry – a dish to which they were all now very used – his words serving to soothe the men's anger. 'What do you think of the news?'

'Well, sir, we was lookin' forward to gettin' at the bastards in Cawnpore, but it seems as though we're too late for that, don't it?' Pegg replied.

Whilst on the march up to Deesa, the officers had been told that Cawnpore had finally been taken on 6 December, but, in the absence of other objectives, it had been decided not to tell the men in case it dispirited them.

'So now we're bound for Jhansi and 'Rutter country – that's another four hundred miles from Cawnpore, ain't it, sir? What will that be like?' Pegg asked the question all the men wanted answered.

'Mahratta country,' Morgan corrected, his stomach leaping at the very mention of Jhansi. 'Well, it ain't going to be like the stuff we've heard about in Delhi and Lucknow, where the mutineers have come out to fight pretty regular. The major part of John Company's Bengal troops have been beaten now or dispersed. Where we're going, though, is vitally important, for unless this bit of country is tamed, rebellions and uprisings might continue indefinitely. There'll be turned sepoys aplenty, you can be sure of that, but we'll also be facing local troops from the maharajas' armies, as well as all manner of irregulars.'

'What, sir, like that bunch o' savages that Colonel Kemp has got with him?' asked Private Sharrock.

Kemp had banded together a couple of dozen horsemen – some civilians, some British and Indian officers whose troops had mutinied – and a hundred or so native irregulars clad in loincloths, greasy turbans and little else. They carried a collection of bows, axes and matchlocks that, according to McGucken, 'would'a done credit to the fuckin' Saracens', and this exotic troupe had mesmerised the men, making Kemp an instant celebrity, everyone wanting an attachment to his posse.

'Yes, a bit like them or that set of clowns that ambushed us on the way here,' Morgan replied, 'but there's one thing I'm sure of: Corp'l Pegg's right, it's bloody miles to Jhansi and there'll be many a Pandy in between, so look to your boot leather and your weapons, lads, an' be ready for a long slog.'

'Aye, sir, an' a merry fuckin' Christmas to you too!' was Pegg's reply as he took a deep pull at the bottle of whiskey.

FOUR

The Battle of Rowa

'Sahibs, very quiet, please,' Rissaldar Batuk pushed his finger to his lips and signalled gently with his palm that the reconnaissance party should lie down on their bellies. 'Be snake now,' and with no further instructions the grizzled Indian NCO wormed forward through the grass in the gloom of dawn.

'He doesn't need to worry about the noise; the bloody insects would wake the dead, so they would.' But even so, Morgan whispered this to McGowan, now promoted from adjutant and commanding a double company of the 10th BNI, as they crept on their elbows and knees through the cacophony of the cicadas' dawn chorus.

'Probably,' McGowan murmured back, 'but we're very close now.'

Indeed they were. After five more yards or so of too close acquaintance with damp grass, ants and scuttling centipedes, the trio came to a lip of land that gave way to a short, steep slope where the trees and scrub refused to grow. There, no more than a hundred and fifty paces away, lay the cramped, fortified village of Rowa, now quite clearly stretched out below them as the sun rose and beamed on the pall of cooking smoke that hung above it.

'See, sahibs.' The rissaldar pointed carefully, slowly, not wanting to draw attention to them by any sudden movement. 'Sentries, there, there and there. Smoking, see.'

This man knows his business. I'd give good money to have my Grenadiers scout the ground like this; I hope not too many of the rebels are as skilful as this fellow, thought Morgan.

The night before, Hume had called Morgan to see him, along with McGowan, whose two Bombay companies had been placed under Hume's command for the forthcoming attack. The general had ordered Hume to lead two of his own companies and the pair of the 10th BNI, along with a troop of guns, against the village that lay about twelve miles from their camp at Muddar, where the troops had paused on their march towards Jhansi. Rowa was said to be full of mutineers who would certainly challenge and harass the column on the route of march unless they were defeated. He told the two captains to take an escort and carry out as thorough a reconnaissance as possible the following morning, then come back to him by midday with a plan of battle.

Rissaldar Batuk, one of Kemp's loyal and experienced NCOs, who had had a brush with the garrison of the village some weeks before and who knew the ground, had told them where to dismount and Lance-Corporal Pegg, Morgan's escort, had been delighted to remain with the horses. Morgan guessed that Batuk was about forty, for his beard and hair were tinged with grey, but he was as slender and muscled as a whip and moved with a practised, silent grace.

The two officers slowly brought up their binoculars, cupped their hands over the top of the front lenses to prevent any reflection, and studied the ground.

'That wall extends right the way in front of the village and up the slope the other side, don't it, Morgan?' They were looking at Rowa from the edge of the jungle scrub on the right flank of the village. McGowan's eye had followed a mud wall that was almost the height of a man for about seventy paces before it jinked away out of sight, re-emerging beyond the reed and grass roofs of the crowd of low buildings behind it.

'Aye, that's right enough, but is there some sort of trench cut behind it?' Morgan answered quietly as he squinted through his glasses.

As both men concentrated, the noise of the cockerels in the village was suddenly joined by the barking of myriad dogs.

'Yes, look there, that carrying party seems to be climbing down into it.' McGowan, though he didn't know it, had seen the sentries' cooked breakfasts being taken out to them by half a dozen cooks. 'I've lost them now. It must be deep.'

'Hmm . . . how many guns can you see?' Morgan tried not to let the white ants that crawled over his wrists distract him.

'Three . . . yes, only three, but there could be one that's masked by the turn of the wall,' McGowan answered. 'Look like light brass horse guns, what d'you think?'

'Yes, sahib,' the rissaldar cut in in a whisper, holding up three fingers. '*Tatt* gun – old.'

'Old they may be, but murder at close range.' Morgan adjusted the focus on his glasses minutely. 'Let's hope the rogues are as dozy tomorrow morning as they are now.'

In the British Army, dawn would have seen all sentries alert – certainly not eating their breakfasts – and gun crews standing to their pieces, portfires lit and barrels trained on the enemy's most likely direction of attack.

'Aye, they're still a-slumber under their carriages.' McGowan could see figures lying under the guns wrapped in some sort of blanket. 'In fact, most of number three gun's crew seem to be absent from their posts.'

'Good, let's hope they're smoking a pipe of bhang somewhere and that they've enough to last 'em another day,'

Morgan said lightly, though privately he dreaded the horrid black muzzles.

'Now, me owd mate,' Corporal Pegg, comfortably seated on a folded blanket to keep the insects away from his ample bottom, leered at Sepoy Suddo Surpuray, 'tell me 'ow yer plan to murder that master of yours, Captain bleedin' McGowan?'

Both of them had been left with the reconnaissance party's horses in a small clearing in the forest, concealed from the main track that led to Rowa. Surpuray, McGowan's orderly, had proved to be a much better horseman than Pegg, both of them doing their best on the baggage ponies they'd been given to keep up with the rest of the group. Now Pegg was taking advantage of the sepoy's almost complete absence of English to unleash all of his prejudices.

'Goin' to creep up on 'im an' knife 'im like you did that peeler back in Bombay?' Surpuray nodded and smiled as Pegg mocked him. 'Mind you, the ignorant twat prob'ly deserved it, didn't 'e, bab?'

The sepoy continued to nod and grin, making a dumb show of firing a rifle, thrusting a mock bayonet and pointing towards Rowa before drawing a finger across his throat.

'That's right, youth,' Surpuray was, unconsciously, providing great sport for the veteran Pegg, who'd loathed McGowan ever since their encounter in Bombay so many weeks ago. 'Shoot the stuck-up sod. It's the only danger he's ever likely to see.' Pegg drew a lucifer across a striker several times before he got the damp chemicals to burn, then sucked hard on his blackened clay pipe. But just as he began to puff clouds of blue-grey smoke from the side of his mouth, one of the horses whinnied quietly and the others pricked up their ears.

Surpuray tensed with the horses and then, with one smooth movement, grabbed Pegg's pipe from his mouth and smothered the bowl with his hand.

'Why, you ignorant . . .' Pegg drew his hand back to slap the sepoy, as he'd slapped many a native servant. '*Tum lakhri, lakhri tum?*'

But just before he launched the back of his hand, Pegg saw that Surpuray had his fingers pressed to his lips, beckoning wildly towards the track. Reluctantly lowering his fist, Pegg listened intently, trying to hear above the whine of the insects all around him, knowing that the native's hearing in such circumstances was vastly more practised than his. Surpuray must also have feared that the fragrance of the pipe, carried on the slight breeze, would have told a sensitive Pandy nose that humans were close by.

The horses continued to fidget but he could just make out the click of hoofs and the jingling of tack. Pegg sensed that it was only one animal approaching; he lifted his rifle whilst Surpuray drew his bayonet from its scabbard and crouched in the bushes, peering through them onto the track like some great scarlet cat.

Then, the sepoy struck. Before Pegg had even realised that the quarry was so close, Surpuray leapt from his lair straight into the path of whatever it was that was coming, grabbing the leather bridle of a mule with one hand and pulled his long spike of a bayonet blade back to strike.

He had no need to bother. The mule bucked and reared with fright, depositing a fat, pyjama-clad native with a solid thump into the centre of the track.

'Keep still, you Pandy sod.' Pegg had thumbed back the hammer of his rifle and, jumping forward, pointed its muzzle just inches from the Indian's face whilst Surpuray fought to control the mule, which now circled and tossed its head against the tension of the harness. 'Or you'll get a Cawnpore dinner, yer will.'

This was how Pegg liked his enemies. The mutinous sepoy – for that's what his broad leather cross-belts and brass regimental plate in the centre of his chest declared him to be –

was bulbous and over forty, as many chins quivering below his luxuriant moustache as there were fingers on the hand he held out in supplication. The fall had winded him; now he sprawled amongst two great kettles of spilled rice, which the mule had thrown at the same time.

''E's no solja, 'e's too bleedin' fat – some sort of cook.'

But the man's lack of martial appearance was no reason for mercy in Pegg's eyes. 'Stop yer mithering, shall yer?'

Despite the fat mutineer's terrified jibbering and his begging hands, the NCO reversed his rifle and caught him such a blow over the right eye with the heavy butt-plate that the man slumped to the ground unconscious.

'Get that bloody moke under control, can't you?' Pegg endeavoured to take command, but Surpuray was already master of the situation. He'd pinched the mule's nostrils together, both to stop it from braying and to make it more compliant. Now, with a resigned reluctance, the ass was pulled and dragged into the concealing brush, whilst the Surpuray did his best to make Pegg do the same with his corpulent prize.

'Coom on then, Pandy.' Pegg hauled at his victim's ankles. 'By, I should o' kept you awake. The exercise might 'ave got some of that blubber off you.' If there were jokes being made about fatness, Pegg was usually the subject, but now he'd found someone that he could mock, even if the sepoy was deaf to his taunts. But then, even as the mutineer's eye swelled to the size of a small, bruised tangerine, he began to murmur and regain his reason.

Didn't do much of a job there; I'll hit the next 'un a damn sight harder, Pegg thought.

Soon they were back in the clearing, the horses snuffing interestedly at the mule, flicking their tails with curiosity. Surpuray soaked a rag, which he took from his saddlebag, in water and pressed it against the cook's wound, slipping his hand under the brass cross-belt plate on the man's chest and holding it and the belts up for Pegg's inspection.

'Aye, son.' The Englishman couldn't understand a word of Surpuray's excited chatter. '"E's from the Twenty-fifth BNI.' The brass plate had a well-polished '25' raised on it. 'They stationed hereabouts?'

But before they could continue the uneven debate any further, there came the noise of several stealthy people approaching from the very direction that Pegg was meant to be covering as sentry. Abandoning his human trophy, the NCO leapt to his post, rifle at the ready, more worried that Morgan would find him absent from his place of duty than frightened of an enemy.

'Who comes there?' challenged Pegg.

'Friend,' came the answer in a familiar accent. 'Captain Morgan and two, as you know fine well, Corporal Pegg.'

It's all right for Paddy Morgan to be all relaxed about the sentries, thought Pegg, but just let me drop me guard for one second an' wouldn't I catch it?

'Well, what have you got here, you two?' Morgan led in the rest of the reconnaissance party, wet from the dewy grass. They clustered round the captive in what was now almost full daylight.

'Cook wallah on his way to the village, I reckon, sir,' said Pegg as Supuray made his report in Hindi to Captain McGowan. '"Eard 'im comin' a mile off, I did; didn't put up much of a fight.'

'Good for you.' Morgan was genuinely impressed by Pegg's initiative. 'He'll be able to give us some valuable intelligence about the garrison of Rowa – if you haven't bashed the sense out of him, that is.'

'Yes, well done, Pegg,' McGowan added.

'*Corporal* Pegg, if you don't mind, sir.'

'Supuray tells me that he couldn't have managed without you,' said McGowan.

The prisoner, now quite conscious, was bound by his ankles under the belly of the mule before the party mounted and trotted off as quietly as possible down the track and back to camp, Pegg muttering reproachfully and Morgan smiling to himself.

'No, sahib, that wallah is a high-caste Brahmin; most of the Twenty-Fifth are like him, but those who prepare the food are from the highest castes.' Rissaldar Batuk pointed towards the prisoner, who was jogging unhappily along lashed to the saddle of his mule in company with McGowan, Pegg and Surpuray.

The rissaldar had insisted that he and Morgan should hang back rather than give an ambusher the gift of the whole reconnaissance party. Now they trotted stirrup to stirrup.

'Light cavalry regiments, like mine, were recruited from all different castes, as skill with horses comes from many backgrounds.' Morgan had noticed that Batuk's English was much more fluent than that of most other Indians of his rank.

'But how do your officers get to understand all the differences and religious needs of the men?' asked Morgan, intrigued by a system with which he was only beginning to grapple.

'Officers, sahib? I am an officer,' Batuk replied coolly.

'Yes, yes, of course, I do beg your pardon. I meant the British officers who come out here barely understanding your language and certainly not your class and caste system,' answered Morgan, embarrassed by his slip.

'No, sahib, it is difficult to understand and easy to get wrong. That is why in John Company's regiments there are native officers who serve to explain the British officers' orders to the jawans and the soldiers' wishes to the white men. In the past it has worked well; our Bengal regiments fought alongside yours in the great battles against the Sikhs.' Batuk pushed out his chest slightly as he said this, making sure that Morgan had seen his campaign medal. 'And the regiments

113

that did best were those whose British officers learnt the men's language and got to know them like a father would his son.'

Morgan had already seen how close to the sepoys the British officers in the 10th Bengalis seemed to be. Those who had mastered the local languages enjoyed a simple intimacy with the Indian troops that would have been difficult to copy in the stiffer atmosphere of one of Her Majesty's regiments.

'But the problems started when the sahib officers were taken away from the regiments for staff and political jobs. That only happened after the Sikhs were beaten. Then there were the soft officers; they seemed to be the ones who were always talking about their own Hebrew God and spending as much time in their temples as they did with the men. Some Brahmins in the infantry regiments took them for fools and began to make free with discipline and custom that would never have been tolerated in my pultan. But the damage was done during your war with the Russians – were you there, sahib?' asked Batuk with a slight smile.

'Yes . . . yes, of course I was. The whole regiment was there; first in, last out.' It was Morgan's turn to show off his ribbons.

'Ah yes, sahib, I am blind. But that war caused too many of your regiments to be sent there and not here; Victoria *bahadur* should never have trusted these people, they need to have the heel of your boot on their necks, sahib. The badmashes had a wonderful time of it with your newspapers, reading of the mistakes and all the problems with supply and reinforcements, and when your men were forced back from before the great Russian city.'

'Not my regiment, Rissaldar,' Morgan interrupted a little too quickly.

'No, sahib, I am sure of that, but it showed your enemies that the *gora-log* could be beaten and all the hotheads and malcontents in my regiment drank it up like sherbert. So, when the rumour spread that British rule would last only one hundred years, people began to say that the sahibs would force us to accept their religion and that's why some of those Hindu fools believed all that dung about the new Enfield cartridges being greased with pig fat. Most of us Muslims could see that was just nonsense,' Batuk continued.

'But if there were right-thinking men in the ranks of experienced, steady regiments, Rissaldar, why did the mutinies happen at all?' asked Morgan.

'Sahib, it was like a madness. Take Kemp Bahadur; he was seen as a man-god in the Twelth – they worshipped him. But even there the disease took hold. That monkey Mangal Pandy of the Thirty-Fourth became some sort of hero and the fools just lost control of themselves. Why, I saw our own officers ride smiling, unarmed into a crowd of men whom I would have counted as brothers, and be cut down whilst scarcely able to believe what was happening.' Batuk shook his head sadly.

'And what are we to expect of our enemies, Rissaldar? Plainly, there are good soldiers amongst the mutineers, and we can't hope that every fort and town will be guarded by sleeping sentries like the ones we have just seen,' Morgan replied.

'You are right, sahib, but I find it hard to answer your question for I have never seen our regiments fight without their British officers. If some great leader springs up who can fan the flames of doubt in the rebels' bellies and unite Muslims and Hindus in their hatred of the English, then we will have a stiff fight. That is what we must watch for – someone of strength and vision who understands the soldiers' weaknesses.' Batuk spurred his pony on gently as the gap with the rest of the group along the jungle track had widened.

'And is there such a man, Rissaldar?' Morgan put his heels to his own horse's flanks.

'Such a man, sahib, or perhaps such a woman. We shall see.'

* * *

'So, Hume, where are you going to site the guns?' Brigadier-General Smith had Colonel Hume and all the officers involved in the next morning's attack on Rowa clustered round a map outside his bungalow at Muddar.

'Well, sir, we'll have them here on the left flank, firing between the two infantry parties.' Hume pointed with a pencil to a rise in the ground identified by Morgan and McGowan during the reconnaissance. 'There should be enough elevation from there to allow our nine-pounders to rake the parapet and keep the enemy's pieces quiet.'

'Quite so, but how will the guns get into position without being fired on by the Pandies?' Smith asked irritably, his brow wrinkled tightly. Although Smith wasn't going to command the four companies and troops of guns involved, this was the first action in which part of his column was to be involved and he wanted it to go well.

'The two Ninety-Fifth companies,' Hume pointed to Carmichael and Morgan, 'will give covering rifle-fire from here . . .' Hume pointed to the wood line directly in front of the village's walls, '. . . whilst the guns take post and McGowan's double company of the Tenth hook round to the left flank.'

'But the point you've selected for the Ninety-Fifth is exactly where the enemy will expect the attack to come from,' Smith said impatiently.

'Yes, sir. The idea is to hold his attention – especially the guns' – before launching a surprise assault from the left, supported by our artillery,' Hume continued matter-of-factly. 'Then, once the Tenth have drawn off any reserve that he might have—'

'And do we know how many men he's got or, indeed, whether he has a reserve?'

Smith was clearly unimpressed with the scheme, thought Morgan, standing close to him where the smell of stale tobacco was almost overpowering.

'Well, yes, we think he's got about two hundred men under arms, and there are about the same number of women, children and old men in the village,' Hume replied. 'It seems as though about half a company are kept here in the central building under the hand of the Pandy commander.'

'And this intelligence has come from where?' asked Smith, doubtfully.

'A prisoner that the reconnaissance party took, sir,' Hume said flatly.

'And how reliable is this man, pray? I hope you're not basing the entire plan on information from one fellow who could, after all, be gammoning you?'

'Sir, the man was questioned most carefully—' There was just a hint of impatience in Hume's voice now.

'With your leave, Colonel,' Morgan cut in, 'I was there when the man was taken; he couldn't have been planted by the enemy, and the questioning was conducted by Rissaldar Batuk, one of Commandant Kemp's scouts who knows the lie of the land well.'

Kemp looked up appreciatively at the sound of his name.

'Oh, really . . . Morgan, ain't it?' Smith took the cigar from his mouth and sneered. 'So you used one of Kemp's irregulars, did you, not one of your drunkards then?'

There was an embarrassed silence from the meeting except for one amused snort from Captain Carmichael.

'Sir, I—' Morgan began stiffly.

'Enough, Morgan,' Hume stopped him. 'General, the information's better than anything we had in the Crimea when *we* were mounting attacks.' Hume paused for effect, knowing full well that Smith had seen no action during that campaign: and it seemed to work.

Smith sniffed hard and puffed his cigar. 'This isn't the damn Crimea, is it? Now listen, all of you.' He turned to the officers. 'I expect you to do your utmost in this attack – no hanging back.'

'I beg your pardon, General, but there'll be none of that from either the Ninety-Fifth or the Tenth, of that I can assure you,' said Hume, his beard jutting out with irritation.

'I'll want to know the answer if there is, Hume.' Smith caught up his slung sword and turned to leave, the audience jumping to their feet. 'Carry on!'

The rangy, peppery man stumped away with an aide, his spurs jangling, trailing an acrid cloud of tobacco smoke.

'So, Morgan, there's to be no hanging back.' For a second Carmichael seemed to be almost comradely until: 'Not even by your crapulous crew!'

'Devil take you, Carmichael,' Morgan spat back, cursing himself, even as he said it, for giving his brother officer exactly the sort of reaction that he'd wanted to provoke.

But Carmichael's reply was just a raucous laugh.

No matter how many times he led columns of men at night, Morgan never managed to slow his pace to a crawl. Now the approach march to Rowa a couple of hours before dawn through the black, humid jungle was just the same. The attacking column had ridden out of camp well before midnight in bullock carts, jerked and plodded in relative discomfort for ten miles or so before dismounting, shaking out into their constituent parts before Carmichael and Morgan's companies plunged into the jungle. At the same time, the guns and McGowan's two companies sloped off as quietly as possible to the west of the village.

Then it was all: ''Ang on, sir, Captain Carmichael's lot's got held up,' and, 'Hold hard, sir, we've lost the back half of our boys.' The native guide from Kemp's irregulars, a particularly emaciated man of uncertain age, wearing nothing but a loincloth and singlet, and carrying a bow with a quiver full of viciously barbed arrows, had to be held back by Morgan.

Eventually, they met another group of Kemp's archers, this

time under one of his rissaldars, who were to guide them to the point in the jungle from which the attack would start. All the while, Morgan had tried to check on the guide by using the compass that he'd bought so expensively in Dublin before they embarked, but the luminous paint on the dial was no match for the inky darkness.

We're making a hell of a noise, thought Morgan, as the column banged and swore through the catching, thorny brush. Those sentries will have to be only half alert – then we'll catch a packet as soon as they can see us.

But as the first glimmer of dawn became visible through the tangle of branches above them, Morgan realised that the noisiest time of the day in the forest was just before the sun came over the horizon, as the insects' day shift took over from the night shift and, for twenty minutes or so, there was double the din.

I suppose that's why they get us to assault at this time of day, he thought as he placed each of his men down into a kneeling position and then showed Carmichael where to spread his company out to the right of the Grenadiers.

Eventually, all the men were placed.

'Right, Colour-Sar'nt, load, please.'

Every soldier set about the smooth task of loading and ramming. Morgan saw how each man's face, battle-hardened or not, was strained with fear and anticipation. He'd read some rot in the papers suggesting that the noise of the ramrods would send 'a thrill of warlike delight through the ranks' – there was no thrill for him, just an instant churning of his guts.

'Yous all right, sir?' McGucken was at his elbow, just where he should be.

'Fine, Colour-Sar'nt.' Morgan realised that he was clumsily fumbling his revolver. 'We'll be firing a good few volleys whilst the guns get into position – have the men untied enough shot?'

'Aye, sir, you know they have,' McGucken replied. 'You told me to check it – an' I did.'

Morgan's knew that he'd ordered a full twenty rounds to be unwrapped from their wax-paper packets in which they were carried, despite the damp of the jungle. He also knew that he'd told the big Scotsman to check, but it settled his nerves a little to go over things again.

'Those savages should beckon us forward once they've found a good enough place for us to open fire at the edge of the trees.' Morgan nodded towards Kemp's men, who were now loping off through the brush, chattering unintelligibly.

'Sir: then we wait for the colonel's signal to fire, don't we?' McGucken answered. 'Two green rockets, ain't it?'

Morgan whirled on the colour-sergeant. 'No, you know it ain't; it's green over yellow!'

But then the officer saw that McGucken was grinning widely, deliberately trying to distract Morgan during the tensest part of any battle, the moments before fire was opened and all the relief that that would bring.

'Look yon, sir,' said McGucken. Whilst they'd been talking, the rissaldar had come back through the trees and was now beckoning to Morgan for the men to advance to the jungle's edge.

'All ready, Colour-Sar'nt?' Morgan looked in the dim light left and right of him as the men saw McGucken's signal to stand; then they raised themselves, their rifle muzzles level in front of them.

'As ready as they'll ever be, sir – an' Whaley's getting Captain Carmichael's lot on their feet.' McGucken had made sure that his counterpart in the next company had seen the signal; he had, and now the entire line of about one hundred and forty men stood ready to move.

With a wave of his hand Morgan indicated that the line should advance: then the red-coated troops stuttered forward in the undergrowth.

It wasn't far, but the jungle was thickest at its very edge where the sun could penetrate and cause the brush to grow even more densely. But as they pushed on, the forest ended abruptly, allowing the shallow grey of dawn to show them the mud walls of Rowa less than two hundred paces in front.

'Right, get them down here.' Morgan told McGucken to halt the line just inside the cover of the brush, where sleepy sentries shouldn't have been able to see them. The NCOs repeated the hand signals, Morgan watching as young Ensign Fawcett placed his men individually at the far left end of the line.

'Green over yellow, wasn't it, sir?' McGucken grinned at Morgan.

Hume had said that he would fire the two signal rockets – the facing colours of the 10th and the 95th – himself when all was set, but now Morgan could see that the slightest delay with the guns or McGowan's flanking move would mean that his men would have to remain undetected, close to the enemy, for an uncertain length of time, just hoping that the sentries on the walls in front of them were as slack as they had seemed during yesterday's reconnaissance.

'A-shoo . . .' Private Sharrock sneezed mightily a few yards from Morgan. The men either side of him tensed, hoping that such a human noise would be covered by the whine of the insects. Seconds passed, nothing happened, except Sharrock's rubbing at his nose with his cuff, energetically enough, Morgan felt sure, to alert every sentry in the whole town.

Morgan knew that there was no room for this attack to go wrong. Quite apart from the danger and possible loss of life, it was the Regiment's first, real taste of action on this campaign and he was under the scrutiny of Hume as well as his rival, Carmichael. On top of that, the brigadier-general seemed to have grave doubts about his and the company's competence, not to mention their sobriety. He tried to hush

121

Sharrock's snuffling with sign language, ten yards away from him in the brush, but he was stolidly ignored.

The most likely danger, Morgan thought, came from a turbaned sentry in an embrasure above them, just to their front. As the light improved, the man's head could be seen bobbing gently, not alarmed but certainly alert. Then, as Morgan watched, he heard a clatter that came from the sentry position and the bulky head disappeared as a shower of arrows skidded off the packed mud wall around the gun port.

'Where, in God's name, did they come from, Colour-Sar'nt?'

'There, sir, them damn savages, look,' said McGucken as a clutch of Kemp's native troops notched another cloud of arrows onto their bow strings, lifted the wooden arcs high in the air, paused for a fraction of a second to judge the range, then let another volley fly.

The lethal, slender barbs winged over the wall this time, searching for targets sheltering behind it, but they were answered almost immediately by a couple of popping shots from the wall sentries' muskets, then a flash and roar from the closest gun and a sheet of canister that shredded the canopy of leaves high over the Grenadier Company's heads.

'Grenadier Company, wall parapet, two hundred, aim low . . .' The horrid lash of canister had almost driven Morgan to ground in the brush, but he had enough experience by now to realise that the crew of the gun in front of them would reload whilst the piece was at the full extent of its recoil, invisible to his men, then have to expose themselves once they ran it out to fire again. 'Await my order.'

Every man twitched at his sights and then cuddled the butt of his rifle hard against his shoulder, waiting in the brush for the company commander's word.

'Wait,' yelled Morgan as his commands were repeated up and down the line by the corporals and sergeants. 'Why did the irregulars let fly then, Colour-Sar'nt?' he said quietly to McGucken.

'Buggered if I know, sir,' he replied conversationally. 'Nae discipline.'

'Indeed, but that'll vex the colonel,' said Morgan, 'and we'll use a whore of a lot of powder and shot now if the Tenth take their time about things.'

'Aye, sir, but thank God we've got Captain Carmichael's lot here to bail us oot.' McGucken looked through the brush down the line of men towards the next company, where Richard Carmichael's pale face could be seen bobbing around, looking worriedly towards them, silently asking why the plan had gone awry.

Then three ragged heads were silhouetted by the early light against the top of the wall as the gun crew ran the four-pounder out.

'Fire!' bawled Morgan, and the jungle was suddenly full of billowing smoke as seventy Enfields bruised their owners' shoulders and a curtain of soft .577-inch lead rounds smashed into the parapet, throwing clouds of dust and chippings up, whining off the stonework and swiping the gun crew away from the brass barrel before they had time to fire another shot.

Ears rang, birds rose with alarmed shrieks and a troop of sleepy monkeys chattered off into the green depths of the forest, swinging from branch to branch as the men toiled rythmically with ramrods, caps and pouches, and the NCOs chanted the rubric that saw the company reload faster and more efficiently than any other infantry in the world.

'Wait for Number One Company to fire now, lads,' Morgan ordered, and heard it repeated by the NCOs, for that was the plan. Despite the premature fire that the irregulars had provoked, Morgan now expected Carmichael's men to fire next, allowing his lads to reload and a constant fire to be kept up on the enemy, so drawing off the reserve and covering the movements of their own artillery – exactly as the colonel had ordered – but only silence and worried looks came from their right.

'Why ain't they firing, Colour-Sar'nt?' Morgan asked as his own men completed the reload and came back into the aim.

'I don't bloody know—' but an uneven wall of lead cut McGucken off, fired by the garrison of Rowa from hard on the Grenadier Company's left flank.

Great sheets of orange flame and plumes of roiling smoke lined the bottom of the town's protective wall, two hundred paces away from Morgan's riflemen, exactly in the spot that should have been raked by their own guns – had they been in position. The undergrowth was shredded all around him, a pattern of leaves falling like a shower of rain, whilst Private Pritchard grasped his neck, spun around just yards from Morgan and fell with a muted curse to the jungle floor, blood spurting between his fingers.

'Goddamn, they're putting down fire from exactly the spot that we thought they might, Colour-Sar'nt.' Morgan and McGucken were now crouching low on the loamy floor of the forest. 'They're better troops than we'd hoped.'

'Aye, sir, turned sepoys, sure enough, but may I suggest a wee volley to soften 'em, then, p'raps, at 'em with the steel?' McGucken was thinking clear and straight, as usual.

'Yes, Colour-Sar'nt,' Morgan gulped. A volley might keep their heads down, but the only way to clear the flank would be with the bayonet – McGucken was right – yet he couldn't expect raw Ensign Fawcett to do the job; he himself would have to. He felt for the hilt of his sword as his mouth became suddenly dry. 'Get a dozen solid lads ready, please, from the right of our line: get them to fix bayonets and be prepared to move on my order.'

If Morgan had expected any help from Carmichael's company on his right, he was to be disappointed. Number One Company just knelt there, the men's heads turning left and right, awaiting orders as the battle developed on their left, yet their commander was silently supine.

'Grenadiers, half left, two hundred enemy infantry at base of wall,' Morgan bellowed, trying to make himself heard above the cries of the NCOs and the insects that were competing with the din of the fighting. 'Ready . . .' seventy hammers were pulled back from half to full cock, '. . . fire!' as another jet of flame and smoke tore through the brush that surrounded them.

But even as the echo of rifle-fire whipped through the trees and off the walls of the town opposite, McGucken had the attacking party ready.

'Here, Sar'nt Ormond, here, on me!' Crashing through the bushes came a sergeant and a dozen men, faces set, bayonets glittering at the high port, lips already grimed where they had quickly bitten off fresh cartridge papers before dashing to obey Morgan's orders. They puffed into a line beside him, crouching down, ready and alert for whatever the officer would tell them to do and wherever he would lead.

'Glad to have you with me, Ormond . . .'

Jesus – Ormond, thank God, thought Morgan. That's the same daft, bloody face that was with me at the Alma and that fucking massacre at Inkermann.

'Right, lads, we're going to scrape those bloody Pandies clean away from the bottom o' that wall. Mr Fawcett will give us some fire as we hook round the left flank of our line.'

I hope young Fawcett will have the common bloody sense to do just that without having it spelt out to him . . . Morgan fretted.

'Right.' He pushed his hand through the damp leather sword knot and pulled the long, curved steel blade from its scabbard, noting the dull orange sheen of rust that the dank jungle had already caused, despite last night's coat of oil.

'Follow me,' as he plunged off with the line of men crouching and stumbling behind him.

'There they are, sir . . . look there,' Sergeant Ormond pointed excitedly to Morgan as the handful of his counter-attack party emerged from the leafy dip in the land on the left flank of the 95th's line. 'There's a damn sight more than I thought, though.'

They'd run, pushing their way through the clinging branches around the back of Fawcett's men with Morgan yelling, 'We're coming to your left, Fawcett. Give us covering fire,' before they shook out into an assault line in a low piece of ground that was invisible to the enemy.

Morgan was rather pleased with himself for having found this bit of ground – pleased until his boys surged forward, weapons ready, only to find that the Pandies were within touching distance in front of him and in much greater force than he'd imagined. Where he'd expected twenty there were now a hundred. He seemed to have succeeded admirably in drawing off the reserve that Hume had told him to, but he'd completely misjudged their numbers and he now had their furious attention all to himself and his dozen men.

He'd heard the volley that Fawcett's part of the line had fired just before his group emerged from the cover that the ground provided, and now the young officer and his NCOs were bawling out the orders to reload. In front of Morgan's party, though, the mutineers had recovered their balance and were set upon driving the British back. There could be no hesitation; the only answer was to attack.

'No, get on, lads, get on!' Sergeant Ormond yelled to the attacking line as the men shied back when they saw the mass of Pandies so close in front of them.

'Come on, boys, stay with me!' bawled Morgan as his every bone, his every sinew tried to drag him down into the protection of the earth. But if they faltered now, he knew that they would be overrun – the great, ragbag crowd of mutineers would be on them, muskets banging, tulwars swinging, hacking and chopping them back into Fawcett's men and rolling up the 95th's line.

Why ain't Carmichael's company firing? thought Morgan as he pushed himself at the Pandies, lungs bursting with the strange growl that seemed to come from someone other than himself. This will be all bayonet and butt work – I hope the lads have the pluck for it.

But there was no time for any more self-doubt. Morgan was conscious of a spatter of shots from over his shoulder, then he was toe to toe with his enemies. Immediately in front of him was a stringy, skull-capped creature whose teeth stuck from his sallow face like yellow fangs. In a pyjama top and long dhoti, the man's sword belt and whistle chain suggested that he was at least a subadar, whilst the way he waved his sabre and snarled at the others marked him as a leader. Now he whirled on Morgan, dropped the point of his sword low and pulled his elbow back to thrust in a practised, soldierly way.

Not again. Morgan had never faced a swordsman before, but he'd seen more angry Russians in circumstances like this than he wanted to. *Let him commit himself first.*

The lithe Pandy threw all his weight into the thrust, allowing Morgan to jink left, but as he did so, he barged into Lance-Corporal Pegg, who'd been making martial noises as he followed just a few safe paces behind his officer.

'Sorry, sir,' Pegg apologised too late, for the collision had spoilt Morgan's riposte, allowing the mutineer to recover himself and to corkscrew back, his blade up and across his body, guarding himself against Morgan's clumsy, weak little counterpoke. With almost no power behind the thrust, the Pandy knocked Morgan's blade to one side in a classic, sweeping parry. Then, in just the same textbook way, the Indian swung his sabre cleanly over his shoulder, keeping his elbow tucked in tight against his chest to protect his vulnerable ribs and face, and pounced hard on his quarry.

Instinct told Morgan not to respond in the way that the sergeant-instructor had taught them at the depot; the manual would have told him to fall back, parry and then reply with 'Cut-Three' – just what his opponent, schooled in the same way, would have expected. So he didn't. Falling to one knee, Morgan grabbed the blade of his sword about six inches below the point with his left hand, ducked under the mutineer's arcing hilt and let the man's own weight carry him onto the curved steel like a spitted pig.

With an explosive gasp and an expression of complete surprise on his face, the subadar slid down Morgan's blade. As the Pandy lunged forward, so the steel jabbed easily below his sternum; as he staggered and wheezed, so the sabre made a tent of the back of the man's shirt, before the bright metal emerged from the cloth, staining it red as it ripped through the grey cotton.

'You all right, sir?' Pegg kicked the cooling Pandy off Morgan before pulling the officer to his feet, whilst the rest of the men tore into the throng with shots, butts, kicks and punches even as the mass of mutineers lapped around and behind them, engulfing the red-coated British in a wave of slashing swords and smoking muskets.

'I am, Pegg, but watch yourself!' As Morgan was pulled to his feet, he saw a mutineer in cross-belts and issued cap come running at the NCO's back with the point of his bayonet levelled at Pegg's kidneys, his lips drawn back below his extravagant moustache.

Morgan tried to push the lad aside, away from the long steel spike, but as the sepoy pounded forward, there was a familiar, shrieking thump and Pegg's assailant was batted to the ground, his head horribly awry and a great, pulsing hole from which a bloody mass of tissue flopped, just below his right shoulder. The musket and bayonet clattered down, before the corpse flopped into the grass, its lifeless legs pumpings, sandalled feet catching at the soil.

'Get down, lads . . . get down, for Christ's sake,' Morgan bellowed at his men, most of whom were following his orders even before he'd issued them. 'Those are our own guns!'

Nine-pound balls skipped and slapped amongst the mutineers, making what the gunners chose to call, 'good practice'. Where bounding iron touched soft flesh it smashed and gouged it, turning vibrant men into bags of offal before their dead bodies hit the ground, whilst the rounds that missed threw showers of grit and spoil in their wake, scoring and pitting anyone that was close. The 95th hugged the earth, as the iron tore their enemies and sent them wailing for the cover of Rowa's walls.

The ground was littered with bags of coloured rags, some moving, some still, some moaning as the mass of Pandies crouched and dashed back through a sallyport in the walls of the fort that had been invisible to the reconnaissance, whilst the guns banged on. The troop of nine-pounders continued to fire round-shot that pitched and leapt around the enemy's artillery.

'Fuckin' good hit that, sir.' Even whilst they were in grave danger from their own side, even as they clung for dear life to the shielding earth, Sergeant Ormond couldn't help but admire his own gunners' competence. As the iron rounds thumped into walls and soil, there was a sudden clang and human yells as a ball caught the muzzle of the enemy gun that was mounted in an embrasure close to where Morgan's lads sheltered.

'Aye, the thing's got wings.' Morgan looked in wonder as the heavy barrel spun off its carriage and whirled through the air and over the wall, landing in a spray of muddy clods.

'Look there, sir, it's a signal rocket.' Even flat on his belly, Ormond saw the finger of smoke reaching high into the early morning sky. 'Which one is it?'

They had, obviously, missed the double rocket that was designed to launch the attack amidst the muddle of the advance – if it had been fired at all.

'I don't know. I can't see the colour of the damn thing: the sun's too bright.' Morgan was squinting hard as the pyrotechnic burst above the distant tree line. 'I guess it must be . . . yes, hark there, can you hear it?'

For an instant the artillery had fallen silent, but even above the noise of rifle-fire a solid cheer came down the wind.

'It's Captain McGowan's lot. That must have been their green rocket,' said Morgan.

'Aye, sir, an' they're heading into the whole mass of the mutineers – the fuckers are now all gathered at that end of the town.' Ormond pointed to the west end of Rowa to where the enemy had obviously realised that the main attack was going to fall.

'You're right.' Morgan licked his fear-dried lips. 'We may have underestimated this bunch of Pandies. They must have worked out that we've tried to pin them from the front whilst a flanking move goes in and now they're massing to resist Captain McGowan's companies. This is a fucking shambles. The poor sods will be cut to ribbons unless we get into the town and behind the Pandies.'

'Why's it always us, sir? Why hasn't Number bloody One Company done owt?' asked Ormond.

Morgan was wondering the same. The plan was for the two 95th companies to fire and manoeuvre and pin the enemy's reserve down. When Morgan had led his group forward, Carmichael and Number One Company should have done their damnedest to menace the enemy from the east end of the town, but there had been only the odd shot, not even a volley.

'You know why as well as I do, Sar'nt Ormond.'

'Sir, it's that useless quim—' But the NCO bit off the disloyal remark.

Useless quim's about right, thought Morgan. I can see his blokes dithering about even now. No doubt he's told them to 'conserve ammunition', the swerver.

'What are we going to do, sir? We can't fanny about out here.' Ormond was right, they couldn't stay out in the middle of nowhere whilst the battle ranged about them. 'Best get back to the tree line, don't you think, sir?'

Morgan would have liked nothing better. If he took them back to the relative safety of the trees and broken ground, they could rejoin the rest of the Grenadiers and sit there sniping safely until Colonel Hume called them forward. In other words, do just what that useless quim Carmichael was doing.

'No, Sar'nt Ormond.' Morgan pulled the cap from his head and mopped at the sweat on his forehead. 'We've got to get into the bloody town.'

'But, sir . . .' Ormond began to protest.

There was nothing wrong with Ormond. Indeed, thought Morgan, he'd be lost without him, just like he would have been lost had the broad Sheffield man not always been on his shoulder in the Crimea. But that was the problem: Ormond had been in too many scrapes like this before and Morgan had no desire to leave Mrs Ormond and both nippers to the mercy of a sergeant's pension – especially when there was another company that had, so far, hardly dirtied its barrels.

'Send someone back to Mr Fawcett and the Colour-Sar'nt.' Morgan was yelling now to make himself heard above the crash of the guns. 'Get them to bring the rest of the company forward.'

'Very good, sir,' The professional NCO had taken over now. Ormond had had his say, but Captain Morgan had spoken – no matter how bloody dangerous the orders were. 'James, on yer hind legs an' get back to the company. Tell the officer to bring the whole lot up to us position 'ere. Got it?'

131

'What, back there, through all this shit, Sar'nt?' James, a solid twenty year old front Northampton, with a reputation as a runner, was as cowed by the flying lead and iron as anyone else. 'I've got a sore leg, me.' James had scarcely mentioned his encounter with a runaway howitzer round six weeks ago, but now was the time to cash in his credits.

'You'll have a sore fuckin' conk in a moment, son,' Ormond growled above the noise. 'Do as you're bloody told.'

James saw that it was pointless to argue, raised himself on his forearms, took another look at the sergeant in case he'd seen reason – which he hadn't – and launched himself in a jerking, darting run, rifle trailing in his right hand.

'Jesus, sir, poor old James: every bugger's havin' a go at 'im.' Ormond voiced the lethally obvious, for as James had risen from a piece of ground where the Pandies had last been seen to swallow Morgan's party whole, all of the attacking force had noticed him. There were rifle balls from Number One Company, showers of arrows came from Kemp's irregulars, a shell from their own gunners cracked blackly over his bobbing head and even the mutineers joined in with a musket shot or two from the walls.

'Can't they see he's one of us?' asked Ormond rhetorically as missiles continued to fly.

But somehow, James got through. He dodged through bullets and darts, every ounce of his sprinting form alive with relief as he reached the clutch of riflemen crouching in the wood line – a wood line that had suddenly seemed a mile away.

It took an age – waiting for anything whilst under fire always did, thought Morgan – then it was all stamping, pounding boots, beefy, sweaty lads and bouncing equipment as McGucken drove the rest of the company forward with his voice, and Fawcett waved them on with his sword.

The guns ceased to fire as they recognised a host of red coats in their sights, but before they could throw themselves down beside him, Morgan was up and leaping along with the wedge of panting men, shouting, 'Follow me. Go for the gate yonder,' pointing to the low sallyport with the tip of his sword. 'Come on, Grenadiers,' every trace of doubt and fear gone as he was caught by the delicious, thrilling spur of leadership.

That same spur saw him right at the head of his men, halloing and cawing like the 'eejit boy' that he knew his father would have called him if he'd been there. All caution melted as he flung his shoulder against the flimsy door of the port, staggered as it flew open and exposed a dirty, puddle-filled lane flanked by houses. But there, not ten paces away, thirty or forty mutineers, armed with every sort of sword, pike and musket, were listening intently to someone in their midst. The men closest to the British glanced over their shoulders at the noise of the gate, looked back to the speaker, then whirled round, mouths open, moustaches hanging low as they tried to take in the sight in front of their eyes.

'Them Pandies don't need to see dinner-time, sir.' McGucken said it almost matter-of-factly, but it broke the spell that had seized the handful of 95th who'd come flailing through the door before skidding to a halt, whilst the rest of the company piled up behind them like a demented rugby scrum.

Pushed almost bodily forward by the bawling troops behind him, Morgan couldn't hesitate even if he'd wanted to. Some outer force seized him; he found himself pulling his revolver from its holster as he stormed along the alley with a clutch of demons either side of him, all of them shouting as hard as he was. The ten paces took an hour as rifles banged and his own pistol jerked in his fist, the nearest Pandies being mowed down by the lead balls, flung against their comrades by the sheer force of the rounds.

'Get tore in, lads,' McGucken bellowed. 'Remember Cawnpore!' And they were amongst them.

A spear was thrown at Morgan when he was close enough to touch its owner, but somehow it sailed harmlessly over his shoulder, as the Indian's face changed from hate to grim fear when he realised that he was now defenceless.

'*Get as close to them as you can before you fire that goddamn pistol.*' Morgan remembered Colonel Kemp's advice to him when he'd been given the Tranter just before he left Cork for the Crimea almost four years ago. '*Best to touch him with the barrel first, if you can.*' Now, though, he didn't even know how many rounds he had left in the pistol's chambers – he hadn't been counting in the mad dash up the alley.

But what brutish satisfaction it gave him as he poked the scrawny little Pandy in the cheek with the barrel of the pistol. He could even smell the man's rank sweat as he pulled the trigger and watched a spray of blood fly out of the man's head, just behind his left ear. All around him the troops were hewing their enemies with just the same savage delight – something that Morgan had never seen in these boys before. Rifles banged, smoke billowed, bayonets flashed and dug whilst butts were swung into yielding flesh with an urgency born of hate. Then it finished as soon as it had started. Those Indians who could, broke and skittered off round a bend in the alley, leaving a dozen of their comrades moaning and twisting on the ground, the panting British standing over them, surveying their brutal handiwork.

'Wait you, sir.' McGucken caught at Morgan's elbow, just as he was about to set off after the fugitives. 'Let's get the rest of the company formed up first.' The colour-sergeant was right, of course, for Morgan only now realised how few men were with him. Most of the Grenadiers weren't even through the sallyport yet.

But then McGucken said something that Morgan had never expected: 'Right, lads, finish 'em,' and that set the bayonets jabbing methodically into the Pandy wounded, their cries of pain ceasing within seconds of the stark order.

Jesus, thought Morgan, what are we becoming? I've seen McGucken with the enemy's wounded before and he's never done that. Why, at Sevastopol he was positively Christian with Russ, treated them better than our own boys. Have we learnt to hate just from what the newspapers have told us? What were the men shouting when we went for Pandy – 'Remember Cawnpore'? But there wasn't a man here who was at Cawnpore – they've just read about it. But if I'm so bloody appalled by the conduct of my own lads, why didn't I put a stop to it?

Morgan was shaken from his reverie by McGucken.

'Right, sir,' the colour-sergeant was using a puggaree for which the owner had no further use to wipe the gore off his blade. 'Reckon we can get after 'em now, if you'd care to lead off.'

Most of the company had now squeezed into the narrow alley, and the guns were firing low over their heads and the roofs of the buildings at targets at the far end of the town. But away to Morgan's left, invisible behind the intervening walls of the houses, there rose the din of battle – the banging of firearms, the clash of steel and the great, wild shrieks of men putting others to death, a noise that he'd come to know and fear.

'Yes, Colour-Sar'nt, sounds like the Tenth are hard at it over yonder.'

'It does, sir, an' judging by the numbers of Pandies we saw earlier, they could be hard-pushed.' McGucken struggled to make himself heard above a salvo of nine-pound rounds that bustled low overhead. 'But have a care in these snickets, sir. They're canny buggers and they know every inch of the ground.'

The town was a mass of runs and alleys that bisected dried mud houses, mostly low and mean, but some of two storeys mixed with squalid little hovels. The ground was pitted and dank, dry in the middle of the paths, but flanked by noisome, scummy puddles and piles of rotting vegetation and filth. Dogs ran and yelped from the advancing British, disturbed in their rootling at slicks of animal and human dung, but of the civilian population, about whom they had been warned, there was no sign.

'They don't get any bloody cleaner, this lot, do they, sir?' Sergeant Ormond wrinkled his nose in disgust.

'No, they don't,' Morgan answered distractedly. 'What's that?' Both sergeant and officer, leading the column of troops, nervously raised their weapons as a shadow fled round the corner in front of them, but offered no harm.

As the urgency of the 10th's invisible battle had battered their ears, Morgan had quickly broken the company down into two columns, sending one half off under Ensign Fawcett with McGucken to help him, and taking thirty or so men and Sergeant Ormond with him. It was clear what had to be done. He'd simply said to Fawcett, 'Get up that alley there as quick as you like and take the mutineers from the left; we'll go to the right. From the sounds of things, Captain McGowan's in trouble, but the Pandies shouldn't be expecting us. Just get stuck in, but for God's sake don't fire into us or the Tenth.'

The youngster had simply nodded, asked no questions and leapt to the front of his newly independent command with admirable speed, the men and McGucken streaming off after him. But now, Morgan wondered, was Fawcett having any more luck finding his way to the fight than he was? The clash of weapons rose close by, but the alleys all led into the centre of the town, channelling them away, not towards the combat.

'Where now, d'you think, Sar'nt Ormond?' Morgan asked as the men behind him scanned the windows above and beside them, rifles ready, pausing only to wipe the sweat out of their eyes.

136

'Boggered if I know, sir,' Ormond replied. ''Ere, you two, cum 'ere,' and he grabbed two frightened-looking privates and made them cup their hands and lift him up above the seven-foot mud wall that stopped them from seeing what was going on. The sergeant's boots scrabbled at the dusty surface, his elbows pumped him up onto the top of it, and there he hung for a moment, his grey shirt sticking out between his trousers and the bottom of his scarlet shell jacket.

No sooner had Morgan seen Ormond claw his way up than he was back down again, pulling at his clothes and belts to restore his soldierly appearance, whilst immediately reporting what he'd seen. 'There's some sod tinkering with a bloody mine or summat, just the other side o' the wall, sir. Big pots, all linked by fuse, an' a Pandy trying to get it lit.'

'Well, come on then, let's get over,' said Morgan urgently, and in seconds he, Ormond and a few others were being shoved up and over the wall by the rest of the men.

As soon as Morgan got his head over the parapet he could see the danger. In a gap in the next wall, only about six paces away over a filthy yard at the back of a wood-framed house, a cross-belted, turbaned man in muddy pyjamas was toiling with a tinder box and a bit of fuse that led into what the more lurid papers would describe as 'an infernal machine'. Just beyond, Morgan sensed more than saw McGowan's men and a press of mutineers, the grunts and screams suggesting a serious bout of blood-letting.

The uproar and his concentration distracted the man who was oblivious to the scratching and scrabbling behind him until a mangy little pye-dog came snarling from the reaches of the yard, bounding up at the wall and yapping at the British. Then, alerted by the noise, the mutineer turned, gasped, took in what was happening and tried to get at his musket, which he had slung over his back, just as Ormond, half on, half off the top of the wall, fired the oddest shot that Morgan had ever seen. With one toe hooked over the wall and his left elbow on top of it, Ormond somehow snapped off a round holding his rifle with just his right hand, the butt scarcely in his shoulder. So precarious was the sergeant's balance, but so urgent was the need to shoot the rebel, that the recoil of the rifle knocked Ormond back over the other side of the wall – Morgan heard him swearing even as he fell. The ball flew wide, just over the man's shoulder, throwing up a great puff of mud from the far wall before ricocheting straight back into the sepoy, hitting him – Morgan guessed by the way that he grimaced and clutched behind him – squarely in the spine.

This gave the British just the time they needed, and as the Pandy jigged in pain, with the blade of his sword Morgan whipped the fuses away from a series of three-foot-high earthenware jars that were brimming with gunpowder. Next to him, meanwhile, a bloody little cameo was being played out.

'Dance on that, you fuck-pig.' Private James – he of the sore foot – jabbed all fourteen inches of his bayonet through the man's belly, stopping only when the point emerged through the small of the Indian's back and ground into the gritty surface of the wall.

There the man hung – spitted – until that same sore foot was raised up and hoofed firmly into the mutineer's groin, allowing James to pull the steel spike clear. Morgan saw how the dying man's eyes bulged, how his tongue, red with blood, stuck straight from his lips as he slumped onto a pile of rotting vegetables. No sooner had James finished the job with a heavy blow to the man's neck with his butt, than Lance-Corporal Pegg was searching the body for anything of the slightest value.

Then Morgan looked round. In the tiny yard there were just himself, two soldiers, a mangy dog and a cooling corpse; Ormond and the others were nowhere to be seen.

'Leave the poor man, Pegg.' Morgan knew that the Pandy deserved no sympathy whatever; why, he thought, he's probably lost count of the number of memsahibs he's ravaged, but the sight of the man's face lolling above the neck that James had just snapped – his still open eyes already buzzing with flies – was indignity enough. 'You can rob the dead when there's a few more of 'em – don't you ever learn?'

Morgan was suddenly aware of how much like a school-master he sounded and how utterly pointless such a lecture was at that moment.

Lance-Corporal Pegg – and he was an NCO, who shouldn't be upbraided in front of private soldiers, after all – hung his head with a muttered, 'Sorry, sir,' and stood up, taking his rifle in one hand but still trousering a couple of coins that had come from the dead sepoy's purse.

'Are you both loaded? Have you got plenty of shot?' Morgan asked.

James nodded quickly – he was wiping his blade on the skirts of his victim's clothes – whilst Pegg's extra ammunition pouch hung down heavily on the waist belt that he'd failed to tighten properly.

'Aye, sir, but there's only the three on us,' Pegg said shrilly just as another volley of shots and shouting erupted from beyond the next wall. 'An't we better wait for the others?'

'Just come on, the pair of you,' and Morgan dashed off through the gap in the wall, deliberately pushing over one of the great jars of powder as he went.

The party emerged into the next alley to find it obscured by dense yellow-grey smoke from the burning thatch of a house that lay next to the town wall. The firing had obviously caused the dry grass roof to catch fire and now the alley served as a funnel for the smoke, which billowed on the freshening morning breeze. In the next alley, coughing and holding a handkerchief to his nose, was Captain McGowan, surrounded by fifteen or so of his own sepoys and a litter of enemy dead and dying.

'McGowan . . . McGowan, we've come to help you,' Morgan spluttered in the fumes whilst tucking his sword under his arm and trying to knot his neckcloth around his face just as the native soldiers had done.

'Well, I'm deuced glad to see you. Any more on the way?' McGowan coughed and wiped his eyes. 'Hello, Pegg – it is Pegg, ain't it?'

Pegg had wrapped a native's puggaree around his face.

'No, sir, you know fine well it's *Corporal* Pegg.' But his bruised *amour propre* went unnoticed.

'Where's the rest of your company, Morgan? We could do with 'em just now.' Desperation wasn't quite the word, but there was real concern in McGowan's voice.

'I wish I knew,' answered Morgan. 'Half of 'em are some-where over yonder under my ensign,' he pointed in the vague direction from which Fawcett should have been approaching over a series of walls and roofs obscured by billows of smoke, 'and the rest should be following up behind me, but I'm –' he was interrupted by the shriek of artillery rounds loping overhead, which made all of them crouch low on the alley floor – 'damned if I know where they've got to now. What of yours?'

'One company's fighting up that bloody trench – it's more than six-foot deep in places and full of hidey-holes, you know,' McGowan answered – 'and I took the other lot off to try to get into the middle of town and find their head-quarters. But, like you, we got split up in the alleys and all the smoke, and then this lot bounced us . . .' McGowan pointed to the mutineers whose wounded had been quietly dispatched by his own sepoys, 'and now we're just pausing to sort our casualties out.'

Morgan looked at the three wounded men of the 10th who were being dressed by their comrades. None looked particularly badly hurt, yet Morgan could more than sympa-thise with McGowan, who was clearly nonplussed by the speed and violence of the fighting that had engulfed his command. But, Morgan thought, if this was McGowan's first time in action, he wasn't doing too badly, especially when he compared the beginner's conduct to his own veteran performance. Not only had he buggered up the assault, he'd now lost his company within minutes of getting into the streets and alleys.

'Right, well, let's you and me go and find out where our boys are. Leave your lads in a defensive position here whilst they sort out the casualties, and we'll have a look-see.' Morgan felt better for taking charge of the situation, whilst McGowan was obviously relieved to have someone to tell him what to do.

'James, you stay here with the Tenth.' Morgan's unspoken message to the private was, *and don't let them run.* 'Corporal Pegg, come with me.'

James nodded, obviously pleased to be in the middle of a well-armed group, but Pegg had other views.

'But, sir, don't you think I should stay 'ere to look after 'em?'

'I'll thank you to remember that we don't need to be looked after by the likes of you, *Corporal* Pegg.' It was now McGowan's turn to be prickly.

'Aye, Corporal Pegg, just get up here, if you please.' Morgan was suddenly impatient with the lad's backsliding. 'Follow me.'

And with that, the patrol of two officers with sweaty Pegg and Sepoy Surpuray as escorts set off up a smoky, sun-baked alley in the general direction of where, Morgan hoped, Sergeant Ormond and his errant mob should have been.

'Listen . . . listen . . .' As they crept up the dirty lane, keeping their backs close to the broken walls that lined it, Morgan brought the group to a halt. 'There, can you hear someone calling?' There was a lull in the gunfire and as the patrol

141

edged forward they approached a junction where, Morgan swore, he could hear English voices. 'Sar'nt Ormond, we're here,' Morgan bellowed, then again: 'Sar'nt Ormond!'

All four of them crouched down by the wall, the two soldiers covering the rear with their rifles and bayonets, just as they had been taught.

'You an' me together again, Surpuray, old lad,' Pegg muttered confidentially to the sepoy, who grinned back delightedly. 'Keepin' an eye on that bloody officer of your'n.'

'Will you button your lip, Corporal Pegg, can't you see I'm trying to listen?' Morgan's anxiety spilt over into another bollocking for Pegg. 'Go forward, if you please, and have a look down the street and see if you can't find our lads, but keep low.'

Pegg licked his lips, considered asking Morgan to send Surpuray instead, realised it was a lost cause and crept off slowly towards the end of the alley where a mean, dusty, sunbleached street crossed it. As he approached the end of the wall, he sank to his knees, just as he'd been taught, and at the very moment that he bobbed his head round the corner, a mutineer did the same, looking in the opposite direction, straight into the alley.

The two men gawped at each other, one from below a smoke-stained forage cap, the other from under a greasy turban, but Pegg was first off the mark.

'Them's fuckin' Pandies, sir!' burst from his lips as he pelted back ten paces down the alley where the rest of the group had paused.

Morgan was just aware of Pegg's panic-filled arrival, of grit being kicked up from his scrabbling boots and an expression that suggested that the devil and all his evil followers were hard on his tail – before the suggestion became fact. A crowd of a dozen grimly silent mutineers spilt round the corner, bayonets and swords levelled, sandals thumping on the earth.

'Run, sirs . . . just fuckin' run,' shouted Pegg as he tore past the other three.

'No, stand firm,' Morgan commanded. 'It's our only chance.'

McGowan shouted something in Hindi that caused Surpuray to catch Pegg by the belts and bring him to an undignified halt, before both officers' pistols banged and banged again, then the three of them were on their feet, sprinting as hard into the charging mutineers as they could go.

As the two groups met, Surpuray fired his rifle from the waist and both Morgan and McGowan snapped off another pistol round apiece, causing a pair of Pandies to clutch at their wounds and fall, others tripping over them in their haste to be at the hated Feringhees. The odds were evened a little, but still not enough. But as the trio charged, Pegg hung back and watched as a wave of war-stained mutineers swept over the others, engulfing their scarlet coats in flashing sword and bayonet blades, bangs and white powder smoke.

Pegg hesitated as he saw both officers knocked to the ground and Surpuray flailing with his butt left and right, trying to stay upright amongst his assailants. He knew that he should stay and help, but just as he was stealing away, he heard a single voice above the tumult.

'*Corporal* Pegg, help us for pity's . . .'

Pegg stopped, turned reluctantly back and saw there, at the edge of the scrimmage, Captain McGowan, bleeding heavily from a cut on his neck, rolling over and over in the dust with a Pandy locked about him whilst another stood by, spear raised like a man out eel fishing, trying to get a clear jab at the officer.

Morgan felt the whole press of bodies suddenly give – just as a rugby scrum does when the ball is kicked clear. His sword had been knocked out of his hand by the stock of an enemy musket when the two sides met and he had been forced down onto one knee by several men who were vying with each other to punch or stab him. He was holding them off with his left forearm whilst poking hard at stomachs and ribs with his now empty revolver, when Pegg threw himself bodily into the fray.

Barging with his shoulder, the tubby corporal tumbled Captain McGowan's standing attacker to the floor who, in turn, cannoned into Morgan's foes. Then, with one of the neatest strokes – almost as if it were a demonstration, thought Morgan – Pegg spiked the Pandy who was above McGowan with just enough steel to disable, but not so much as to cause the blade to get stuck. The man fell off McGowan shrieking in pain, allowing Pegg to turn on the next mutineer.

That was some feint, thought Morgan as Pegg, now standing astride McGowan, allowed an Indian swordsman to overreach himself before neatly stabbing the man in the kidneys, but that next bastard'll have him.

Morgan threw the mutineer who was trying to wrench the pistol away from him to the ground, stamping on his hand so hard that he heard the bones snap whilst yelling through fist-bruised lips, 'Look out, Pegg!' as another Indian with a short spear came at the NCO's back.

But Morgan needn't have worried. He'd never seen Pegg in such a fluid frenzy. Ducking under the shaft, the lad brought his bayonet squarely up underneath his attacker's chin, the blade entering the skin under the jaw and thrusting up into the roof of the Indian's mouth and then straight into the brain; his assailant was dead before Pegg had even managed to get back on his feet and shake him off his blade.

But still the fight raged. Morgan could see Surpuray hard at work with the butt of his rifle amongst a clamour of enemies, whilst he tripped over a body in his haste to help Pegg protect McGowan. Sweat and curried breath surrounded Morgan as he thrashed and punched at the struggling, shouting sepoys, but the next move by Pegg was his best yet.

Morgan had no breath left to warn Pegg of another attacker as the lad stood like a rock over McGowan. But some sound, some sense must have warned him as a Pandy with a curved knife stole up on him from behind. Just as the blade was pulled back to strike, Pegg turned, dropped his rifle to waist height and shot the sepoy in the middle of the chest. Morgan marvelled as the round ripped through the back of the man's shirt and threw him to the ground – not at the marksmanship but at Pegg's self-discipline in a ruck like this. Morgan knew that he would have fired his rifle – his only round – in the first tight corner, yet Pegg had saved it for a real emergency.

'Sir, get the officer, shall yer?' shouted Pegg as Morgan stumbled through the wreckage of bodies that now surrounded him. 'Surpuray, get here: we'll hold 'em.' And as Morgan grabbed McGowan's unconscious body by the armpits, Englishman and Indian stood shoulder to shoulder, jabbing, stabbing and kicking, falling slowly back down the alley. Finally, what remained of the mutineers broke and ran away, disappearing around the corner from where they'd first emerged.

With the immediate danger gone, Morgan let McGowan down under the cover of a mud wall and reached for his water bottle. As he sucked at the contents, Pegg and Surpuray staggered towards him, falling into an exhausted heap besides the groaning McGowan.

'Fuckin' 'ell, sir, that was a bit sharp, wan't it?'

Pegg seemed uncharacteristically calm, thought Morgan. The young NCO had lost his cap and at least two gashes were matting his hair, whilst the grey cloth of his shirt stuck out from a long tear in his jacket just above his waist belt.

'Young Surpuray here did a grand job, din't you, bab?'

The Indian soldier smiled and winced as Morgan poured

a little brandy from his flask onto a long sword cut on the back of Surpuray's hand, before binding it with a clean bandage that he'd taken from the sepoy's own haversack.

'You weren't bad yourself, Corporal Pegg,' said Morgan. 'How many did you see off?'

'Dunno, sir, but you mustn't go back to loot 'em.' Pegg smiled weakly at Morgan. 'They'll be wanting to finish the job once they've rounded up a few o' their pals. Cum on, sir, we'd best move; an' you, Surpuray, get yersen reloaded.'

Pegg was suddenly in charge, pulling Morgan to his feet, lifting the semiconscious McGowan up and draping his arms over both their shoulders, and telling Surpuray to guard their backs. But no sooner had the tattered little gang started to move than a storm of shots and shouts broke out fifty paces away at the alley junction behind them.

'Christ, they're back. Put him down, sir,' Pegg told Morgan as Captain McGowan was allowed to slump to the floor and they all reached for their weapons again. But instead of charging sandals, boots thumped the dirt, a British cheer met their ears and a storm of red coats swept past the end of the alley. Leaving the sepoy to guard his officer, Morgan and Pegg ran as fast as their leaden legs would carry them back to the junction. There was Sergeant Ormond and half the company with fresh blood on their bayonets and powder about their lips.

'Well, there you are, sir. We was just starting to get worried about you,' Ormond grinned widely, delighted to have his officer back and in charge. 'You haven't been letting him get into mischief again, have you, young Pegg?'

'So, just to be clear, the brigadier-general was called a what?' Hume, tired by the fight and now exasperated, asked.

'"A battle-shy whoreson", sir,' Morgan replied. He'd tasted a bit of this sort of treatment from Hume before, where the

146

application of excoriating reason – not anger, just reason – could reduce him in seconds to a naughty schoolboy.

'And that he had what?'

'"More mouth than a cow's got cunt", sir,' Morgan muttered.

It had been a long day. Rowa had finally fallen and, even now, just before sunset, the Sappers were still blowing in the walls and trenches. Hume had called Morgan to him to explain a litany of things: why the assault had started before his signal; why the enemy's reserve had not been stopped from attacking McGowan's men; why the 10th had taken so many casualties as a result; why the guns had been masked by the Grenadier Company; why there had been no signal passed by Morgan's men to tell Carmichael's company to move; who had ransacked the treasury building and where were the contents.

'I know how difficult the fighting must have been inside the town, especially when most of the buildings were set a-fire,' Hume continued as Morgan stood to attention in front of him, covered in mud, black with smoke and with his scabbard still empty. 'I know how the men got their dander up and became very difficult to control . . .'

'Difficult to control', not 'you lost control of your troops', thought Morgan. The man's even courteous when he's tearing a strip off me.

'. . . and I know that it was the first, serious action for most of the soldiers . . .' Hume paused for effect.

'If only you knew the half of it, Colonel, thought Morgan. If only you'd seen McGucken shoot a Pandy at full stretch more than two hundred paces away; if only you'd seen Fawcett leading the boys over a blazing roof as if he'd done it all his life; if only you'd seen Ormond pull Kemp's savages off the three girls they'd found hiding in that cellar and if only you'd known the sweet joy of leading those lads then you – Colonel, my jewel – could forgive anything.

147

'. . . but why, when we know how much the general abhors drunkenness; why when he's just paying a cursory visit to see how the day has gone, why does one of your poets have to abuse the gentleman at the top of his gin-soaked voice and then run off and hide?'

'Well, sir, the men don't seem to like the general very much . . .'

'I don't suppose he likes them very much either, after having to listen to all that,' Hume snorted, 'and you haven't been able to find out who it was?'

'No, sir,' Morgan lied. The whole company knew that it was Matthew McGarry, who'd found 'a wee drop o' juice,' in a native still, and who had no great respect for authority even when sober, but then, he'd killed three Pandies all by himself that morning and, well . . .

'Hmm . . .' Hume was too wise a man, too good a leader, not to know when he was wasting his time. 'Well, you'll just have to convince the general somehow that you command my Grenadiers, not a parcel of sots. Other than a list of things that you and your men have learnt not to do again and ways not to address the general, is there anything creditable to come out of all this?'

Morgan thought hard and thought quickly. 'Well, yes, sir, I believe there is. Sepoy Suddo Surpuray fought well and saved several lives, and whilst I know that a native soldier can't receive the same decorations that our people can, we should do something for the man. And there's Lance-Corporal Pegg, sir—'

'I said anything *creditable*, Morgan.'

'I know you did, sir,' Morgan paused, 'but I believe his actions today deserve the Victoria Cross.'

'The Victoria Cross . . . Pegg?' Hume drew a deep breath. 'Pegg, the man who shot the priest outside Sevastopol, the man who lies for a pastime, the man who covers every native girl he can and the man whom you yourself said ought to be reduced from lance corporal because he "sets a bad example under fire". You think that he deserves a decoration from the hand of the Queen herself?'

'I do, sir.'

'Very well.' Hume sat down on an empty ammunition box and motioned Morgan to do the same. 'Persuade me.'

FIVE

Clemency

'So, Colour-Sar'nt, what does the manual tell us about execution by firing squad?' Morgan tried not to let his revulsion show, for McGucken was being utterly pragmatic about the whole business.

'Damned if I know, sir. This is one of those jobs that you just make up as you go along,' McGucken answered dispassionately. 'You ready yet, Corporal Pegg?'

'Almost, Colour-Sar'nt.' Pegg – after his experience gained with the executions in Bombay – had been charged with tying the prisoners to five wooden posts set in front of a sandy bank. ''Old still, Mr Bogger.' The fourth condemned man in the first batch struggled a little as he was triced up by Private Beeston. 'One more to go.'

After the capture of Rowa almost two weeks ago, General Smith's column had flogged over one hundred dreary, moonlit, humid and rain-soaked miles to join a much larger force that was destined to push hard into Rajputana to try to deal with brush-fire mutinies and uprisings amongst the maharajahs that threatened to spread right across Mahratta country. Great had been the excitement when the troops were told that the fort of Awah (stuffed full of gold and jewels, it was said) was to be attacked, but not as great as the disappointment in Morgan's Grenadiers when they were left in ignominious, unprofitable reserve.

In fact, there had been no real fight, for two thousand rebels had decamped during a torrential downpour, leaving much loot for everyone, except the Grenadier Company, and a couple of hundred prisoners. Whilst the fort was reduced to rubble and the spoils divided amongst the lucky ones, Colonel Hume had been told to court-martial the prisoners.

'So, how many of these lads did the commanding officers have to try, sir?' McGucken asked conversationally as the last man had his arms lashed to the billet.

'Nearly two hundred. There were all sorts of folk taken in the town, mainly by the Eighty-Third, but by some of our lot as well,' Morgan answered. 'Couldn't get their belts off fast enough, all claiming, of course, that they was about their own business. Anyway, it was the fastest assize since Pontius Pilate – so Captain Bazalgette said – but the colonel reckoned twenty-five of the rascals had been "taken under arms and in open rebellion against the State", and now we've got to deal with 'em. I blame McGarry and his escapade in Rowa.'

'Probably right, sir. We made no friend of the general that day,' McGucken continued calmly, 'but how d'you want it done?'

Morgan looked at the five men just yards in front of him. They were soldiers, right enough, their bearing and tattoos showed that, and they all seemed to be of high caste. Two were lightly wounded, with filthy dressings covering their hurts – they both seemed to be in pain – but they all faced the waiting ranks of British troops with quiet dignity.

'Do you think three rounds per man is enough, Colour-Sar'nt,' Morgan wondered, 'or should we give 'em five apiece in order to make sure of it?'

'Waste of good powder and shot, if you ask me, sir.' McGucken was beginning to get impatient with his officer: it would be dark soon and there were a thousand things to do before he could get a swally or two inside him. 'But it's kinder to get on with things rather than hing aboot, sir. If we put two men on each Pandy then the boys can get their weapons cleaned and see their blankets all the sooner, sir.'

'Aye, you're right. Sort it out, please, Colour-Sar'nt,' though Morgan wondered just how much more of this sort of butchery the Queen's Commission would require him to do.

Then the killing started. Morgan's sword rose and fell five times as fifty lead balls fired at ten paces removed twenty-five former servants of the Honourable East India Company from the ration-roll. At that range a single Enfield round would have done the job for, as Morgan saw, none of his men flinched, no barrel wavered, they fired straight and true, two lead balls ripping the vitals of each prisoner, throwing him against the wooden post, leaving every one hanging dead in the ropes that restrained him.

Corporal Pegg and his working party didn't even bother to clear the bodies between each lot, untying the corpses and leaving them beside the stakes in the certain knowledge that friends or relatives would bear the bodies away for burning as soon as possible. In fact, they became quite expert, each set of five mutineers dying before the powder smoke had even had time to clear between volleys.

'All clear, Corporal Pegg?' McGucken asked as the NCO – who still wore a bandage on his head long after he needed to – turned the torn body of the twenty-fifth man to make sure that he was properly dead.

'Aye, Colour-Sar'nt, good as gold.'

'Right, fall in. Detail complete, sir. May I have your leave to carry on, sir, please?' As the light failed, McGucken went through the ritual, stamping smartly in front of Morgan and slapping the sling of his rifle.

'You may, Colour-Sar'nt. I inspected weapons last night, so just rod and oil them: carry on, please,' and Morgan returned the salute before the firing party turned to their right and swung off towards their camping ground.

'Right, lads, march at ease. Smoke if you want.' McGucken's words came down the still air to Morgan as normal and routine as if they had been at musketry exercise.

Morgan asked Ensign Fawcett to stay with him as an escort and they both mounted their horses and walked slowly back towards the town, as explosions echoed dully and fires lit the twilight.

'Distasteful business that, Fawcett.' Morgan felt obliged to talk to the lad.

'Yes, I suppose so, Morgan. But it's just part of a soldier's job, ain't it?' Fawcett replied without much enthusiasm.

All part of a soldier's job? I feel more like Judge Jeffries than a soldier, thought Morgan. Seems odd that we've just executed twenty-five: nice round number, that. I suspect the colonel is as sick as I am about all this and spared as many as he could: two dozen was the least he could get away with. But the men – what's happening to them? This fellow and most of the troops are just boys but they're having to do things out here that nothing could have prepared them for, yet they do it without blinking, killing the Pandies like they was slaughtering sheep. Still, at least they're beginning to see that not every Indian's the same; the fight at Rowa made the troops look at the Bombay lads in a different way.

But the failing light made a stand of peepul trees look decidedly odd as the two horsemen rounded a corner in the road. Tropical darkness was falling fast and under the mottled, leafy boughs Morgan could see vast fruits hanging everywhere. Below them a gaggle of men stood and talked quietly, their voices drowned by the crackle of flames in the fortress. The smell of wood smoke and turned earth drifted down the breeze, and Morgan could see tiny red dots at the mouths of the speakers, cigars glowing in the dark.

'Are those what I think they are, Fawcett?' asked Morgan as their horses slowed to a shuffle.

'Looks like a whole lot of Pandies have been strung up,' replied the young officer flatly.

The voices continued, there was even a muted chuckle as the riders drew close, and then from the loaming came a distinct voice, one that Morgan recognised.

'And that cheeky sod even tried to bribe Rissaldar Batuk here with a pot full of gold pieces.' A bulky arm pointed up into the tree towards one of the dead, who turned very gently at the end of his rope. 'I don't know what he thought he might achieve, because no sooner had he shown Batuk the money than he was marched off down here, had a noose around his neck and up he went – and I can tell you that the gold wasn't left to rot, oh, no!' Commandant Kemp's voice growled from the shadows.

'Commandant, is that you?' Morgan steered his horse through ankles and limp, dirty feet that hung about his head. 'It's me, Morgan of the Ninety-Fifth, with my ensign, Fawcett.'

'Goddamn, boy, it's good to see you.' Kemp grasped Tony Morgan's hand as he dismounted amidst a group of heavily armed older men.

'Listen you lot, this is Morgan, son of a friend of mine back in Cork. Brevet majority at Sevastopol and now leading a company in that bunch of rogues some call the Ninety-Fifth.' There was a laugh all round. 'Well met, boy. Ain't seen you since Rowa. Here, let me introduce you: Moore, he was my quartermaster in the Twelfth; Dr Stockwell from Baroda – more used to a sabre now than a scalpel; Rees the railway; Breen of the Light Horse in Gwalior; you know Rissaldar Batuk from the fight at Rowa – oh, just make yourself known to the whole lot. You're right welcome.'

Distant firelight fell on the grinning, whiskered faces all around the pair of officers as their hands were pumped enthusiastically. It was like the start of a race meeting, or introductions in a gentlemen's club, so cordial were the smiles, so friendly were the embraces. But there was no racing or rounds of port here, just orange flashes from the town and swinging corpses. All of these men had harrowing stories to tell of butchered babies, mutinous troops and narrow escapes, but they were dubbed 'free-lancers' by the regular forces, sneered at for their extravagant arms and clothing, and kept at arm's length despite all their local knowledge.

So free and fast was the talk that Morgan almost forgot the dead all about him until he saw Fawcett, still in the saddle, catch hold of a foot and gently twist its owner so that he could get a better look at the face. Morgan looked too: in the dark it was hard to see the features – like all the rest the head was set at an unnatural angle and the tongue lolled from blue lips – but this man was old and snowy-haired, a cropped grey beard hung down his chest. He must have been sixty if he was a day, thought Morgan, and so painfully thin that he looked incapable of shouldering a musket, still less swinging a sword.

'Seems a bit ancient to be a Pandy, don't he, sir?' Fawcett said conversationally, but the group suddenly went silent. 'Wish those rascals we met in Rowa had been as flea-bitten as this old boy. Why, I'd—'

'Oh, young 'un, so one little skirmish in a fart-arse of a place that no one's ever heard of makes you an expert on the Queen's enemies, does it?' Kemp instantly cut across Fawcett's callow remark, his good humour vanishing along with his friends' banter.

'No, sir, not a bit of it,' Fawcett answered gamely, but he was given no chance to continue.

'No damn cheek from you, you bloody griff,' Kemp exploded. 'They don't have to be in belts an' scarlet to be our foes. Why, if you'd been in Jhansi with us you'd have seen what the fuckers did: one minute they were our loyal servants, the next they were defaming our women and catching babes on their bayonets. I'll take no lectures from a kid straight off his mother's tit.'

'Commandant, young Fawcett meant no offence,' Morgan intervened, gently taking the furious Kemp by the elbow and steering him away from the boy. 'Off you go, Fawcett: check the sentries; I'll be back shortly.'

'But I was only asking—' Fawcett was as much confused by Kemp's angry reply as he was offended.

'Don't argue, Mr Fawcett, be off!' Morgan felt how the group's mood had swung and the best way to assuage it was to be rid of the cause. With a stiff salute, Fawcett trotted off into the dark, leaving a resentful silence behind him.

'I'm so sorry about that, Commandant,' said Morgan. 'He's too green to know how much your people have suffered.'

Kemp's gang had dispersed, leaving their commander, his rissaldar and Morgan to talk beside the road under a canopy of deaf witnesses.

'Well, he needs to keep a leash on his tongue, does that tyro.' Kemp shook cheroots from a worn leather case, offered them to his friend's son, to Batuk and then lit them from a single match.

All three puffed appreciatively into the night air for a moment before Morgan judged that Kemp had regained his composure.

'We had to shoot twenty-five prisoners after the court martial; how many was you told to hang?'

'I know, I heard you wasting good lead on the bastards. We stretched about forty-odd necks today – don't know exactly, not enough anyway. Take a tip from me, Morgan, don't burn good powder when you've got rope at two annas a yard; besides, shooting's too quick for 'em. Just put some hemp round their necks and pull 'em off the ground; gives them a bit of time to reflect on their sins and lets their pals see what's in store for them unless they mend their ways.' Kemp looked up at one of his victims and blew a cloud of smoke.

'I'm sure you're right, Commandant, but didn't the court specify the manner of execution?' As soon as he'd asked the question, Morgan knew what answer he'd get.

'Court? What bloody court? The only trial they get is the same sort of trial that Neeta got, or Dr Stockwell's twin girls, come to that. And as for all that dung about clemency that Canning gave us – well, the only clemency that I'll give this lot is a short drop or a bit of good Birmingham steel – that's called Kemp's clemency.'

There was a chill in the air as Morgan trotted back into Awah alongside Batuk, whom Kemp had instructed to act as his escort.

'The commandant seems hellbent on sorting this whole mess out single-handed, don't he, Rissaldar sahib?' Morgan peered through the dark at the man in the saddle next to him to see how his comments would be received.

'He, like so many of us, sahib, has been deeply hurt,' Rissaldar Batuk answered quietly.

'Aye, but this uprising will be brought under control – it's only in one presidency, after all – and then the whole country will have to get back to whatever passes for normality here. Wholesale bloody murder of people is only going to sow hatred for years to come, ain't it?' Morgan was suddenly aware that he was sounding like Lord Canning.

'Sahib, you don't understand – you can't, you haven't been here long enough. Kemp Bahadur and I have eaten the Company's salt all our lives, fighting its wars and carving new lands out of wilderness and savages. We heard the grumbles and the rumours, and we knew of the troubles that there had been with sepoy regiments back in the years when your queen was young, but we thought that was just part of the normal music of the army. But we were wrong, and the men we trusted turned into the very filth they had helped to beat.' Batuk drew heavily on the last stump of his cheroot before tossing it away into the dark, its glowing tip lost against the flames in Awah. 'Now we must have no mercy, for if we do, my "brothers" will see this as a sign of weakness and peace will never return.'

'But half those men we saw hanging from trees were not mutineers, Rissaldar, they were old folk, villagers—' But Morgan wasn't allowed to finish.

'Yes, sahib, just like the men who killed my family up in Nowgong – not sepoys, just dung beetles who hate the *goralog* and have no respect for what you have brought us; ignorant monkeys who listen too much to the babus and suck up Hindu poison. Kemp Bahadur saw the massacre at the Jokan Bagh at Jhansi, and I saw the bodies of Turnbull sahib, Burgess, Taylor, Gordon, your friend Mr Keenan of the Twelfth and all the other fine gentlemen, their memsahibs and – ask the gods for mercy – the children. Most were not soldiers and they were not killed by soldiers; they were hacked by butchers' axes and knives, by scum drunk on the words of evil men. That, sahib, is why these things are being done and why you must understand that this is our war more than yours, that those owls from the Tenth Bombay will learn to cut with the sword of vengeance just as well as your white-faced men and see that many here in Bengal need to be punished for what they have done.' There had been an intensity in Batuk's words that left Morgan feeling foolish and naive.

'I see, Rissaldar.' Morgan paused before adding, 'There are many hard things for us from England to grasp here. I thought I knew war, but not this sort of war, not this sort of hatred; you'll have to help me to understand things better, Rissaldar sahib.'

'Morgan sahib, I will try. Now, here's the way back to your own men; be safe, sahib.' Rissaldar Batuk pointed towards a clutch of buildings in the dark and saluted with a smile before turning his horse and trotting away.

What had seemed clear and simple in daylight – and even with the rissaldar's directions – was now confusing and difficult in the dark, for as he'd left the main body of the 95th to carry out his duties, their camping ground was only just

158

being established amongst a clutter of battered buildings and yards. Now it all looked so different and all he wanted after the nastiness of the executions, Kemp's theories and Batuk's cold realism was some food, a drink, no pestering from the troops and as much time in his blankets as he could get. He thought he could see the outline of a tower lit by flames, near to which the company had been billeted, and spurred his horse towards it.

'Hookum dear?' was suddenly yelled almost beneath the hoofs of his horse, but as he reined in hard there was a yellow flash in the night, a deafening bang and a ball sang past his ear.

'Goddamn you, stop that bloody nonsense,' Morgan shouted in both outrage and fear, his horse jibbing and plunging at the noise. 'Friend . . . friend, stop shooting, won't you?'

His angry words brought a sheepish sepoy from the shadows, weapon at the shoulder, grinning with embarrassment, his left hand coming to an uncertain salute.

'What the hell do you think you're doing, man?' Morgan knew that if one sentry started firing in such circumstances there was a very good chance others would follow suit. Experience had taught him that the best way to avoid another dose of fast-moving lead from a frightened sentinel was to be as imperious and confident as possible.

'You're Thirteenth BNI, aren't you?' Morgan could see the numbers on the sepoy's brass cross-belt plate. 'Bertram sahib shall hear about this.'

The sepoy pricked up his ears at the name of his commanding officer, but obviously understood nothing else that Morgan was saying.

'And don't just yell nonsense like "*Hookum dear?*" It's "Who comes there?" "Who comes there?", do you understand? Go on, say it after me.' Morgan got the soldier to repeat the phrase a number of times, but was not convinced that the man was any the wiser. 'And don't open fire before you get a reply – you'll bloody kill someone like that, understand?'

The sepoy stood rigidly to attention, nodding and grinning at the sahib's lecture. Eventually, though, Morgan had had enough and left the soldier chastised but, he suspected, just as likely to do the same again to the next innocent that approached.

The road into Awah was deserted and Morgan was still uncertain of his route until he stopped a passing file of fresh sentries from the 83rd, the corporal in charge of which, to his amazement, knew where the 95th's camp had been sited. Mercifully, his own men didn't attempt to murder him as he asked for directions to the building that had been pressed into service as an officers' mess. It was a tired and dispirited young captain, though, who finally dragged himself into a large, stone-flagged room that was lit by a cooking fire of planks and splintered timber. Looking round, Morgan could see that the place had once been magnificent: there were rich murals of hunting scenes and the remains of heavy curtains at the windows, but the walls had been scored with bayonet blades or defaced with charcoal into crude portraits, vast initials or regimental numbers, the universal graffiti of passing British soldiers.

'Now, the officer commanding our bold Grenadiers . . .' Bazalgette was the only officer present other than a few snoring forms in the corner, wrapped in sheets or light blankets, '. . . plate of stew, dish of tea and a splash in the hand would go down well, I'd say? Your man has brought in your bedroll.' He nodded towards Morgan's strapped bedding and haversack that lay by the wall.

The presence of his friend lifted Morgan's mood, but his servant was nowhere to be found, so he unbuckled his own sword and pistol, levered off his own worn boots and scrabbled in his bags to find his native slippers and a flask of brandy.

'I'm glad to see you, Bazalgette. Here, have a wee bit of this.' Morgan poured some cognac into his comrade's outstretched silver beaker. 'Oh, thank you, Hambleton,' and he took a china plate of lamb stew from the mess servant.

'We've been pulling down buildings all day and dismantling the armoury. Here, look what I took . . .' Bazalgette showed Morgan a splendidly chased flintlock pistol that was set with gems of some sort; the fire flickered off the stones. 'It's been the devil's own job to stop the troops from making off with more loot than they can possibly carry . . .' But Bazalgette could see that Morgan wasn't really listening. 'You've been on a firing party, ain't you?'

'I have and, by God, I'm low about the whole sorry affair.' Morgan spooned some gravy into his mouth and noticed that the servant was hovering in the shadows.

'Is there any more of this, Hambleton?'

The man scraped the ladle round the stew pot and slopped a mouthful or two onto Morgan's plate.

'Thank you, that's grand. Please leave us now, Hambleton, you'll need your sleep if you're for guard later.' The man knew that Morgan's thoughtful words really meant that he was to get out of earshot; he wiped his hands on a grubby apron, settled his dusty cap, saluted and withdrew into the dark.

'We carried out Hume's orders, shot twenty-five and left 'em for their mates to collect and burn. That was bad enough, although the Pandies died with courage and as much dignity as they could muster – you've seen what they're like – but at least they'd had some sort of trial before punishment was meted out—'

'You're right, but the colonel's sticky about the whole business of summary justice,' Bazalgette interrupted. 'You can see it on his face, and he only ever condemns the least that he can.'

'Aye, that's my impression too, and I respect him for it, if

I'm honest. No, the problem came when Fawcett and I rode back and we knocked into Commandant Kemp . . .'

Morgan related the whole story of Kemp, the hangings and the wild gang with whom he was scouring the country-side, bent on destruction.

'Whilst I can understand his thirst for revenge, the need-less murders sicken me, yet what could I do? You're aware that he's a friend of my father – I've known him since I was a boy in Skibbereen – that his record against the Sikhs was second to none and that, if the stories are to be believed, he kept the resistance going up in Jhansi pretty well single-handed. But, that doesn't excuse his behaviour, does it?'

'No, you're right, it doesn't,' Bazalgette answered. 'But the trouble is that Kemp's too bloody senior and wise to the ways of this country to be gainsaid. And it doesn't help that we treat the John Company officers as if they're second-rate folk. That, of course, suits Kemp perfectly, for no one is prepared to dirty their hands on him and his band of cutthroats. Did you see what those archers of his did after Rowa fell?'

'You mean the Pandies' heads they brought back? I did; took me a while to realise that they weren't coconuts they'd been harvesting,' Morgan shuddered, 'and he all but ignores Hume and the general. That bit in *The Times* ain't helpful, either; all that tosh about the "light of just vengeance" in his eyes just gives him more bottom.'

'You're right, of course.' Bazalgette, now puffing at his pipe, nodded thoughtfully. 'No, I suspect that everyone will turn a Nelsonian eye to him until the whole business has burnt itself out.'

'Possibly, but that may not be so easy for me.' Morgan leant over to his friend and lit his pipe from Bazalgette's. 'You see, Kemp gave me a very fair exposition of how he saw the rest of the campaign up here unfolding. He says that Tantya Tope,' Morgan looked to see whether the name of

162

the mutineers' commander in the field registered with Bazalgette, 'will certainly defend Kotah, Chundaree and Gwalior, and expect us to try to take them by deliberate siege or storm.'

'Just a minute . . .' Bazalgette went to his kit and retrieved a map, spread it out, taking a lantern to let them both examine it. 'Yes, we've got to if we're to pacify the place.' His finger traced the main centres of rebel resistance.

'Not according to Kemp. He says that the moving spirit behind the whole rebellion in the Mahratta lands is the Rhani of Jhansi, and that if a fast-moving column could bypass the places where the enemy expect us to attack and go straight for her headquarters here . . .' Morgan pointed to Jhansi some one hundred and fifty miles east of where they were, '. . . and take the bitch alive, then the spunk would go out of things and we could probably wrap the whole campaign up in weeks.'

'Well, he may be right. He knows the place inside out – that's why, as we've just said, no one dares to stop him – and we've now got three regiments of native cavalry as well as de Salis's Eight Hussars who could push deep and fast.'

'Yes, and, of course, he sees the general letting him have command of all that lot to go and destroy her.' Morgan sipped at his drink. 'And if Mary and Sam are to stand any chance of survival in the Hades that's going to be unleashed, I'm going to have to be with the gentle commandant.'

'What? I know you're a friend, but why on earth should you want to—' Bazalgette scoffed until he paused and thought. 'Ah, of course: Mary and the boy . . . of course.'

'Keep your voice down, for God's sake,' Morgan cautioned him.

'But are you sure that they're both – I'm sorry to have to say it – still alive?' asked Bazalgette awkwardly.

'I believe so. According to Kemp, Mary and the Rhani were pals long before all this horror – and now Mary's acting as her physician, but how willing she is to do that and how much is against her will is far from clear. The commandant's people in Jhansi report that Sam is being kept close-hauled with the Rhani's lad, Damodar; so I suppose that if they've got the boy, the mother will do her damnedest to stay with him. Leastways, I hope that's the case; I can't believe that she'd throw in her lot with the enemy – but she's so bloody headstrong I'd put nothing past her. But I just can't believe that. She knows that the Pandies murdered her husband, James Keenan, and now there's no one to shift for either her or the lad. It's clear where my duty lies.'

'Clear to you, perhaps; I wouldn't put money on our lords and masters having the same clarity,' Bazalgette responded. 'And, seeing what I've seen, I'd put a year's pay on Kemp and all his loons being wiped out before they got anywhere near their objective. The man's mad with grief and vengeance, and it clouds his judgement; he'll want to move at speed so he won't be able to take any decent guns with him, and infantry would just slow him down. He won't be given more than a handful of regular cavalry, so he'll be fighting the sepoys on pretty well even terms except that there's a plague more of them than there are of his crew. No, my friend, I can see what you think you should do, but being close to Kemp is the surest way to an early grave that I can imagine. He's looking for eternity; I should steer as clear of him as the Pope does of the pox.'

But before they could discuss it further, the mess door banged open, accompanied by a cloud of swearing.

'Dutton, Dutton, where are you, blast you?' Richard Carmichael, in tearing bad humour, came bursting in. 'My goddamn storm light's gone out and I've fallen in every bloody ditch. Dutton . . . Have you seen the wretched man, Bazalgette?'

'So, your fellow's made himself as scarce as mine has,' said Morgan, 'and in view of his master's mood, it's probably a wise move.'

164

'Oh, hello, Morgan, didn't see you there,' Carmichael said gruffly. 'Your lazy bugger absent too? No matter, where's the duty cook? Any food left?'

'No, Hambleton was called for guard and all the stew's long gone,' Morgan glanced at Bazalgette, his mood rising at Carmichael's frustration, 'but there's a bottle or two of porter over yonder.'

'Porter? I'd sooner drink camel piss. I've some brandy in my kit, though. Where's Dutton put it?' This set Carmichael off on another furious, fruitless search until Bazalgette took pity on him and poured him a generous measure of his own precious spirits.

'And what have you two been plotting?' Carmichael pushed at the fire with his boot, then settled down next to the others.

'We was just discussing Commandant Kemp and his views on how the rest of the campaign should be conducted,' Bazalgette replied.

'Kemp; man's no better than the bloody sepoys he commands – or did, that is, until they saw the error of their judgement and threw him over,' Carmichael sneered. 'Leadership in war should be left to gentlemen, not damned tradesmen and Paddies who come out to this shoddy country because they can't cut it back at home.'

'Kemp's a friend of my father, Carmichael . . .' Why, Morgan wondered, did he always let himself rise to the bloody man's bait? '. . . and he may be a common fellow from the bogs of Cork, but he was besting the Sikhs when you were still at that damn school of yours.'

'Envy's such an ugly emotion, Morgan. Quite twists your features, y'know,' Carmichael retorted quickly.

Bazalgette put a restraining hand on Morgan's arm just as a clever counter that was guaranteed to throw Carmichael into confusion utterly failed to roll off his tongue. Instead, he rose and walked as calmly as he could from the room, making sure that he closed the door soundlessly behind him.

Outside his anger subsided with each puff that he took of his pipe. The sky was alight with stars, the Pleiades bright above him. He opened his shell jacket and thought of Mary's fingers pulling at those same hooks and eyes in the camp before Sevastopol on the afternoon three years ago when their son, Samuel, had been conceived. Now he wondered if she was gazing into the same firmament.

Flames that were licking up beyond a building in the distance suddenly belched more fiercely upward, throwing a bouquet of orange and silver sparks into the night sky and making the breeze fragrant with the scent of burning wood. Then, quite clearly, came the tenor of Corporal Patrick Brick from Sion Mills as the troops entertained each other around their cooking fires. Morgan had heard him make wonderful music with a fiddle, but he'd never listened carefully enough to appreciate how beautifully the man sang.

> *A-thirsting to avenge, my boys,*
> *The bloodshed that was done.*
> *On poor defenceless women,*
> *Ere Delhi had been won.*
> *We made the Pandies for to know,*
> *And caused them for to feel,*
> *That British wrongs should be avenged,*
> *By sterling British steel.*
>
> *When a-hunting we did go, my boys*
> *A-hunting we did go.*
> *To chase the Pandies night and day*
> *And levelled Delhi low.*

SIX

The Relief of Kotah

'What time are you wanted by the brigade commander, sir?' Colour-Sergeant McGucken asked Morgan.

'Noon, Colour-Sar'nt. He wants to give all the assaulting company commanders their orders whilst there's still some daylight, so we can get a good look at Kotah before tomorrow's attack.'

Morgan and McGucken were crouching low behind a tussocky bank and staring hard at the great fortress that lay five hundred yards away across the greasy, sluggish Chumbal river. The pair had come forward for their own reconnaissance, rather than waiting to be told.

'It's going to be a real pig's bastard if we have to storm them walls, sir. They must be sixty foot high in places and the Pandies' guns can rake the river from downstream when we try to cross it. Has the general had a good look at this, sir? Does he know what he's asking us to do?' asked McGucken, a note of real concern in his voice.

'Well, I hope so, Colour-Sar'nt. I'll know the precise details later on, but I gather that we're to be ferried across the river at dead of night into the main citadel where the forces that have remained loyal to the Rajah of Kotah are holding out against the rest of the natives, who have mutinied. The general slipped a few hundred of our men into the place three days ago to support the Rajah's lads and, well, you've heard the firing that's been going on ever since as well as I have,' Morgan replied quietly, continuing to scour the ground opposite with his binoculars.

'Aye, sir, that all sounds grand, but if one of them Pandy guns catches wind of the fact that we're crossing in boats, night-time or not, there'll be the devil to pay,' muttered McGucken, studying the opposite shore just as carefully as his officer.

'You're right, Colour-Sar'nt, but it'll be as well not to let on too much of this to the men. They seem to have recovered well after the march from Awah, don't they?'

'They have, sir, but I had me doubts about some of the younger lads. Twenty-four fuckin' awful night marches and no shaggin' sleep to speak of during the day soon takes it out of you, but I was pleased by how few fever cases we had, especially when the rest of the Regiment joined us: they was full of it, wasn't they?'

Morgan nodded his agreement. The journey up to Kotah had tested them all, but they had been cheered when the other wing of the 95th, who had sailed on another transport and followed a separate route up-country, had formed up with them soon after the march had started.

'Well, they've had a chance to rest now, haven't they? Someone must have thought this attack through pretty carefully, for this is the first time that I've seen the infantry being given the time to draw breath whilst the guns and engineers do all their preliminary work,' said Morgan.

'I hope you're right, sir. The boys have done well so far and they deserve a chance to get at Pandy and have a bit of loot and a drop o' drink, but I still don't like the look of the guns that can cover the river. Anyway, sir, I dare say the general will have some devilish clever plan. Seen enough?' McGucken wormed his way down below the cover of the bank.

'I have, Colour-Sar'nt,' Morgan followed suit, moving carefully so as not to attract the attention of an enemy marksman. 'I have every confidence in the tactical ability of our lords and masters, just as I know you do.'

'You're right, sir, my cup of confidence overfloweth. Come on, sir, you don't want to be late for your orders, do you?' McGucken grinned sardonically as the pair moved carefully into the cover of some bushes.

The attack had been set for dawn the next day, 30 March. Thirty or so officers now sat, smoked and studied a looted easel on which was set a hand-drawn map of the target. Against the wooden trestle lay a pointer-stick with which Brigadier-General Smith would, doubtless, draw their attention to the features of the defences themselves that lay no more than five pistol shots away across the river.

'Right, gentlemen, relax; smoke if you wish.' Smith started well, for most of the audience were concealing pipes or cigars that were already well alight. 'We were lucky not to encounter the enemy on the march up here . . .'

Shame, thought Morgan, might have given me the chance to save my reputation.

'. . . but now we've got some real opposition. You all know how the Rajah's men turned on him under the leadership of a rogue called Hira Singh, then they burnt the British residency. You're also aware that the Rajah holds the citadel and a portion of the town next to the river yonder . . .' Smith pointed to a vast keep surrounded by high ramparts; it was faced on all except the side next to the Chumbul by houses and other buildings which sprawled within an outer curtain of lower walls, '. . . and that he's besieged by about seven thousand rebels in the greater part of the town: the newspapers have been calling for us to relieve the poor man for weeks and now, with the guns in place and a good reserve helping to stiffen the Rajah's resolve, we're ready to cross the river, enter the citadel, break out into the town and let Pandy catch a Tartar.'

Morgan couldn't like the man and his irascible, charmless style, but he had to admit the general's plan seemed well thought through, although, like McGucken, he was still uneasy about a river crossing under the enemy's nose.

'Every gun we and the Rajah have got will fire as rapidly as possible from dawn tomorrow until the assault is ready to start . . .' Smith illustrated the positions of their own batteries using the map, '. . . then the three columns, which will have crossed the river in the dark, will attack from out of the citadel into the town. The sappers will be on hand to blow breaches here and here . . .' Smith used the map again, '. . . for the first two columns, whilst the third column will start from the Kettonpore Gate – you may need a bit of powder to clear that as well.' Smith looked directly at Colonel Hume, who was to command the third column. 'The first column will take the Pattadar and Zorawan bastions, and the second will secure the Surajpole Gate, drawing off the enemy and allowing the third to go for the centre of Hira Singh's reserves.'

Smith paused and looked at his column commanders. 'I trust that it's now obvious that your column, Hume, will get the lion's share of the fighting. Once you've blown your way through the Kettonpore, you're to hook left and go straight for the heart of the enemy just here.' Smith pointed to a tight group of buildings on the map. 'I know you're aware of how crucial your part of the operation is, so please dispose your troops carefully.'

'Sir, we're very honoured,' said Hume; only those who knew him well would have detected any sarcasm, thought Morgan.

Each column consisted of a mixture of British and native troops, the third one being made up of four companies of the 95th and four of their comrades from the 10th Bombay.

170

There were a strong troop of engineers to support them, both in getting out of the citadel and in clearing the barricades that the mutineers were said to have erected amongst the streets and alleys, whilst two howitzers were to bring up the rear for close-quarter work.

The plan may be sound, thought Morgan, but I wonder how far forward our precious general will place himself. Pound to a pinch of shit we see nothing of him once the Sappers blow those breaches. Anyway, it don't signify; all that matters is what's in store for me and the boys, but it's about time that bloody Carmichael was given a bit of work to do. We've had more than our share of 'honour'.

There were more details from the general about where and when the boats and rafts were to be picked up, which enemy batteries were thought to be the most lively, and how their foes would be cut down by the cavalry once the defeat became a rout. But Morgan had ceased to listen once the parts of the plan that involved Hume's column had been covered. Eventually, Smith had finished, called for questions – which none dared to ask – and stamped off with his staff, leaving the column commanders to speak to their officers. As if to signal the end of the general's diatribe, the British batteries fired a salvo at those of the enemy – ranging, Morgan thought, for the morning's onslaught.

'Right, gather round, gentlemen.' Hume had been given plenty of warning of his column's tasks by Smith and now there were just the formalities of tying up which company was to do what, some timings, details of feeding, extra ammunition and assistance to the Sappers and Gunners. The group of a dozen captains and subalterns stood by expectantly with their notebooks ready.

'As you've heard, we're to form the third column, and it will be lead by the four companies of the Ninety-Fifth and followed by your four companies, gentlemen.' Hume looked towards the officers of the Tenth. 'Carmichael and Massey, your companies will form the main body.' The two captains both nodded, though Morgan thought he detected a certain paleness around Richard Carmichael's gills. 'Bazalgette, I want your company to be prepared to act as an immediate reserve, with the two howitzers acting under your command. Your troops will move just behind the main body but I want you, Bazalgette, up on my elbow so that you'll know exactly what to do once I deploy you as the fight develops, is that clear?'

'Sir, very clear.' Bazalgette replied, but there was something low, flat about the way that he said it, a tone that made Morgan look hard at his friend.

'Now, the Grenadiers,' Hume paused and looked Morgan directly in the eye, 'as befits my senior company, you are to form the storming party.'

Morgan's balls and guts tightened. It couldn't be worse. Another dose of 'honour', he thought. How will I tell that to the men?

'You'll have both Sapper parties with you until we've broken out of the citadel; I want you to go hard for the initial enemy guns and barricades, seize and hold them. Then, when you give us the signal that routes of advance are clear, I'll bundle Carmichael and Massey through you. I can't tell you how important this first stage of the assault is, Morgan. If you run into really stiff resistance, I'll put Bazalgette and his company under your command with both howitzers. Any questions?'

'Sir, no questions except for the crossing of the river. The enemy guns that are downstream, firing from the outer part of Kotah, can easily rake the bend of the river where we are to cross. One or two canister rounds will tear us to shreds once they know we're there.' Morgan tried not to sound too worried, but he had to make sure that his seniors knew the dangers of what was about to be attempted.

'Yes, I've looked over that piece of ground and river myself

172

with the general, and that's why we're going to mount the crossing at night with no artillery bombardment that might put the enemy on the qui vivre. We'll just have to use the cover of darkness and trust to John Pandy being asleep on sentry – nothing new there. Does that make it clear?' Hume looked steadily at Morgan, his eyes betraying the danger of the task, but his voice as steady as if they were discussing horseflesh. Morgan could see that there was no room for further debate,

'Very clear, sir.' And it was clear, the Grenadiers and all his powers of leadership were to be very seriously tested: how honoured he felt.

'Well, Morgan, our forefathers must have upset people thoroughly for their sins to be visited on us like this.' Bazalgette and Morgan, now that Hume's orders had finished, were taking one last look at Kotah's walls and bristling batteries before they went back to give their orders to the men.

'Aye, that bugger there could give us a problem if they tumble to the fact that we're so close to them.' Both officers had turned their binoculars onto the enemy battery that McGucken had identified during the earlier reconnaissance. 'Lucky that we'll have plenty of darkness, because it's only about four hundred paces upstream,' Morgan muttered, more to himself than to his brother officer.

'I know, it could be dangerous if it sees us, but have you heard anything about the strength of the enemy inside the town?' Bazalgette asked with none of his normal cheerfulness.

'No. Well, nothing beyond what we've just been told: about seven thousand under this character Hira Singh, who's already seen more blood-letting than he should. But the reports that the Rajah's men have been passing back suggest that we're going to have a right good shindy.' Morgan tried to make light of his own dread.

'Look, Morgan, please don't think less of me . . .'

Bazalgette was behaving oddly, thought Morgan. Usually, before battle he was calm; indeed, he'd seen him more worried over a cricket match than going into action.

'. . . but I've got the most awful feeling about this business. I just don't think I'm going to pull through. I'm not an imaginative or religious man – you know I'm not – but you can call it a presentiment or whatever you like, but I believe that I shall be killed.'

'Oh, nonsense, Bazalgette; why—'

'No, please take me seriously. I'm not going to pass you a final letter or give you my watch – you'd only pawn it –' Bazalgette tried valiantly to make a weak, little joke – 'but if I'm right, please send my things to Miss Gabbett and tell her whatever sweet lies you think she'd like to hear.'

Morgan thought of the plain but lively girl that his friend had met in Dublin. Bazalgette had been particularly impressed by the way that she showed no revulsion at all to his scaly, wounded hand – something that so many other girls tried to avoid.

'You're talking utter rot, old sport,' Morgan put his arm on his comrade's shoulder and tried to reassure him, 'but I'll do whatever you want. You know, don't you, that this time tomorrow we'll look back on your "presentiment" and laugh? Now, come on, we'd better get back to the troops. Don't you go being all morbid with them: save that for me.'

'Why do we always have to be closest to the Pandies, Colour-Sar'nt?' Lance-Corporal Pegg and his section of men were sitting uncomfortably on the boards of a raft that was now starting its voyage across the river Chumbul.

The craft was connected by stout ropes to another in front, which in turn was being towed by two rowing boats crewed by oarsmen from the Rajah's forces. The whole of the Grenadier Company, thirty-five men on to each raft, crouched there, scarlet coats now faded, faces deeply tanned. The only things that shone in the dawn's first rays were the well-oiled barrels of their Enfield rifles.

Downstream, to their right, were the other three companies, crossing on similar rafts, Carmichael's Number One Company closest – about fifty yards away.

'It's an honour, that's why, Corporal Pegg.' Colour-Sergeant McGucken had had much the same thought as Pegg. Captain Morgan had pointed out the enemy battery that would be most dangerous to the flotilla the evening before, saying that if they made too much noise, it might open fire, but the darkness should protect them: but that was before the delay. The crossing was meant to have started at three in the morning, but the Rajah's men were late and now they were sitting in the early morning light like geese on the Clyde. 'And anyway, them rebels will still be a-fairtin' on their charpoys at this time o' day.'

'Well, if that's the case, what's caught our Paddy's attention?' Pegg could see how Morgan was hooked over in the leading raft, trying to steady his glasses, squinting hard at the far battery.

'Probably spotted some bint washing her itcher in the shallows,' McGucken's joke relieved the tension a little, 'and it's Captain Morgan to you.' But Corporal Pegg was right, the company commander was studying something, thought McGucken, and if he screwed his eyes up, he reckoned that he could just make out some movement in the nearest embrasure.

'Now, Corporal Patsy Brick,' the men on Morgan's raft were just as tense as those behind him as the sun banished the sheltering dark, 'd'you think your shooting's as good as your singing?' For the benefit of the men, Morgan tried to sound as light-hearted as possible, despite the shiver of fear he felt as he scanned the enemy battery.

'It is, your honour. I guess you'd be wanting me to put a

pellet or two at yonder Pandies.' Brick, like everyone else afloat, had seen the danger, but, winner of the company musketry prize in Bombay, he was probably the only man who was capable of putting a round through an eighteen-inch-wide gun port at such a range. 'I'd say it's about four hundred, maybe a wee bit more. May I suggest you have a few *bandooks* ready, sir, then I can fire rapid, like.'

'Yes, of course.' Morgan immediately felt better once he was doing something useful. 'Set your sights at four fifty and aim low; I'll watch your fall of shot. You lot, load your fire-locks and be ready to pass them to Corp'l Brick once I give the word.'

The men scrambled around to make room for Brick who, having loaded, lay prone on the decking with Morgan next to him, his glasses trained on the bastion. Brick settled himself, carefully adjusted his iron ramp-sight and aimed it at the stonework at the bottom of the black oblong of shadow where, he guessed, the enemy gun must be.

'Them rowers is jerking us a bit, sir.' Brick's face was twisted with concentration as the light improved with every passing second.

'Aye, but you don't want me to tell 'em to go any slower, do you?' Morgan asked. They were about a quarter of the way across the river now, all the boats and rafts were beginning to feel the tug of the current when, clear in Morgan's lens, he saw a smudge of great black crows rise from the walls, clawing up into the air, disturbed by some sudden movement.

'I sin them birds, your honour: just give me the word,' said Brick.

'Steady, we'll have to let them fire first,' Morgan replied. His every instinct was to fire now before the enemy; but, despite the light, there was just a possibility that the mutineers hadn't seen them and he dare not spoil any chance of surprise that might still exist.

176

Almost immediately, though, in the depths of that same dark shadow, there was a fizz of a spark, a pause and then the image in Morgan's binoculars was full of silent smoke and flame.

'Fire, Brick, fire!' yelled Morgan as the report of the Pandy gun echoed across the water and off the walls of the fort, followed instantly by the bark of a rifle.

Gunners had often told Morgan that if you were sharp enough you could see a gunshot in flight along with the swirl of hot air that the ball left in its wake. He'd never seen it – not until now. He was concentrating as hard as he could on the embrasure, obscured as it was by smoke, to see where Brick's bullet might land when the picture in his glasses was dominated by a black disc that grew by the second, followed by a mirage of contorted air. It looked to Morgan as if it were coming straight at him.

'Dear God . . .' Morgan only had time to lower his binoculars before the ball struck the water some twenty paces upstream of the raft, and skipped like a skimmed pebble low over the top of them. 'Get down!' But they couldn't get any lower.

The round-shot hummed as it passed, lightly showering them with spray, but it missed by a mile compared with the narrow shave that Number One Company got. The ball could only have been a few feet from Carmichael's raft, Morgan thought, as he twisted his head to watch. A great sheet of water was thrown over his neighbours, all of the troops shying away as if the iron had actually hit them. But one figure clung lower and harder to the planking, his eyes closed tighter, his knuckles whiter than anyone else's – Captain Richard Carmichael.

'Ay-up, sir, best get off an' swim!' A loutish voice was raised up from the craft behind Morgan – Pegg's for sure.

But there was no time for any more distractions, as Corporal Brick needed his help.

'Where was that one, sir?' Brick had grabbed another rifle and fired again, but even his naked eyes could not see whether the lead had flown true or not: he needed Morgan to spot for him.

'Sorry, missed it. Try again,' Morgan apologised.

Brick took a cocked rifle and fired another shot; Morgan just saw the flash of the round in his glass before a puff of chippings was thrown up on the bottom sill of the embrasure.

''Bout two foot low and six inches left, Corp'l Brick.' As Morgan said it, there was another cloud of smoke from the bastion and, almost immediately, a cracking boom.

'Got it, sir. Gimme more rifles, yous 'en!'

Even as the shot bowled towards them, Brick was grabbing, aiming and firing, hurling lead back at the gunners as fast as the rest of the men on the raft could load.

Morgan crouched as low as he could, but the second round flew high and just behind them, throwing a great gout of spray between the two rafts.

He looked round to see McGucken grinning – quite unaffected – mouthing, 'They should be using canister, sir. Them Pandies is useless without us to help 'em!'

But now Brick had found the range and Morgan guessed each round was humming squarely amongst the gun crew. Certainly, the enemy was silent whilst the rafts pulsed forward through the water with renewed energy as the oarsmen tried to get out of danger as fast as they could. But with only yards to go before they were under the cover of a rocky bank, the gun fired again. Morgan thought he could hear every man suck his breath in and hold it; certainly, as the ball yawed wide, skimming harmlessly over Bazalgette's company away downstream, all seventy Grenadiers breathed out as one man.

'Well done, Corporal Brick. Reckon you put a stop in a rebel or two there; good shooting.' Morgan was both relieved and delighted as the Rajah's men leapt from their cutter and pulled the rafts towards the shore.

'Well, sir, not a bad morning's work, even if I do say so meself.' Brick was rubbing at his shoulder, which had been bruised by a rapid succession of recoils. 'Might there be a drop o' grog in it?'

The steps up to the citadel were steep and uneven; Morgan found himself panting as he led the company up and into the fort from the strip of shingle where they had landed.

'Them rebel guns was a bit too close for comfort, wasn't they, sir?' Pegg rebuked Morgan as they toiled upwards, even as their own artillery started the preparatory bombardment.

'You're alive, ain't you, Corp'l Pegg . . .' Morgan was impatient with the NCO, due as much to his own relief at having got across the river without casualties as anything else, '. . . what more d'you want?'

'Ten days' leave and the thanks of Parliament would go some way to mekin' me feel appreciated, sir,' came the riposte.

'Well, I wouldn't put a sovereign on that, young 'un,' was about all that Morgan could manage as they eventually reached the square at the centre of the fortress. Then Bazalgette and a bugler, who were moving ahead of the main body of his company, suddenly appeared next to them.

'Now, how's yerself?' Morgan was trying to jolly Bazalgette out of his self-imposed misery. 'That rebel gun was firing wide of the mark, was it not?'

'It was, but it was close enough to wet our pants,' replied Bazalgette flatly. 'Good job they was boss-eyed.'

There seemed little that Morgan could do to cheer his friend, and before he could think of anything more to say, the Sappers had arrived, heavily laden with sacks of blasting powder, the Board of Ordnance arrow boldly stamped on the linen, intent on finding the best places to blow holes in the citadel's walls. Morgan was only concerned with his own

179

objective, however, and leaving the men under the care of Ensign Fawcett, he called for McGucken and an Engineer sergeant and set off to find the Kettonpore Gate.

'Well, sir, the Rajah's boys seem to have made a good job of it.' McGucken was looking at the pile of stones and loose masonry that had been piled inside the vast oak gates and stone towers either side, which marked the limit of safety. 'You'll need a fair pinch of powder to shift that lot, Sar'nt Hamilton.'

'I will, Colour-Sar'nt,' replied the Sapper as he produced a dog-eared manual from within his haversack and started to look at a series of tables and charts that would tell him exactly what weight of charge he would need, 'but I'll want some of your lads to help me get the bangers in place.'

'Fine, just tell us what you need,' replied Morgan impatiently as the Sapper mumbled to himself and drew a dirty fingernail over his rubric.

'Sir, I'll need fifteen of your finest, please,' and at this the trio traipsed back to the square and the waiting company.

'That's enough, ain't it, Sar'nt?' Corporal Pegg and his men had been told to help the Sappers with the preparation of the clearing charge. 'There's plenty of bang-stick in there now; it'll get us to Aus-bleedin'-tralia.' Pegg's men had toiled with endless sacks of chemical-smelling powder, which, at half a hundredweight apiece, had left them all pouring with sweat, their grey shirts now black with the effort.

'Aye, that'll do.' But the Sapper was distracted from his task with tarred detonating cord and flash initiators by a gaggle of other Engineers, who were talking to him earnestly.

'I need to speak to your officer, serious now. Where is he?' Sergeant Hamilton was unhappy. The news from the other Sappers was not good: the citadel's walls, which were due to be breached for Columns One and Two, were judged to be too thick and too well constructed for the amount of explosive that they had carried forward.

'Sir, I don't see owt else for it.' Sergeant Hamilton stood stiff and tense in front of Colonel Hume, to whom Morgan had taken him when a change of plan had become necessary. 'The Kettonpore Gate's the only exit from the citadel that's possible with the time and gear we've got. I've spoke to me troop officers an' they've given us the go-ahead.'

It was difficult for infantry officers to understand the amount of authority that the Sappers placed in a mere sergeant, expert though he might be, although Hume had the experience to listen.

'Very well, Sar'nt Hamilton, I'll tell the brigade commander; I'm sure that he'll have a view,' said Hume.

'Obliged to you, sir.' Hamilton was relieved to find a foot-plodder, particularly a colonel covered in gongs, who was prepared to respect his expertise. 'Just be aware, sir, a native came in whilst we was a-tinkerin' with the charges an' said that Pandy had already mined the gate – but from the outside. Just thought I ought to mention it.'

'Very good, Hume . . .' It was now about half-past ten, and the enemy guns had started a desultory fire on the citadel, having seen, Morgan was sure, the assault forces forming up inside. But Smith, the brigade commander, did not seem to be daunted by the changed circumstances that the Sappers had identified, '. . . the other two columns will follow your boys through the Kettonpore once it's been blown. That means that the enemy will be able to concentrate solely on your leading company – bit of a challenge. Who's in the van?'

'My Grenadiers, sir,' said Hume softly.

'Ah, very good, your stalwarts.' Smith positively chortled at the idea. 'That's that Irish lad, Morgan, ain't it? Giving him a chance to make up for things after Rowa, are you? Bit of a "forlorn hope": death or glory, is it? Take me to him, if you will, Hume.'

By the time Smith reached the Grenadier Company, the

roads and alleys leading to the Kettonpore Gate were crushed full of troops. With all three columns now converging on just one exit, over fifteen hundred infantry as well as the artillery – who were to hand-wheel their howitzers and extra ammunition into the assault – were packed tightly together. Nor was the situation made any the easier by the thunder of their own guns overhead and the occasional round-shot from the mutineers whining high over the walls in front of them.

'Well, Morgan, are you all set?' Smith and his staff, with Hume in close attendance, had pushed their horses through Bombay regiments, a couple of sombre-looking companies of the 83rd, boisterous Highlanders of the 72nd, gunners, artificers, signallers and, most crucially, the Sappers, whose demolitions would signal the start of the assault.

'Set as we'll ever be, General.' Perhaps Morgan didn't deliver the line with quite the thrilled pleasure that Smith expected; certainly, McGucken cast his officer something of a sideways look when he said it.

'Well, I hope you know just how important the job is that's been entrusted to you?' Smith was obviously not pleased with Morgan's manner.

'I do, sir, and you can depend on the Ninety-Fifth's Grenadiers to do it.' Morgan knew that this reply sounded much better.

Sadly, Lance-Corporal Pegg undid things: 'Just like we did at Alma, Inkermann and The Quarries, sir – you remember.' Pegg's observation wasn't intended to annoy the general; indeed, it was said in such an open manner that Smith paused for a moment, weighing the words for an intended slight.

But any doubt was cast from his mind when a faceless brogue came from the rear of the throng: 'How would he remember? He wasn't there at all!'

Smith's face flushed puce with anger. For a second Morgan considered turning on Private Matthew McGarry – for there was no doubt that's whose voice it was – but he knew, as Smith did, that it would be impossible to prove.

'Sirs, would you get back as far as you can, please?' Luckily, a scurrying Sergeant Hamilton of the Engineers intervened. 'We've got about four hundred pounds of powder ready, gentlemen, but your troops is awful close. Please get 'em back, sir.'

'Aye, Morgan, get your men as far away as possible, but once the charge has gone, you mustn't hang back: get straight through the gate and amongst the Pandies,' roared Smith above the noise of the overhead fire.

'There'll be no hanging back from this company, sir, you may be sure of that,' Morgan replied, making no attempt to hide his anger.

'Well, be sure there isn't,' Smith almost snarled back as he pushed his horse through the press of men, getting himself to a place of safety.

Things weren't helped when the same anonymous voice piped up, 'It's that way to the rear, your honour!' Followed by a peel of derisive laughter from the rest of the men.

'Right, shut yer rag-holes, yous.' McGucken's bellow hushed the mockery. 'Check your pouches; hammers at half cock, an' any twot whose spike falls off in the rush will have me to answer to.'

The men busied themselves with final preparations whilst Morgan pulled his sword from its scabbard and his watch from his pocket, and glanced to see how close they were to the appointed hour of eleven o'clock.

'You're late, Sar'nt Hamilton.' Morgan immediately regretted heaping any more pressure on the man as he paid out a long spool of fuse, but it distracted him from the brusqueness of his brigade commander.

'Sir, an' if you'd just 'elp me by getting your blokes into some form of cover, we can get a move on things.' Hamilton was equally testy.

'Yes, get the men back as far as possible, Morgan.' Hume had appeared silently out of the crowd, smiling slightly, speaking calmly, patting the men gently on their backs as he passed. 'Then at 'em with the steel as you always do and, Morgan . . . Godspeed.' Hume had obviously heard the exchange with Smith and realised how unsettling Morgan had found it. Now he, the colonel, was right here at the front, rubbing balm into his men's wounded pride, setting exactly the right example.

But even as McGucken and the NCOs harried the men back behind rubble and any bit of wall or masonry they could find, Hamilton was tinkering with a fat, green-tipped match that eventually sputtered, flared into life and set the fuse burning with a racing plume of blue-tinged smoke.

'There, y'are, gents . . .' Hamilton looked with satisfaction at the spluttering fuse, '. . . 'bout twenty seconds. Put yer fingers in yer ears an' keep low.'

Morgan hunkered down next to McGucken behind a low bank of dirt and bricks and, self-consciously, lay his sword down and clamped his hands over his ears. He was glad he did, for in much less time than the promised twenty seconds, the light was blocked out by a tearing cloud of smoke and grit that ripped his breath away. At the same time the earth shook with a violence that he'd never expected, still less experienced, which left him sprawled on his back, McGucken draped half on top of him.

For several seconds both men lay there, enveloped in the cloud and dust, ears ringing, heads bursting with the concussion.

'Jesus, we was too close . . .' McGucken was the first to regain his senses. 'You all right, sir?'

Both men looked as though they'd been dipped in flour, so thick was the dust that clung to their clothes, skin and hair.

'I . . . I think so, Colour-Sar'nt.' But Morgan's concern for himself evaporated as Sergeant Hamilton came staggering back through the reek towards them. Every bit of him was grey with dust except his eyes, which blinked in shock from a dirty mask. His hat was gone, his hair seemed to stand on end, thick with grit.

'Are you hurt, Sar'nt Hamilton?' Morgan heard himself asking, but it was as if he was talking underwater, so numb were his ears.

A thin trickle of blood came from one of the tattered NCO's nostrils; he shook his head as if trying to clear the stunning effects of the explosion. Finally, he answered, his speech slightly slurred: 'Sir . . . ahm all right . . .' he swayed slightly, flexing his fingers, '. . . must indeed have bin another mine by the gate.'

It certainly looked that way to Morgan. As the dust and smoke cleared slowly, where once the Kettonpore Gate and towers had stood, there was nothing now except heaps of shattered stone and fallen masonry that smoked slightly in the sun. The great teak gates, built by the Moghuls, were now nothing more than matchwood, whilst a telltale crater and collapsed trench showed where the mutineers had laid their mine.

'Come on, sir.' McGucken picked Morgan's sword up and pressed it into his hand. 'Them bastards'll be even more shocked than we are. Let's use the advantage.'

And with that, at a stumbling shuffle over the heaped debris, Morgan set off, doing his best to shout, 'Follow me, Grenadiers,' through a mouth that felt as though it had been punched raw.

As he topped the piled obstacle in front of him, Morgan gulped, expecting a storm of enemy fire – but none came. As he paused he stared down onto a rubbish-strewn junction surrounded by shot-torn houses, improvised barriers at the mouth of every street, but of the enemy there was no sign. Suddenly lonely, he looked round to see who was following. At his elbow was McGucken, who was frantically waving and shouting at the others to close up – but there were remarkably few. Instead of a reassuring mass of beefy lads, there were just a few men carefully picking their way forward over the broken mound – all new boys, he noticed, for the older hands had learned to keep a cautious score of paces to the rear.

'There, sir, look.' McGucken pointed at a barricade no more than thirty paces away. 'A fuckin' gun; that's ours!'

And he was right, for a brass muzzle stared unblinkingly at them, obviously sited to eviscerate any sally that came from behind the gates.

A gun, goddamit, thought Morgan. Instant glory, there for the taking.

There'd be no mistaking who'd snatched this prize. Greed and ambition overcame any lingering shock, and Morgan found himself positively scampering down the slope of rubble, a crazy shout on his lips and his sword oustretched.

He was over the breastwork of spoil and sticks of furniture in an instant, ignoring the pair of concussed gunners who moaned harmlessly below the gun's carriage, desperately trying to scratch '95' into the wooden trail. But a sabre was designed for no such work, so he rummaged in his haversack, produced the clasp knife that he'd bought in Cork four years ago and started to whittle away. The wood was hard, though he was determined that there would be no arguments over who'd captured it.

By the time he'd made even a passable impression on the timber, a gaggle of men were around him, the enemy gunners had been dispatched without hesitation and McGucken was issuing rapid orders.

'Get 'ere with that spiking nail, ye great jessy.' Private Beeston was the butt of McGucken's impatience, yet again. 'Go on, get it in the touchhole.' Beeston was groping around the unfamiliar breech of the gun. 'You'd find it soon enough if it had hairs on it. Gi' it here,' and with that the Scotsman seized the nine-inch iron needle and banged it home with a handy lump of stone.

'Look at this lot, sir.' Pegg was distraught; one of the other soldiers had beaten him to the pockets and purses of the dead sepoy gunners. But in his search around the area, he'd found three earthenware pots full to the brim with a mixture of nails, iron studs, lead pellets and all manner of other scrap. 'The bastards were going to fire this lot at us – mek yer bloody eyes water, that would. Right, you lot . . .' Pegg turned to his men, '. . . put that one on the slate as another score to settle.'

But even as the troops tutted with outrage, a bullet sang off some broken masonry close by, pricking Sharrock and Coughlin's faces with a dozen tiny shards of stone and sending the rest of the party scuttling for cover.

'Where's he at, Colour-Sar'nt?' Morgan looked down the closest road. It was lined with two-storey mud and brick thatched houses with a shallow drain running down the centre.

'There, sir, 'bout two hundred, puff of smoke by that upper window just—' Even as he said it, a further volley of shots erupted from the same house, jets of smoke coming from all the upper windows, lead balls humming and whining all about them.

'Bugger me . . .' Private James, who had thought himself safe behind a wall after the first single shot, was amazed to find that he was wrong, '. . . they've shot me water bottle!' A round, distorted by hitting the brickwork, had skimmed off at an angle, clipping James's big, blue-painted canteen and splintering a hole through the wood, out of which his precious water now poured.

'There's a gang of 'em in there, Colour-Sar'nt.' Morgan looked round but saw no sign of the companies that were supposed to be following them. 'We'll have to deal with it.'

'Aye, sir, you fire us in from here an' I'll take some lads round the flank and flush 'em out,' said McGucken.

'No, Colour-Sar'nt. You stay here with Mr Fawcett and show him how to give covering fire. I'll come at 'em from behind the building and try to drive them towards you, then cut 'em down.'

'Sir, ain't it time that Mr Fawcett took an assault in?' McGucken looked at Morgan intently as he made the suggestion.

Why the hell does he not want me to lead the attack? thought Morgan. He doesn't think I've turned sticky, does he?

'No, it's too soon to tell him to do that . . . just get me half a dozen lads, please.' But even as Morgan said it, he knew that Lance-Corporal Pegg and his men would be detailed off for the job. He just hoped that the lad would be in the same fighting fettle as he had been the last time they met Pandy together.

Under the constant hammering of their own guns, McGucken took Fawcett, showed him where to place his riflemen to best advantage, and then shepherded the attacking party towards Morgan, who was crouched behind a breast-work, checking the chambers of his pistol.

'Ah, Corporal Pegg and the heroes of Rowa.'

'Aye, sir, that's us,' Pegg answered and then, more softly, 'The only names the bloody officers know.'

'We're going for that building from over on the left.' Morgan pointed to the objective. 'Loaded and ready? Right, single file, last man cover the rear, follow me . . .' and the line moved off bent almost double, staying under the cover of the walls as Morgan led them through a gate and into an unknown alley.

They trickled forward cautiously, running past gaps, eyes roving over windows and doorways. Another volley came from the house, confirming for Morgan precisely where it was, for, seen from an angle, it was suddenly so much more difficult to recognise. But a steady rhythm of fire was now coming from Fawcett's party, McGucken's shouted orders just audible over the din, whilst balls chipped at the masonry and richocheted away, showing him exactly where his enemy lay.

On they pushed, rifles level at waist height, ready for any unexpected enemy interference when, just as he passed a sunken doorway, screams pierced the din of musketry.

So close was the noise that Morgan whirled automatically, pulling his pistol back to his waist and taking first pressure on the trigger. But there, no more than two feet away, were two girls, great kohl-painted eyes showing white and terrified from above the veils they had pulled across their faces.

'Jesus, you silly bints, d'you want to die?' Morgan pulled back as the pair cowered against the wood of a yard door. 'Go on, be off with you.'

'Shall I deal with 'em, sir,' asked Coughlin even as they skittered out into the lane, little bells jingling at their ankles.

'Deal with them, Coughlin?' Morgan realised that this normally decent, quiet young Dubliner was asking if he should kill them. 'Jesus, no; they're only girls,' to which Coughlin just shrugged in reply as the pair made their escape.

Within minutes the Grenadiers were below the windows of the mutineers' stronghold.

'Here, you two, help me get this out the way.' Morgan enlisted a hand to get a pile of furniture and rolled curtains full of earth out through a ground-level window, whilst the rest of the group protected them.

Just as they pulled at a stave of wood, however, Pegg fired his rifle deafeningly at the upper window just above them.

'Fuck, missed the sod.' He went into the automatic routine to reload his rifle, whilst his eyes never left the space. 'Some twat in a turban just shoved 'is 'ead out for a look-see . . . eh, tek care.' Pegg suddenly yelled, 'Geddown!'

Morgan just saw a grubby hand reach out and release a wooden pot from which stuck a spitting fuse. It fell foursquare at his feet, rolled a little, then lay there fizzing before he found himself pushed hard in the back by Private James, who hoofed the spitting demon away across the street on the toe-end of his grimy boot.

The flash and hollow boom of the home-made grenade threw Morgan against the wall of the house as long, rusty nails spun harmlessly past him.

'Get in here, lads, lend a hand.' Morgan could see how carefully the mutineers had prepared themselves for this battle and knew that if they stayed outside the stronghold that they would be treated to more of these horrid, dangerous things. So, by dint of boots and shoulders, they eventually managed to force their way into the lower storey of the building.

'This must 'ave been the stable, sir.' Pegg looked around at the straw, ropes and rude, wooden mangers that lined the place. 'They've tekken the ladder out so we can't get at the trapdoor.'

'Come here, Coughlin, get on my shoulders.' Morgan selected the lightest of the men and staggered with him to a point below the trapdoor. 'Get a round or two in there if the door gives,' and with rifle barrels covering them, the pair tried to push open the trap in the ceiling. But it was no use, the enemy had blocked it and, sensing something going on below them, hurled another bomb, which exploded noisily but safely in the street outside.

'Right, we're in a bit of a fix here.' Morgan could hear the rest of the company keeping up a desultory fire at the floor above them. 'Pandy knows we're here but can't get at us unless we run for it into the street, but we can't get at him.'

'Set fire to the bastards, sir.' Pegg was kicking the straw that lay around the floor into a great bundle. 'Get these

190

'urdles down, lads,' and in no time the men had pulled the tinder-dry wooden byres down, splintered the timber with hefty kicks from their boots and garlanded the lot in yards of old rope.

'Bit o' ghee 'ere, sir.' One of the other men began to sprinkle the fat from a jar onto the pyre.

'Aye, lads, but we'll fry ourselves before we smoke that lot out above.' Morgan could see that the pile would catch fast and burn well, but the floorboards would give some protection to their enemies from the flames and smoke, whilst the room they were in would very quickly become overwhelmed.

'Naw, sir, it'll work a treat. See 'ere . . .' and before Morgan could forbid it, Pegg had split open one of his cartridges, scattered the contents on the heaped junk and set light to it with a lucifer, the whole thing catching with a *whoose* of flame and a white puff of gunpowder smoke.

But that was as nothing compared with the conflagration that followed. In seconds flames had caught the straw and vast billows of acrid yellow smoke, tinged with an oily black, filled the room, a tongue of fire flicking six feet in the air and tickling the seams of the boards above.

'Pegg, you bloody idiot . . .' Morgan struggled to find a handkerchief to press to his face, amazed by the speed of the fire. 'Quick, get outside,' he coughed and mumbled, immediately seeing that it was better to brave whatever the sepoys might throw at them than the flames in the building.

Coughing, choking, dragging tendrils of smoke with them, the handful of men tumbled over the windowsill and out into the street, all danger forgotten whilst they sought the clean air. No sooner had they said a silent prayer for having got away from the flames, though, than a series of rifle shots whistled past them; in the smoke and confusion, they must have looked like the very enemy whom Morgan had told the rest of the company to mow down.

'Keep back hard against the wall, boys,' Morgan spluttered. 'Maybe Mr Fawcett will get bored with shooting at us in a moment. You'll be the death o' me, Pegg.'

'Sorry, sir.' Whilst Pegg had seemed rather pleased with himself when the fire took hold, he now pressed his considerable form as flat as he could against the wall of the house. 'S'pose that's what you'd call "out of the frying pan and into the fire".'

But no one had any time to appreciate Pegg's adlib, for as they trembled there, a mutineer leapt from the window above, ushered out by a vast billow of smoke and landed heavily on the packed earth below, coughing almost as hard as the British. The man hardly had time to stand before Pegg put a bullet into his guts that sent him staggering into a nearby drain.

Then, like lemmings from a cliff, the other mutineers followed, spluttering and cursing, tumbling into the smoky street, stumbling and rolling just before each was torn by the bullets of the covering party. Hectic minutes passed with the building and roof behind Morgan's party now blazing hard and lead flashing past within inches of their bellies until a dozen or more rebels lay still or writhing on the ground in front of them. Finally, the stream of sepoys came to an end and, as Morgan desperately shook his handkerchief to indicate his position to the others, so did the firing.

'See, sir,' grinned Pegg. 'Just like I said, worked a treat.'

'Neatly done, Morgan.' As McGucken and the rest of the company had trotted up to join the group, so Colonel Hume, the adjutant and Bazalgette had come running and crouching up behind them. 'Where's the rest of these rascals?'

No sooner had the first stronghold fallen than more shots had come shrieking through the air towards them, singing off brickwork, one catching Private Spoor in the throat and spinning him into a moaning bundle on the ground. Now the men were ranged around the yards and byres, spotting, ducking and replying to the mutineers as Morgan decided what to do next.

'There, sir, keep down, look . . .' he peeped round a wall with his head just six inches off the ground, Hume following his example, '. . . in that big building at the road junction; you'll see the musket smoke . . . yes, there . . .' another volley came from the upper storeys at the end of the street, '. . . and there's movement behind that bigger window.'

'Which bigger window? There's any number of 'em,' said Hume impatiently, irritated more with his inability to grasp exactly what his company commander meant than anything else.

'Here, sir, watch for my fall of shot.' McGucken understood Hume's frustration and leant over the top of the wall where the officers crouched, and carefully aimed his rifle. 'Sixty paces, second floor, plain wood sill below two open shutters; just beneath that . . .' and the rifle barked, throwing up a cloud of dust and chippings directly under the target, '. . . seen?'

'Seen,' Hume answered in textbook style.

'Reckon they've got a wee gun or something in there, sir,' said McGucken, who was now back below the cover of the bricks, hastily rodding another ball down the barrel of his rifle.

'Yes, I can make out something there in the shadows with my glasses. What I'm planning to do, sir, is—' But Morgan wasn't allowed to finish.

'You and your boys have done enough for the time being.' Hume looked across at Spoor, who was now lying silently whilst two medical orderlies wound lint round his neck. 'I'm going to pass Bazalgette's company through you to take that next position. You're to give covering fire from here; Bazalgette, I suggest you move one of those howitzers up here and leave it under Morgan's direction . . .' Hume rattled off a series of orders to both his captains, specifying the route that Bazalgette was to take and a host of other details.

'So, are you clear?' Hume asked, as the three of them remained huddled in cover.

'Sir,' said Bazalgette in the same flat tone that Morgan had heard him use before the attack started.

'Yes, sir, but once Bazalgette's been committed, d'you want my company to become the reserve?' asked Morgan.

'No, I should have told you about that. You're to link up with Massey and be prepared to move forward on my orders. Carmichael's company has, somehow, got tangled up inside the fortress. I'll pull them up as the reserve once they're sorted out.' Hume looked straight at the officers, his face betraying nothing. 'Tell your men what to do. We'll start on your signal rocket in, say, forty minutes, Bazalgette – is that time enough?' Hume asked calmly.

'Sir, that should be. I'll fire red over yellow, if you please.'

'Fine, good luck to you.' Hume paused before he moved off, 'And no hanging back, now!' he grinned.

'No, sir,' Morgan laughed back, 'no hanging back.' But whilst Morgan had appreciated the commanding officer's poking fun at the general, the joke appeared to have fallen flat with Bazalgette, who merely nodded as Hume and the adjutant scrambled away.

The two friends lay for a few moments looking at the next enemy strongpoint, discussing where he was most likely to have sited his riflemen, whether there was, indeed, something sinister behind the big windows, and which direction of attack was better.

'Best thing is to blow him to buggery with that howitzer, just before you assault.' A little to their rear an artillery crew had arrived wheeling the squat gun forward over the fallen debris with much swearing and sweating. 'I'll direct his fire when you launch a second signal. I guess that'll be from somewhere beyond that clutch of huts yonder?' Morgan paused and looked to his friend for confirmation.

'Yes, yes, I suppose so,' Bazalgette answered hesitantly.

'I suggest you use canister; at this range it'll clear the whole house with a couple of rounds,' Morgan continued, though still concerned with his friend's lack of interest.

'Yes, all right I will. Might there not be innocent natives in the house, though?' Bazalgette asked without any enthusiasm.

'Look, Bazalgette, you must show some drive. We'll be firing you in, but if the boys detect any lack of certainty from you, the whole damn business will fail. You know what they're like: if the officer hesitates, they'll just down tools or, worse, run – and that we can't have.' Morgan put his hand on the other's shoulder. 'Come on, this isn't you at all.'

'Forgive me, Morgan,' and Bazalgette straightened up, licked his lips and strolled away back to his company as lead balls sang around him.

'Where d'you want this gun, sir?' McGucken had one ear on the company commanders' conversation and another on Mr Fawcett's fire control orders. 'Did we ought to keep it out o' sight until Captain Bazalgette's signal, sir? It'll attract shot like flies round shit, sir, an' tell Pandy what's coming his way if we show it too early.'

'You're right, Colour-Sar'nt. Bring the gun team's sergeant to me, please. I'll brief him. Meanwhile, redistribute our ammunition. I want rapid fire when Number Two Company's assault starts.'

'Sir.' McGucken had anticipated all of this. 'Don't mind me askin', sir, but is Cap'n Bazalgette all right – he don't seem normal?'

'He's fine, Colour-Sar'nt. Don't worry about him.'

But as McGucken watched the officer brief his subalterns and NCOs a few dozen paces further back down the street, all the fire, all the energy seemed to have gone out of him.

'Right, Colour-Sar'nt, almost time . . .' Morgan snapped the cover back on his half-hunter, '. . . twenty past the hour. Number Two Company should start the attack any minute; have the gunners ready to move, if you please.'

Captain Bazalgette had disappeared from Morgan and McGucken's sight at the head of his company down an alley that led round the flank of the next strongpoint. When the pair of rockets appeared from Bazalgette's position, they would be ready with the loaded howitzer, then, when the next rocket rose, they would help to push the gun into position to blast the house and open a rapid rifle-fire with every man of the Grenadier Company.

'He's late, sir.' McGucken was looking at his own watch. 'The colonel won't like that.' Five minutes had now passed since the appointed hour with the attack that Bazalgette was to lead acting as the signal for the other two columns to close on their targets as well.

'You're right, and the general won't like it either,' Morgan fretted. Then, more quietly:

'Come on, man, don't fanny about.' Almost as if he'd heard him, Bazalgette's rockets rose high in the sky above the smoke of the burning town, accompanied by a cheer.

'Right, yous, stand by,' McGucken yelled above the noise of gunfire to the howitzer's crew. 'Next rocket, I want you up here and a round in that pox-ridden house sharpish; then reload as fast as you like an' give 'em another.' The crew were already braced at the spokes of the gun's wheels, a bombardier holding the trail-spike ready to lift it clear of the ground. The artillery sergeant stood behind a low bank of debris, peering hard at the target.

They heard a burst of musket fire from the next street and the crack of Number Two Company's rifles replying, some shouting, then silence.

'Come on, man.' Morgan licked his lips, urging on his

friend's invisible progress as another burst of fire broke out. 'What's holding you up?'

It was impossible to judge the other company's progress, so they all hung on the next signal rocket, hoping that the sporadic firing meant that Bazalgette's men were getting close to their target.

'Any moment now, lads,' Morgan yelled to his own troops and the gunners, who were still crouching in cover. 'On my order, up into your fire positions and lace into the Pandies.'

But a great, tearing ripple of shots, like nothing that Morgan had ever heard before, suddenly rose from the far side of Bazalgette's objective, along with a cloud of powder smoke that billowed slowly over the intervening walls.

'What, in God's name, was that, Colour-Sar'nt?' The dense firing was accompanied by more shots and shouts of glee from the mutineers' stronghold.

'Dunno, sir, but it sounds as though Cap'n Bazalgette's in trouble, so it does.'

Morgan knew McGucken was right and that something had to be done. The rebels would be concentrating on Number Two Company and if he launched an attack straight up the alley, sixty or so paces in front of them, they might just catch Pandy off balance. But the charge would have to be straight in front of their own howitzer, preventing it from firing more than one round – and they would be sprinting directly into the arc of the horrid little gun that he suspected the enemy was keeping as a lethal surprise.

That same indecision now gripped Morgan that he'd experienced before. The stealing, icy fingers of doubt clutched at his guts just as they had done at Sevastopol – and what had been the answer then?

It's a damn sight better to do something, to go forward, than to dither about, he thought. Just look at the men's faces, they're wondering why I don't take a bloody decision . . . Jesus.

'I think the only thing to do is to boil up a wee bit of a charge, sir . . .' McGucken had seen the doubt in the men's faces too, Morgan thought to himself, '. . . I'll get the company ready to follow you, sir, once the gun's done its bit.'

So, there's my decision made for me, thought Morgan. Here we go again . . .

The hilt of his sword was slick with sweat and he'd forgotten to check how many rounds he'd fired from his pistol.

Don't bother yourself; that howitzer will scrape any bastard away from the windows and it'll just be a wee trot up the street and into a house full of dead men – the thought was meant to reassure him, but it did nothing to make his bowels feel any less watery.

'Get that left wheel forward a bit.' As the crew pushed the howitzer over the broken ground and into the mouth of the alley, the gunner sergeant had straddled its trail, crouched down behind the barrel, and now, one eye shut, ordered the gun to be inched left or right and aimed by lay of metal directly at the open shutters just yards away down the street. 'No, come forward a bit more.' The gunner beckoned his straining men with an outstretched palm until the piece was aiming just where he wanted it.

Morgan stared at the building. The side facing them seemed quiet, though the firing from the other side, at right angles to his forthcoming attack, was growing in volume. Then, just as the sergeant took the slack off his firing lanyard and began to lift his leg clear of the trail, the air was filled by shrieking metal, bouncing and singing off the howitzer's barrel, the window bay full of smoke and three of the gun crew rolling on the ground, shrieking, the sergeant thrown backwards, twitching by the trail.

'So, you was right, sir.' McGucken, taking cover next to Morgan behind a broken fence, looked dispassionately at the blood-stained artillerymen. 'They have got a gun up yonder; best get at it.'

'Aye, before they can reload,' said Morgan, trying not to let his courage leak away. 'Follow me, lads.'

How fast can they get another dose of shot rammed into that thing? Morgan's boots scrabbled on the packed earth of the alley. *If I can just get close enough to the bottom storey, they won't be able to depress the barrel enough to hit me, but the lads will be all bunched up behind, a perfect target . . . oh Jesus.*

Every pounding pace he took he imagined his enemies thrusting powder, musket balls and fuse into their gun, lowering the barrel to sweep the British away. A quick glance to the rear revealed a scarlet and dusty wave of men hard after him, a pack of drumming feet, shouting mouths and glittering steel pressed together by the buildings on either side of the alley – food for the gun's maw.

Then he was against the lower window, tearing at staves and planks.

'Here, Suttle, Williams, lend a hand . . .' just like the last building they'd stormed, the window bay was blocked with rolled mats and carpets filled with earth – improvised sand-bags – which were hard and heavy to shift, '. . . get your shoulders to it.' But with the officer leading the way, the three of them toppled the obstacle and tumbled into the room to find themselves staring at two Pandies, muskets levelled, who stood at the bottom of a flight of wooden stairs.

As Morgan dived to the filthy floor of the room, four weapons banged deafeningly in the confined space; his two men firing as they clambered over the sill, the two mutineers – one of whom was still in his red coat – doing the same from the stairwell. One Pandy staggered forward, dropping his weapon, clutching at his leg, whilst the other scuttled back up the stairs to his comrades around the gun. Even prone on the floor in a room now filled with powder smoke, it was an easy shot for Morgan. Lifting himself on one palm, he stretched out the Tranter, it bucked, the sepoy clutched at his thigh with a yell and then tumbled back down the stairs in a tangle of belts and pouches, knocking his wounded, whimpering comrade to the floor.

'Leave them, leave them alone.' The poky, sordid room was suddenly full of his men, all jostling to finish the wounded Indians with bayonets and kicks. 'Fire into the ceiling.' Morgan could see the men's eyes full of blood lust, but if they shot up through the boards into the room above, they might just stop the gun from firing down the street again.

Shots splintered the wood overhead, making sore ears ring again, but a shriek came from above and, in a rush, Morgan and a clutch of sweating men were up the short flight of wooden stairs and fanning out into the big room.

Well, that's our second piece today, thought Morgan as his men fell to their brutal work on the crew who surrounded a boat's iron swivel gun mounted on two great blocks of teak, which the rebels must have manhandled up the stairs.

An Enfield round fired through the floor had hit one of the gun crew somewhere in the calf, and now the man hopped about the boards, clutching at his wound. What no one realised, however, was that he'd spilled loose powder all around the muzzle of the gun and when Private Henry Robinson brought his rifle up to put the man out of his misery, the muzzle-flash licked at the explosive, causing a vast, slow, yellow flash and belch of smoke that caught the mutineer at its centre.

'Someone kill the poor soul, can't you?' Morgan shouted in the din of shouts and bangs around him as the rebel, now burnt from head to toe, hair and beard singed off, his clothes smouldering and still hobbling on his wounded leg, shrieked with pain.

McGucken was instantly there. In the confined space filled with scrabbling bodies, he reversed his rifle, butted the man to the ground and then thumped his bayonet squarely through his stomach so hard that it stuck in the wooden board below. For an instant the Pandy squirmed, spitted until the colour-sergeant stamped a boot onto his victim's ribcage and worked the blade free from the flesh.

'That wee thing'll look good at the entrance to the big hoose, sir, wouldn't you say?' asked McGucken.

The room was now silent except for the heaving lungs of the Grenadiers, who stood over the torn and bloody bodies of the gunners, the colour-sergeant routinely cleaning the gore off his bayonet whilst casting admiring glances at their latest prize.

But Morgan could only nod, amazed by the man's sang-froid, before another storm of shouting and firing broke out down the corridor that linked this room to others on the further side of the house.

'Sounds like Cap'n Bazalgette's a-tryin to break in, sir.' Again, McGucken had read the battle perfectly. 'Might we lend him a hand?'

'We shall,' said Morgan, and with that it was all pounding boots and cries of dismay from the Pandies as the Grenadier Company caught them in the rear just as Number Two Company broke in on their flank. Morgan hadn't seen anything like it since the butchery at Inkermann. His men went at the enemy with bayonets, boots and butts, Ensign Fawcett with his sword, McGucken killing methodically, dispassionately like the deadly professional that war had made him.

'I'm obliged to you, old friend.' Bazalgette grasped Morgan's hand as they stood together in a smoky room full of dead and wounded rebels. 'Did you hear that damn thing go off?' The victory seemed to have restored Bazalgette's verve. 'We had just taken a bit of lead when they fired it, 'bout forty musket barrels all lashed together and fused to fire simultaneously. Poor George Green was killed outright,

God rest him, another three wounded . . .' Morgan saw how two of the soldiers crossed themselves at this news, '. . . and Green was right next to me. It all looked pretty tricky until we heard your attack go in.' Then, more softly: 'The boys just didn't seem to have their normal stomach for the fight – until we heard you getting behind the bastards.'

But there's nothing wrong with the boys. They was picking up that reluctance from you, Evelyn Bazalgette; I told you they would, thought Morgan.

'Now what, in God's name, is that?' Bazalgette asked as the noise of brass instruments and drums suddenly became audible.

'Why, it's "Don't You Remember Sweet Alice," ain't it?' said Morgan as both officers moved to the window closest to where the music came from and looked out at a dusty square about one hundred and fifty yards away, deep in the rebel-held part of the town.

'Sounds like it. Which regiment's brought its band up with it? I'd have thought the bandsmen would have had their hands full acting as stretcher bearers, anyway,' said Bazalgette. 'But there's your answer.' A full forty bandsmen of one of the native regiments marched trimly across the square in front of them, their instruments harmonious, the drummers' sticks rising and falling together.

'Well, I'm damned if I know who they are, but—' Morgan wasn't allowed to finish.

'They're fuckin' Pandies, sir, that's who they are,' said McGucken grimly at the officer's elbow. 'Look yon!'

Marching behind the band came file after file of infantry, keeping time with the music, in step, with their Colours flying bravely in the centre. But only a few red coats and shakos remained, and no British officers. Every man had retained his belts and haversack, but most had acquired swords or long daggers stuck untidily in their waistbands, giving them the air of brigands, despite their ranks and even step.

'Fire, men, to your front, fire!' Morgan and Bazalgette

yelled together, and after a few uneven shots, the men of both companies lined every window and roof, firing, reloading and firing again with a steady rhythm whilst below them Hira Singh's men fell like corn to the scythe.

'Did you see that bugger on the bloody great 'orse, sir?' Lance-Corporal Pegg was full of the battle. 'Leapt right over the battlements, 'e did; dead as mutton, they were; waste o'a good nag, that – worth a few bob. Did you see it?'

'Yes, Corporal Pegg, I saw it, thank you,' Morgan replied quietly.

'And don't ever doubt that these Pandies can be first-class troops when they put their minds to it, young Pegg,' McGucken reproved him. 'May not be our way o' doin' things, but leapin' to certain death rather than falling into the hands of us Feringees takes a bit o' guts.'

McGucken's right, it was brave, thought Morgan, . . . but I wish I hadn't seen it.

As they'd volleyed into the enemy from the safety of their firing points, both companies of the 95th had watched as one of the mutineers' leaders came galloping through the square into which they were shooting, leaping over the dead and injured, going hell for leather, crouched low in his saddle, towards one of the battlements of the Salumbah bastion, and leapt clean over it. They all assumed that the rider knew a safe route out, but once they moved forward into the square, an excited gaggle of the 10th BNI stood by the stone breast-work, some pointing downwards, whilst others took pot shots into the distance.

I saw that man and his chestnut all twisted up fifty feet below us, Morgan remembered. What can he have been thinking of? He must have known that that would be suicide. And I saw those poor devils on the island – nowhere to run, no cover from our bullets, but no sign of surrender, brave, stupid bastards.

Streams of mutineers had run past the muzzles of their rifles through the open expanse of the square, driven on by the bayonets of the other columns. The Grenadiers had shot more than he could count, firing and firing at an easy target for almost fifteen minutes until the men had complained about the heat of their barrels.

'They may be good troops, Colour-Sar'nt, but not good enough to dodge an Enfield ball.' Pegg rubbed ostentatiously at his blue-bruised shoulder.

Morgan continued to ponder the slaughter. Where did they think they was going to go once they'd got down the ropes? That island looked like a morgue once we'd finished with them . . .

On the other side of the battlement the mutineers had prepositioned long ropes down which those who escaped the British fire had slid – until too many got on at once and they broke – before splashing and wading out to an island in the middle of a wide ornamental lake. There was the Kishor Sagar – a miniature palace – in the middle of the island, but no other cover.

The battlement had been crowded with British and Bombay troops alike, shoulder to shoulder, firing as hard as they could into the defenceless sepoys at less than two hundred yards from their muzzles.

The men just wouldn't stop firing. Morgan, appalled more by the sight of the dead horse than its rider, had just stood and watched as the men tore at the Pandies with round after round. If we hadn't have run low on shot, the boys would be at it now, and the Tenth were just as wild.

The boys just tore in to them – even the wounded got shot at time and again until they stopped twitching. I should have put a stop to all that – it was no more or less than murder, and I'm no better than Kemp and his moss-troopers.

Now what remained of the mutineers were being pursued by the cavalry outside the walls of Kotah, whilst the infantry hunted down the last of Hira Singh's men and set about the systematic destruction of the fortress. McGucken had ordered weapons to be cleaned, ammunition and water to be replenished and feeding to begin, conscious that the men were chafing to start the search for loot, yet at any time they could be ordered forward in pursuit. Leaving the NCOs in charge, though, he took a carrying party back to the Kettonpore Gate to collect the body of Private Spoor, for the medical orderlies had been unable to stop him from bleeding to death.

Morgan, sickened by the carnage and wanting to be away from the excited chatter of the newer men, had chosen to go with his colour-sergeant, knowing that Ensign Fawcett would soon send for him if new orders were received; he also wanted to see the gun that he had captured.

Now they walked back down the route their attack had taken, rebel bodies lying huddled against the shot-pocked walls, smoke drifting from the blazing roofs.

'See what's making that noise, will you, Sullivan?' From the compound of a tiny battered temple came the bleating of what sounded to Morgan like a very hungry sheep.

Sullivan, five-foot nine of Tralee tough, a moan never far from his lips, but always on your elbow when the lead was flying or loot was to be had, doubled away immediately, only to emerge minutes later with a dirty, slightly emaciated ram trotting along behind him on the end of a rifle sling. Round the animal's neck a brass bell, as big as a fist, tinkled forlornly.

'He's as friendly as you like, your honour,' said Sullivan as Morgan bent to pat the animal's lanolin-sticky fleece and looked into its strange, elliptical eyes.

'That'll make a grand mascot for the company, Sullivan.' Morgan was comforted by the ram's friendliness and simple trust. 'Just like the Forty-First and that damn goat they took in Russia.'

'Can it be ate, sir?' asked Pegg, feeling the animal's rump for meat.

So the dusty group wandered on, an officer, four battle-stained men and a shabby sheep, only McGucken giving them any sort of martial air.

'Who's that lot yonder, Colour-Sar'nt?' Morgan could see red coats milling around the debris near the Kettonpore Gate where their lethal day had started.

'Number One Company, sir.' McGucken waved back to a familiar figure. 'There's Colour-Sar'nt Whaley.'

Whaley had been a sergeant in the Grenadier Company before being promoted and moved to be Richard Carmichael's most senior non-commissioned officer. He'd shared danger and hardship with Morgan and McGucken, and remained a firm friend of both, not least because he now had to endure the misery of Carmichael's leadership.

'Hello, sir, Jock.' Whaley saluted Morgan. 'Good to see you. The Grenadiers have obviously been in the thick of things again. We've not fired a shot all day; been hanging around here in bloody reserve after Cap'n Carmichael misunderstood what the colonel wanted.'

'Sure it was a mistake, Colour-Sar'nt Whaley?' asked Morgan. McGucken had looked uncomfortable at Whaley's outright disloyalty to his company commander in front of another officer, despite the bonds of shared experience, so Morgan had answered in the same style.

'Well, you know how it is, sir; the lads are bloody seething at not having a go at the loot.' Whaley shrugged. 'Anyway, we looked after your boy for you.'

Private Spoor had been laid straight, arms folded across his breast, under his own grey blanket. Morgan stooped and pulled the cloth back to look at his face, whilst McGarry and Sullivan crossed themselves.

'Did any of you know the lad at all well?' Morgan asked the men whilst looking at the waxen face of the nineteen-year-old. The rebel's slug had hit the boy in the lower throat, tearing one of the great arteries, Morgan guessed. Now the bandages and his collar were soaked through, a wide russet stain had spread on the earth below him and a long drop of black, coagulated blood hung from an ear lobe.

'Aye, your honour, he was my messmate,' Matthew McGarry said gravely. 'The ink was 'ardly dry on his 'list-ment papers.'

'Well, take a lock of hair for his mam, McGarry,' said Morgan, dropping the blanket back into place and disturbing the cloud of flies that had rushed at the boy's wounds.

'Then put young Spoor into his blanket, boys, an' let's get him back home.' McGucken was quietly matter-of-fact, knowing just how heavy the corpse would weigh on the mile or so back to his comrades.

'Now, where's that gun of ours?' Morgan knew that he should have tried to be more sombre in the presence of the dead for, hardened to death as they had all become, the men still treated their own fallen with an almost exaggerated respect.

'What gun's that, sir?' asked Whaley hesitantly.

Morgan smiled. 'That brass bugger over there that we took this morning; don't give me any more of that gammon.'

'Ah, yes, sir,' but Whaley really was embarrassed. 'That'll be Cap'n Carmichael's gun, the one that he's told me to guard with my life whilst he goes to register it with the prize agents – is that the one, sir?'

'Carmichael's gun my arse.' Morgan still thought Whaley was fooling. 'Why, McGucken spiked the thing and I scratched the regimental number on the carriage. Look here.'

But Whaley didn't want to look 'here' or anywhere else, for as Morgan ran his fingers over the deeply etched '95', he saw the initials, 'RLMC' emblazoned just as thoroughly above it.

'Why, the scrub!' Morgan exclaimed. 'The useless knob,

I've a mind to—' But Morgan's fury was interrupted by the racket of a knot of horsemen riding up.

McGucken and Whaley had been standing by, embarrassed by one of their officer's anger at another. It was a relief for them to shout, 'Stand up!' and quiver to the salute as Brigadier-General Smith and his brigade-major, Charles Bainbrigge, approached.

'Good day to you, gentlemen.' The brigade commander looked down from his saddle, crisp in a blue linen frock coat, polished top boots and snowy white sun helmet. 'It's been a most satisfactory affair, has it not?'

How the devil would you know? You look as though you've not left your tent all day, said Morgan to himself.

'Morgan, isn't it?' Smith suddenly recognised him. 'You led the assault, my "forlorn hope": how went it?'

'It went rightly, sir, thank you.' Morgan knew he had to sound cheerful. 'We lost Private Spoor – here – and had a few men lightly singed and struck, but we took a gun or two and, just as you said, Pandy caught a Tartar.' Morgan despised his own simpering tone, but there was a lot of ground to make up.

'Musket-shot or gunfire?' The brigadier general dismounted, his Turkish decorations catching the sun as he did so. He bent towards the dead man, but his horse shied at a distant explosion, pulling Smith slightly off balance as the reins tightened.

''Ere, McGarry, hold the general's mount for him.' After their last encounter, Pegg saw some strange bond of friendship between Smith and himself; now he was all solicitude.

'No, not you McGarry,' McGucken started, suddenly worried that there might be another bout of ventriloquism, but it was too late, the little Irish soldier had already taken the general's reins and was soothing the sleek, black hunter.

'Hit in the throat by one of their muskets, sir.' Morgan

208

and Smith now looked at the dead man. 'Just nineteen, Warwickshire lad, sir; joined us in Dublin.'

'Aye, well, Morgan, there's no room for sentimentality in war, you know – an omelette can't be made without breaking eggs. Collect his personal effects and make sure that you write and get one of his friends to write as well – try to find someone who can use a halfway decent pen – comforts the family, y'know.'

There was a mute loathing in the men's faces as they listened to the brigadier-general – and profound shock. Morgan saw McGucken bite back a reply, swaying almost imperceptibly with the effort of self-control.

'Sir,' was all that Morgan could manage. *Have I really just heard this swerver make light of a man's death and try to teach us our duty at the same time?*

'And that's a fair-looking gun. Did *you* spike it, Morgan?' Smith ran his hand over the blocked touchhole.

'Well, I took it, sir . . .' he darted a look at Colour-Sergeant Whaley, who grinned back, '. . . but Colour-Sar'nt McGucken, here, actually nailed it.'

'Hmm . . .' Smith mused. 'You might have been better to turn it on the rebels, don't you think? D'you know how to handle artillery in such circumstances?'

'I do, sir,' McGucken replied quietly. 'Cap'n Morgan here learnt us all that before Inkermann.' His hand strayed, as he said it, to the Distinguished Conduct Medal that hung on his chest.

'Did he, indeed?' Smith saw the big Scot's gesture but, Morgan guessed, missed his silent scorn. 'Right, Bainbrigge, get a limber up here and take this gun back to headquarters, if you please.'

'Very good, sir.' The brigade-major, still in the saddle, dashed a note in a pad. 'To battalion headquarters, Ninety-Fifth Foot?' Bainbrigge, a fellow infantryman, had always been a particularly welcome guest in the Regiment's mess.

'No, dammit, *my* headquarters.' Smith's irritation boiled to the surface. 'But you didn't get very far once you were through the gate, Morgan, did you?'

'Sir, yes, we did—' Morgan spluttered, but wasn't allowed to continue.

'Well, I don't call a hundred paces or so outside the Kettonpore very far.'

'Sir, these men aren't my company, they're—' but Morgan wasn't being listened to.

'In the attack, Morgan, you must show drive. You mustn't allow yourself to stall when you take casualties. All very sad, I know, but the men will take on dreadfully if you let them. You have to push hard.' Smith stuck his foot in the stirrup, took the reins from McGarry and swung up into the saddle. 'It doesn't do to hang back. The Pandies'll fold if you just keep at 'em, you know.'

'Sir, that's not—' But Morgan spoke to the brigadier general's back: he was already engrossed in discussion with Bainbrigge.

He was engrossed until his horse began to jib and toss its head; he was engrossed until he had to turn every bit of his attention to the horse's sudden kicking and bucking, then he was engrossed in trying to stay in the saddle. Even the finest cavalryman would have been hard-pushed to curb the furious animal – and Smith wasn't that. Despite much cursing, despite the application of spurs and crop, the general just couldn't hold on: the big hunter sent him flying over its shoulder onto the packed and filthy earth of the lane along which he and his staff were trotting. There he was, sprawling in the dust, sword anyhow, pristine helmet rolling in the gutter.

Morgan's party and the whole of Number One Company hooted and laughed out loud at their brigade commander; even the ram looked at him balefully and squeezed out a few dry pellets.

As the general picked himself up with the help of an aide,

the laughter suddenly died away as the men quickly found themselves busy with weapons and chores.

Only McGucken saw the danger. 'No, McGarry, not a word . . . not a word now!'

'I don't know what you mean, Colour-Sar'nt. I ain't said a t'ing.' And, indeed, McGarry had been unusually taciturn. 'A wee bit of thorn under yer man's saddle has spoke loud enough.'

SEVEN

Presentiment

'Well, you old worry-guts,' Morgan smiled at his friend Bazalgette, who was sitting scraping mud off his boots on the veranda of a shattered bungalow, 'so you're still with us. No more dreams of doom; no more gossiping with the Grim Reaper?'

Number Two, Bazalgette's Company, had been told to pause on the riverbank a couple of miles outside Kotah and wait both for orders and for the Grenadier Company. There had been much moaning by the troops when they'd learnt that they would not be allowed to remain in the town and join in the orgy of looting. But, they were told, serious things were afoot, and serious things required serious troops.

'Well, take the rise out of me all you like, you Irish lout,' Bazalgette grinned back at him, 'but it was the strongest of feelings, you know. And, I tell you what, when that goddamn thing went off right next to me, I thought that I really had breathed my last. Did you see it?'

'Not directly, but I saw the smoke and flash; it must have given you a wee bit of a tremble.' After the fighting had died down, Morgan had made a special point of examining the great bundle of musket barrels that the mutineers had strapped together and placed in such a way that they would catch any advance on their flank.

'Aye, it did. Riddled poor Green; dead before he hit the ground, and it wasn't the best of things that all the other boys had to pass him as we went into the attack. Right bloody next to me, he was.' Bazalgette shuddered at the memory.

'P'raps, but it didn't stop you, did it?'

'Well, no, but the lads paused a bit . . .' Bazalgette wrinkled his brow. 'You know how it is: they'll be heroes one minute, full of deeds and glory, but if the least thing goes wrong they're just as likely to run like rabbits. You must have seen that?'

Seen it? thought Morgan. I've come close to running more times than I can count. The boys saw me hesitate today, and if McGucken hadn't kicked me on we'd have left you so deeply in the mire, my friend, that your goddamn presentiment would probably have come true.

'Aye, I've seen it – and felt it.' Morgan looked directly into his friend's face before continuing, 'But did your men detect anything wrong with you this morning, Bazalgette?'

'What are you suggesting, Morgan?' Bazalgette replied slowly, a little stiffly.

'Well, I know how much you've been through out in Russia and now here, and I'm suggesting that you need a rest.' Morgan could see his friend bridling. 'Take a job on the staff or at a depot until your "presentiments" go to blazes.'

Bazalgette started to rise up to be at Morgan's level, his face angry, but just as suddenly he sat back down with a thump. 'Aye, you're right . . .' It was as if all the fight had gone out of Bazalgette. 'But don't you ever wonder if the next bullet, the next shell, the next fucking spear or whatever it is, will get you and you'll end up like Green today, wrapped in a blanket in a filthy bloody alley in God-knows-where?'

'Of course I do, but I try not to let the men see,' said

Morgan. 'Once they've tumbled to the fact that I'm scared, they will be as well.'

That's a bloody great bit of hypocrisy, Tony Morgan, he thought. You know how difficult you find it even to stop your hands trembling sometimes.

'Yes . . . yes, you're right, of course; and it must be even more difficult for you with Maude and . . . and, well, the other situation,' said Bazalgette, looking at the ground in embarrassment.

Maude – God, I've hardly given the girl a thought now for weeks . . . The mail, usually so efficient in India in peacetime, was now dreadfully delayed. Just as it reached one of their stopping points, the column would have moved on again, leaving the men frustrated and feeling even more isolated than they needed to. *The baby will have been born weeks ago; boy or girl? And what of Mary and Samuel – are they even alive?*

'I try not to think about it,' Morgan lied; he'd gone far enough with this discussion. 'At least we're both better off than Burton and his sons.'

They were talking on the steps of the bungalow that had been the home of the British Resident, Major Burton, until he and his two toddler sons had been butchered there. It had been burnt out, but deep, red-black splashes still covered the veranda and the lower part of the walls.

'There'll be no Christian burial for those poor souls, any more than there will be for that lot, there.' Bazalgette looked at the Chumbal, on whose banks the bungalow lay. In midstream the first crop of rebel bodies had begun to drift by. All young men, many still in the red and white of the John Company regiments that they'd betrayed, they eddied and whirled down the river, limbs outstretched, reaching for each other in the comradeship of death.

'Yes, they'll stink by morning and then won't the shite-hawks have a spree?' Morgan looked at the bodies; most,

214

he guessed, had died after being thrown seventy feet over the battlements of Kotah. Even if they'd survived the fall they would have drowned. But there was time for no more reflection as the brigade-major, Bainbrigge, came jingling up the path between files of Morgan's Grenadiers.

'Ah, gentlemen, idling the day away after hanging back this morning?' Bainbrigge asked with a broad grin.

'Steady, Bainbrigge,' replied Morgan, 'or I'll get one of my men to hold your horse for you.' Both laughed whilst Bazalgette looked on bemusedly.

'And before you ask so kindly,' the brigade-major continued, 'General Smith is well – if a little bruised – and in fine ranting form. More to the point, he has a job for you that I've cleared with Colonel Hume, who's happy for me to seek your services.' Bainbrigge was careful to make the officers understand that he wasn't operating outside the formal chain of command.

'Just over that hillock is the hamlet of Kinaree.' He pointed to a smudge of smoke that rose about a quarter of a mile away. 'Half a company of the Tenth are in there and they report that it's stuffed full of powder, shot and fuses. The rebels seem to have been using it as a magazine and they're worried that they haven't got the manpower to stop a Pandy or two creeping up after dark and sparking the place. Just as importantly, we need the ordnance for our own guns.' The brigade-major paused to open a map.

'Morgan, I'd be obliged to you if you'd set off first and put a cordon around the place, tight as a duck's arse. Then, once that's done, would you, Bazalgette, get your lot into the place, smoke out any badmashes lurking there, and then secure any stores, and, if possible, list what you've got – you know how the general likes his lists. I'll be down as soon as I can – probably won't be until after dark, now – to get your report. Can we move off sharpish with the Grenadiers ready to secure Number Two Company in, say, sixty minutes, gentlemen?'

Both officers had now been joined by their colour-sergeants, who listened intently to the major. There was much checking of maps and pocket-watches before the pair of captains agreed to Bainbrigge's orders.

'Right, gentlemen, I'm very grateful to you.' Bainbrigge settled himself in the saddle. 'By the way, Morgan, the brigade commander told me to say how very trim that gun of yours looks outside *his* tent!' Everyone laughed, Morgan a little ruefully.

'You're sure the boys have got their slippers on when they're in the buildings, Colour-Sar'nt?'

Morgan and McGucken had removed their boots before making their way into a little thatched building that lay next to the main road from Kotah into the village of Kinaree.

'Aye, sir. Those that ain't got 'em or have lost 'em will just have to pad around wi' bare tootsies, won't they?' McGucken replied with characteristic sympathy.

Even from the outskirts, the Grenadier Company could see that most buildings were full of powder in open chatties, fuses, copper initiator tubes and all manner of other, dangerous 'bang-stick', as the men liked to call such things. There was a real fear that a nailed boot might strike a spark on a stone floor, so slippers had been ordered.

'And please make sure, Colour-Sar'nt that there is no cooking inside buildings and no open candles. If you're content, we'll use this building as our joint mess tonight; I hope we can get back into Kotah in the morning.' Morgan had lit a storm lantern now that darkness had fallen; it shed a cosy glow over the scruffy interior, which was dominated by a hearth, some rags and cooking pots but, apparently, no munitions.

'Fine, sir. I'll get your, my and Mr Fawcett's servants up

here wi' some cold food; let's hope the place ain't crawlin' with lice.' The last temporary mess that the sergeants and officers had shared before the assault on Kotah had left them all itching and scratching for days.

Morgan took a chance and stretched out on the stone floor, asleep almost before his head touched his haversack, which he was using as a pillow. Neither the shouted commands of Number Two Company as they sorted out the munitions deep in the village, nor the crashing of the servants as they arrived and unpacked the officers and senior NCOs' food and personal items disturbed him, but Private Beeston did.

'Now then, sir, stir yersen.' Beeston shook his company commander awake whilst the servants looked on, thoroughly amused by what was likely to happen next. 'Coom on, you'll like this, yer will.'

'Beeston, just bugger off, will you . . .' there was a ripple of mirth from the men at Morgan's understandable anger. 'Can't a man have a damn bit of sleep without being—'

'Hush, sir. There's some mail for yer.'

Mail, thought Morgan. . . . We don't get that any more. I was only thinking about that just a few hours ago.

'Some bogger loves you, sir,' and with a casual salute, the big, awkward Nottingham man withdrew, leaving a thick wedge of envelopes for the officer.

There was the normal clutter of bills from tailors, saddlers and veterinaries; his solictor had written about something complicated at Glassdrumman, and a farrier had asked him for a reference. There was a clutch of delicate envelopes in his wife's rounded hand but one letter in particular seized his attention and made his stomach shrink. He recognised his father's spindly hand; he recognised the Cork postmark; he recognised the seal in the wax but he knew what the thick black line that ran right around the envelope suggested. His hands trembled, one filthy fingernail being pushed under the paper flap, ripping it open.

'My Dearest Son, it's with the heaviest of hearts . . .' Morgan could hardly bear to read any more of his father's letter, '. . . that I tell you that your beloved wife is now safe with her maker.' Maude had died in childbirth on New Year's Day 1858 after, 'a difficult labour bravely borne.'

I can just imagine what that labour must have been like, thought Morgan. It may have been bravely borne, but it killed the poor girl – the poor girl whom I've barely thought about for the last few weeks. And now I'm a widower and a father again – and free to pursue Mary . . . But the unworthy thought shrivelled in his mind even as he had it.

'William Anthony is a fine, stout lad and we'll be baptising him at Saint Thomas's the week after next, as I know you and Maude would have wanted . . .'

As you, Billy Morgan, want, he thought. Heir to a Protestant dynasty and now utterly under his grandfather's influence whilst his papa is away at war. But I'm a father again and this time the lad can bear my name. But what sort of a husband was I that I can feel no more than a pang of remorse for the poor girl? Despite all this, though, Morgan felt a surge of pleasure penetrate his guilt and shame.

'There y'are, sir.' The door of the hovel was thrown open with a crash, disturbing Morgan's misery. 'Sorry to upend you, sir, but I've got Major Bainbrigge waiting outside for you.' Lance-Corporal Pegg was in charge of the picket on the main road, just next to Morgan's headquarters.

'Thank you, Corp'l Pegg.' Morgan scrambled to his feet, scattering papers and envelopes over the floor. 'I'll be with him directly. All quiet?' he asked as he buckled on his sword and reached for his cap.

'Aye, sir, I think so. Cap'n B's lot are doing a lot o' shouting and bellowing in the town, but nowt else,' Pegg replied, wiping a dirty hand over his red-rimmed eyes.

'Any sign of Pandy?'

'Not a thing, sir. There's this old hag who keeps mitherin' the lads for some embers, sir, but she's 'armless enough.' Pegg pointed in the dark. 'There she is now.'

Just across the road from them was an ancient woman who seemed, in the starlight, to be bent almost double with age. She was shuffling about, mumbling.

'She looks as though she's lost her wits, Corp'l Pegg; don't allow her near the men if you can avoid it – and don't let them mistreat her. She's old enough to be their great-granny.' Morgan was under no illusion about the potential for nastiness that the man had.

'Ah, Morgan, there you are . . .' Major Bainbrigge was accompanied by an orderly; neither had dismounted and it was clear that he was in a hurry. 'All quiet? Where's Bazalgette, d'you know?'

'All's as quiet as can be, thank you, sir,' Morgan replied, saluting and using the formal term in front of the men. 'Bazalgette was last seen in the two-storey building yonder.' Morgan pointed down the road a hundred paces, where a tiled roof could be seen outlined against the night sky. 'If he ain't there now his colour-sar'nt – Judd – will know where he's got to. Come in for a stiffener once you've seen him, if you like sir?' Morgan tried to push the bad news he'd received to the back of his mind.

'What, and return to the general stinking of grog? I'll tell him I got it from the Grenadier Company, Ninety-fifth, shall I?'

Morgan did his best to laugh at the quip as Bainbrigge walked his horse off in the direction that he'd been shown.

'Right, Corp'l Pegg, make sure the men are fed and rested as best you can and keep an eye on that old bint.' Morgan spoke automatically, his mind now returning to Maude's death once the welcome distraction of Bainbrigge had passed.

'Will do, sir. That bloody ram eats more of us rations than the rest o' the mess put together. What you goin' to do with it? Patsy Coughlin said it could be trained to fight proper; I saw him take 'is horns to a pye-dog today, sir, an' there was no contest there, I can tell you. Might make a bit o' money out of 'im, sir.'

But even Morgan's interest in 'the fancy' couldn't be stimulated tonight. 'I haven't decided yet, Corp'l Pegg; just don't roast the poor lamb, is all I ask.'

'Won't do that, sir, we ain't got no mint sauce.' Pegg, delighted with his own wit, saluted as Morgan withdrew morosely into the privacy of his mess.

A plate of rice and cold chicken was pushed into his hand as soon as he returned, but the letter from his father, which still lay on the floor, guaranteed that he could not eat it.

'Now, sir . . .' the door opened again, bringing the welcome sight of McGucken and another, '. . . all's well, an' I found Mr Fawcett blundering about jumping at shadows.'

The young ensign grinned at the colour-sergeant's good-natured joke. 'That was no shadow, Colour-Sar'nt, but a bloody odd old crone that was buzzing around near Corporal Aldworth's position, annoying the men.'

'Yes, she was around here as well. I told Corp'l Pegg to keep her at arm's length,' said Morgan.

'I think she'll be safe enough, even from Corp'l Pegg's depravities.' Fawcett was pleased with the word. 'Why, I've never seen anyone quite so ugly, not even—'

But he got no chance to finish. Through the narrow windows a flash lit the room like dawn, followed straight afterwards by a rolling boom that blew a clump of thatch out of the roof.

'God, that's a magazine going up – and bloody close.' Morgan scrambled to his feet. 'If you see a native, just shoot. Bloody Pandies must have got back into the town somehow.'

The three of them picked up their weapons and tumbled out of the room, to be greeted by a pool of flames and a pyre of smoke belching up into the sky at the end of the street. Where a substantial, two-floor mud-and-brick building had stood, there were now just shattered walls no higher than a man's waist.

They ran as hard as they could, seeing no one except two sepoys of the 10th, who had been carrying a big basket of what, in the dark, looked like fuses until they had been blown clear off their feet by a great wall of flame and heat. Both were moaning on the ground, badly scorched, and Fawcett paused to help them.

'No, sir, leave them,' yelled McGucken, 'there's nothing to be done for that pair; just keep your eyes peeled for rebels.'

In no time they were at the seat of the explosion where bricks, earth, tiles, roof timbers and burning straw lay in a terrible muddle, flames licking up almost prettily, smoke drifting across the stars.

Then, round the far side of the shattered walls, came Colour-Sergeant Judd, unarmed, in his shirtsleeves, with his hair and face dripping wet.

'Y' all right?' McGucken grasped his friend's arm as they all looked at the myriad fires.

'Aye, Jock; think so . . .' Judd was obviously shocked. 'I'm a bit deaf from the bang, like . . .' Judd shook his head as if to clear it, '. . . I'd just got me kit off an' was having a wash in that shack next to the magazine, when there was this fuck-off bang an' all the thatch an' tiles got pulled off of the roof. Thank God it was only a bit of all this stuff and the rest of it in the other buildings didn't go off. Where's the officers?'

'We were just going to ask you that, Colour-Sar'nt,' said Morgan, wrinkling his nose against the smell.

They'd all noticed it; but each of them had enough experience not to comment. In the same way that India's normal scent was a combination of rotting vegetation and dung, her battles smelt of wood smoke and roasting flesh. At first, the men had greeted the aroma with comments like, 'Ay-up, that smells grand,' and, 'Frying tonight,' until they realised what it meant.

'Cap'n B and Major Bainbrigge was in the building there, where we've got us mess.' Judd pointed to the now roofless shanty from which he had just emerged. 'Told me to get me 'ead down whilst they looked around for some report that the general wanted. They went out an' I was just getting a swill when it happened.'

Whilst Judd had been speaking, McGucken had been poking at something on the ground with the toe of his boot. The shadows hid its exact nature until he lifted it into the light.

'What's that you've got there, Colour-Sar'nt?' Morgan asked as McGucken held the thing up and stared at it against the fire.

'Not sure, sir. Ain't seen anything quite like it before.' The Scot turned an inch or two of narrow piping over in his fingers. It was strangely ribbed and the flames made the matter that held it together pinkly luminous.

'Looks like a bit of an oesophagus, Colour-Sar'nt.' Morgan remembered the lessons at school about the body's organs and his delight in their complex names; whilst he'd never seen such a thing in the flesh, instinctively, he knew exactly what it was.

'A windpipe, d'you mean, sir?' asked McGucken calmly. '. . . Aye, that looks about right,' before he quickly tossed the bit of gristle into the flames.

'That's right, but whose is it?' asked Morgan, as his heart fell.

'Oh Jesus, sir, look here.' Judd had found another gruesome fragment.

He showed them a complete hand that still had a cuff of a grimy white shirt at its wrist where the explosion had severed it. There was no blood – the heat of the bang had cauterised the neat amputation – but the two lower fingers were curled in a scaly, familiar way.

222

'May I see?' asked Morgan, and Judd was only too pleased to rid himself of the horrid thing. 'Look here . . .' Morgan pointed to the scarred palm and fingers, and to the signet ring, surprised that the flesh was still warm to the touch. 'I fear that this is Captain Bazalgette's hand; look, these are the wounds he received under the Colours at the Alma.'

'You're right, sir, and this is Major Bainbrigge's wallet, ain't it?' McGucken was holding a buckled piece of black leather about ten inches long and eight wide. It was the brigade major's sabretache.

'It is, Colour-Sar'nt. We've lost two very fine officers, gentlemen –' Morgan was interrupted by shouts and yells arising from the ground floor of another house close by.

'Sir, that's the lads from the Tenth. They've nabbed some bugger, by the sound of things,' said McGucken, not even waiting for his officer's approval as he bounded the short distance to the fire-lit walls of the next house.

'*Rook jao; hat jao!*' McGucken roared at the clutch of Bombay men who were pushing and slapping at someone in their midst. The sepoys froze as the colour-sergeant's bellow echoed off the walls of the squalid little room.

'*Theek hai, sahib.*' The naik in charge of the group stiffened to attention at the sight of the British officers, moving the unsheathed bayonet that he held in his right hand to his left before sketching a salute.

'Who have you got here, naik?' Morgan asked, pushing the bodies away in the darkness to try to get a glimpse of the sepoys' captive.

'It's that old woman I was telling you about earlier, Morgan.' Fawcett recognised her stooped form immediately. 'You know, the one I said had been pestering Corporal Aldworth, begging some fire.'

'Yes, indeed. Corp'l Pegg had seen her as well,' said Morgan, studying her. She was bent like a sickle, her skin a deep, wrinkled brown and her hair wispy below a tattered shawl. A trace of blood seeped from her hooked nose, but the eyes that stared at Morgan burnt deep and intense.

'Come here.' He beckoned her towards him but as she took a shuffling step, the sepoys cried out in alarm, thrusting her back.

That's damned odd, thought Morgan. The mutineers have done unspeakable things to women, but I've never see these Bombay lads treat them with anything but respect, deference almost, yet they've obviously roughed her up and want her nowhere near me.

But whilst Morgan tried to guess what had been happening, McGucken had been in a spirited conversation in his best pidgin Hindi with the sepoys, who were pointing excitedly at a scorched patch on the floor.

'They say she fired a mine, sir . . .' McGucken broke away for another explanation from the naik. 'Look here, there's a wee bit of bamboo sticking oot the floor, sir, burnt at the top. The jawans say it's a fuse that was pre-laid under the road, bamboo full o' powder that must have led to all that bang-stick in the house opposite.'

'Well, no wonder the old bitch was so anxious to get hold of some of our embers.' Morgan now recognised the hate in the woman's eyes. 'How else would she have lit the fuse?'

'How, indeed, sir.' McGucken shook his head slowly as the woman stared her mute defiance at them all. 'She must have bided her time here, keeping her sparks goin' until she saw Cap'n Bazalgette and the brigade-major walk inside and then lit the fuckin' thing.'

'What have we done, Colour-Sar'nt, to make them hate us so much?' Morgan was genuinely puzzled. Surely, British rule must have improved life immeasurably for elderly folk like this woman – hadn't it?

'Aye, sir, as you say, they must just bloody hate us,' replied

McGucken flatly. 'Best if we deal with this rather than leave her with the Tenth, sir, by your leave?'

'Yes, you're right, Colour-Sar'nt,' Morgan answered distractedly, for he was still pondering the depth of loathing that such an old, dessicated creature could harbour. 'Carry on, please.'

As Morgan turned to leave the room, he missed the colour-sergeant putting his wishes into practice. All he heard was a gasp from the sepoys, a crack that experience had taught him could only be that of fracturing bone, and the noise of a body collapsing to the floor; then just silence.

Morgan turned to look: there was McGucken standing over a clump of rags that, only seconds before, had been the old woman. His bayonet was dug hard through her nose and palate, the steel nailing her skull to the floor, whilst her eyes were still open, still hating.

'Fire!' shouted Morgan for the third time.

The first volley, fired by twelve picked men of Number Two Company had sent the crows cawing from the trees and the parrots rocketing out of their evening roosts in the date grove. There had just been time for the birds to calm themselves, to stop their panicky flapping, to eye the branches to which they might return, before the next dozen shots banged above the coffin. But the third volley was too much. Every set of wings, be they sable or flashing green, sought a quieter perch for the night.

'Order . . . arms.' The Two Company men had done their best to look clean and tidy on their company commander's last parade. They'd begged trousers that still had unpatched knees, sponged the mud off their scarlet shell jackets and washed the filthy covers of their caps until they looked almost white. Colour-Sergeant Judd had even got them to scrub their leather belts until they were an even, dun colour. Now they all waited for the words of command as they buried their officer, and Morgan buried his friend.

There'd been a spirited argument after the explosion. Whaley had assembled a working party to scour the ground for further body parts – a search that had gone on into daylight by men anxious not to let Captain Evelyn Bazalgette and Major Charles Bainbrigge provide any nourishment for the pye-dogs or shite-hawks – there were plenty of dead Pandies who could oblige on that account. But when both officers amounted to no more than a mess-tin full of offal it had been decided, after much discussion, that one crude plank coffin, hastily knocked together by a native carpenter, would do.

'Party . . . ready.' Colour-Sergeant Judd had now taken over. Six men, three either side of the coffin, took the strain on the ropes with which they would lower the box into the grave.

'Sir, if you please.' Judd gave Morgan the signal to step forward.

He returned his sword to its scabbard, marched to the grave-side, halted and briskly removed the faded yellow silk from the top of the coffin. The subalterns had slipped the Regimental Colour from its pike and suggested to the commanding officer that it might be used to cover Bazalgette on his last journey.

And I remember you beneath this flag four years ago, thought Morgan as he carefully furled the cloth into a neat rectangle. . . . Up there, you were, on the banks of the Alma, bullets and shot all around you, and you cheerin' like the hero you were, even when you had a couple of canister rounds through the fist . . . He looked at the brown stain at the corner of the flag, where his friend's blood had daubed it so long ago. And now look at you, and that grand man Bainbrigge alongside: blown to splinters by a withered old witch – and for what?

'Lower!' The box disappeared into the ground as the priest

took up his prayers where he'd left off and both company buglers sounded the Regiment's farewell.

Goodbye, my friend, thought Morgan as his hand quivered to the salute. Miss Gabbett shall have this . . . he felt the signet ring in his left palm that he'd taken off Bazalgette's dead hand . . . and she'll never know how we mocked your presentiment.

EIGHT

Jhansi

''Scuse me, sir, orderly from the commanding officer for you,'
Private Beeston spoke as softly and respectfully as he could,
trying not to stamp on Morgan's sorrow.

The drums had rattled and the fifes had squealed as the
companies had dispersed back to their duties once Bainbrigge
and Bazalgette's grave had been shovelled full of soil and
two wooden crosses knocked into the earth at its head. In
the deepest reaches of despondency, Morgan had marched
the men back to the pickets around Kinaree, knowing that
he'd lost not just a friend, but the only person who knew
all the details of his tangled circumstances. Now, whilst both
the Grenadiers and Number Two Company continued the
tedious business of clearing the village, he slumped onto his
bedroll in the improvised mess, took his flask and poured a
long measure of brandy into its silver cap. But he wasn't
given the chance to slip too deeply into misery.

'Sir, Colonel's compliments, sir, and would you be so kind
as to attend upon him up at the Rajah's palace in town at
four o'clock, sir, please? Brigadier-General's got some instructions to give out, sir, but the colonel needs to speak to you
first.'

Morgan had heard the pony that had brought the young

private from the orderly room with the message. He recognised him as one of the men who had joined in Dublin last year; in the initial tests for all new draft from the depot, his literacy had stood out and he was immediately whipped away to be one of the adjutant's clerks.

'Thank you. I'll be there . . . remind me of your name.' Morgan was careful to treat the adjutant's messengers well. 'And d'you want a swallow of tea whilst you're here, son?'

'Groves, sir; I will, thank you.' As Morgan yelled for tea and for his horse and an escort to be prepared, he looked at Groves. The lad stood only about five-foot six, but he was broad and sun-burnt, with the clearest blue eyes peering through the gloom of the little room, and whilst his first trade was scribbling, a bandage on his left hand showed that he'd taken as fair a share of the fighting for Kotah as any of the men with the companies.

'Any idea what it's about, Groves?'

'Sir, not really, sir. I know the brigadier-general is giving orders, sir, and I've just had the devil's own job finding Colonel Kemp who's been blown for as well, but I think it's just the pair of you and Colonel Hume what's going to be there.' Groves reached slightly timidly for one of the two mugs of tea that had appeared in Private Beeston's beefy hands, for he wasn't used to being treated with such civility by lofty creatures like Morgan.

'I think you've taken leave of your senses,' Hume told Morgan.

Kotah was burning and the smoke drifted low over the few buildings that hadn't been torched. Hume had established his own headquarters besides one of the fort's bastions in a huddle of low buildings from where he could look out over the countryside beyond and attempt to see the cavalry chasing the remnants of Hira Singh's men.

'I understand that Kemp has persuaded the brigadier-general

that he's the only man who knows the Rhani well enough to be able to hunt her down, and I quite see that her death will prick the damn Pandies' confidence . . .' Hume looked exhausted, thought Morgan, '. . . but your persuading the gallant commandant that you have to be in at the kill is a bit too much to swallow, ain't it? Isn't the command of the Grenadiers enough for you, or have you suddenly tired of the boys that have stood by you and the Regiment that's acted as your wet nurse?'

'Colonel, I think I've got some explaining to do.' Morgan gritted himself and was about to plunge into a full explanation of his private life when Hume cut across him.

'Oh, no, Morgan, you don't need to puke up all that stuff about you, the late, brave James Keenan and his wife, nor about the boy you and that girl have sired. No need; I've known all about that nonsense since you was tupping her before Sevastopol. I wasn't going to intervene, it was too distracting watching Richard Carmichael working himself into a horny lather over it all. I've also heard the news about your wife – and I'm damn sorry about it – but your tomcatting will threaten a promising career.'

Morgan stood and gaped at Hume. He had no idea that the commanding officer knew every last detail, including the fact that he was now free to pursue Mary.

'But you're experienced enough to make those decisions for yourself,' Hume fixed Morgan with a hard stare, 'and I quite understand that you would want to try to find Mrs Keenan and your son in the Hades that the bloody Rhani has created. No, that's not my concern at all. Kemp's half mad – driven that way, I dare say, by the grief and misery of what's happened to his command and to his family – but he's lost his flint and will probably end up getting himself and you killed . . .'

That was exactly what Bazalgette had said, thought Morgan.

'. . . and on top of that, General Smith eats out of Kemp's hand; wouldn't dare tell him to face about. Now, of course, with Rose knocking on Jhansi's door . . .' Morgan had heard great things of Sir Hugh Rose, the newly appointed commander in Central India, who was gearing up to take the Rhani's fortress by storm, '. . . Kemp has sown the idea in the generalissimos' minds that he can cut the head off the serpent by stamping on the Rhani. The danger is that the whole thing will just end up in a suicidal blood bath, which would suit Dick Kemp down to the ground.'

Morgan thought back to the Kemp he'd met all those years ago at home in Glassdrumman. He'd listened to his stories of the Sikh Wars and seen the fierce joy he'd had in reliving dangers and glories past, yet there had always been an brusque kindness there. But the Kemp he'd met again out here in mutinous India was different. There was still the rough-hewn exterior, the ready smile and genius for leadership, but all mercy had gone from him, any compassion had been swept away on a flooding need for revenge. The colonel and Bazalgette were right – Kemp would be a highly dangerous man to be alongside, yet his path led not only to the Rhani but also directly to Mary and to Sam.

'Anyway, Kemp's sold the idea to Smith, and he's written to Rose about it so, unless you decide to stay with the lads who've served you so loyally,' Hume paused and looked at Morgan coolly, 'you'll be off post-haste to Jhansi once Kemp's got his troops together. Now, whilst you're gadding about playing Richard the Lionheart, I shall be a company commander down, and that leaves me with no alternative than to give Captain Carmichael command of a double company – the Grenadiers and his.'

'But, Colonel, you can't do that to my company,' Morgan remonstrated.

'Too late. They're not your company any more. You've made your decision and I have no choice, Morgan. With

Massey taken to replace Bainbrigge as brigade-major, and now your haring off after love's sweet dream and away from me, what's to be done?' Hume's frown turned into a smile. 'But don't worry too much. Young Fawcett has made a capital start to things and as long as McGucken isn't struck down your precious Grenadiers should survive.'

Should survive, thought Morgan. Jesus, I don't want to be the man that breaks the news to Jock McGucken that he's to be under Richard bloody Carmichael's command again. There was drama enough out in Russia.

'Now, gentlemen, I know that most of you are only too painfully aware of how things stand, but there are some newcomers,' Brigadier-General Smith looked past Hume, Kemp and Morgan, concentrating on his two new staff officers, 'who might benefit from knowing a bit more of the overall situation. Whilst the main centres of the rebellion, Delhi and the other cities, are now mostly under our control, here in Central India, the six Mahratta-controlled states of the Central India Agency have thrown their lot in with Tantya Tope – that devil who massacred General Wheeler's people in the Ganges at Cawnpore – and have become a serious thorn in the side. The most influential of these territories is Jhansi and the Rhani who rules it, not so much because of its military prowess, but for other, strategic reasons. This bold young Jezebel has now sunk her differences with Tope and the pair of them will be a bloody pest unless we snuff them out right sharp.'

The man may not like the sound of lead, thought Morgan, . . . but he can hold an audience's attention right enough.

'Anyway, there are two crucial points about Jhansi,' Smith went on. 'First, the commander-in-chief, Sir Colin Campbell has got quite enough worries about the rest of Bengal without having to keep looking over his shoulder all the time. The fortress dominates Sir Colin's lines of communications and didn't need to be concerned about it until Tantya Tope teamed up with the Rhani and a gang of other ruffians. Now that the place has been fortified and garrisoned we've got to take it, for if we don't we can never be confident that our rear areas are secure, nor where the next brush-fire mutiny will break out.' Smith pointed to the map. 'You see how Jhansi's central position must have distracted Sir Colin during that nonsense around Lucknow. Now, Sir Hugh Rose has just started his first moves against the place – parallels began to be cut yesterday – but there'll be serious fighting to be done once they decide to storm. We'll be too far distant to get there in time – it's a least a dozen forced marches away – but a small party on fast horses will be there in five days.'

Five days' hard riding, thought Morgan. . . . That'll leave us with raw arses and the nags with sore backs . . .

'The second point is the Rhani herself,' Smith continued. 'You all know what a Jezebel the papers have made her out to be – and quite rightly so after her perfidy with Skene and the other Europeans – but Kemp knows the woman in the flesh. Tell us about her, if you please.'

'There was a time when I really would have liked to know her in the flesh, General, for she's a tasty little bint . . .' Kemp looked round at the audience, most of whom grinned, but one or two – Smith included – frowned disapprovingly, '. . . but the bitch played us false and murdered – well, you've heard enough about the blood-letting that she started. Thing is, she's damnably persuasive and strong-willed. She's got all the native princes eating out of her pretty little palm because she's brighter than the lot of 'em put together, understands us lot – the British – and all our weaknesses, and she don't lack courage. She was brought up like a boy and taught to fight Mahratta-style; why, I've seen her myself on her Arab pony with a sword in either hand controlling the damn thing with the reins looped round her toes. The shave is that she's now leading her troops herself, dressed like a man in a mail shirt and steel pot; the only way to identify her is that she has her eight-year-old son, young Damodar, on her saddle-bow when she goes into action. And there's something else: she protected Mrs Mary Keenan – wife of one of my sub-alterns who was murdered – and her son when the rest of the Europeans were put to the sword. Mrs Keenan . . .' Kemp paused as he looked at Morgan, '. . . some of you know her, I believe, was already a pal of the Rhani's before this unpleas-antness started. She became a sort of unofficial physician and confidante, I'm told, and now she and her young lad are being held hostage by the Rhani.'

'And it's because of the Rhani's pivotal influence, and the fact that you know what she looks like, that I'm asking you to go after her,' said Smith. 'It's vital to remember, Kemp, that the whole moving spirit of the mutiny in and around Jhansi stands or falls with the wretched woman. If she's destroyed I guess that the wind will go out of many of the rebels' sails, so no playing the gentleman. Find the traitorous drab and kill her.'

'The pleasure will be all mine, sir,' replied Kemp, a vulpine smile on his lips.

'Very good, sir,' McGucken greeted the news woodenly.

'What d'you mean, "Very good, sir"? It's very fucking bad news indeed,' retorted Morgan, at bursting point with his colour-sergeant's insouciance.

'Very good, sir,' the Scot repeated as they stood in the doorway of the house in Kinaree that they were using as their company headquarters. 'You've given your orders an' I'll obey them as best I know how.'

'I'm sure you will, Colour-Sar'nt, but it's Captain bloody Carmichael who's to take over; half the men in the company served under him out East and loathe the sod. Quite apart from which, he left you for dead at Inkermann and I have no doubt that he'll find every excuse to misuse any Grenadier that he can,' Morgan blurted, guilty that he was abandoning both McGucken and his own troops.

'Very good, sir,' was all that McGucken replied.

'Will you stop repeating that goddamn nonsense, Colour-Sar'nt?' Morgan was yelling loud enough now for the sentry on the roadblock close to where they stood to move away to a distance that looked as though he could no longer hear his superiors arguing, whilst straining his ears for every syllable. 'You'll be run ragged by the bastard.'

McGucken took Morgan by the arm – a thing unheard of between officer and NCO – and almost dragged him into the shabby house, telling their soldier-servants to make themselves scarce as he did so.

'All right, sir, so you want me to be honest with yer?' This was as close as McGucken was going to get to informality, Morgan realised. All the months of heat and danger here in India, on top of the horrors of the Crimea, had forged a friendship between the two men that nothing could dent, yet the gulf of rank between the two of them still yawned. Besides, McGucken was what he was – a Glasgow keelie who owed his life and wellbeing to the army and its creed – and if that meant exchanging the finest officer he'd ever met for the worst in the regiment, well, that's the way it would have to be.

'I dinna want to lose you as my company commander when we've barely started taking this sharny place back from the Pandies; I dinna want to have that fucker in command of me again after what happened in Russia; I dinna want to have to watch Mr Fawcett doing the company commander's job for him – for we both know he'll have to; and I dinna want to watch you going off on some arse-bag job having to look after crazy Colonel Kemp.' McGucken paused to see what effect this burst of undisciplined candour was having on his officer. 'But I understand that you want to get to Jhansi and find Mrs Keenan and your lad. So, I'll just carry on and it'll be, "Yes, Captain Carmichael; just as you wish, Captain Carmichael", an' not a mention will be made of all the swerving that has gone on; no, sir, it'll just be, "Leave to carry on, sir; salute and turn to the right", and hope to God that not too many of the boys catch it along the way.'

It had been an impressive speech: McGucken at his long-serving, regimental best, but it gave Morgan no comfort. A few words of cheerful resilience would have done perfectly; it would have allowed him to go off with Kemp with his conscience slightly more at ease, but that wasn't what McGucken had wanted. His next comments made things no easier.

'And don't you go getting yourself kilt, neither, sir. Yon Kemp ain't got nothing to live for – you've seen how he serves the prisoners an' how he's always at the front of the fighting: that's not bravery, sir, it's just desperation. No, sir, just give him as wide a berth as you can when you're up Pandy way. Mark my words, for he's a billet looking for a bullet, so he is.'

Morgan had noticed Kemp's blood lust, not just during the execution of prisoners, but in every action and skirmish in which they had been involved. Whether mounted or on foot, Kemp could be relied upon to be everywhere when metal was flying, yet Morgan had just assumed that it was gallant zeal. But Bazalgette – God rest him – Hume and now McGucken had all seen something that he had missed: a misery that was driving Kemp to self-destruction.

'Anyway, sir, you've made yer bed so you'll have to lie in it. I've told yer servant to get both your charger and your pony ready, saddlebags packed, and I've robbed one of them cavalry carbines for ye with a hundred rounds. Oh, and yer escort was only too keen to volunteer for the adventure, sir.' McGucken smiled slightly.

'Good, thank you very much, Colour-Sar'nt; I'm sorry to leave you at such a time as this, but I've no choice, really,' Morgan lied. 'Who's coming with me?'

236

'Why, Lance-Corporal Pegg, sir,' McGucken's face now split into a broad grin. 'He's a good enough horseman, sir, and, besides, he needs to get some rest; the bint he's got never lets him get a minute's sleep.'

'Lance-Corporal Pegg; thank you, Colour-Sar'nt. I can't thank you enough,' Morgan replied, divining the subtlest form of revenge in McGucken's choice of escort.

'It's not that I mind coming, sir, it's just 'oo's going to look after the ram and 'elp Cap'n Carmichael when 'e teks over, sir?' Pegg was unhappily hacking along on a quartermaster's whaler that he'd been told to sign for that morning. Now his kit, water chatties and rifle banged about untidily around him.

'Well, you've changed your tune, Corp'l Pegg.' Morgan was rising and falling easily in his saddle as his heavily laden mare, Emerald, trotted along the dirt track outside Kotah towards Kemp's horse lines. 'You couldn't stand the thought of the man when you last served under him out East. In fact, I have a memory of you gobbing on the man's boot at Inkermann.'

'Aye, sir, but that's a long time ago an' somcone will need to be around to 'elp the sprogs, won't they?' Pegg wasn't going to give up easily. He'd detected that the regiment was in for a long period of idleness – safe idleness, when no one was going to shoot at him – and he wanted some of that. Besides, there was Cissy to look after.

'Well, I think you can leave all that in the safe hands of Colour-Sar'nt McGucken, who, you might recall, is more than aware of Cap'n Carmichael's foibles.'

'Foibles, sir, what's them?' Pegg replied, mystified.

'It doesn't matter, Corp'l Pegg. Just sit up in the saddle and try to look soldierly.'

Morgan had seen one of Kemp's sentries, evidently a long-serving daffadar from one of the mutinous Bengal light cavalry

237

units who had decided to stay true to his salt. His turban was wrapped exactly, his moustaches and beard as freshly oiled as the carbine that sat easily in the crook of his arm. Even the standard challenge was well delivered in fluent English as the stumpy smooth-bore was brought to the ready'. Behind him milled twenty or so British hussars, all trying to stow fodder and shot on mounts that were already overloaded.

'Captain Morgan and one, detached from HM Ninety-Fifth Foot, looking for the commandant, Daffadar.'

The cavalryman drew back, pulling his feet together – now in sandals where once there would have been good, solid boots – and saluted before pointing mutely further down the road. As the two infantrymen trotted past, Morgan swore that the Indian's lip curled as Pegg bumped and wheezed in the saddle.

They pushed through what seemed like half a troop of the 8th Hussars, once smart in blue shell jackets, tight overalls and white cap covers, but now dusty and blinking as they stamped musty hay into nets and strung it across saddles and bat-ponies.

'Mr Morgan, sir . . . Mr Morgan . . . well, I never,' a raucous female voice called from the press of horses, men and weapons.

Morgan looked down towards the noise, but all he could see at first was a farrier-corporal strapped about with sword and pouches, his carbine hanging down by his side from its cross-belt and hook. The horse-soldier sweated as he struggled with a girth strap, his tanned face slightly familiar. But beyond him peeped a great, chubby, ruddy face of a woman who looked as though she could be in her forties but, in reality, had yet to see thirty. A floral cotton dress clung to her, wide stains of sweat making the armpits black, her bun in disarray as her mousy locks broke loose. But even as she pushed the hair back with a damp wrist, Morgan was still at a loss.

'Oh, sorry, *Captain* Morgan.' The woman had spotted the

stars and crowns on Morgan's collar. 'It's me, Betty Martin
– our Tom's missus.'

The hussar stiffened and saluted.

'You know, sir, Mary Keenan's pal. We was at Ballyklavy
together. You must remember when our Tom got sliced by
them Russians an' Mary helped our surgeon.' But Morgan
was still struggling. 'You must remember, sir. We was always
up at your camp with Mary – saw you there more times than
I can think.'

Morgan looked round guiltily, but he needn't have worried
for no one here was aware of his and Mary's secret – or if
they were they had better things to think about. He studied
her again.

Of course, you're that nosy little hussy that was always
hanging about Mary's neat warm hut, just when we wanted
a bit of privacy, he thought.

'Yes, of course, Mrs Martin, how could I forget? What a
delight,' said Morgan. 'But you're not coming with us on
this little sally, are you?'

'Oh, no, sir . . .' Corporal Martin was impatiently showing
his wife where to hold open a saddlebag, whilst all Betty
wanted to do was to gossip with the 'quality'. '. . . I'm just
mekin' sure our Tom's got enough comforts before he sets
off on his latest adventure.'

'Well, Corp'l Martin, if the ride ahead of us is as hard as
I reckon it's going to be, I expect we'll need a farrier above
all else; have you seen Commandant Kemp?'

Morgan now remembered the man. He'd visited him in
hospital whilst on a spurious trip with Mary down to
Balaklava. He could just see the curling, shiny scar that
reached down below a clipped ear lobe where a Russian
sabre had gouged Martin so deeply.

'And don't be taken in by the bitch if you get close to her.'
Kemp trotted along easily next to Morgan, his khaki pyjamas

and light cork helmet a contrast to Morgan's dusty scarlet and worn blue overalls. 'I tell you, if you get near her she'll be all sweet reason and, "I was forced to fight the British because of my precious Jhansi and boy," but that's just balls.'

They were two days into the journey now, riding through the heat of the day as well as the cool of the night. Only when the mounts needed rest, water or food did they pause, the thirty or so men having to shift their needs and fatigue to suit the animals.

'Well, what is the truth exactly, Commandant, about the Rhani and why she turned on us?' Morgan was just starting to feel saddle sore after almost thirty-five miles of jolting, choking roads, thrown shoes and lame baggage ponies. All the frustrations of moving horse soldiers fast over a long distance had come to the fore, but they were still making remarkably good time. 'The papers have made her sound like the worst sort of she-devil.'

'Aye, lad, and that's not too far off the mark. There's some,' Kemp replied, 'who still believe that the whole thing's our fault, but I know Lakshmi Bai better than most and she was always a conniving, scheming little quim. The fact is that despite nearly fucking her ancient husband, Raja Gangadhar Rao, to death, they couldn't have any kids – his pencil had run out of lead. So they adopted a boy from a good family, Damodar Rao, but when the old boy chucked in the towel in late 'fifty-three, the authorities fell back on the rule that says that any rajah here in the Agency that dies without an heir, forfeits the land to British rule. Now, our Rhani seemed to accept all this with a good grace at first. Retires to her little palace in the middle of Jhansi rather than the fort and makes out that she's the model of loyalty.'

'Do you know her well, Commandant?' asked Morgan, intrigued by the prospect of this big, horse-smelly man hobnobbing with the elegant, duplicitous princess.

'As I say, I knew her well enough for her to unburden herself

240

of all her grievances – not that she was ever too direct about it all, mark you. She'd insinuate herself with me and Skene, try to weave her charms about the injustice of things and how, with her properly at the helm she would turn Jhansi into some sort of beacon for loyal co-operation with John Company. But if you want to know the Rhani really well, talk to your sweet little cushion, Mary Keenan.' Kemp cast a sideways glance at his companion as he came out with this, but Morgan didn't rise. 'Now she got to know her in detail. Two clever, lonely women, one with a young 'un, the other with a babe-in-arms – they spent a lot of time together, Mary learning the lingo and Lakshmi Bai getting to trust her more and more as an amateur quack. The Rhani had all sorts of problems with her itcher – probably needed a trip to the armourers for a rebore, I'd guess – and Mary was frightfully good at all that sort of fanny-doctor stuff, so the memsahibs tell me.'

'And you're sure that the European garrison was butchered on her say-so, are you, sir?' Morgan watched Kemp as the older man thought carefully.

'I'm not convinced,' Kemp eventually replied, 'because the whole affair lacked any sort of finesse and was just a blood bath. I'm not going to go into all that horror again – I told you all the details weeks ago. But, case in point was the way that Lakshmi Bai made sure that Mary and Samuel were spared – but I really don't care. She's so damn clever, so damn persuasive, that the rest of the princelings will do as she says. That's why the whole area remained loyal for as long as it did – on her orders. And that's why, if we want to kick the wind out of the rebellion in these parts, we've got to destroy her; and that's why I'm telling you not to let her persuade you otherwise – was you to get into a position where that might be possible.'

Morgan nodded his understanding, not liking the idea, but seeing both its logic and the gleam of vengeful hatred in Kemp's eyes.

'She'll not be good and Christian with your two, neither. If Mary's outlived her usefulness, or she can use her as a shield, as sure as the Pope's in Rome, she will.

'Now listen, boy, when did you last hear from your father?' Kemp changed tack.

'Just a few days back. I got a long-delayed letter from him about Maude's death and the birth of my son – we discussed it.' Morgan had sought some comfort from Kemp when the news had arrived, not really expecting much, but just needing to share the contents of the letter with someone who knew the people and Glassdrumman. In fact, Kemp had been remarkably sympathetic in a rough, soldierly way.

'As I thought. I got a letter from Billy just before we set out, dated two weeks ago. It said some pretty bald things. He knows about James Keenan's death and assumes that Mary and Sam are alive; he also assumes that you'll seek 'em out and do your duty by them. But he wants you to be under no illusion about the reception that'll be waiting back home if you turn up with a papist lass on your arm and a fatherless child, particularly now that you have a legitimate son and heir. He's asked me to reason with you because of my own circumstances – well, my former circumstances.'

Morgan rode on besides Kemp, silently furious that his father would choose to communicate with him over such matters via someone else – but he might have expected as much.

'Point is, I chose to marry a Eurasian girl because I loved her – I still do, and I'll make those heathens weep for what they did to Neeta and my family. Anyway, I knew that marriage to a native girl would make it impossible for us to make our way back home in Ireland, and that's why I always came home by myself. Now that was my choice – and it was a hard one – but at least I could look to India as an alternative place to raise a family where few people would cock an eyebrow at us and at our children – and those that took exception could go hang. But it ain't going to be like that for you back in Cork, married to a Taegue. Most will assume your bastard son really is a Keenan and he will have to be raised Roman whilst your own boy will be one of us. Mark my words, lad, it won't work. The bloody lot of you will be miserable and – unlike me – you'll have nowhere to run. If you can't resist the lass – an' God knows I can see she's prime – set her up on the estate somewhere and be discreet. Skibbereen ain't London, nor Dublin, even; just don't lay yourself and Mary open to sadness that can be avoided.'

Morgan was at a loss. Kemp was his father's oldest friend – that he understood – but how dare the old man delegate such a discussion to an outsider? Why couldn't he put all this in a letter to him, his only son?

'That's as maybe, Commandant, but I've got to find Mrs Keenan and the boy alive first, and – from what you say – they're likely to be hard alongside the Rhani, so both our ventures are linked,' replied Morgan, trying hard to hide his fury with his father's typical clumsiness.

But just as he was trying to think of a suitably frosty reply, one of the leading scouts, a dust-wrapped sowar on a handy little pony, came skipping down the track, his body alive with tense excitement.

'Sahib . . . sahib . . .' was all that Morgan understood as the soldier pointed over his shoulder further up the track, gabbling in Hindi to Kemp.

'Spot of fun for us here, Morgan; take your mind off the things we've just been discussing,' said Kemp, waving the hussars to a halt and beckoning for his own posse of officers to join him.

'Moore, will you take the left and sweep around that stand of trees yonder?' Kemp spoke to his former quartermaster quickly, economically, the man instantly understanding what was needed and, beckoning for his orderly to follow, spurred his horse into a canter, creating its own individual cloud of dust.

'Breen, be so kind as to hook round from the right; stop the bugger from running down that nullah.'

The light cavalryman, younger than most of the others, knew at once what Kemp wanted, drew his sword with a rasp from its scabbard and with a simple, 'Very good, Commandant,' rode off in a wide circle towards the top of the dried stream bed that Kemp had pointed out, one of the sowars following him without any spoken orders that Morgan could detect.

'Right . . . Rees, Dr Stockwell, Morgan, form left and right of me and keep your pace nice and steady. Those two flanking parties should make him run towards us if they do the job right. Just don't let him break the line. No, Rees . . .' the civilian railwayman had drawn his revolver from its holster on his saddle and was checking the priming, '. . . no musketry. We'll be too close to each other for that; I've seen more accidents with pistols and ricochets than I can count – sabres only.' They all drew their blades, the afternoon sun winking off the curved steel. 'All ready?'

Morgan nodded with the rest of them, not wanting to show his complete ignorance of precisely who they were about to kill, whilst hoping that it wasn't another of Kemp's murderous ideas.

'Come on, then, keep the line straight and close; when he comes he'll run hard and fast.'

And with that the four horsemen trotted forward towards the clump of trees and brush, swords glittering, whilst the troop of stationary hussars looked on with almost as much bemusement as Morgan. The faces of the other three were hard and set, their eyes narrowed as they squinted at the tangle of brush and thorns ahead of them. When they were still sixty paces from the cover, trotting smartly but cautiously forward in a tight-drawn line, Breen and his man, invisible to Morgan from over on right, let out a series of shouts and hoots. Kemp tensed in the saddle, tightened the reins and flicked his sword down from where it had been resting on his shoulder. The point hovered low, just above his horse's rising knees; Morgan saw how the commandant tightened his grip on the hilt in silent anticipation.

'There . . . see there . . . there's the bastard!' Kemp yelled in delight, and kicked his mount into a gallop. 'Stay close.'

Morgan saw how no one doubted Kemp's leadership; they obeyed his word without question.

As all three of them surged forward trying to keep up with their leader, Morgan braced himself for battle. But where he'd expected to see some desperate mutineer, musket primed and ready, steeling himself for one last throw of hate, there was something very different.

Jinking and swerving out of the thorns came the biggest, blackest wild sow that Morgan could ever have hoped to see. The hackles on her shoulders stood up like a scrubbing brush, her hoofs scraped at the ground as she turned this way and that, whilst her vicious, curling tusks were held just as low and ready as any of their swords. In the dust that she raised followed four piglets, their tiny hoofs drumming as they tried to keep up with their mother; but where she was menacingly silent, the young ones squealed in alarm.

Morgan caught a flash of her eyes – they were tiny, black and determined, set above long, bristled cheeks that ended in a surprisingly pink snout. As he watched she turned and bounded directly for the gap between Kemp and him, gathering speed as she came, a ribbon of speeding forms spreading out behind her.

'Fall back to my right, Morgan,' Kemp bellowed. 'I'll slow her, you finish her,' as naturally as if Morgan had been slicing bacon from a fast-moving horse all his life. But there was no time for doubt as the sow turned hard to her right almost under Kemp's hoofs, causing the colonel to lean low to his left, and making a powerful blow from his sword all but impossible. Kemp's blade cut a bloody line across the pig's nearside shoulder, causing her to yelp in pain and stagger in the dirt, but no sooner had she stumbled than she was back on the attack, driving a tusk firmly above one rear hoof of her attacker's horse. Rearing and neighing in pain, Kemp's grey rose on wounded legs and tossed his rider clear, the big man landing with a thump, thickening the dusty air.

A younger, leaner Kemp might have mastered the situation, but the fall was heavy and so was he. Winded and stunned, the commandant was at the angry sow's mercy. Now, as her brood scattered around her, she gathered her bleeding haunches, lowered her sharp ivory and charged her tormentor. Morgan saw the danger.

Use the point, man. Don't slash at her; it simply won't stop her, he thought as memories of human enemies, whom he'd wished he'd stopped dead with his sword, flashed through his mind.

The target was difficult, being so low to the ground – which was why spears were normally used to deal with dangerous wild pigs – so Morgan leant as low as he could, dug his heels into Emerald's flanks, aiming a couple of yards in front of the dashing sow that was heading for Kemp. She came fast, diagonally across Morgan's front as the commandant raised himself on a bruised elbow and looked into a pair of furious, button eyes that were coming straight for him.

Hold the goddamn thing straight. Morgan's sword arm made one long rigid line with the steel. *Use her weight to run onto the blade, don't chop at her.*

Morgan knew it would be tight. The sow hadn't seen his galloping horse, so intent was she on her victim, but he knew that he had only a few feet to intercept her: too far left and he risked trampling Kemp; too far right and he would miss the careering pig completely. This time he got it right. Holding tight to the saddle's pommel with his left hand he lowered himself ever further, and as the great, bristled flank was under

Emerald's nose, his sabre sank into it, pushed deep by the combined momentum of horse and pig.

The speed of the quarry almost pulled him from the back of his horse, but as the sow shrieked in pain, blood shot from her mouth and nose, flecking Kemp as he pulled his arms up to protect himself. Even as the point of the sword emerged through the ribs on her right side, the animal was dead, her weight bringing horse and swordsman to an abrupt halt.

Kemp hauled himself to his feet, sword dangling by its knot from his right wrist. He banged some of the muck from his clothes, stooped for his soiled topee and stared up at his saviour.

'I thought they'd taught you to be faster with wild pig, my boy.' Morgan was still struggling to free his sword blade from the sow as Kemp threw his head back and chortled, 'You mustn't hesitate with these brutes. You can afford to be much rasher!'

The piglets were especially good, thought Morgan, as the British orderlies – for none of the Indians would touch the profane creatures – carved hunks of pale meat off the spitted animals. The knot of 8th Hussars had been particularly assiduous, a fire being lit to prepare a bed of cooking embers and butcher's knives at the ready almost before the sow and her offspring had been dragged back into the clearing where a camp had been established. Now the British and a pair of Eurasian telegraph clerks from Kemp's party sat in a gaggle around the fire, gorging themselves on the fresh meat.

'I'll tek a look at your charger's off-rear, sir. She's got a bit of a limp there.' Farrier-Corporal Martin was sitting cross-legged on the ground next to Morgan, charred pork and chapatti jutting from his mouth. The NCO was difficult enough to understand even when he didn't have a mouthful of food, for the sabre cuts that the Russians had administered to his skull had left his speech slightly slurred, just as the surgeon had said it would.

'Thank you, Corp'l Martin,' Morgan replied, just before he stuck a piece of crackling and mango into his mouth. 'I thought she seemed a bit uneven during the chase. She'll be good for another couple of day's march, though, won't she?'

'Aye, sir, so long as you let me get at her hoof. I've got some linament that them chasseurs learnt us how to mix in the Crimea; wonderful, it is,' Martin replied.

'Is that all it is, sir, two more days before we get to Jhansi?' Lance-Corporal Pegg had not enjoyed the journey so far. The horsemanship that he'd been taught on a Derbyshire hill farm had served him well enough there, but the techniques of horse husbandry, the stowage of kit, fodder and weapons were all new to the infantryman. He'd found the notion hard to accept that at every stop, or even the slightest pause, the horse's needs came first; Morgan had to tell him time and again to water his mount before he even thought about refreshing himself. On top of that, the inside of his calves and thighs were rubbed almost raw in places, making him bad-tempered and hard on the bit.

'Well, it should be, but unscheduled stops like this don't help,' replied Morgan. 'You can see how fretful they make the commandant.'

It was true. Kemp had driven the small force remorselessly, not allowing even the shortest halt for a little gentle looting when they had passed by ravaged villages. But the wild pig had been different. Now their leader sat on a saddle-cloth spread out on the ground, gnawing at a roasted rib as fat dribbled down his chins. Even in the firelight, Morgan could see how his eyes were half closed with pleasure as the meat disappeared down his throat at remarkable speed.

'Aye, sir, the commandant's a bugger for 'is grub, ain't he?' Pegg was no amateur either, for he'd already tucked away more than his fair share, by Morgan's reckoning. 'But you know what he's like: there'll be no rest once this food's done. 'E'll want to use the cool o' the night to get a league or two behind us, won't 'e, sir? Don't see what all the rush is about, I don't. But you know what the army's like, sir. It's always, "Not a moment to be lost," then, "Rush to bloody wait," ain't it, sir?'

'Most times, yes,' answered Morgan between mouthfuls, 'but that galloper that came in earlier put the toe of his boot up our arse.'

Whilst the hog and piglets were being bled and the hairs singed off their pelts, the whole group engrossed in the forthcoming feast, a trooper and one of Rose's aides – a cornet of Scinde Horse – had come cantering into their camp.

'General Rose was expecting to start the assault on Jhansi yesterday. It was a question of whether they would have enough artillery ammunition to begin the bombardment and then sustain it. Our political people suggest that the Rhani is still in the main fort. They think she's been seen there with her bodyguard, tearing around the garrison trying to put some mettle into 'em,' said Morgan, 'but it also seems that Tantya Tope and an army of several thousand Pandies may be advancing to help her. Now, you know how important she is to the enemy's cause . . .'

'I've 'eard she's a sweet little piece, sir, well titted out an—' but Pegg wasn't allowed to continue.

'Yes, thank you, Corp'l Pegg, but I think that the Rhani's contribution to the spirit of the rebellion may go just a little further than the size of her poonts. As I was saying,' Morgan continued, 'Rose is going to have to decide how he handles both the siege and any force that may be coming to raise it; that's why he needs us sharpish, to find the woman and to destroy her. So, Corp'l Pegg, enjoy that meat, for I suspect you may be right. Once the commandant's had his fill, it'll be "boots and saddles" and away.'

Pegg was, indeed, correct. No sooner had Kemp thrown

the last pig bone into the fire than he was up and impatient, stirring the others to their duty, to mount and ride into the night.

There's those goddamn stars again, thought Morgan as the jolting of his horse brought another, meaty belch bubbling from his mouth. I wonder if Mary knows that I'm not far away. And I bet Carmichael's ordered double sentries when there's no need to, just so that his precious sleep won't be disturbed . . . bloody man.

'Who's the Bombay Europeans then, sir?' Pegg asked as they fed and watered their tethered horses in a shell-pocked yard in the town of Jhansi.

'The Third Bombay Europeans, Corp'l Pegg, are the lucky set of people yonder,' said Morgan as he pulled the strap of the nose-bag tighter over Emerald's ears so that she could get to the oats at the bottom of it, 'who we're going to grace with our company during the assault on the fort.'

A last storm of artillery rounds thundered overhead as the evening light began to fail, striking the enemy gun emplacements hard and accurately in the walls of the fort that towered forty feet above them. The occasional shot was returned, but the garrison seemed to have been thoroughly overwhelmed by the weight of metal that was being hurled at them.

Sheltering behind broken walls and buildings was a crowd of infantrymen, busily lashing shorter pieces of bamboo to longer staves with thick quartermaster's twine. As they tied and knotted, so long light ladders took shape, which they would soon have to throw against the heavily defended walls, before clambering up into the teeth of the mutineers.

'But they ain't Queen's troops, nor are they natives,' said Pegg, swiping at a cloud of mosquitoes, which had gathered about his sweaty face for an evening treat, 'an' they're full of piss an' wind, they are. I told one cheeky bogger to 'old me 'orse – friendly, like – and 'e just flicked me the fingers, 'e did: 'e could see me tapes, an' all. Tempted to give 'im a punch in the gob, I was.'

'They're just like the Bombay Artillery in our column, Corp'l Pegg: Britons recruited over here or attracted by a bounty back in England just to serve in India in the Company's white regiments,' Morgan explained. 'They're not bound by Queen's Regulations so they tend to get above themselves. We'll see whether they can fight, though, for we'll all be up and at the fort in a few hours' time.'

After six days' hard riding, Kemp's people had arrived at Jhansi in the middle of the afternoon of 3 April, where they found that the storming of the town had already started. Kemp had been snatched away to receive orders from General Rose himself, before returning and leading his men up to this courtyard on the right flank of the forthcoming night attack on Jhansi's main fortification.

'Well, sir, why can't they attach us to the Eighty-Third or one of the proper regiments, then?' Pegg was genuinely affronted by the devil-may-care approach of the Bombay Europeans, whose lack of respect for 'real' soldiers (were they blind, couldn't the ignorant bastards see his Crimea gongs, Pegg wondered) was unthinkable.

'Because the Rhani is said to be inside one of these bastions over here on the right of the assault,' Morgan pointed up to the slope and the louering stone elevations that lay a hundred or so paces in front of them beyond the cluster of mud and brick shanties, 'and our little gang has got to go and get her.'

'You'll have the devil's own job getting up that ladder under the Pandies' fire, you will, sir.' Pegg looked up at the battlements in the loaming. 'Them sepoys won't be too welcoming to you, will they?'

'No, it'll be bloody murder, but we've been through worse at Inkermann, and in The Quarries, ain't we, Corp'l Pegg?'

'We 'ave, sir, an' don't you worry, sir, you'll be all right.'

'I know we will, but I'd prefer to have our own men with

us, wouldn't you, Corp'l Pegg?' Morgan replied. 'I'll need you right behind me if we're to be over the wall smartly; you'll need to have an eye on this Bombay lot and keep 'em up to the mark.'

But Pegg's face dropped. 'On the ladder, sir? Me, sir? Oh, no, sir, I'll 'ave to stay behind with the 'ussars, sir, keeping 'old of the nags in case you wants them.' Kemp had told the 8th Hussars to stay out of the brutal business of a deliberate storm by the infantry, preferring to keep them intact for any mounted pursuit that might be necessary. But Pegg thought that his part in active operations of war was at an honourable end; he saw himself now more as an observer and advisor, a sounding board for his officer's tactical decisions. He was going to be disappointed.

'Shift over a bit, can't you, mate?' As the assault parties crouched in the gardens and yards for the signal to surge forward in the darkness, a beefy Bombay European elbowed Morgan to one side as the men tried to balance the weight of the twenty-foot-long lattices with that of their weapons.

'I'm not your mate.' Even in the darkness of almost three in the morning, there was no excuse for the soldier not to have recognised him as an officer, thought Morgan. 'I'll thank you to keep a soldierly tongue in your head.'

Morgan had never had to use such terms in the 95th, where an officer was automatically treated with respect. This Bombay lot was different, he thought; even Pegg had noticed their scant sense of discipline and general rowdiness. There was no apology, though, just a slight snigger from those who had heard the exchange above the noise of the shells, reminding Morgan of the times that he had seen Carmichael being scorned and laughed at by a squad in the anonymous dark.

'Right, lads, I'm Captain Morgan of the Ninety-Fifth; Corp'l Pegg and I will be leading you up the walls of Jhansi as soon as the signal is given.' Morgan did his best to recover from the unfortunate beginning; the last thing he wanted was resentful, surly troops at a moment like this. 'See that flag yonder?' Morgan pointed to a great green cloth that hung limply from a pole in the dark above them, just visible each time the guns flashed. 'I've a bottle of best Irish in my saddle-bags for the man who pulls it down.' That was better; they all seemed to be grinning at the thought of the grog, except for Lance-Corporal Pegg, who had been deeply taciturn ever since he'd been told that he was to be at the forefront of the attack.

'Don't be fixing your bayonets, any of you.' Morgan made sure that the Bombay men all got an eyeful of his ribbons. 'At Sevastopol we found it a mite disconcerting to be pushed onto one of our own men's spikes.' It was worth playing the veteran, Morgan thought; he'd never even seen a scaling ladder before, let alone climbed one, but he could remember reading something about officers falling onto their own men's steel during one of the Peninsular sieges.

'Don't you worry yourself, sir,' a strange, grinding Lancashire accent came from the dark. 'You're with the Third Bombay now; we was stuffing Sikhs long before you got a sniff of a Russian. We'll have that rag off its stick sooner than you'll know, and a-hangin' in the Lord Canning's quarters.' There was a ripple of, 'ooh, clemency, clemency, please,' and a general laugh of approval at this retort, which immediately made Morgan feel more comfortable with these rough-necks.

'I hope you've got plenty of shot to hand, lads?' Morgan looked at his fellow stormers in their khaki linen trousers and tops. Their shirts had obviously been run up by a local contractor; they were light and comfortable with generous pockets on the chests, which the men now patted.

'Aye, sir, an' our pouches are brimfull, too,' the leader of the group, who wore no badges of rank, Morgan noticed, answered.

'Good men. Water bottles full?' Morgan had used this device before on the verge of action: distract the men – and himself – with petty checks and questions; anything to stop people from pondering their fates too deeply.

'Sir, will you stop mithering us – we're not children.' The non-commissioned officer – for that's what Morgan guessed he was – would have continued had not three red rockets sprung into the air from over to their left. 'Eh-up, there's the signal, c'mon, boys,' and with no more reference to the officer the whole gang of assault men and covering party set off at the best gallop they could up the steep glacis below the fortress's walls.

'Get going then, Corp'l Pegg,' yelled Morgan, embarrassed at being caught unprepared. Pegg, however, had taken his officer's hesitation as just the sign he wanted, and hung back behind the cover of a particularly solid piece of masonry. As Morgan drew his sword and dashed forward, though, Pegg saw that it was useless to resist and, shoulders hunched like a man stepping out into a storm of hail, he left the protection of the building and trotted reluctantly after the attackers.

The walls spurted flame and lead, flashes coming from loopholes and embrasures, bricks, stones and hunks of wood studded with nails showering down on the men's heads and shoulders like lethal sleet. Then it was all: 'Don't let the ladder drop, boys,' and, 'Pete, get 'ere, Taff's down . . .' mixed with cheers, shouts and cries of pain as their boots dug into the slope and the missiles swept down upon them.

With no burden and no rifle, Morgan was soon at the head of the rushing crowd, mouth as dry as his arse was tight, shoulders pulled as high as nature would allow, dreading the next boulder or ball. As he looked to the ladder party, the long spokes were parallel to the ground as the men sweated and grunted it up the slope; then it dropped, the feet digging themselves into the soil as the front man buckled and fell silently in the dark.

'Get on, lads, get on.' Morgan dashed to the front of the party, pulled the arms of its wounded leader out of the rungs and stuck a wooden leg squarely on his shoulder. 'Just a few more paces, come on.'

As they scrabbled up to the foot of the walls, Morgan could see how the rubble caused by the gunfire both helped and hindered them. No proper breaches had been punched through which the attackers might pour – there simply hadn't been time for the guns to concentrate their fire against the fortress in the running fight for Jhansi, which was now in its fourth day. The artillery had mauled the walls badly but not fatally, the piles of broken masonry making an uneven platform at the top of the glacis upon which they could lodge their ladders, yet the heaps of spoil meant that there was no cover from the defenders above.

'Here, just here . . .' Morgan thumped both timber feet into a heap of brick and broken stone work a yard or so from the base of the fractured wall, '. . . heave, get your shoulders behind it . . .' and the wobbling bamboo fingers reached six yards up into the night sky. '. . . bed it in . . .' Morgan could picture how the window cleaners at home would settle their ladders and make sure that the tops were firm against the walls of the house – but no lead or iron flew there.

This is like something out of the Dark Ages, he thought. Now I see why Hume said I was off playing Richard the Lionheart. Indeed, he caught sight of a flash of steel and swirling robes on the battlements above that would not have looked out of place in the Crusades.

'Corp'l Pegg . . .' Morgan had one foot and hand on the ladder's crosspieces, hoping that his weight would drive the legs more firmly into the rubble, '. . . Corp'l Pegg, where in God's name are you?' Morgan yelled in competition with all the crashes and bangs around him.

Curse the little sod, he thought. Just when I need him in

the same fighting trim that he was at Rowa, he bloody well disappears.

But at the third time of asking, Pegg's pale, sweaty face peeped round a file of the protection party.

'Get behind me, Pegg, and keep close. Don't fire whilst you're climbing up.' Morgan looked at Pegg's long Enfield rifle and realised how unlikely that was anyway. 'I'll clear any badmashes with my pistol, but I'll need you ready to shoot as soon as we're on the parapet; got it?'

Pegg gulped and nodded unhappily.

'Right, no more than four on the woodwork at any one time, and you men,' Morgan turned to the squad who were snapping rounds at the top of the wall whilst doing their best to avoid the shower of rocks and bricks that were being thrown blindly from inside the fort, 'hold your fire. Give me a volley just as I get to the top, understand?' But before they could reply, Morgan was hard at the rungs, climbing as if he were born to it, sword dangling from its knot on his right wrist, his pistol clenched between his teeth.

I must look like some bloody pirate, he thought as he scrambled on, remembering how his father had always insisted that they were descended from another Captain Morgan altogether, but I'm all but defenceless now unless I spit this Tranter at them.

The wood bowed below his and the other men's weight, the tops of the tines scraping up and down against the gritty stone of the walls, but on he climbed, hand over hand, the whole structure yawing despite the men below trying to hold it steady. Then he was suddenly aware that more was going on outside the bubble of his own fear and excitement. Morgan had heard another splintering crash against the brickwork ten paces off to his left, but all his attention had been focused on the enemies above his own stretch of wall.

Then he heard a bellow: 'Remember Cawnpore! No mercy, my boys!' and Kemp, like a great khaki ape, was swarming up the rungs, two pistols dangling round his neck from a single lanyard. But even as he stared at Kemp, he sensed a dark figure leaning far out of a shell-cracked fissure just above the highest reaches of his ladder. Something sang and flickered in the dark – a tulwar blade had come within a shave of the top of his head, cleaving the air but nothing else. Morgan trembled and clung to the ladder, even as the blade was swung again; it missed, but it forced him to duck and slip back down a rung. There was little that he could do now except hope for a bullet from the covering party to clear the way. But even as he dithered, Corporal Pegg below him gave the most ghastly shriek.

'Sir . . . sir, for pity's sake.' The yells pierced even the booms of gun and musketry, Pegg hanging, dying horribly and slowly, Morgan had no doubt, from some hideous wound. 'Oh Jesus, sir . . .' the cries redoubled, '. . . you're standing on me 'and.'

Then came the volley. Bullets chipped and whined around him, throwing up a cloud of dust from the bricks, a rifle ball hurling the defender back from the gap, allowing Morgan to leap forward and on to the firestep beyond the parapet, sword in one hand, his pistol, slimy with spit, in the other.

Even as he was taking his revolver from his mouth, trying to find his footing on the broken slabs deep in shadow behind the parapet, he heard a shout and drumming feet. Looking towards the towering flagstaff that lay further along the breastwork to his right, he could see wounded and dead lying in twisted heaps – victims of the artillery shells. But over them came a slight, fleet figure, running hard, robes streaming out behind, a glittering blade high above his greasy head, his mouth twisted into a mask of hate.

Then every fencing lesson that Morgan had had as a boy asserted itself, for he reached for his sword rather than his pistol and flicked his blade in a high, protective curve over his head, dropping to one knee as he did so. The tulwar scythed down.

Don't snap now, you useless bit of cutlery, thought Morgan as the Indian's sword clanged against his own. He'd always mistrusted the standard infantry officer's weapon, but this time it stood the test, his opponent slewing past him, staggering over the broken floor. He twisted round, pulled his own sabre back to deliver 'cut four' and struck.

'Ow . . . you bastard. Ow!' Morgan found himself shouting as he swiped hard enough at the back of the man's shoulder to sever his arm, yet merely bounced off his victim, jarring his hand and wrist painfully. There was a similar yelp from his target, but the blade failed to bite.

'Stand clear, sir.' Pegg barged his officer to one side: steel flickered and the native sprawled on his face, with the NCO's bayonet – which he must have fixed at lightning speed – dug fatally deep into the man's spine.

'I'm obliged to you, Corp'l Pegg – once again.' Pegg could be an awful shirker sometimes, Morgan thought as he fought for breath, but he was good in a roughhouse. 'But did you see that: my blade didn't even touch the sod.'

'Sir, I did. But look at this.' As Pegg pulled the bayonet from the dead man's back, so a span of tight, metal links came with it, showing through the rift in the native's jerkin. 'chain mail, sir, crafty heathens. You won't cut through that, but a good poke with a bit of Birmingham's best will do the job.'

I was right, I am back in the Dark Ages, thought Morgan as he looked at something that he'd last seen in a London museum.

'Come on, you two, stop fannying about.' Kemp with Rissaldar Batuk at his side, swept past them, just as a great gang of the Europeans came barrelling along the walkway in their wake, shouting and yelling at the tops of their voices. Morgan sprinted to overtake them; if they were going to haul down the Rhani's colours, he wanted to be there.

'Follow me, boys.' Now the troops were panting to keep

up with Morgan. 'Leave the dead; they'll do you no harm.' Morgan wanted the trophy, but the 3rd Bombay Europeans had very different ideas. Not a body or wounded man was left unturned, each corpse being expertly rifled, purses found in cummerbunds, mohurs in turbans and the linings of skull caps. As he reached the shot-splintered flagstaff and began to fumble with the halliard, the crowd just carried on going, tumbling down a flight of steps that led from the walls into the depths of the town.

'Stand firm, you men,' Morgan shouted after the disappearing forms; he and Kemp needed some form of protection from the bodyguard that the Rhani was bound to have with her – if she could be found.

'You stand fucking firm, mate.' And the pride of Bombay hooted off into the shadows, smoke and flames of Jhansi.

'Don't waste your breath, lad.' Kemp stood next to Morgan at the pole, scanning a pile of corpses at its base, his revolver hovering, ready. 'Those boys are after grog and gold; they won't be listening to you or any other officer. Leave them. And stop buggering about with that rag . . .' the big flag now lay in a pile at Morgan's feet, '. . . there's a better prize for the taking.'

Morgan looked at Kemp. The bulky, wheezy old warrior had gone; there stood a man twenty years younger, every fibre of him alive with what the popular newspapers called 'the joy of battle' (though Morgan had yet to experience such a thing), his eyes alight, his body just an extension of the pistol in his hand.

'*Namskaar . . . kahaang hai Lakshmi Bai?*' Kemp spoke clearly and firmly as a tattered native rose from the pile of dead men, grinned and made *namasti*.

'Jesus, sir, it's a bleedin' ghost.' Pegg pulled his rifle into the shoulder and aimed directly at the native's belly, but Kemp beckoned for him to lower the weapon as he and Rissaldar Batuk poured out more questions and instructions.

Another ripple of musketry lit the night as a further storming party straddled the battlements, but the Indian continued to grin and bob. Finally, Kemp reached into his shirt, pulled out a small cloth bag, heavy with gold and threw it across to the man; he caught it neatly and with no more ado, scampered off down the same steps that the Europeans had found, signalling for Kemp and the others to follow.

'Sorry about the delay, gentlemen.' The commandant turned on the steps and ducked as a shell burst to their front. 'Spot of haggling to be done. The Rhani's people don't come cheap. Just keep up with our friend here; he says he knows where the bitch is. But don't go picking any fights, we ain't got the muscle.' Pegg looked relieved at this last instruction as he stuffed the flag that Captain Morgan had told him to carry into his haversack.

The five men picked their way cautiously down a darkened alley, hearing the shouts and fire of what they could only guess was the Europeans' progress some way to their left, but paying it no attention. They rounded a corner; light from a burning building showed a junction ahead that led into some sort of open area or square, their guide flattening his palms in the universal sign for caution.

'Stay here, you three.' Even one of Kemp's whispers demanded instant obedience. 'I'll go on with this bucko for a look-see.' The two figures, one stick-thin and stealthy, the other stout but nimble as a leopard, crept forward, eventually lowering themselves onto the gritty earth and peeping round the corner of the alley just inches off the ground.

All Morgan could see was the two men lying side by side and watching something beyond them that was lit by the flames. Then the guide pointed slowly, tensely, before he put his lips close to Kemp's ear and murmured, Kemp almost immediately signalling the others to join him.

'Come on, stealthy now.' Morgan had already sheathed his sword, but he checked his pistol, making sure that none of the six percussion caps had fallen from their nipples. 'Crawl the last few paces.' The rissaldar and Pegg nodded their understanding and in minutes the three of them were creeping their way up to the junction.

A poky square no more than fifty paces across lay before them, three sides of which were dominated by high merchants' houses – one blazing fiercely – whilst the fourth consisted of the wall of the fortress, pierced by several embrasures. In the middle of the open ground stood a dozen or so nervous, shifting horses, some with riders, others being held by a variety of native troops. The firelight reflected off scabbards and carbine barrels, off long-rowelled spurs and polished metal helmets.

'Look there, Morgan.' Kemp had taken off his topee; now his long hair hung down over his brow as he mouthed, 'What do you make of that?'

A handful of darkly robed men were in the saddle, others stood by their horses' heads, but in their middle was one mounted, helmeted figure who was obviously giving orders. On a pony to the rear of the group seemed to be two children astride the same saddle and, close to them, half obscured by the other riders, a fair-skinned, willowy figure.

'I think there's a memsahib there, Commandant . . .' Morgan felt as if the breath had been knocked out of him by the sight, '. . . at the back of the gang . . . look; and there's two boys on that pony, ain't there?' The blood thundered through Morgan's head. After all this time, all these dangers, there was his woman and the son he'd never seen, just yards from him.

'No, damn them. That's the little bint I'm interested in, there in the centre, giving voice – just as you'd expect.' Kemp pointed to the person in the midst of the group whose face was obscured by the metal of a nose-piece and a curtain of chain mail. 'Pegg, I'd be grateful if you'd pass me your rifle. Is it primed?'

'It's *Corporal* Pegg, if you don't mind, sir.' Pegg checked that the hammer was at half cock as he passed the weapon forward. 'An' of course it's ready. I'm not some bloody crow, you know, sir,' he bristled.

'Aye, well, an Enfield ball should cool her ardour.' Kemp moved carefully into the kneeling position, pulled the long rifle into his shoulder and thumbed the hammer back in one smooth movement.

As he curled his finger round the trigger and squinted at the easy target, there was a lull in the artillery fire, a sudden quiet, in which the Rhani's high, commanding voice was clearly audible. Those should have been the last words she ever said, but as the hammer came down there was just the pop of the cap's detonation. The rifle had misfired.

'Devil take it. Use your pistols, for Christ's sake.' And in an instant Kemp had let the weapon drop and was on his feet firing his revolver, with Morgan hastily doing the same whilst the rissaldar, smooth as silk, snapped a shot off from his carbine.

Only Rissaldar Batuk's round found a mark, wounding one of the escort whose yelp ripped the night. But the other bullets did no damage at the forty or so yards from which they fired, except to frighten the horses. A few balls came in reply, flying equally wide, but by the time the powder smoke had cleared, all Morgan could see were frightened faces and sparking hoofs as the knot of cavalry spurred towards the far wall. In the middle of the group rode the other woman. She was doing her best to keep up with a bearded mutineer, still in his John Company coat, and on a big chestnut, who was dragging the pony and its cargo along with him by a leading rein.

'Mary . . . Mary Keenan!' Morgan yelled and, for an instant, the girl slowed her mount and stared, wide-eyed and beautiful through the dark, looking straight into his face. She pulled her horse to a standstill, her mouth open, trying to form words, but then she turned to look as her son was led away, and in an instant she was kicking hard at the flanks of her horse and following the rest of the galloping party straight towards the battlements.

'God, they're not going to jump that, are they?' Kemp gasped as the dozen riders put their beasts up the wide flight of steps that led to the walls and then, one by one, bounded through the gun embrasures, and disappeared from sight. 'They'll bloody kill themselves!'

As they ran towards the stone breastwork, Morgan remembered the horseman who had leapt to his death at Kotah. Lungs heaving, he reached the parapet and looked over, expecting to see a tangle of smashed bodies far below. But even in the dark he could see that the jump, though severe, was possible, as a grassy bank reached up to a point no more than twelve feet below the wall. It had claimed one victim: a horse whinnied pitifully with a broken leg, a sowar lying motionless on the ground alongside, but in the light of the half-moon, Morgan could just see the rest of the group riding off towards a point of the siege lines that he knew to be thinly manned.

'Damn her to hell,' growled Kemp. 'The bloody woman must have had that planned to perfection. Right, men, the only one of us who can shoot is the rissaldar. So, back to the horses and let's get after her.'

NINE

Pursuit

''Oo exactly was that native, anyway, sir?' Pegg's face was creased with incomprehension, his voice lurching each time he thumped uncomfortably on his horse's saddle. 'An' why did the commandant knife 'im like that?'

As soon as Kemp, Morgan, Pegg and the rissaldar had joined up with the rest of the party, they had galloped off as hard as they could in the wan light of dawn, keen to find their enemy's trail. But Lance-Corporal Pegg was perturbed. Eight months into this, his second campaign, he was hardened to most things, but after the Rhani's escape over the fortress walls he had witnessed an act of cold brutality that he simply did not understand.

'As far as I can gather, he was a spy – someone close to Lakshmi Bai – who'd been bribed by the commandant to tell us where she was.' Morgan hadn't been made privy to the details of the betrayal.

'Well, sir, if 'e were on our side, why did the commandant destroy 'im?' Pegg wasn't going to let the issue go. 'Wouldn't it 'ave been useful to keep 'im with us whilst we was giving chase?'

'I suppose, Corp'l Pegg, the commandant felt he couldn't trust him; if he was willing to sell out his own queen, he could just as easily turn on us.' Despite this emollience,

Morgan had been horrified to see Kemp grab the native – who was still crouching at the throat of the alley when they had left him in the skirmish with the Rhani's troop – drag him bodily to his feet and then push a long sliver of steel under the man's sternum, stabbing up into his aorta. The native died silently, just a look of surprise on his face as Kemp let him drop. Then he'd reached into the man's belt and retrieved the purse of money with just a mumbled, 'Ah, the wages of sin . . .'

'Bloody 'ell, sir, remind me not to get on the wrong side o' Clemency bleedin' Kemp, won't you?'

And that sentiment came from Lancc-Corporal Charlie Pegg, thought Morgan, the man who would ransack his dead mates' kit before they were even cold; the man who'd shot a priest out East without blinking. As everyone had warned him, Kemp was turning into a very tricky confederate indeed. Morgan was trying to think of something loyal but sympathetic to Pegg's view when the NCO spoke again.

'Ay-up, sir, it looks as though you're wanted.' Down the files of trotting hussars and irregulars, came Kemp, holding his big grey in check whilst the rest of the cavalrymen passed by. In the early light, Pegg and Morgan's red coats stood out especially starkly in the files of blue and khaki; now their leader reined in alongside.

'Rissaldar Batuk's found their hoofprints; he reckons they're about an hour and a half in front of us, but the Rhani will insist on stopping to pray and eat at about midday.' The bulky officer sat comfortably in the saddle, almost an extension of his horse, in contrast to Pegg's ungainly posture. 'Reckon you can keep this pace up, young Pegg?'

'It's *Corporal* Pegg, sir. Course I can. This is nowt to what we did in Russia, sir,' Pegg puffed in reply.

'Hmm . . . I'm sure. Be a good fellow and make yourself scarce for a while, would you, son?' Kemp jerked his head for Pegg to leave him alone with Morgan.

'Yer what, sir?' Pegg was confused by the commandant's subtlety.

'Just fuck off for a minute, will you? I need to speak to Captain Morgan privately,' Kemp replied.

When Pegg had at last grasped what the officers wanted and kicked ahead to join the hussars in their cloud of dust, Kemp slowed his horse, pulling it a little way away from the jangling column, Morgan alongside him.

'I'm glad we've got a chance to speak alone, sir.' Ever since Kemp's lynching of dozens of prisoners outside Awah three months ago, Morgan had been trying to screw up his courage to speak to the man about his excesses. Perhaps he might have found the careless murders more acceptable if they had been committed by someone he didn't know, but Kemp was his father's best friend – the only link out here with Glassdrumman and rainy civilisation. The shocked face of that man in the alley, though, had been too much for him; Morgan couldn't connive any more. 'That native you killed back in the town—'

But Morgan wasn't allowed to continue.

'Aye, I saw the look on your face – and on his. He was a traitor, Morgan, just like all these damn Pandies, and this one had outlived his usefulness.'

'But he was—' Morgan tried to interrupt.

'No, hold your tongue, boy.' Any geniality had gone from Kemp's voice. 'He was just another piece of scum who's better off cold. And you can't know this, but that lad in the red coat was – I'm pretty sure – Sepoy Lolemum Dunniah, formerly of the Company's Twelfth Regiment of Native Infantry, the very man who ate my own salt and then butchered my wife.' Morgan had seen Kemp's bitter, unreasoned hatred before. 'And now that we're talking about betrayal, what do you make of the lovely Mrs Keenan's conduct, for that's who it was in the Rhani's party, was it not?'

'It was, Commandant.' Morgan's belly tightened at the memory of the fleeting glimpse he'd had of the girl. 'Why, she's a hostage, is she not? She's being held against her will by Lakshmi Bai, ain't she?'

Morgan had scarcely admitted to himself that Mary had fled just a little too readily, her horse spurred on just a little too keenly. Why, he wondered to himself, would she want to see him? There was the child, for sure, but a child he'd never seen and a child that James Keenan had treated as his own. He'd hardly tried to pursue her, had he? And he knew how strong-willed – cussed, some would say – Mary could be. Others had thrown in their lot with the natives, after all.

'Is she, though?' queried Kemp. 'She could have made a break for it back in that square, I fancy. And it's mighty queer company she's keeping: murderin' Pandies and rene-gade rhanis. Not without risk, I grant you, but then that leap over the battlements was bloody dangerous too. Dressed as a native, she was; wouldn't any loyal woman have made a run for it there and then, particularly once she'd grabbed an eyeful of you? I suspect that your comely friend might have "gone bush", been spending too much time with the bloody natives and caught a nasty dose of treachery. There's plenty of examples, you know. Look at that white sergeant-major who was fighting with the enemy in Lucknow.'

'Aye, sir, I've heard those stories as well, but it's much simpler than that. You saw those two boys on the pony, didn't you? I can't swear to it because I don't know either by sight, but I'll wager that they were Damodar – the young pretender – and Mrs Keenan's son. Roped to the saddle, as far as I could see, and being towed around by that pug-ugly that you now tell me is Dunniah. What mother's going to abandon her child in such circumstances?' But Morgan had wondered when Mary galloped off with scarcely a backward glance and then dared that appalling leap over the castle's walls.

'You think? You really believe that a woman of spirit like Mary wouldn't take every opportunity she could to get away from these savages?' Clearly, Kemp's mind was made up. Morgan suspected that the commandant saw treachery round every corner – yet he harboured many of the same doubts.

'Of course she wouldn't, sir, not if her child was being held,' Morgan replied, trying not to let his own worries show.

'Hmm . . . I wonder. Well, we shall see, won't we, for I'm expecting the next round of this contest very shortly.' The harshness had gone from Kemp's voice. 'Then, perhaps, we shall have a chance to judge where Mrs Keenan's loyalty really lies.'

The sun was hot in the sky now, the dust as dense and choking as ever. Where Jhansi had been mostly green and fertile, the further they got away from the fortress town on the road to Gwalior, the flatter, browner and increasingly parched the landscape became. The few villages that they passed through, though, were remarkably untouched, for this part of Mahratta country had yet to see any real campaigning. Other than a little marching and counter-marching by the local princelings' troops as they jockeyed for position whilst the British were distracted, the country had been left alone. As a result, the natives were still naïvely friendly, turning out to line the road and gawp as the column of grey-powdered horsemen clattered by. Roly-poly children with great, curious eyes came to watch the cavalcade, whilst cadaverous chickens ran squawking from the horses' hoofs as they pounded on without check. In normal circumstances – if these times could even begin to be described as normal – thought Morgan, such places would be ripe for the torches and blades of Kemp's men, but the urgency of the pursuit spared them.

Half blind and choked by the swirling grit, sore from the saddle and dazed from a night without sleep, Morgan failed to spot the pair of horsemen who came tearing back to report to Kemp at the front of the column.

'Bit of a *ramasammy* goin' on up front, sir.' Pegg pulled the handkerchief that he'd knotted about his mouth to one side. 'Commandant's all a-fluster, look.'

Kemp was like a hunting dog, thought Morgan, as two of his scouts – both loyal Indians from one of the disaffected cavalry regiments – pointed excitedly towards a stand of trees that were just visible above a low bank. The commandant stood in the saddle, every sinew taut, quivering as he first raised his arm for the column to stop, then flapped his hand in the field signal for 'Dismount and await orders'.

''E wants you sir.' Pegg had seen Kemp tap his shoulder and then place his hand on his helmet – another set of silent hand signals meaning 'Officers to me'. 'I bet 'e's got the scent of that Rhani lass.'

'I trust you're right, Corp'l Pegg and it's not another bloody porker,' said Morgan as he pulled Emerald from the line of march and gently nudged her into a trot with his spurs.

'Right, you lot.' Kemp's irregular gentlemen crowded around their commander just as Morgan arrived. They were all filthy, their faces and beards masked with grime, the miscellany of swords and pistols that stuck from sashes or hung from cross-belts all covered with a thin layer of powdered dirt. 'Our boys reckon they've found her. Stay in the saddle, let's just walk forward a few paces and have a look. Slowly, no dust cloud, now, and shield your field glasses. Her sentries will be as shagged out as we are, but I don't want any flashing lenses to alert them.'

The clutch of riders moved cautiously forward until they were just peeping above the scrub-covered bank. Along with the other half-dozen, Morgan pulled his binoculars from their leather case that hung around his shoulder and raised then gently, his hands cupped over the ends. About a mile away, he could see a clump of date palms that were dense in the middle, sparser at the edges, concealing, he thought, some sort of walls or buildings. Down the wind came the faint cawing of rooks and crows, which had been disturbed by something below them; now they circled on black, tattered wings high above.

'Wind's pretty well in our faces, boys. She'll have dogs out with her sentinels so any move from behind – upwind – will have to be quick and hard. If we give her any warning at all, she'll be away as fast as light. Right, here's the plan. Cornet Breen, I want you to keep our boys,' Kemp pointed to the thirty dishevelled irregulars, who were now squatting in the cover behind them, most watering their horses, 'and half the hussars to form a firing line on that bund yonder.' Kemp pointed out a thorn-topped bank, which wobbled in the sun about eight hundred paces to their front. 'You'll need to move now, slowly, and some of the way on foot if you're to get there unseen. Soon as you're there, Morgan and I will assault from the left, from that bit of village.' Again, Kemp raised his arm slowly in order not to attract attention, and pointed way off into the distance. 'We'll go in with the sabre and pistols. I want you, Breen, to drop any of the bastards that run with carbine fire. I expect there'll be a bit of a set-about with her bodyguards to let her and her followers get away, and that's when you've got to make every round count: fire at the nags and we'll deal with the survivors.' Kemp looked deliberately at Morgan. 'Shoot everyone, Breen; control your fire. I don't want any gaps whilst you reload. Any questions?'

There were no questions – everyone understood their lethal tasks. Morgan just sat and stared numbly; in the chaos that was about to be unleashed, there would be no quarter for Mary or for Sam.

'Fuckin' mongrel's giving it some, sir.' Pegg, along with the dozen 8th Hussars, Kemp and Morgan, was picking his way through the deserted village that lay about one hundred paces west of the clump of date palms. In the twenty minutes that it had taken them to skirt round to this flank, all had been quiet. Breen's troops seemed to have moved undetected and this barking was the first sign that the rebels might have had that something was in the wind. 'There's some movement in the brush, sir.'

Pegg pointed to a flash of light-coloured robes in the tree line. As the assault party had first ridden, then walked carefully round in a broad hook, Morgan had seen how the covert had changed shape. Dense at the southern side, from where he had first scanned it with his glasses, the trees thinned out to the north, broadening into a tear-drop of cover some two hundred and fifty paces long and seventy wide. Thorns and low brush gave way to an open area in the middle where a tiny dilapidated Muslim temple stood, its white walls and wood-shingled roof now crumbling. There were at least two thin columns of hazy smoke rising from behind the walls.

'Yes, I can see it, and those bloody birds are off again.' Morgan caught Kemp's elbow and pointed as they peered round a low mud wall.

'Well spotted, Corp'l Pegg,' Kemp muttered as he studied the target. 'Bloody lookouts know something's up now. Is Breen in place yet, Morgan?'

How in God's name am I supposed to know? thought Morgan. 'He should be, sir. He's had plenty of time and there's been no disturbances.'

'Well, it's too late now.' The dog had worked itself into a frenzy of barks. 'Use these walls for cover, mount, form line and move on my signal, if you please, Cap'n Morgan.'

Farrier-Corporal Martin was leading the dozen hussars; now he looked up keenly from under the peak of his covered cap, grasping Morgan's hand signals perfectly and shaking out his file of men behind the screen of the tattered buildings. As the last man mounted, Kemp – crouching low in the saddle – trotted down the file and broke cover as he put his horse up a ditch and onto the dirt road.

With a rasp he pulled his sword from its scabbard, pointed it at the enemy and, abandoning all caution, yelled, 'Come on, the Balaklava Boys. Give these Pandies what you gave the fucking Tsar!' touching just the right nerve with the 8th Hussars, jealous as they were of their record.

The men responded, horses skittering right and left of the commandant, blades singing from their sheaths as they prepared for battle, hoofs scrabbling at the dirt, leaping from a standstill into a fast canter. From the tree line two balls of smoke blossomed as the sentries fired at their attackers, both rounds humming high over the line of horsemen as sabre blades fell and a long, low snarl came from the lips of the Irish 8th.

'What d'you want me to do, sir?' panted Pegg as he dug his heels into his horse's ribs; he was unarmed except for the Enfield rifle slung across his back. 'I'll go back an' wait for you, shall I?'

Morgan hadn't given a thought to Pegg, still less supplied him with a suitable weapon. His eye was sighting down his blade at one of the Rhani's men, who was sprinting as if his life depended upon it – which it did.

'No, damn you, just keep up with . . .' But he was too distracted by the tricky business of running a moving man through from the saddle to give Pegg any more attention. Nothing he had ever done had prepared him for this. Fencing lessons as a boy were one thing, and high fences with the West Meath were another, but he'd never combined the two. Point or edge – what had Finn the ex-lancer always said to him? But there was no time to try to remember as the Indian ducked under his horse's nose, and the powerful slash that had been designed to cleave his collarbone met nothing more solid than fresh air. The effort nearly unseated Morgan as he struggled to keep his feet in his stirrups.

Then came a cry from behind: 'There, yer bastard!'

As Morgan wheeled his horse for another go at his foe, he found that Lance-Corporal Pegg had dealt with him without the benefit of expensive fencing lessons; indeed, without even the benefit of a weapon. He'd kicked the man firmly in the mouth with a steel-shod toe. Then a hussar reached low and finished the job with a neat thrust from his sabre. But even as they wheeled and turned around the corpse, a spatter of bullets flew around them as Kemp and the rest of the troops fell on the Rhani's people.

From the look of things, thought Morgan, the princess and her bodyguard had done just as they had expected and paused around midday for prayers and food. The temple had probably been a defendable convenience rather than preplanned stopping place, and, judging by the doused fires and the speed of the Indians' reactions, they had just been about to mount and move on. Now all was chaos as a knot of men knelt and fired at the British, others tried to load the last bits of kit onto their saddles, whilst the rest fought with frightened horses to get their feet in their stirrups and turn to face the attackers.

'Sir, look, the commandant's got 'is 'ands full.' Pegg, unarmed as he was, and to his enormous credit, whacked his horse with the ends of his reins and set off towards Kemp, who was cutting and thrusting for all he was worth against three mounted opponents.

'Come on, Corp'l Martin, follow me,' cried Morgan as the NCO, another hussar and he plunged into the hoofs and flicking blades that surrounded the commandant.

Martin was hard up against his left stirrup as Emerald – gutsy little mare that she was – barged into one of the mutineer's chargers, sending horse and rider sprawling on the ground. The impact threw Morgan's aim, but next to him, Corporal Martin pulled his arm back and thrust just as his horse came level with the back of one of Kemp's assailants.

All the Indian's attention was focused on his quarry; he'd just been parried by Kemp and was pulling his arm back for another jab when Martin's sabre hit him squarely in the back of his left lung. Morgan could only admire the way that the farrier-corporal turned the blade at the last moment so that it could slip between the cavalryman's ribs without jamming. Indeed, there was a look of impressed surprise on the victim's face as the reddened sword emerged through the front of his tunic; he dropped his tulwar and reins and feebly groped at the steel before tumbling out of the saddle, Martin pulling the sabre from the dead man with one smooth movement.

'Neatly done, Corp'l Martin,' gasped Morgan, as his horse danced to avoid the bodies on the ground below them. 'Have a care!' But even as he warned Martin about the third sowar, who had realised the danger and was reining his mount back and preparing to defend himself, the commandant struck. It was a roundhouse blow, a catharsis for every bit of his hatred for the mutineers and all their works. Kemp, Morgan noticed, had acquired an ordinary cavalry private's sword, the blade of which he had honed at every opportunity; now he put sixteen stone of venom behind the sickling steel as he brought it from behind his left shoulder in a great, slashing arc. As his arm straightened, so Sheffield's best hit the sowar just below the left ear and sheared the top off his head. Away went a dome of bone, skin and hair with a skull cap clinging to it, just like a knife slicing through a soft-boiled egg.

Even as Morgan shook himself clear of this scrimmage, he became aware of another party of riders putting as much distance as they could between themselves and their pursuers.

'Look there, sir.' Morgan tried to seize Kemp's attention, for the older man was still marvelling in the sight of his decapitated victim. 'I fancy that's the Rhani and her retinue making off.' He pointed to twenty or so horsemen who were still just visible through the trees some hundred paces away.

'Aye, most likely. The bodyguard have done a good job

of delaying us,' the hussars were rounding up the few sowars whom they had decided not to hack or stab, the prisoners begging pathetically for mercy, 'but Breen will settle the Rhani's hash once they leave the cover of the trees,' Kemp chuckled.

Aye, and anyone else who's with her, thought Morgan, railing at his own impotence.

'Deal with those Pandies, will you, Corp'l Martin.' Kemp casually condemned the captives. 'Come on, Morgan, let's see what practice our sharpshooters make,' and off he set, spurring his horse just as the Rhani's party left the cover of the trees and broke into the open ground.

What in God's name can be done? Morgan felt sick as he thundered after Kemp. *Is she there at all – I can't see her?* But he knew he was grasping at straws. If Mary were a valuable hostage she wouldn't be allowed to go free, and if she were with the Rhani willingly, there she would stay, especially if her son was with her.

The fugitives, now only thirty or so by Morgan's reckoning, kicked up their own smudge of dust as they galloped across the plain, making it hard for Morgan to see the details of any riders at all in his binoculars.

'Can you see any sign of Breen's people, Morgan?' Kemp and he had pulled up at the edge of the trees, the commandant shielding his eyes from the sun. 'They should open fire any minute now.'

Morgan dragged his glasses away from the fleeing horse rumps with great reluctance and slewed them round to find the covering party. He searched the top of the bank, where he knew they were meant to be, without success whilst, as each minute passed, the Rhani's party lengthened the range for the waiting carbines.

'Where the devil have they got to?' cursed Kemp. 'They'll be safe away unless Breen stirs himself.'

But even as he spoke, a carbine popped, another, two

more, then silence. Morgan's stomach dropped at the sound, but as he studied the puffs of smoke that flew from the bank, he could see hussars and irregulars rushing up, throwing themselves down, scrabbling with their weapons. The covering party had obviously been slower than Kemp had hoped and Morgan had dreaded. Far from being poised and ready for the target to cross their front, they had had to sprint to their firing positions, snatching potshots rather than firing deliberately at properly estimated ranges. The result was predictable: the Rhani and her people flew unscathed – whilst a rush of guilty relief swept over Morgan.

'God dammit to hell . . .' There were no histrionics from Kemp; he was too good a soldier for that, thought Morgan. His plan had failed so he would design a new one without further waste of time. 'We've missed her again. Right, Morgan, gather up our folk that are back at the temple; Corp'l Pegg, hack off to Mr Breen and ask him to be good enough to join us at that tank . . .' Kemp pointed to a pool of stagnant water some little way to the front, '. . . as soon as possible. We'll run the bloody woman to ground yet.'

With Pegg bumping away to pass Kemp's message to the covering party, Morgan trotted back into the trees and buildings, pleased to be by himself even for a few minutes. But as he reached the temple he found the hussars and their NCOs milling around, some in the saddle, dithering, others picking over the half-dozen corpses that littered the ground, and two dismounted, pointing their carbines at four dishevelled prisoners, one of whom held his hand to an arm that bled badly. There was fear in the Indians' eyes, their clothes were torn and travel-stained and their hair and beards matted with dust; they pressed themselves together for comfort whilst the British decided upon their fate.

'Are all your men unhurt, Corp'l Martin?' Morgan saw

the look of relief in the hussar's face when an officer arrived and took command.

'Sir,' Martin stiffened in the saddle, 'we're all fine, sir. Just wondering about these prisoners, I am.'

'The commandant told you to deal with them, didn't he?' Morgan knew the answer to his question.

''E did, sir, but . . .' the soldiers looked at their corporal, as did the prisoners, with wide, mute, pleading eyes, '. . . I'm not sure what 'e wants exactly. We can't tek 'em wi' us but we can't just shoot 'em, can we?' Martin was desperately hoping that Morgan would make the decision for him. 'They all fought fair, sir, an' it's not as if they're mutineers exactly – they've been loyal to their queen.'

Morgan was surprised to see such a sense of fair play in one of the men; he thought that all notions of justice had been swept from their heads by the brutality of the fighting, by the newspapers and windbag politicians baying for revenge.

'Let the poor devils go, Corp'l Martin. You've beaten the fight out of this lot. They've no weapons and you've taken their ponies, ain't you?'

'We have, sir.' There was no mistaking the burden that fell from Corporal Martin's shoulders as the decision was made. 'We shot four and kept the only two mounts that are fit, but they'll do for us baggage.'

'Well done.' Morgan saw the two guards lower their weapons and shoo the prisoners to freedom, the Indians scuttling away like rats let free from a sack. 'But fire a few shots to hurry them on their way, won't you?'

'Why's that, sir?' asked Corporal Martin.

'Just do as I say, man,' replied Morgan quietly.

'Sir: you four . . .' Martin had cottoned on, '. . . fire a round each into the ground.' The order was followed immediately by shots from the soldiers, who understood Morgan's ruse precisely.

'Get your men moving then, Corp'l Martin,' Morgan hoped

that the fleeing prisoners would have the sense to stay in cover until Kemp was far away, 'for Himself wants the hide off the Rhani.'

'One of their nags is hurt, Commandant.' Cornet Breen, still smarting from his earlier failure, was keen to regain some credit. At first he'd seen just the odd spot of blood amongst the earth churned by their quarry's hoof's, but as the pace of the relentless chase had increased, so the spots had become splashes. Now there were florin-sized, sticky gobs of gore every few paces. 'And they've got no spares.'

'You're right, Breen; she'll keep going overnight and as long as we don't lose her in the dark we'll have her by morning, for she's got to slow down. Pass the word for the farrier, if you please.'

They'd continued the chase as quickly as they could after the failed ambush, Kemp rounding his people up, issuing fresh orders and directions, and pushing on as rapidly as possible, but the Rhani had taken every advantage and put as much distance between herself and her pursuers as she could.

Morgan looked at Kemp as they trotted side by side. Little sleep and sparse food and water seemed to suit the man, despite his being the oldest person in the column by far. Most of the others were wilting under the merciless sun and the pace that the commandant was setting; more than twenty hours of chasing and fighting without a pause would test the finest of horse-soldiers.

'Sir, you blew for me.' Martin, slurring his speech as ever, reined in beside Kemp and saluted.

'I'd be obliged, Corp'l Martin, for your thoughts on our mounts and their weaknesses.' Kemp had been impressed with Martin's quiet skills over the last few hectic days and nights.

'Sir, all the mounts is tired and Private Fenn's has got a

278

split developing in his nearside rear hoof.' Martin was even more attentive than he'd realised, thought Morgan. 'But I can shift him to one of the bat-ponies if there's no great chase a-coming, though you'll not get more than another night's march out of most of 'em, sir, if you continue spanking along like this.'

'We've done well to get this far with only a couple of thrown shoes, thanks to you, Corp'l Martin.' Kemp was genuinely pleased with Martin's husbandry. 'Shift Fenn, and I guarantee you that we'll halt to rest and mend if we've not overtaken the Rhani by mid-morning. Meanwhile, keep your eye on every nag, for we've a hard night ahead of us.'

And a hard night it was. There was little moon by which to follow the blood and hoof trail and Kemp ordered fifteen minutes' trot in every hour rather than the fast walk that had been the norm during every other night-march. They'd paused to water the horses shortly after midnight in the cover of a grove of barren fruit trees, but they had to stop again almost as soon as the chase resumed after a man was found to be missing. Corporal Martin, to his intense embarrassment, had to admit to leaving one of his soldiers behind: Private Ford had dismounted and fallen fast asleep, not even stirring once the column moved out. He was only roused when a boot was applied to his softer parts. But that was the only distraction. The periods of trotting seemed to come more and more often to Morgan as every man – except Kemp, of course – strained to stay awake and alert in the saddle.

Dinners and hunts, deeds and misdeeds from the Sikh wars, Billy Morgan's doings and great horses they had known helped to pass the time as Kemp and Morgan walked and trotted their horses at the front of the column. This was the old Kemp, the fine soldier and good companion, though Morgan still expected some sally from the commandant about Mary and her loyalty. But, perhaps because of Lance-Corporal

Pegg's insistence on riding within earshot of the officers' conversation, he was spared.

Other than for Kemp's regular, 'Trot-march . . . pass the word,' the pair talked of nothing but Billy Morgan and mutual friends, bringing Glassdrumman to life whilst they traversed mud and dust, grit and pebbles, through swamp, brush and glade, always accompanied by the steady tide of sweat beneath their belts, the click and hum of insects and the smell of damp saddle leather. Every hour, one of the two scouts who rode a few hundred paces in front of the main column would be replaced but, other than that, there was nothing to distract them from the tedium and the tiredness. Just as first light approached, Morgan noticed that even Kemp began to flag. His prattle dried up as the deep blue of the night gave way to the dove-grey of dawn, and the glittering stars began to fade.

'Walk-march . . . pass the word,' was given, the column slowed with a, 'Thank fuck for that,' mouthed by Pegg but echoed, Morgan had no doubt, by every man in the saddle as a torpor settled over each weary soldier and horse.

It's still bloody dark in here, thought Morgan as the track led them into a dense grove of broad-leaved trees. This would be a grand place for a quick halt and a drop of water before the sun gets up. Morgan had let himself drop behind Kemp. He spurred Emerald forward.

'Commandant, don't you think—' But just as Kemp turned a sleepy eye towards Morgan, the shadows were lit by a volley of flame, and the din of cicadas drowned by crashing gunfire only a few paces away from them.

Yells and screams came from their rear as the ambush hit hard at the centre of their column where the troopers and baggage ponies were most tightly grouped. Morgan just had time to peer behind him, to see hussars and others being tumbled from their saddles whilst exhausted horses fell over, shot, or bucked and jibbed in terror. Then Pegg charged alongside him, slapping Emerald's bottom as hard as he could, driving her into a gallop to get away from the chaos, hurt and noise.

'Come on, sir, get yer se'n out of 'ere.' Pegg's horse was going as hard as Morgan's own petrified mare now was. 'It ain't healthy. Get after the commandant, move yerself, sir!' And Pegg was right. The last place that Morgan needed to be was wheeling back into the cacophony of bangs and screams behind him. The commandant's instinct was – as usual – right: he was hunched low in the saddle, arcing swiftly through the dark scrub away from the ambush party, hoping to loop round their flank and counterattack – no matter how few horsemen he had with him.

'Bloody woman, sharper than I thought. The scouts should have seen those bastards whilst they was waiting for us – and I should have been ready for something like this.' Other than for the odd pop of the hussars' pistols, the gunfire had all but ceased now. NCOs' brazen voices were trying to reorganise the shattered party. 'Now those buggers will try to sneak away before our people can regroup. Their horses will be held somewhere over there, I'd wager.' As they circled back on themselves as fast as the clinging branches of thorn and scrub would allow them, Kemp pointed with his pistol barrel towards denser bushes some yards back from the track up which thy had just trotted. 'If we can shoot their nags . . .'

Morgan had come to much the same conclusion, but as they edged past a dark, dense stand of brush, a gout of flame seared itself onto his eyeballs, a pistol boomed just feet away and the commandant clutched at his shoulder with a half-formed curse as his charger tried to bolt away from the noise.

'Get at 'em, Corp'l Pegg,' roared Morgan, digging his spurs in hard and firing his own pistol blindly into the bush. 'Come on, man.'

As Emerald collided with a bigger horse, another flash and

bang erupted almost in Morgan's face. The yellow streak of flame lit the scene for a fraction of a second.

'Dunniah, you bastard!' yelped Kemp, grabbing at his wound and trying to control his frightened horse.

Morgan glimpsed the bearded, red-coated horseman clutching a heavy, double-barrelled pistol that, had it not been for the impact of the two mounts, would probably have gone off right against his chest. Now the Indian scrambled to stay in the saddle as the ball hummed harmlessly away into the edging dawn, his horse anchored by a cat's cradle of reins to another pony upon which sat, as far as Morgan could see in the semidark, two children, who were bawling at the tops of their voices. The more Morgan urged his horse forward, the more the three animals became entwined. Before he knew what was happening, he was thigh to thigh, saddle to saddle with his attacker, and both men had dropped their pistols, grabbing and gripping one another, trying with desperate strength to wrestle the other to the ground.

Morgan felt the breath being squeezed from him by strong limbs that now had his head in a fierce lock. Rasping, curry breath enveloped him as he tried to pull his arms back far enough to get a decent punch at his assailant. But Dunniah saw his advantage; the more space he gave the Feringhee, the more dangerous an opponent he would be, so he held on tight to the white man's neck as the horses whinnied and the children screamed about him.

Try as he might, Morgan could not get himself free.

It's just like being at the bottom of a rugby scrum when the bloody thing collapses, he thought inconsequentially as his lungs shook at his ribs in protest. This is no way to go.

Then: 'Get off of my officer, yer dirty, fuckin' Pandy.' Fluent Wirksworth was being growled as punches perfected in the Bear and Billet found their mark. 'You 'eathen bastard,' completed the refrain as Pegg and his horse joined the mad merry-go-round of grunting men, tangled horses and shrieking boys.

282

Pegg's onslaught took effect. Under a flurry of blows, the bruised mutineer let go of Morgan and kicked his horse far enough away from those of his two attackers to allow him to draw his tulwar.

'Have a care, Corp'l Pegg!' Morgan alerted the NCO as the blade flickered in a semicircle, striking nothing, but driving both Britons back and allowing the sepoy to drag the pony and its terrified cargo clear. For no more than a few seconds, the three men sat on their horses, glaring at each other, trying to get their breath, whilst the sword blade hovered menacingly.

Any order that might have been restored, though, was stillborn. Just as Dunniah reached to shorten the rein that attached the children's horse to his own, confusion returned.

'You *barnshoot!*' This, bellowed at the top of a powerful voice, accompanied thunderous hoofs that seemed, to Morgan at least, to have come from nowhere. 'That's Damodar. I'll nab the little brute; get that fucker Dunniah.' Kemp, wounded and bleeding as he was, had immediately grasped what Morgan, Pegg and he had stumbled upon. The horses that were beginning to settle started bucking and prancing again as the big man and bigger horse flung themselves into the mêlée. Morgan could see that Kemp was in no condition to tackle Dunniah, but he grabbed the larger of the two boys and began to pull at the child for all that he was worth, for he realised that by seizing her precious son he could disable the Rhani as a commander in the field.

Pegg and Morgan had little choice but to launch themselves again at the muscular Dunniah before he had a chance to cut at Kemp. With a shout they pushed their horses forward as the Indian tried unsuccessfully to manoeuvre his horse back and out of reach. But he'd forgotten the reins that bound him to the other pony. Neither had Kemp accounted for the ropes that were tied to the boys' ankles and passed under their mount's belly. The more he tugged at Damodar, the more the creature and the boy objected; so did poor, two-year-old Samuel, sandwiched between his deeply alarmed elder, and sixteen stone of sweating, cursing, bleeding colonel of irregular cavalry. There was utter chaos.

As Kemp swore and pulled, Pegg and Morgan tried to get inside Dunniah's guard, ducking and swerving at each flick of the man's steel. In the dark and confusion, Emerald caught a slight gash across her nose that made her throw her head up high, whinnying in pain as she did so, but as the sword flashed back in the other direction, Morgan, even as he reached across to draw his own sword, found his reins slack in his hand. They had been cut and he had no more control over his wounded horse than his heels could provide. Game as she was, the mare needed the bit to keep her head towards the fight, but with no control from her master, she swerved away.

In the dark and pandemonium, Morgan – to his eternal regret – saw only flashes of the next vignette. Just as he lost control of his charger, another rider joined the jostling mob. The arrival of a further fury only became obvious when yet more curses were added to the bedlam.

'Keep your hands off them wee 'uns, you feckin' thing.' From the sound of it, an angry daughter of Erin had joined the uproar, and a familiar one at that. 'Get away, you dirty bowsie!' The virago went straight for Kemp.

Morgan was doing his best to help Pegg in his unarmed assault on the sepoy so he sensed more than saw a flurry of whirling hands slapping, punching and clawing at Kemp's head and his wounded shoulder, and the commandant's shrinking from the attack with uncharacteristic speed. Morgan could not mistake the dark demented figure, for he'd heard and seen that temper too many times before – although in rather different circumstances – to need to be told that Mary Keenan had joined the throng.

'Leave off, you crazy bitch.' Kemp was grunting with pain

as the she-devil battered at him. 'I'm on your side.' He did his best to hold Mary at bay and shield his head with an arm. Meanwhile, Samuel took his cue from his mother and added his infant fists to the tattoo that was now falling on the commandant's stout form.

Soon, the combination proved too much for Kemp, who wheeled his horse from the fray and, in doing so, released Dunniah and the pony's last anchor. Seeing that he now had only one Englishman to deal with, the Indian brought the knuckle bow of his curved sword into crunching impact with Lance-Corporal Pegg's nose, knocking the NCO from his saddle, and then kicked violently at his horse, which hauled the pony and its passengers away from the brutish scene.

'Mary . . . Mary, it's me!' Morgan stuttered as, maddeningly, his filly turned in exactly the opposite direction that he wanted her to. He saw the woman hesitate, look directly at him and bring her fingers to her mouth in indecision.

But then came the eldritch shriek, 'Mama . . . Mama!' from Samuel, whose fat little arms reached out beseechingly – and that won the day. As the rebel soldier headed off into the dawn at the best speed that his trailing charge would allow, Mary kicked hard at her horse's flanks and followed Dunniah as fast as she could.

As Morgan fought to control his bucking horse, he stared after Mary. She was lying low in the saddle, making the smallest possible target of herself; she looked neither left nor right nor back at him; she just rode hard into the shadows and the dust.

But there was enough light now for Morgan to see what a sorry sight the three of them made. Pursuit was pointless as Kemp slouched astride his horse, clutching at his shoulder.

'Are you badly hit, Commandant?' Morgan could see a dark saucer of blood staining the older officer's khaki shirt just above the collarbone.

'No, it's bugger all; it's nothing compared with what I'm

going to do to that murderer Dunniah.' Although the grimace on Kemp's face suggested something rather more serious. 'Corp'l Pegg needs your help more than I do.'

Morgan, still numb from the sight of his lover, looked down at Pegg. What the NCO lacked in style in the saddle he made up for with the common sense of survival and he had kept his reins looped about his wrist even when he was unseated. Now he clutched at his bridle with one hand and his nose with another. Morgan noticed simultaneously how the blood dripped from Pegg's nostril whilst a great clump of grass and dirt protruded from the blocked barrel of his slung rifle where it had rammed into the ground during his fall.

'Fuckin' India, never did want to come to the bleedin' place,' Lance-Corporal Pegg groaned nasally. 'Leaves a man nothing but black and fuckin' blue, it does; it's just a flyblown shite-house, it is.' Morgan had to admit that Pegg had had more than his share of misfortunes since the beginning of the campaign.

'It'll be good for your pension, though, Corp'l Pegg,' said Kemp through clenched teeth as Morgan started to dismount.

'If I ever fuckin' live to see a fuckin' pension, sir.' Pegg was swearing even harder than usual.

'I'd get my reins knotted together before I'd do anything else, Morgan,' said Kemp before: 'Jaysus, look there,' as he brought his pistol up with his good hand.

Whilst shouts and commands had continued in the wake of the ambush, dark shapes of horsemen had been slipping past the battered trio. Morgan looked up at half a dozen horsemen riding as fast as they could along a nearby track through the scrub in the same direction that Dunniah and Mary had taken. At their head was a noticeably slim figure in a metal helmet, whose nose-piece glinted in the first rays of light.

'It's the Rhani – the little whore!' As Kemp spoke, he fired two quick shots from his revolver, the second one of which wounded one of the group's mounts, causing the beast to rear and throw its rider. Morgan was to remember that moment for the rest of his life, for even as Kemp fired he knew that he should have tried to stop him, as the three of them were in no condition to face the swirling hell that now descended.

The riders jerked off their course to charge down on them. They needed no orders, understanding their leader's intentions instinctively, simply following the point of her heavily curved, outstretched sabre and rousing their horses to a gallop. They were only thirty paces away when they swerved into the attack, so the three soldiers didn't even have time to form a hasty defence. Each man reacted viscerally. Lance-Corporal Pegg shrank behind a thick tree trunk, experience reminding him to reach for his bayonet – the only effective weapon he had. Meanwhile, Morgan still had one foot in the stirrup when Kemp opened fire, so he dragged his mare down to the ground, groped for his carbine, which hung from the swivel on his cross-belt, and made as small a target as he could behind Emerald's saddle and haunch.

Mother of God, Hume was right. Morgan thumbed the carbine's hammer back and checked that his percussion cap was in place, *That man must be tired of life.* He watched as the wounded Kemp jerked his reins as best he could with his gouged left arm, thumped his heels viciously into his grey's ribs, and with his revolver outstretched, surged straight for the Rani as she thundered directly at him. Kemp fired two more shots as the range closed, but neither found a mark.

I hope he's counting his rounds, thought Morgan, and I wish I'd loaded with ball. On the advice of Cornet Breen, Morgan had primed his carbine with pellets rather than one single lead shot so that he would have more chance of hitting a fleeting target during a mounted fight. But now he needed the power of one solid bullet to bring an attacker to a standstill, not just wound him. Most of all, though, he wanted his pistol and its six chambers, which now lay abandoned somewhere in the scrub.

But if Morgan wanted a revolver, he wouldn't have chosen Kemp's, for the Adams jammed at the critical moment. As the two riders closed on each other, Morgan watched the commandant aim straight at the Rhani's throat and squeeze the trigger when they were no more than two horses apart. The heavy ball should have lifted the princess from the saddle, but instead there was just an empty click.

'You useless lump of junk!' yelled Kemp as he hurled the pistol and watched it bounce harmlessly off the Rhani's shoulder.

But in throwing the now redundant bit of steel at his attacker, Kemp had raised his arm and exposed his ribs as he did so, giving the Rhani the classic cavalryman's target.

Morgan knew that a handy British trooper would have dug his straight, regulation blade into the soft target point first, but the woman's curved sword was designed for slashing and that was exactly what she did. The thin steel blade sighed through the air, carving a neat seam below Kemp's arm from which the blood instantly sprang, but there was something else, something sinister, about the way that she handled her horse. Morgan saw a cruel, foot-long, dagger in her other hand. She was controlling her mount with reins attached to her feet, just as the Mahrattas were said to do. Now she drew her elbow back and pushed the poniard hard into the already stricken commandant, the tip of the blade darting quickly into his vitals before being drawn out again just as fast, but now dull with blood. Morgan saw his commander topple slowly from the saddle and fall with a dusty thump amongst the pounding hoofs. But he had no time to see anything more, for his own hands were suddenly very full.

The charging horse seemed enormous, its knees and hoofs pumping gigantically, its mouth open far enough for Morgan to be able to see its yellow tombstone teeth. So much of his vision did this leviathan take up that Morgan could barely see the rider: a skull cap showed above the charger's ears, a ragged beard framed an open mouth above two hate-filled eyes, whilst a slashing blade was held high above his attacker's head. It may not have been much of a target, but the officer threw the carbine into his shoulder and fired without pausing. Even at this short range the thirty lead slugs fanned out enough to catch the top of the horse's head and pepper the Indian's face at the same time, making the mount scream, rear and throw its rider, whose hands were clutched to his face. But as the cloud of powder smoke cleared, Morgan could see that two men and horses down was enough for the Rhani. Now her party sheared off quickly, whacking their ponies' rumps with the flats of their blades in order to make good their escape.

From first shot to the last chasing round from an 8th Hussar, the whole affair had lasted no more than two and a half minutes.

'Well, she's seen us off properly, ain't she, Corp'l Pegg?' Morgan urged Emerald to her feet, looped her reins over his shoulder and plodded off, exhausted, to examine the commandant.

'She bloody 'as, sir.' Pegg turned over the moaning sowar whom Morgan had wounded. 'What d'you want me to do with 'im?'

Morgan was distracted by the mayhem of the last few seconds, the glimpse of Mary, and Kemp's inert form.

'Destroy him,' Morgan barely noticed the way that he was using the irregulars' patois, 'then get over here and help me with the commandant.'

Pegg slipped the long steel shaft of his bayonet casually behind the wounded Pandy's collarbone, the sowar ceasing to moan and twitch once the tip plunged into his heart. Then Pegg took a minute to wipe the blade on his victim's kurta and run a hand over the man's waist to check for a purse before obeying the officer's orders.

One of Kemp's feet remained in the stirrup whilst the man lay quite still, twisted on his left side. As his horse cropped at the patchy grass, both Morgan and Pegg reached down to Kemp and turned him gently on his back,

'They've made a right mess of 'im, ain't they, sir?'

Morgan couldn't disagree with Pegg, for the commandant seemed to be bleeding from every point of his body. He'd been shot in the shoulder, slashed across his side, his nose and mouth streamed redly, but the neat, blue little hole in the left side of Kemp's groin that hardly bled at all was the wound that worried Morgan most.

'That's a nasty jab he got from that dagger.' Morgan had pulled Kemp's breeches down and, as feared, the puncture seemed deep and grievous. 'He lives, but it'll be nip and tuck.'

'No, my money's on Queen Victoria. Look at her – ain't she got a sting like a lance, though?' Morgan was quite certain of his choice.

'Balls. Prince Albert's the boy. It's not the sting that matters really, it's the pincers. The lad who can get the strongest grip will come out on top, you mark my words. Who do you fancy, Pegg?' asked Kemp from his wicker chair.

'It's *Corporal* Pegg, sir. Why, I'm with you, sir. Albert's smaller in the body, but 'e's got a right pair of grippers on 'im. I'm in for two rupees,' Pegg replied.

Morgan knew not a blind thing about scorpion fighting, but it was worth a few coins just to oppose the bloody old curmudgeon. In any event, he would have paid just to watch the sport, let alone wager, so bored had he become with Kemp's moaning and this aimless hanging around.

'I'm buggered if I know how 'e don't get stung.' Pegg marvelled at Rissaldar Batuk, who, having first held an armoured insect in the thumb and forefinger of each hand and shown them to the audience so that they could see which they fancied more, was now tying a piece of coloured thread to Victoria's tail. 'You wouldn't catch me doing that – oh, no. Mind you, that string's a good idea. Lets you know which is which when they set to partners, don't it?'

'Aye, it's an old trick, that. D'you know, there was a sepoy in the Twenty-Fifth who used to fight scorpions and his speciality was to hold the creature and tie the thread with just one hand. In fact, after Aliwal I saw . . .'

Morgan ceased to listen as Kemp chased yet another memory. Like Pegg, he was fascinated by Batuk's skill with the venomous black horrors.

'Where should I put my money, Rissaldar sahib?' Morgan called.

'Where your wisdom tells you, Morgan sahib; both are evil little whores,' Batuk replied with a grin.

These two were some of the biggest that Rissaldar Batuk had ever seen caught. Victoria, at about two inches, was longer than Albert, but without the massive claws that Kemp had identified as the deciding factor in the coming battle. Usually, they only managed to catch creatures of sporting size one at a time; then the unlucky things were put on a specially prepared stone slab with a circular channel etched in it that was filled with raw spirits. The scorpion was placed in the middle, the circle of liquor ignited and bets won or lost according to how long the sacrifice lasted against the clock before it stung itself to death. Morgan thought it a very crude entertainment, but it had its following.

No, whilst this was no substitute for rat baiting or what his father would call 'the spurs', scorpions answered well enough whilst the soldiers licked their wounds here in Seepree and waited for the campaign to sweep them up again in its arms.

'There's no real rules for this, sir, is they?' Pegg asked, all his attention fixed on the two tiny knights as the rissaldar and one of the other daffadars placed them carefully opposite each other in the ring. 'Not like ratting?' The lance-corporal had become almost as keen on that other noble sport as Morgan, in the few brief months that the 95th had been in Dublin before setting out for this campaign.

'No, Corp'l Pegg,' Morgan answered, just as engrossed by the forthcoming combat, 'the ring's usually the same dimensions.' He looked at a thick piece of rope spliced into a circle like a quoit about fourteen inches across. 'They just insist that the dirt is packed down and smooth so that the little heroes can't sneak out underneath the twine. Then they just go at it. Watch now . . .'

The rissaldar had glanced for approval at the bandaged Kemp, who sat on his chair like an emperor of Rome at the amphitheatre. He waited for the minute hand on his pocket watch to be set and then nodded – the signal for the contest to start. The whole audience – hussars, irregulars, officers as well as rank and file, almost all the dog-eared survivors of Kemp's column – strained in one scruffy, ill-dressed mob to get a glimpse of yet more death and suffering. They were not disappointed.

The royal pair circled for a moment, horrid segmented tails arched above their bodies, twitching slightly as they scuttled in the grit. But then Morgan realised how sinister these tiny gladiators were. Terriers and rats had living eyes that betrayed fear and emotion; even cockerels' black marble orbs had some flicker of character in them, but these ghastlies had just two hoods on top of their heads and then rows of other dot-like things that looked utterly soulless.

Certainly, Victoria's first charge was seen off easily, Albert sidestepping as she darted at him, throwing his tail and sting towards his opponent but not physically connecting. They whirled to face each other again as the audience sighed with anticipation.

'Right, see this. Albert will grab that other bugger as it passes next time,' Kemp opined. 'Canny little sod.'

And to Morgan's disappointment he was right. Victoria was more energetic and bigger, but less skilful. As she lunged and overshot again, Albert grabbed one of her legs with his left pincer and then, quick as light, sank his other one into Her Majesty's thorax. Morgan watched transfixed as the horny, black carapace dented and crumpled under the claw and a drop of clear liquid oozed from the wound.

'Go on, my son, crown 'er; that'll teach 'er to keep yer short of yer greens,' some waggish hussar observed, to the amusement of the crowd, and Albert obeyed. First he pulled his opponent slightly towards him, her legs leaving tiny furrows in the dust, then he drove his sting expertly between the joints of two, shiny segments. In seconds all the fight had gone from the Queen. Her forelegs stiffened in a last ecstasy, then the body settled on the ground as Albert stung her again and again, his tail flicking in a series of lethal darts. Slowly, Victoria's own tail, coloured thread and all, went limp; death had arrived.

'Hmm . . . not bad, seen better. Just shy of two minutes.' Kemp snapped the cover of his watch shut. 'Right, Rissaldar, to the victor the spoils.'

This encomium could only add laurels to the commandant's Caesarean image, Morgan thought, for rather than taking the winner and subjecting him to a ring of fire, the poisonous little insect received quite a different reward: the rissaldar simply put the sole of his riding boot firmly on his tough shell, crushing the life out of him. Morgan seemed to be the only man in the audience who noticed. Everybody else was scrabbling for their winnings.

'I feel just about right, now.' Kemp was walking with the aid of a stick along the baked earth of what passed for a main road in the village of Seepree. 'Smith's brigade should be with us any day now, don't you think, Morgan?'

'You may think you're well enough, Commandant, but we nearly lost you after that last tangle with Herself,' replied Morgan.

This was only the third time that Kemp had felt able to stump around one or two sentry posts in the burnt-out village that lay on the main Jhansi to Gwalior road. The mutineers had fallen on it and its inhabitants in early April – at about the same time that Kemp and his men had been dealt such a stinging blow by Lakshmi Bai – and razed the place. Now all that was left of it was a series of blackened shells of buildings, collapsed roofs and shallow graves where the local people had buried those whom the rebels had deemed to be loyal to the British. But even now, at the start of June, the situation was still so unstable and the village's position on the main road so important that it had to be garrisoned.

'You mustn't open that wound, you know.' Morgan was uneasy with the scar on Kemp's abdomen. 'That dagger went deep, and you had blood in your piss for an age afterwards.'

Even as the party was trying to recover from the ambush – now seven weeks ago – a strong troop of 1st Bombay Lancers had passed close by whilst harassing the fugitives after Jhansi had fallen. Morgan, with two dead hussars and six wounded (including the gravely ill Kemp) had ordered them to detach some of their spare horses and after three difficult days in which the commandant and one of the irregulars had slipped in and out of consciousness, they had eventually arrived back at Jhansi. Morgan had had to report to General Rose.

'Tell me again what the chief said.' Morgan had gone through the conversation between himself and Rose for Kemp's benefit many times already.

'Well, as I've already told you, Commandant, the general was full of congratulations for what you'd achieved. He said he quite understood why Brigadier-General Smith spoke so highly of you.'

'Get on with you. He didn't really say that, did he?'

Kemp's faux modesty had become a little wearing, thought Morgan.

'Yes, he did. He told his staff that if any man was going to able to rid him of that turbulent woman it was Commandant Dick Kemp; how you'd come within an ace of achieving it; how he was sorry to hear about your wounds; how he hoped that the case of claret he was sending you would set you up rightly; and how a wee bit of rest at Seepree would be just what you and all of us needed. I've told you all this a dozen times, sir.' Morgan had, but he found himself both repelled yet intrigued by the vanity of the old war-horse and he was amused by Kemp's childlike delight in the compliments.

The onward journey of forty miles or so south-west to Seepree had really worried Morgan, though. The worst hurt irregular had recovered well, as had all the other wounded who travelled in bullock carts, except Kemp. Dr Billings, who had been attached to them, had even called a halt the second day out of Jhansi, clearly fearing for Kemp's life when his nonsensical rants had stopped and he had lapsed into a sweaty coma. But, after two ounces of blood had been drawn from him with leeches, the commandant had rallied and the little column had lurched on until it reached its charred and desolate destination.

'Well, we've had enough bloody rest now. Everyone thought that when Kalpi fell to our lads a couple of weeks ago that the whole thing would fizzle out.' Kemp, once he'd recovered sufficiently to appreciate the isolation and ugliness of Seepree, had quickly begun to chafe. 'But once the Gwalior troops defied their own maharajah and went over to the rest of the Pandies, it was bloody obvious that Rose would have to see the thing through to the bitter end. He couldn't just ignore the Rhani when she was putting some spunk – ha, if you see what I mean – into all the other useless princelings, and pretend that she'd bugger off somewhere obscure and we'd all live happily ever after. No, there's a deal more fighting to be done yet.'

A deal more fighting, Morgan pondered. I've seen more of that than I want to, and I can never delight in it like Kemp does, but once you're in amongst them, once you're trading shots or blows with the Pandies, it's so much easier than it once was.

Morgan remembered how he'd dreaded the prospect of battle at first – not so much the idea of death or injury, but the prospect of letting his men down. Now, he knew that he could do it – his balls still tightened every bit as much as they did back in the Crimea – but he knew that the men depended upon him to lead and set an example. And that expectation was a powerful thing. He could no more shy away from a fight whilst his soldiers were watching, yet he could never relish danger like this madman Kemp.

The advantage of being on the main road was that every galloper and aide who passed could be interrogated. One such, a young lieutenant of Native Cavalry from Rose's staff, had been lured into Kemp's convalescent web just over a week ago and, with the help of some of his master's claret, had been thoroughly interrogated. So it was that they had found out about a further defeat of Tantya Tope at Kalpi in May and how, at first, many had thought that the enemy had little further fight left in him. But then, the Gwalior troops had mutinied against their own Maharaja Scindiah and marched off – with the six brass guns presented to the Maharaja by John Company – to throw in their lot in with Tantya Tope and the Rhani. Then, the slightly foxed sub-altern had told them, 'The whole damned parcel is now marching on the impenetrable fortress of Gwalior.'

'Do you know Gwalior, Commandant?' asked Morgan as they approached a sentry position manned by a dismounted 8th Hussar.

'Aye, it's a grand-looking place, but it'll be a devil's bastard to attack. It sits on a great plug of rock sticking out from the surroundin' plain and the walls are sheer. It makes Kotah – and even Jhansi – look like a pimple on your arse; Rose will need to use every bit of guile he can to stop Lakshmi Bai and her confederates from making a stand there that would cost us dear in both time and blood. A deliberate attack must involve heavy casualties, so he'll try to avoid it – and that's where we'll come in, I guarantee it, and that's where we'll not only catch that woman, but we'll get that sod Dunniah.' Once Kemp's mind reverted to the subject of bloody revenge upon those who had wronged him, all his ills seemed to be forgotten.

'Yes, Commandant, but he's obviously expecting a right good fight – that's why he's blown for General Smith's brigade and the Ninety-fifth,' replied Morgan, for word had reached them almost immediately when Smith had been ordered to start the long march to Seepree.

'Perhaps, but he'll hope not to have to lay siege to a town like that. Mark my words, he'll have special work for us to do again and I, for one, will be damn glad not only to get away from here, but also to even the score with that heathen woman and her godforsaken followers.' Kemp rubbed at the scar beneath his armpit.

You're a capital soldier, Dick Kemp but you're bored with life, you bloody old lunatic, and I'm not yet bored with mine, thought Morgan. It was dangerous enough trying to find Mary and the boy and not getting chopped when you were fully fit, I don't want to have to do the same whilst nurse-maiding you. I'd be damned glad to be safely tucked up with the Regiment – but then who will get Mary and Sam back in one piece?

The last few weeks had been intolerable as Morgan had thought about the glimpses that he had had of Mary and his boy time and again; now he tried to thrust them out of his mind.

'Now, Pollard,' Kemp greeted the sentry, who kept his back to the officers – no salute, undistracted, stolidly watching his arcs of responsibility, just as the manual said – 'how are you? Heard anything from Bristol?'

He may be a lunatic, but he's damn good with the troops, thought Morgan. It's all I can do to remember the names of the hussars' non-commissioned officers, let alone the privates and where they come from.

'Sir; the missus has had the babbi an' called 'er Jane, sir. Din't ask me, just named 'er; what d'you make of that, sir?' Private Pollard continued to stare out of the sandbagged sentry post, carbine in the crook of his arm.

'It's a fine name, Pollard,' Kemp replied genially. 'Just be glad that they're both fit and well.'

'Aye, sir, but *Jane*. I wouldn't call a dog that, sir, I wouldn't,' Private Pollard maundered on, his eyes never leaving the distant wood line that he had been charged to observe.

'Watch your arcs, Pollard, and dream of the loot that you'll be able to take when we catch up with the Rhani.' Kemp, Morgan realised, was mentioning all the troops' most important touchstones – family, home and undreamed-of wealth. 'You'll be able to sign off, buy a nice ale house in Clifton or somewhere, and bore any poor bastard who'll let you with tales from brother Pandy,' Kemp chuckled.

And it worked. Private Pollard had been flattered by the officers' attention, reminded of his most cherished possessions and ambitions and, at the same time, fired up for the strife that lay ahead. Morgan was just turning this neat little device over in his mind when, once they were out of earshot of the sentry, Kemp returned to the attack that he'd been expecting for some time now.

'So, Morgan, there it is. Smith will be with us any time soon. I'll be told to go and have another go at capturing that harlot and that'll leave me in a right, bloody quandary, so it will.' Kemp had stopped and turned to face Morgan.

'You're right, Commandant. You know that you need more time to get over those knocks properly—' But Morgan wasn't allowed to finish.

'Balls . . . I'm as fit as a butcher's dog – you know I am. No, my problem is you, young brevet major hero-of-Sevastopol, son of my best friend, Morgan. You're the boy who lets fucking Pandies run free, who encourages the men to shirk their duty by not putting this scum to the sword – don't think I don't know that you told Corp'l Martin to let those four rebels go at that ruined temple when we was hard on Lakshmi Bai's tail back in April,' Kemp said coldly. 'No, don't interrupt me, boy, and you're the feller who's so infatu-bloody-ated with a piece of skirt that he can't see the truth of what's happened to the lass.'

'But, Commandant—' Morgan tried to protest.

'No, lad, hold your tongue. I know what the girl means to you – and that lad of yours is a spirited little sod; he gave me a right pummelling when we met up in that wood that day – you wouldn't be risking your career and inheritance if she wasn't important to you, but you must see where her loyalty and future now lie. For whatever reason she's plumped for a native way of life. It happens so often with the lower orders, especially the Taegues who come out here and get swayed by all the religious hocus-pocus – all those damn statues and graven images are pretty well what Rome gives 'em anyway. She's gone across just like my own boys murdered Neeta and her people: you must try to understand it. You've lost her as surely as if she'd perished back in Jhansi with that brave bore of a husband of hers last June. If I'm wrong, why does she fuck off with the Rhani even when she can see that you're there to save her?'

'Commandant, we talked about this in Deesa; you're right about my feelings for Mary and my son – I realise how much is at stake and how odd it must seem to anyone else . . .' Morgan did his best to hide his own doubts.

'No, lad, just remember what I did. I loved and married a native woman – and I don't care if she was Eurasian, she was a native as far as "Polite" society saw her – and raised children by her who could never be seen in Ireland or take their place in the society in which I grew up, so don't think I don't have some understanding of your tupping a Catholic chamber maid but remember, when it came to it, you *married* one of your own rank and creed – and quite right too.'

Morgan was stunned into silence by Kemp's insight. It was too easy to write him off as a hate-filled murderer: that he might be, but when his blood had cooled, he was intelligent and intuitive, thought Morgan.

'But the fact remains that if you're to be by my side whilst we run the Rhani to ground, you must remove the goddamn blinkers that tell you that Mary-bloody-Keenan is still a faithful subject of Miss Vicky – she ain't. Twice now we've seen her stirrup to stirrup with Herself; I've even felt her blows. So, make your mind up, young Morgan. You're either with me or you're not. We can't ride stirrup to stirrup on our next jaunt if you're still thinking that Mary Keenan's outright treachery is just a misplaced expression of motherhood; dear God, the thought makes my tits burl.'

'But you're putting me in an impossible position, Commandant.' Morgan was thoroughly discomforted. 'Whether what you say is right or not, someone needs to save Mary either from herself or from the Rhani, and nobody can do that except me. I've known the lass for years now – she's part of home – and whilst I've wronged her and her late husband, I love her still. So, whether you like it not, whether you trust me or not, I shall be there.'

'No, lad, I've every faith in Captain Anthony Morgan of

the Ninety-Fifth,' Kemp fixed him with one of those looks that made him squirm, 'but I worry about that other feller, young Tony who cares more for quim than for his duty. I don't need him beside me in a fight.'

Morgan was about to boil over with anger, but before he could think of any sensible riposte, there was the crash of boots as Lance-Corporal Pegg came to attention besides the officers, his hand quivering at the band of his cap.

''Scuse me, gennelmen.' Corporal Pegg now had a scaly strip of skin running over the bridge of his nose to remind him of his last encounter with the Rhani's troops. 'Mr Breen's compliments, sirs, but a galloper's just arrived from that bugger Smith's – beg pardon, sirs – General Smith's brigade to say as how he's marching through the day an' 'e'll be 'ere by nightfall and wants a full account of the situation.'

'Sit yourself down, sir, have a swally o' this . . .' Colour-Serjeant McGucken passed a precious bottle of pale ale to Morgan as they sat in the ruins of one of Seepree's burnt-out bungalows that had been allocated to the 95th. 'One of the sutlers brought us a whole lot a couple of days back.'

Smith's brigade had arrived only a few hours ago after five days on the march. The 10th Bombay had been the vanguard, followed by the 95th, then the guns and Engineers with the baggage train and its menagerie of animals being protected by the cavalry. Where the village had been eerily scorched and quiet, it now burst with life and noise, even after darkness had fallen.

'Thank you Colour-Sar'nt.' Morgan poured the golden liquid carefully into a glass. 'This is a rare treat.' He sipped appreciatively at a drink that had evaded all of them even here on the main trunk road.

'Pleasure, sir. But look at you, quite the card in your mufti, ain't you?' McGucken's amusement at Morgan's khaki pyjamas had been immoderate when they first saw each other.

His scarlet shell jacket and regimental trousers had all but fallen apart after the last few weeks, so, once they had reached Seepree, he'd bought four suits – two for himself and two for Corporal Pegg – from a passing contractor and slipped into the irregular mode without any backward glances.

'Perhaps it's a little daring for Her Majesty's Ninety-Fifth Foot, but hark at you lot: the men look more like gypsies than soldiers. I'm surprised at you, Colour-Sar'nt.' The barb went home as Morgan knew it would, even though it was meant to be good-natured. For long-serving regimental non-commissioned officers, the sight of the men in their weather-beaten kit, sun-faded coats and worn out boots was genuinely painful.

McGucken almost took the bait, but just pulled himself back from the brink chuckling, 'And there's not a damn thing me or any of the NCOs can do about it. As I keep sayin' to Cap'n Carmichael, as long as the weapons is bright and clean an' there's shot in the lads' pouches, we can manage, even if we do look like a mad woman's shit.'

Certainly, the troops' appearance had quite shocked Morgan when they'd swung into camp. The horsemen weren't in such bad order, but the 10th BNI and his own regiment were simply threadbare, many of the men having thin native slippers on their feet, their issue boots having obviously worn through.

'How's he been?' Morgan had waited to ask until he'd got McGucken on his own. The servants were too busy getting the officers and senior NCOs' food ready to listen too closely, whilst Ensigns Fawcett and Wilkinson and Colour-Sergeant Whaley had yet to appear.

'Honestly, sir?'

Morgan nodded.

''E's been a fuckin' bastard, 'e 'as. 'E's been halfway decent to 'is own boys from Number One Company, but since the colonel formed double companies after Kotah, a Grenadier's only got to fart an' 'e jumps down 'is throat, 'e does.' McGucken was instinctively loyal and would never have spoken like this in front of the men, but he knew Morgan well – perhaps too well – and they had both suffered under Carmichael when he'd acted as their company commander in the Crimea.

'No, sir, there's been all sorts of problems. First 'e wanted to shoot the ram that you told Sullivan to get at Kotah – said it was yet another mouth to feed. 'E was right, but the men had got awfi fond of the thing an' you know how soft they can be with animals. Anyway, the colonel got wind of it and took Derby – that's what they're calling him now – to Battalion Headquarters as the mascot for the whole Regiment. I think the commanding officer only did it to scunner Carmichael.'

'Well, I'm pleased to hear about our tame sheep; what else has he done?' asked Morgan.

'You can probably guess what happened when the brigadier-general visited during our pause at Goonah. McGarry was at the centre of it, sir,' the colour-sergeant continued.

'Ah, some act of grossly discourteous ventriloquism, I imagine – haven't you managed to stop him doing that yet, Colour-Sar'nt?' Morgan guessed.

'Aye, sir . . . I mean no, sir: he's a wee hero to the men and he fights like a bloody lion when he's sober. We'd just come to the present an' Cap'n Carmichael had stepped forward to report to the general when an officer-like voice calls out from somewhere, "Learnt how to stay in the saddle yet, General?". You know how good he is at it and there was no trace of his own accent, there wasn't. Well, sir, everyone laughed – even the commanding officer was having trouble keeping a straight face – except for our company commander, who turned on young Stout, who was in the rear rank just a few paces away, and tells Corp'l Bennett to take his name and assures the general that he'll be flogged. Now, if you'd done that the troops would have known that it was all a sham – something just to shut the general up – but Stout starts calling the odds there an' then: "It weren't me, sir, honest." Cap'n Carmichael tells me to arrest the lad on the spot, the troops start a-mutterin' an' I thought he'd tell me to blow a couple from the muzzles o' guns next, so bloody angry was he. Anyway, I'd just fallen in a couple of the NCOs to grab Stout, when McGarry steps forward as bold as you like and says, "No, sir, I said it, not Stout, and I'll say it again if Himself wants; stick the lash on me, not Dan Stout."' McGucken shook his head.

'Well, did he flog McGarry?' Morgan didn't know whether to be entertained by the discomfiture of the general, impressed by McGarry's sang-froid, or horrified by a scene that should never have happened in a company that was happy and well led.

'He did, sir. McGarry got ten of the finest, courtesy of Drummer Robinson,' McGucken could see the well-muscled musician laying on even now, 'and when he finished, the big, daft Mick spat the stop from his mouth, flexed his shoulders – bloody as they were – and just laughed. Sounds quite funny now, sir, but it's left a bad taste in the lads' mouths and there's a number of 'em who are just pushin' McGarry on to make Cap'n Carmichael look even more stupid. You'd best get back as soon as you can.' McGucken topped up his officer's glass.

TEN

Kotah-Ki-Serai

The ram looked up from the patch of balding grass where he'd been tethered, blinked his grey eyes at Morgan, shook his head to rid himself of flies and then returned to a sparse feast. Morgan saw how the sun shone off the animal's freshly oiled, curling horns and that a leather water bottle sling had been fashioned into a collar. The dull brass bell that had been around the creature's neck at Kotah had now been polished to a bright gleam. He patted the bony head, was acknowledged by nothing more than a flick of the ears, and then turned his attention to the two sentries who had crashed to the 'present' outside the three tents that were serving, here at Seepree, as Battalion Headquarters.

'Carry on, please, lads.'

Morgan returned the salute and the soldiers brought their rifles to the 'order' before, on a sibilant, 'Tss . . . tss,' the pair stood at ease, their feet stamping at precisely the same time as the senior soldier hissed 'silent' sentry orders, just as if they were back on the barrack yard.

Both men had done their best to turn their shabbiness into something approaching smartness for this duty, but the thread-bare state of their clothing and the thin, cracked leather of their boots couldn't be ignored. Morgan was about to try a little easy banter with the men – despite both privates' wooden regimental expressions – when the thump of hoofs on the road distracted him.

'Ah, Morgan, I'm obliged to you.' The sentries went through their minuet again, whilst Morgan brought his hand level with the peak of his cap as Lieutenant-Colonel Henry Hume and his adjutant trotted up. 'I won't detain you long.' The commanding officer looked thinner than when Morgan had last seen him at Kotah in April, almost two months ago, browner, immeasurably more worn and creased, yet none of the energy or sparkle had deserted the man.

'Carry on, please, you two,' Hume said to the sentries. 'Good work, Saunders; have you had to borrow those boots?'

'I 'ave, sir, but Franklin 'ere 'asn't: 'ee just sits on 'is arse all day, sir,' the senior soldier replied, whilst stamping into the drill-book stance of 'stand easy.'

'Well done anyway. You're both a credit to Number Four and I trust that we'll get new boots before the week is done,' Hume smiled back at the troops.

He's just like Kemp; how does he know the name of that man? wondered Morgan. He's got over five hundred men under his command and he speaks to that lad as if he's his own son. And look at the way that Saunders is trying not to grin with delight – that's made the man's day, it has.

'Come on in; I fear that everything here is a bit temporary.' Hume led the way through the big ridge tent that served as the orderly room – he waved the clerks to sit down as he passed through – to the smaller bell of canvas that was his own quarters. 'Have a seat; I need some porter – will you?' But without waiting for a reply, Hume reached into a bucket of once-cold water, pulled out two bottles of India ale and poured them carefully into Russian silver beakers, souvenirs of a different struggle.

'Now, I've spoken to Commandant Kemp; I've heard all about your last few weeks and a pretty warm time you had until you let Himself get poked about. I did warn you, didn't I?' Hume half-smiled at Morgan and took a deep pull at his drink.

'You did, sir; it was exactly as you said it would be,' Morgan watched as Hume raised his eyebrows in acknowledgement, 'and I'd like to commend Lance-Corporal Pegg, and Farrier-Corporal Martin of the Eighth Hussars for conspicuous service—'

'Yes, yes, that's important but it'll have to wait,' Hume interrupted him. 'I don't know what you see in that lout from Derbyshire, but I've written him up for something after what he did in Rowa, just as you asked; now we'll have to wait on the pleasure of milords to see what bauble they give him – if any. Anyway, I'm glad I've got you back; there's work to be done.'

Morgan's stomach tightened. So he was to be brought back to regimental duty, as one half of him wished and the other half feared.

'Yes, you'll recall that Massey was grabbed by the brigadier-general to be his brigade-major after Bainbrigge – God rest him – was killed?'

Morgan nodded as he savoured a mouthful of ale.

'Well, we've had to leave him behind with a dose of ague, and provide another officer to take his place. That was not a difficult choice – I've sent your friend Richard Carmichael to be the general's boot-black and – I can say this to you . . .' Hume swivelled his eyes at Morgan, '. . . the young gentleman couldn't get away to the safety of Brigade Headquarters fast enough. Just had time to mutter something about his previous staff experience being invaluable, not a word about the men, about McGucken or Whaley, nothing about the two subalterns who've both been bricks – just snatched up his dunnage and was away.'

Morgan didn't know what to say. The colonel was being unusually candid about another officer; Morgan knew the contempt in which Hume held Carmichael, but he couldn't weigh in against him, for that would sound quite wrong. So, he settled for the British Army's portmanteau answer, a non-committal, 'Sir . . .' and waited for more.

'Now, I've done a deal with the brigade commander – Carmichael to his staff, you back to the Regiment – and any more hare-brained schemes to spike the Rhani can be the preserve of the good Commandant Kemp – and the good Commandant Kemp alone. Mind you, the poor man looks more like a bloody colander than soldier after you let the Pandies have their way with him. You'll have to tell me the mad-arsed details of what happened later. It's enough to say that General Smith's delighted with what Kemp's little band of cutthroats managed to achieve – and that's not a great deal as far as I can understand – and you've retrieved a bit of your reputation in his eyes, though I cannot see why.'

At first, Morgan was baffled by this. Then he realised that the commandant – God bless him – must have been using his considerable sway to help him. Kemp must know how appalled Morgan had been by wholesale murder and his disdain for mercy, but for an officer of the commandant's stamp, the bonds of tribe and creed were everything.

'Sir, thank you. Am I to take over both the Grenadiers and Number One?' Morgan thrilled at the idea of a double command.

'You are; let's just see what their returns look like.' And with that, Hume sauntered across to the stifling orderly room tent and asked for the leather-bound book that contained the carefully inked details of each company's strength and readiness for duty.

'Yes, more or less as I thought . . .' Hume grasped the bottom of his beard as he held the book into the direct light of the sun, '. . . one hundred and two bayonets, seven corporals, four sergeants, two colour-sar'nts and four drummers mustered as fit for duty, and only seven sick. That sick list is a wonderful achievement by McGucken and Whaley. You know, the men were falling like skittles on the route up, mainly fever, but some of the day marches were appalling in the sun. We've had four men die outright from sunstroke and I was worried about McGarry after he was flogged. And that's another thing Morgan, I won't hold with punishments of that sort in this climate without your consulting me first.' It was clear that on matters like this, Hume would brook no argument. 'There's a place for the cat but it's a damned rare place in this regiment; we shouldn't need to beat the men like oxen and I won't have it.'

Morgan was grateful to McGucken for having told him about the McGarry incident, for he hadn't realised that Carmichael's arbitrary punishment had upset Hume so badly.

'No, sir, if the men need to be brought to order, there's better ways of doing it than that,' Morgan agreed.

'And it's bad enough that we're stuck in the middle of all this needless brutality anyway, without our inflicting more suffering on the poor, bloody men,' added Hume. 'Don't you wonder how we got mixed up in all this murderous nonsense in the first place?'

Morgan had never seen Hume like this; he was used only to the dedicated, kindly but professional commanding officer, not this reflective, slightly morose one.

'I do, sir. I never could reconcile how we were able to blow those characters from guns in front of their comrades when we landed in Bombay and then expect the rest of the Regiment to behave loyally – yet they have. And being along-side Commandant Kemp's an education too, sir. You never know quite who's on his side, who's in his pay, what caste they are, what tribe, what religion or heaven knows what,' Morgan replied.

'I know, it's a bloody maze, ain't it? I sometimes think we should pack up shop and just let these John Company wallahs sort out their own mess. I'm sure India's a grand place for chasing game, guzzling grog and lording it over the natives – just let me get back to rainy, foggy England and—' But before Hume could finish his gloomy thoughts, a deep, rolling bleat came from just outside the doorway of the tent and caught both their attention.

'I gather that the ram that we took has had a bit of promotion, sir,' said Morgan.

'Aye, he's a boy, ain't he?' Hume smiled broadly as he strode out of the shadow of the tent into the glare of the sun where the ram cropped at the grass. 'The men did well getting you, didn't they, Private Derby.' Hume squatted down next to the animal and stroked his ears and chin as he might a dog. 'And to think, Carmichael was going to have you sent to the knacker's yard, wasn't he?' This was another bit of odd behaviour from Hume, thought Morgan. 'No, you may be just a conceit, my lad, but you look grand at the head of the Regiment.' Hume raised himself up and rubbed his hands together to clean them of the lanolin from the ram's fleece. 'So, go and get a firm grip of your command, Morgan, for Sir Hugh Rose is advancing with his troops from the east,' Hume pointed in the opposite direction from where they stood, 'and we march for Gwalior the day after tomorrow to try and close on the enemy from both sides at once.'

'Very good, sir.' Morgan saluted and turned to leave, just as Hume started a sham pushing match with Derby, whose tail flicked in time to the commanding officer's delighted chuckles.

'That was a good 'un, wan't it, sir?' Lance-Corporal Pegg, now returned to his command of half a dozen Grenadiers, was as tired as he could ever remember being, having stuttered and started over twelve miles of dust, mud and grass throughout the hours of darkness. Now the whole regiment – or the five hundred or so men that the sun, wounds and sickness had left fit to march – had arrived at a resting point which the map showed to be Kotah-Ki-Serai, been dressed off by companies and told to prepare breakfast.

'I've had easier walks, I must admit.' Ensign Fawcett had found the brigade's long flog towards Gwalior every bit as irksome as the men. 'Those bloody oxen need a shamrock every other pace, don't they?'

'A shamrock's too gentle by 'alf, sir; the fuckers want shooting.' Pegg, like all the others, had spent the night cajoling and prodding the baggage animals which, everyone was sure, were in the pay of the mutineers. 'D'you want to look at the men's feet now, or can we cook fust?'

'No, boots off now, please.'

The men, overhearing the conversation, were already throwing themselves down in the lee of a sun-dried ridge, even as the first beams of light stretched out from behind the great fortress of Gwalior, sitting high on its rock pedestal two miles or more from them.

'Get some of the cooked rice and dates you're carrying down you, but don't let the lads waste too much time brewing tea. Every minute of sleep will be valuable.'

'Right, sir.' Pegg noticed how the young officer had grown in confidence even in the few weeks that he'd been away with Morgan and Kemp. 'Come on, you lot, get yer trotters in the air for Mr Fawcett to 'ave a stare at.'

Each soldier sat amongst a scatter of belts, bottles and bayonets, their rifles already quickly oiled, rags pulled over the locks against the dust, all linked together by their muzzles into orderly pyramids of three.

'So, that big castle yonder is what they want us to take this time, is it, sir?' Private Beeston sprawled on his back, his naked left foot extended, both hands linked below one knee so that his right foot might be seen by the officer more easily.

'It is, Beeston; any complaints?' asked Fawcett as he routinely eased the soldier's big toe away from the next one in a search for blisters or jungle rot.

'No, sir, so long as there's some loot to be had – an' a bit of that wouldn't go far wrong, either,' Beeston nodded at Cissy, the cook wallah, who was gliding around with a big animal-skin water bag, refilling the men's wooden canteens.

'No, you clown, any complaints about your boots, feet or your pox-ridden body in general?' retorted Fawcett with mock exasperation.

The troops had all received new boots before the march began from Seepree, along with three fresh pairs of socks. They had tallowed the coarse wool and done their best to knead the new leather, but soreness and rubbed feet were inevitable.

'Fine, sir. Too much service to be caught out by that sort of thing, sir.' Beeston had instantly sown his two long-service stripes to the cuff of the pale canvas smock with which they had each been issued. 'Not like this red-arse 'ere, sir.'

'You're all right, Beeston, but *you've* lost a bit of juice, ain't you, Coughlin?' Fawcett had noticed how the young Dublin lad had been limping, but he hadn't expected one of his socks to be quite so red and wet.

'No, your honour, it's nothing . . .' Coughlin's left heel was raw, a flap of blistered skin as big as a florin swilling blood, '. . . nothing that a dod o' plaster won't sort out.'

'Hmm, . . . perhaps. Keep your boots off for the next couple of days – you've got slippers with you, ain't you?' Coughlin nodded. 'And take every chance you can to ease the leather. If you're not happy with the size of Coughlin's boots, Corp'l Pegg, get 'em exchanged.'

'Sir,' said Lance-Corporal Pegg, scratching in a notebook.

'Now, James, let's have a—' But just as Fawcett lifted another pink, scaly hoof into the light, there was a beastly hum, a horribly familiar shiver in the air, followed by a distant thump of a gun. As the enemy ball bustled over their heads, everyone was scandalised into action, bare-foot men scampering gingerly to get their weapons, others pulling at socks and belts, whilst the air was full of fluent swearing.

'Get hold of their weapons and lie them down please, Colour-Sar'nts.' Morgan had allowed himself the luxury of riding through the night march rather than plodding along on foot. Now he was glad he had, for he was able to be up and amongst his enlarged command without any waste of time as soon as the first round swept over them. Spurring up to the right of the Grenadiers' line, he dismounted just as another ball hummed by, making him want to duck low in his saddle despite the fact that it flew many feet high.

'Can't see where the buggers are firing from, can you, sir?' Colour-Sergeant McGucken had come doubling up the line of crouching men, as trim and taut as if he'd just come from the sergeants' mess rather than from a back-breaking night march.

'Not yet, Colour-Sar'nt,' Morgan had passed his reins to a private soldier and scrabbled to the top of the gritty bank behind which the troops – some of whom were still struggling with straps and laces – were sheltering, 'but just let me get my glasses on them.'

McGucken had crawled up beside his company commander and was trying to get his own telescope from the front of his smock. Both men were soon scouring the low, flat ground that lay to their front, its ditches and shallow banks, its ribbons of trees and clutches of buildings, which suddenly gave way to the huge block of sandstone and Gwalior's fort that loured on top of it.

'There, sir, there, look at yon temple thing left of that date grove about six hundred paces away.' McGucken brought Morgan's attention onto a white building with a domed roof in the middle distance. 'There's a drift o' powder smoke there, ain't there?'

Morgan gently fingered the central wheel on his field glasses, bringing the swathe of ground into clear focus as the brassy light of a new day swept across it. McGucken's glass was old, cheap and worn – Morgan knew it almost as well as its owner – whereas his own binoculars were the very best that Berlin could make, and their well-milled lenses confirmed what the colour-sergeant suspected.

'There is, and I fancy that there's a bit of a sandbag wall and some gabions just to the left of the temple as we look . . . there, goddamn, see that?' As Morgan spoke three gouts of smoke spat in unison from a slight rise in the ground, followed, just seconds later, by a heavy wallop and then the same grinding roar as fast-moving iron passed high over-head.

I've had my fill of that, thought Morgan. No matter how wide it is, I'll never be as cool a hand as McGucken and his like. He lowered his glasses and watched as his colour-sergeant poured every ounce of concentration into spotting where the Pandies' guns were, bothered by the shrieking ordnance no more than he was by the morning's patrol of mosquitoes.

'Sir . . . Cap'n Morgan, sir . . .' Lance-Corporal Pegg was kneeling up at the bottom of the bank a few yards behind his superiors, surrounded by his recumbent command; he pointed off to his left, '. . . the brigade commander's a-coming.'

A cloud of dust boiled around four horsemen, who were cantering down from the centre of the long line of men and mounts that was now shaking out into battle formation behind the slight ridge.

'There's General Smith, his trumpeter and the new brigade-major at a guess, Colour-Sar'nt, but I don't know who the fourth man is.' Even at two hundred paces, Morgan could see how all the riders were tensed over their horses' necks.

'You don't need to say it, sir.' McGucken had read his officer's mind perfectly. 'I'll no' let McGarry anywhere near him,' and he scrambled away to usher the visitors into the vantage point that Morgan and he had already found.

In seconds the party were reining in alongside McGucken, who stood like a signal mast, showing the general where he could get the best view of the enemy. But as the quartet thundered up towards him, Morgan saw how the sprawling soldiers looked away, or even rolled on their sides presenting cold, reproachful backs to the group.

Well, there's a thing. Morgan could feel the troops' resentment towards Richard Carmichael. . . . *A better officer would smell the men's scorn at a mile, but not Captain bloody Carmichael. He'll think the boys are just trying to keep out of the sun, if he's got thoughts for anything but the safety of his own hide. But who's that with them?*

As the cloud of flying grit subsided and the horsemen walked their horses just far enough forward to be able to see over the ridge without exposing themselves, Morgan recognised the generous proportions of the fourth rider. Commandant Dick Kemp was obviously well enough to be back in the saddle and obviously trusted enough to be at the brigadier-general's elbow.

'Good morning.' Smith hailed him as Morgan slithered down the bank to report himself. 'What have you to tell me of the enemy's metal, Morgan?'

'Good morning to you all, gentlemen.' Morgan was damned if he was going to let Carmichael detect just how done up he felt by the trial of the last few hours. Bracing himself to use every ounce of sang-froid that he could muster, he continued, 'Three Pandy guns firing from the foot of that temple at six hundred, sir; quarter left, see where I'm pointing . . .' Morgan stretched his arm in the approved manner, '. . . they've got a wall of bags and baskets to protect themselves, but their shooting's not worth a damn, it ain't.' Morgan did his best to control the tremble in his voice. 'They'll fire again any second; just watch for the signature, sir.'

And as if they had heard his cue, the mutineers obliged with another salvo of three guns that not only showed Smith

315

exactly where his enemy lay, but also had Captain Carmichael cringing low over his saddle bow.

'Are you quite well, sir?' Kemp enquired with false solicitude of the brigade-major. 'Ate something that's disagreed, have you?'

Morgan felt almost sorry for Carmichael. To know Kemp's disapproval for being merciful was bad enough, but he could only imagine his excoriating contempt for cowardice.

'How are you, Commandant?' Morgan greeted Kemp. They hadn't seen one another since the brigade had marched from Seepree.

'Well enough, young Morgan. Just remind me to keep away from you when Pandy's going large. You're too rash for your own good, you are,' Kemp – ever the leader – smiled, saying this loud enough for the Grenadiers who lay thereabouts to hear quite clearly, so burnishing Morgan's reputation still further.

'What d'you make of it, Morgan?' asked General Smith, who was now standing in his stirrups, straining to get a view of his opponents through his glasses.

'Three-gun emplacement, sir, probably nine-pounders. They'll be trying to delay us closing on Gwalior, I'd guess, to buy a bit more time for the defences to be improved there.'

Morgan was rewarded by a nod from Smith. 'What do you say, Kemp?' Smith was sweeping his glasses left and right of the enemy position.

'Aye, Morgan's right, sir, but with Sir Hugh coming at them at the same time from Morar in the east, I'd wager that the Rhani will have strong forces thrown out and concealed on all the approaches to the *kila*. She'll probably try to lure us in by making those guns look like easy meat for a quick *coup de main* by our infantry and have her horse poised to cut up our lads as they go in.' The group all listened respectfully to Kemp's depth of experience. 'Better step a bit gingerly here, I'd say.'

'I agree. We'll use a couple of companies to take the guns and screen them with a squadron of the Eighth Hussars.' Smith lowered his glasses and smiled a rare smile. 'Morgan, are your men sober enough for such a task?'

'Well, it's the break of day, sir, and, as you can see, they're normally drunk as lords by now.' Morgan's riposte provoked a chuckle or two from the troops and another half-grin from the general.

'Good; Carmichael, send an order to Hume and de Salis telling them of my intentions. I'm detaching Morgan's double company and need a squadron of hussars ready to move in five-and-forty minutes. They're to assemble by that stand of trees yonder.' Smith pointed to some scrub just to their rear. 'I imagine that we'll approach from the right, but we'll need to reconnoitre that route first.' He looked at his watch. 'Yes, we have time. Got all that, Carmichael?'

Carmichael, once he had got over the shock of distant danger, had been scribbling away at a sheet of notepaper balanced on his sabretache. Now he nodded glumly.

'Very good. I shall lead the attack myself.' Smith spoke loudly enough for the men to hear him, but Morgan just had time to cast a warning glance at Private McGarry, who seemed to be bursting to voice some witticism. 'You have your charger with you, Morgan? Good. Well, let's see if we can find out what the Rhani has up her sleeve for us.'

Smith stowed his glasses in their case and loosened his pistol in its holster. 'Where are you off to, Carmichael?' he called after his brigade-major, who was just turning his horse away from the enemy.

'About to deliver your orders to the commanding officers, sir,' replied Carmichael a little sheepishly.

'No, man, use your head; send one of Morgan's corporals. I need you with me on the reconnaissance,' Smith barked, to the delight of the surrounding Grenadiers, who smirked at their former commander's discomfiture. 'Come along, everyone, there's not a moment to lose.'

Just as Smith gathered his little group around him, the mutineers' guns fired again, one ball, this time, falling short and skipping over the bank some thirty yards away from where they stood, just as McGucken spoke up.

'Sir, excuse me, sir. Hope I'm no' speakin' out of turn, but don't you think you'd find your escort handy, sir?'

Smith and Kemp looked rather surprised to be reminded of such a fundamentally important point by a colour-sergeant.

'You're right, Colour-Sar'nt. Can't imagine what I was thinking about. Parkyn,' Smith spoke to his trumpeter who, up until then, had been sitting at a safe distance behind the ridge, 'blow for Sar'nt Poole, if you would.' At once the bugle called out, summoning the twenty-strong escort to join their master. 'Good. Now we're complete, we must waste no more time. Sound "form fours: advance", please, Parkyn,' and as the notes carried on the dawn air, the little column jangled off, silhouetted against the rising sun.

The party swept wide and fast through the scattered bush and thorns, passing by a mud-walled hamlet where only a handful of scrawny chickens greeted them and a troop of monkeys ran chattering away from the sour apricots that they were trying to filch. Morgan glanced at his watch: they'd been gone ten minutes and skirted round the right flank of the rebel guns, which continued their disciplined cannonade, firing precisely as the second hand reached each three-and-a-half-minute mark, just as their British instructors had taught them. But as they trotted to within a quarter of a mile of the enemy position, Morgan became aware of a low belt of mist, which lay obliquely across their approach.

'Goddamn, this can't be passed in a hurry.' General Smith reined in alongside the bank of a deep, wide drainage ditch that protected the enemy battery from any rapid assault from their left. A thick haze rose from the scummy water, whilst mosquitoes hummed in clouds just above the surface.

'Sar'nt Poole, take an escort, will you, and see if you can't find a ford or passing place closer to the enemy.' As three hussars trotted off, Smith called the officers in around him to look at the map that he'd spread out on the saddle in front of him. 'You see, this ditch ain't marked, and if we can't find a crossing pretty quick we'll have to delay things and look for a covered approach on the guns' other flank.'

'And that's exactly what the Rhani will want, sir.' Kemp had his horse hard against the general's and was tapping at the chart with a stumpy finger. 'Buys her time and makes us flog around in the worst heat of the day. She's no fool—' But his eulogy was cut short by the arrival of Sergeant Poole.

'General Smith, sir,' two Crimea medals bounced on the senior NCO's chest as his right hand came to the salute, 'there's a corduroy bridge what spans the ditch 'bout two hunned paces up ahead, sir.' He and the two privates with him had unclipped their carbines and had them at the ready across their saddles. 'Only light wood, but stout enough to take a farm bullock or two, so I reckon it should bear the weight of our mounts so long as we keep spread out, sir.'

'Good, well found, Sar'nt Poole.' Smith rapidly folded his map away. 'Will it allow us to get around those guns?' Another salvo made the air jump.

'As far as I can see it will, sir,' the sergeant replied.

'Have a care, General; seems a strange mistake for a bird of the Rhani's feather to have made.' Kemp looked at Morgan, silently asking for his support. 'May I suggest that half a section of the hussars move in front to prove the route; if that bridge is mined—'

'Good point, Kemp. See to it, Carmichael. But we are beginning to run short of time. We'll take a quick look at this last part of the route, then we need to get back to the troops. They should be forming up even now.' Smith rattled out his orders, the escort divided into halves, heels were put to horses' flanks, and off they trotted along the banks of the scummy, greasy ditch.

The files slowed and concertinaed as they approached the logs that had been felled and pegged across the ditch. Morgan could see just what Kemp meant, for the guns lay behind the twisting beck, screened from their view by the scatter of buildings, now less than a quarter of a mile away. To leave this bridge intact was a remarkable mistake. Or, he wondered, was the commandant right, and it had been mined?

The hussars were obviously having the same debate.

'Come on then, nothing to be frit of 'ere.' Sergeant Poole was having some difficulty with the two leading soldiers.

'Well, you go, then, Sar'nt,' said one of the privates who was keeping a tight rein on his horse whilst covering the brush around the narrow bridge with his carbine.

General Smith had obviously not heard this exchange, Morgan realised, being further down the column. He spurred his horse forward – the only way that the reconnaissance would be completed in time was for an officer to lead from the front.

'Follow me, Farrier-Corporal Martin.' Morgan had spotted his old friend as soon as the escort had ridden up. 'These young 'uns need a bit of help.' He hardly slowed Emerald's pace as he trotted by and, to his immense relief, as he glanced over his shoulder, he saw how the NCO was following him without any hesitation, pulling his carbine free of its clip, his face full of eagerness.

But as he bustled between the leading troopers who dithered just short of the bridge, his guts tightened.

Why am I doing this? I can't see a thing against the rising sun, and the bloody Pandies will have their fuses lit to blow the bridge to matchwood no sooner than I lay a hoof upon it. The hussars should be doing this, or that arse Carmichael, thought Morgan, as he and Corporal Martin came within yards of the crossing point. No point in hanging about; the faster I go the less of a target I'll be. And with that he kicked his mare as hard as he could, making dirt fly before her metal shoes thumped on the spongy wood.

'Get on, me lovely,' said Corporal Martin, hard behind him, and in seconds they were across and clear, with not a sign of the enemy.

'Nice as ninepence, that, sir,' panted Corporal Martin, obviously as relieved as Morgan, as he beckoned the rest of the escort forward. 'The Pandies have missed a trick 'ere,' he added, as the leading horsemen spurred across the bridge.

Morgan turned to study the gun position. From here he couldn't see the artillery pieces, – they were hidden by the temple and its outbuildings – and if he could get his men to this point unseen, they would be able to fall upon the gunners from an unexpected flank.

'That was bravely done, Morgan.' The brigade commander on his great, black stallion was suddenly by his side.

Praise from Himself? Perhaps that bit of foolhardiness was worth it after all, thought Morgan.

'This will be a capital forming-up point for your men, and we'll screen your right flank with the Eighth; seen enough?' asked Smith, being almost cordial. 'Time's short.'

'Aye, sir. I thought the same and—' But Morgan's sentence was never finished, for a volley of shots crashed from the thicket of bushes and brush thirty yards away beside the bridge.

Lead tore the air apart, something pulled at Morgan's cap, but before he could gather his senses, Emerald was barged hard by the general's horse, which dropped in a welter of kicking hoofs and bridle-work.

He has a bad habit of falling off his horse. But even as it came into his mind, Morgan realised what a ludicrous thought it was, for Smith was rolling in the dust, apparently unhurt but clearly shocked by the impact of another fall.

Lying low over the mare's neck, Morgan grabbed his revolver from his holster and fired all six chambers into the middle of the cloud of smoke that clung to the leaves and undergrowth. Then he circled his horse between the ambushers and the brigadier-general to give him some protection, before swinging to the ground.

'Here, sir, here . . .' Morgan grabbed Smith by the arm and pulled him towards Emerald's empty saddle, '. . . take my beast.'

'Where's my goddamn revolver?' The general had recovered quickly; he was stripping maps and binoculars from his own horse, which had now ceased to kick and thrash as the blood stopped pumping from its nostrils and its great, soft eyes glazed over. 'Help me find the bloody thing.'

The pair of them scuffed the grass and poked about as chaos exploded around them. A few hussars returned the enemy's fire with their carbines, but the ambush had been well planned, with only part of the escort across the bridge and the rest still back in the relative safety of the brush that covered the further bank. Horses whinnied and circled, one hussar was down, lying still on the ground, his mount shivering with confusion as she sniffed at her master's body.

Then, in the bedlam, a familiar voice shouted, 'Fours about . . . fours about, follow me!' as Captain Richard Carmichael set his gelding as hard as he could back across the bridge in an effort to save himself and anyone else that was quick enough to follow. Some men obeyed, some didn't, but in the flying dirt and smoke, Morgan saw nothing except that he and his brigade commander were stranded within feet of the enemy, unarmed, and with only one horse between them.

Afterwards, all Morgan could remember was his shouting, 'Leave the bloody thing, General: for the love of God, just get on the horse!'

Then the thunder of another artillery salvo, a spatter of shots from the Pandies in the bushes, a hussar shrieking as he was thrown over the back of his horse by a musket ball, and a deep, distant voice bawling, 'No, you bastards, get back and earn your pay. Come on, you fuckers, get amongst 'em . . .' And then Kemp was pushing and barging a knot of bemused cavalrymen back onto the bridge, his great beefy face red both with fury and the joy of battle.

The commandant mastered the confusion just as Morgan had seen him do a dozen times before.

'NCOs, get a grip of your men – what's got into you Balaklava wallahs?' His chaffing was enough to return some normality to the uproar. 'Form line behind me, draw swords.' His sonorous voice calmed the corporals and steadied the dozen or so privates; and it was as well that it did, for with all eyes on the ambush, the drumming of hoofs, a drift of dust, and the flash of steel was only noticed when a fistful of horsemen were suddenly within a hundred paces of them, charging at their right flank out of the rising sun.

Morgan watched the crisis unfold, powerless to do anything except send his brigade commander to a point that was slightly less dangerous. No sooner had Smith thrown his leg across Emerald's back than Morgan smacked her rump, setting her off like a bung from a barrel towards the bridge, just as Kemp made the only decision he could. With invisible enemy in the bushes to his left and a cloud of howling devils bearing down hard on his right, Kemp chose the course that Morgan knew he would – he attacked.

'Right marker, stand firm, right wheel . . .' Kemp's voice galvanised the hussars, who reacted as the hours of drill and sword exercise had taught them to do: their line swung like a gate and as it at last faced the enemy, he commanded, '. . . charge . . . come on, my boys, charge the heathen sods!'

The earth flew as British hoofs dug at the ground, launching themselves into a desperate attempt not to be thrown into ruin by the momentum of the mutineers' assault. Morgan was between the two bodies of horsemen, so he pulled his sword from its scabbard and sank to the ground, knowing that he was going to be overrun by the enemy before his own troops could possibly reach him.

How do I get myself into scrapes like this? he wondered as the faces of the charging Indians became clearly visible ... My only hope is to lie doggo – I'll be too low for a sword thrust but the bloody horses are even more dangerous. And he dropped into a dusty rut, trying to make the smallest target of himself that he could whilst gripping his hilt with one hand and the blade of his sword with the other, just a few inches below the point.

On came the enemy, shouting for all they were worth, curved steel outstretched, some with shields, some with helmets, a red coat here and there amongst the flying cotton robes, all bent upon hewing the hated Feringhee. Then the rider on the outside of the group seemed to notice Morgan and jerked his rein to give him a little more space from the next sowar, drawing his tulwar across his left shoulder and sitting up in the saddle ready for a low slash at his victim, who was so close to the ground.

If I can just keep clear of his cut, and then jab upwards ... But Morgan had no more time to think, for his attacker was upon him, slicing the air, snarling through greasy beard and betel-nut-stained teeth, but too high to kill his man. Then, as the honed steel arced harmlessly above him, Morgan thrust home. He pushed the tip of his sabre into the soft, balding belly of the horse, the point entering the animal's flesh just behind the last rib, carving a scarlet furrow as the creature ran onto the blade, and exiting just below a muscular thigh. Blood fountained, the horse screamed and veered hard into its comrades, knocking another down and crushing its rider as it rolled over him, its legs still pumping even as it died.

Shaken, and flecked with horse blood, Morgan twisted and watched the two groups meet. Kemp's men were one or two stronger than the enemy, but the mutineers had the advantage of speed and surprise, and, he realised with a start, they were led by a slight, helmeted figure in a shirt of mail.

'The Rhani!' Even above the clash of steel meeting steel, of snorting, frightened mounts and the clatter of iron shoes, even above the leather-lunged commands of NCOs and howled Hindustani, Kemp's voice boomed clear and loud. 'Kill the bitch!'

Morgan ran into the mêlée just as the heavier men and mounts of the hussars began to push the native horses back. Since Balaklava he'd heard nothing like these grunts and ring of tempered steel, the jangle of harnesses and moans of pain, the bangs of pistols and the feral noises of men butchering each other. Now the same troops practised their lethal trade, hacking and jabbing, kicking and punching with the determination that he'd seen on the faces of the 8th Hussars almost four years before. He saw one trooper dig his blade too deep into the ribs of a mutineer and hang, inextricably linked to his victim, whilst another sowar cut deep into the soldier's neck with his tulwar. A mutineer plunged to the ground as his horse was shot quite deliberately behind the ear by one of the soldiers who had jibbed at the bridge earlier that morning, forcing Morgan to skip to one side as the animal's legs cartwheeled just in front of him.

Morgan finished the stunned sowar with a quick poke of his sword into his vulnerable armpit, then he danced and dodged through the press of horse legs and withers, looking for another mark. As he crouched and skittered on the edge of the fight, he heard Kemp's voice again.

'Dunniah, you treacherous rogue!' And he watched as the murderer of the commandant's wife and family parried first a slash and then a drill-book thrust from his former master.

He's not himself, thought Morgan, who would have expected a blow from the enraged Kemp to carry all before it, his wounds have left him weak. And as Dunniah collected himself in the saddle and pulled his sword back to riposte, straining at the seams of his scarlet coat, Morgan intervened. Cutting down with all his strength, he sliced into the leg sinews of Dunniah's horse, the steel grating on bone and hamstringing the animal so effectively that it collapsed at Morgan's feet, slamming the angry rebel into the dust.

'Handsomely done, Morgan,' Kemp boomed. 'Now finish the job.' But there was no need, for the sepoy lay still, caught below the thrashing, squealing body of his crippled horse.

Pulling a service pistol from Dunniah's saddle holsters, Morgan scrambled out of the mayhem, just in time to see the hussars complete the work that Kemp had started weeks before. In her mail and helmet, the Rhani had been bruised but safe from the thrusts of the Eighth, giving better than she got with neat, controlled strokes of both her sword and dagger. But one powerful swipe from Private Hoyle had numbed her sword arm and now, as the hussars pressed hard against her bodyguard, she was surrounded by three, sweaty men, hacking and slicing at her.

The last blow was less than elegant, though. Morgan watched as the iron links stopped first a cut to the Rhani's ribs, then a second to her forearm, but there was a distinct crack, her painful flinch announcing that bones had been snapped. Now she was easy meat.

'That's for Cawnpore!' grunted Farrier-Corporal Tom Martin as he pulled his right fist back to his shoulder and punched her as hard as he could on her nose-guard with the iron basket of his sword. Never taught by the instructors and never practised except in battle, Morgan had just seen the favourite blow of the British cavalryman.

The Rhani's head snapped back, she folded over her horse's tail and slumped to the ground, one foot dragging at her reins and stirrup.

'Get on, Sable, get on!' Then Corporal Martin and the other men delivered a brutish *coup de grâce*. The horses didn't like it, but with tight reins and steady spurs, the hussars forced their chargers to trample the slender body with iron shoes, each hoof crushing and kicking the life from the fallen queen.

'Have you found her, Corp'l Pegg?'

Morgan, exhausted by the ambush and amazed to find a shot-hole in his cap cover, had flogged back to the company on a borrowed horse and just had time to give quick orders to the officers and NCOs before moving off to assault the gun battery. Brigadier-General Smith, very spry considering his fall and narrow escape, had been intrigued to hear of the Rhani's death (recounted in gory delight by Kemp), but was still not convinced that she was no more. Now, streaming with sweat, the infantry had advanced, unseen by the guns, over the very ground that Morgan had just ridden and as they shook out to attack, there was one, grisly task that had been insisted on by Smith.

'Aye, sir, I think so.' Pegg, rifle and fixed bayonet in one hand, great circles of sweat staining the khaki of his smock at neck and armpits, pulled at the corpse. 'It's a tart anyway, but she's in a bit of a mess, she is.'

Colour-Sergeants McGucken and Whaley were chivvying the men into an extended line, trying to be as quiet as possible as they approached the screened guns, with the usual advice just before they moved into the assault: 'Check your caps, lads. Spare rounds handy – you'll need 'em in a minute. Keep the line good an' straight when the officer gives the word,' and the normal miscreants being cajoled and gripped: 'Get a hold o' that damned weapon, Price; you look like a duchess holding a copper's cock.'

As the men milled and scrambled about them, Morgan and Pegg crouched next to the stiffening body.

Tart? thought Morgan. *I don't think so. Bloody brave girl, I'd say . . .* He swiped at a cloud of flies that rose from the coffee-coloured skin of her bruised and scraped face.

'Bet that stung a bit.' Pegg looked at the bloody lips, the swollen, closed eyes still with traces of kohl, and the surface of her cheek where a broken sinus bone poked through. 'Got 'er kipper stamped on, by the look of things, but that wouldn't 'ave finished 'er, sir, would it?' Pegg glanced at Morgan with not a trace of sympathy, just professional interest. 'That would, though.'

'Aye, you're right.' Morgan saw how her shirt was red with blood at the waist, how the iron links of mail below it were ripped and distorted. 'A bloody great cavalry whaler pounding up and down on your guts will do the job.' Morgan could imagine the queen's last moments as the metal shoes crushed the life out of her.

'Corp'l Pegg, do you have to? Have you no respect?'

The young NCO had pushed his finger through a delicate gold hoop that pierced the Rhani's left nostril. His first attempt to rip it clear had failed, so he'd tried again using a little more force, tearing the skin – yet no blood came from a heart that had long ceased to beat.

'Well, Her bleedin' Majesty don't need it, does she?' Pegg looked up, genuinely perplexed by his officer's sensitivities. 'Do you want the earrings – 'ere, tek 'em?' Two smaller gold rings with tiny stones had been snatched from the Rhani's lobes even as Morgan objected.

'No, I don't.' Morgan shook slightly at the sight of the body. 'No thank you.' There was something desperately repellent in the sight of such bravery, such nobility being reduced to offal.

But there was no more time to reflect. General Smith had been insistent that the Rhani's death should be confirmed, reasoning that once the rebels came to hear of it, much of the will to resist would desert them. Morgan understood that and he could see why Damodar's fate needed to be known as well, for if the Pandies had a prince to replace a queen, they might still be inspired to fight. What he hadn't expected to see, though was the captive sepoy Dunniah being systematically tortured by one of Kemp's daffadars right under Smith's allegedly civilised nose, just before they set off to attack the guns.

I never thought I'd see a so-called Christian gentleman do that, I thought Morgan. I know that Dunniah's a murderer, but taking the arm that he'd broken in the skirmish and twisting it until you could hear the bones crunching – in between the poor creature's screams – was enough to turn the stomach. Still, I suppose it got the answers we needed – Morgan's heart had leapt when the intelligence was passed to him – and now we know that Mary's safe, treating the wounded rebels up in the fort with Sam and Damodar alongside her. But where does her heart lie? Is she still with us or, as Kemp says, has she turned? Morgan sagged at the thought of Mary having gone over to the enemy. And now a sun-addled army, bent on hatred and revenge, is about to storm the very place where she is, led by Kemp, the maddest of the mad. Unless I'm hard up alongside him, she'll be given no quarter; she'll be treated the same as the mutineers treated the commandant's wife and his family.

'Right, sir, all's set.' McGucken, somehow less hot and sweaty than anyone else seemed to be, reported to Morgan. 'Spare ammunition to hand: when you're ready, sir.'

Morgan looked left and right at his command. More than a hundred sleepless, heat-dazed men poised in two lines on either side of him, every fold of their smocks and caps dusty and stained, nothing bright or glittering except their steel and their eyes.

'Any sign of the cavalry yet, Colour-Sar'nt?' Morgan had little fear of the enemy's infantry, but he knew how quick and aggressive their horsemen could be and how well they used the ground – he'd seen just that in the ambush earlier that morning. Now he was acutely conscious of his vulnerable flanks.

'Aye, sir, they're just a-coming up to our rear.' McGucken had spotted the leading files of the 8th Hussars some couple of hundred paces away.

'Good,' said Morgan, though he knew it wasn't. He was about to commit his men yet again to a deeply perilous task from which not all of them would return – including himself, perhaps – and he was both sorry for it and frightened at the same time. 'We've got some spiking nails to hand, ain't we?'

'Yes, sir, you know we have.' After countless fights and skirmishes, McGucken knew his officer well enough to expect this sort of fussing from him. He understood that it helped him to calm himself in the doubting, dry-mouthed moments before the fight started. 'An' we learnt the boys how to use them after Kotah, sir, so dinna worry.'

'Aye, Colour-Sar'nt, you're right.' Morgan looked at the plain over which they were going to attack. One hundred and fifty paces to their front, across hard-baked, cracked earth lay the clutch of buildings behind which the Pandies had built their battery. A dry nullah scored the ground obliquely just in front of the closest, mud walls. 'Call the subalterns to me, please, Colour-Sar'nt.'

And with that, McGucken, rather than use the customary bugle call, sent two runners dashing away to collect the young gentlemen. Both of them had been expecting such last-minute instructions and arrived – Wilkinson neat and quiet, Fawcett ruddy and clearly very excited – holding tight to their sword scabbards rather than trip in front of the men.

'On my word, Mr Wilkinson, you go first and lead Number One just to the right of the temple. I want you to provide volley fire from there for the Grenadiers' assault on the battery from the left of the buildings. As soon as you're ready, let me know and I'll signal with a flag to tell Fawcett to move up: are you clear?'

Wilkinson gave a silent nod in reply.

'Mr Fawcett, when we see my signal, be up and off without

any delay. Watch that nullah to your front – that'll foul the men's dressing – and I want you ready to assault by echelon as soon as I give Wilkinson the order to open fire. Any questions?'

Fawcett licked his lips, blinked, then asked, 'Sir, where will you be moving, please?'

'Between the two companies with Colour-Sar'nts Whaley and McGucken,' replied Morgan. 'I'll start off just to Wilkinson's left and rear. Once Number One's opened fire, you move up with the Grenadiers, then I shall be with you in the assault. Are you both content?'

Content . . . content? thought Morgan. How can any sane man be content at a moment like this? These youngsters will think the bloody sun's got to me.

But the only reply was, 'Sir,' from both ensigns who, thought Morgan, might have been slaughtering rebels since they left their mothers' tits.

'Well, good luck, then,' said Morgan, remembering just such a parting with his company commander when he first tasted battle at the river Alma. Then Eddington had clasped his hand and been dead within minutes, his head taken off by a Russian thirty-two-pounder. He shivered at the thought.

But neither lad replied. They both looked him hard in the eye and then they were away, leaving him to sweat and worry, to play with his sword knot and, for the hundredth time, to check the priming in his revolver.

'Sweetham, have you got that flag to hand?' Morgan asked his bugler. When silent signals were thought necessary, the buglers relied upon white flags set with a blue line; now the eighteen-year-old pointed to the short stick tightly furled in cloth.

'Aye, sir, ready when you are,' replied the lad, who'd joined straight from the slums of Leicester.

'Stay close . . . come on then,' and as Wilkinson leapt up in front of his men and beckoned them to follow with the blade of his sword, Morgan followed, just a few paces behind the billowing line of men and outstretched steel.

'They don't know we're coming, sir.' Just as McGucken spoke, the enemy guns fired again, neatly in unison, great plumes of smoke jetting out from beyond the buildings, but firing at the brigade that was holding their attention, and not aimed at the 95th who were stalking them. 'They've forgotten all we've taught 'em, daft buggers. There's not a sentry to be seen on this flank, is there, sir?'

And he seemed to be right, for the line swept on, Morgan and both colour-sergeants trailing a few paces behind on their extreme left, keeping as straight and regular as the grass and dry fissures would allow. A covey of partridge hummed away from the soldiers' boots, one gamekeeper's son raising his rifle and pretending to fire two barrels at their tails, but no shot came, none of the shrieking metal that Morgan hated so much. Then, with a spasm of relief, he saw how Number One Company broke into a trot, filed into a wooden-railinged sheep byre and was deployed by their subaltern in such a way, he hoped, that the enemy battery could be taken in enfilade.

'In here, sir.' McGucken pointed to the end of the nullah, where it shrank away, levelling out to nothing in a patch of scrub and thorns. 'Let's get into a bit o' cover until Mr Fawcett comes up.'

With his usual eye for ground, McGucken had seen how the very end of the nullah provided a useful dip in which Morgan's men could conceal themselves whilst the Grenadier Company advanced into the open, covered by Number One.

'Right, Colour-Sar'nt, lead on. Sweetham, are you ready with that flag?' But before the bugler had time to answer, just as the little party panted into the notch in the earth that the banks of the dry stream bed provided, the very sound that Morgan dreaded slapped their ears as a musket ball cracked past them.

'Come on, sir, let's have the fuckers,' and even before Morgan had gathered his wits, McGucken, with Colour-Sergeant Whaley hard behind him, was thumping down the dry gulley, grit and dust flying from the soles of their boots, both men uttering strange, wild yells, leaning over their bobbing bayonet blades.

Then Morgan saw the five young sepoys, no more than thirty paces away, struggle to their horrified feet, grabbing for their weapons. Obviously, four had been resting in the depths of the nullah – there was a jumble of belts, drinking pots and clothes strewed about them – whilst the fifth had been on sentry halfway up the bank. He'd been dozing, oblivious to the advance of a hundred, heavily armed British infantrymen, and now he was about to pay the price.

'He's mine. Get the others, sir.' McGucken spoke more out of respect for Morgan's rank, for the other colour-sergeant had already weighed things up and was almost upon the stupefied, main group who, Morgan could see, were still undecided about whether to fight or run. But McGucken's victim was given no choice.

'On guard!' McGucken yelled the drill-manual phrase at the terrified sepoy. Morgan saw how the lad understood enough English to respond – he probably hoped that the senior NCO in front of him was about to give him a harmless, impromptu lesson in bayonet fencing – for his blade now came up hesitantly to meet the Scotsman's. With a quick flick and a clash of metal, McGucken dashed the Indian's bayonet to one side and the boy staggered on the steep bank, leaving himself wide open.

'That's a fucking useless parry, that is, Pandy, my lad,' spat McGucken. Morgan had seen his colour-sergeant do this before. It wasn't that he was playing with his quarry, it was more a demonstration of the man's skill at arms, a supremely confident, professional killer at work. Even as Morgan closed with his own man, he noticed the flash of McGucken's

333

bayonet, a bolt of metal aimed at the sepoy's throat, a killer blow that avoided buttons and buckles, which might deflect a low thrust, and the bone of the skull, which might resist a higher one. No, it was a perfect attack: the sepoy crumpled on his back as fourteen stone of whiplash-muscled Scot dug the long spike into him, paused, stamped a boot onto the dying lad's chest and then pulled the weapon clear, red in the sunlight.

Then a sea of grunts and oily bodies engulfed Morgan. As he had stumbled down the stream bed towards his opponent, Morgan recognised the fear and indecision in the boy's eyes. The four dozing sepoys had been dragged to consciousness by the sentry's panicky shot and now Whaley, Sweetham and himself were already pounding down upon them in a spray of dirt and dust, weapons at the ready. In the few, brief seconds that their crazy charge had taken, Morgan noticed his chosen target pull his slippers properly onto his feet, grab a blade that looked as if it had been designed to carve the Sunday roast, glance at his comrades to gather what their silent, joint decision would be and then elect to stand and fight. It was a poor choice: as the youngster poked the knife out half-heartedly towards Morgan, the officer skidded into him, slammed the muzzle of his pistol straight into his belly and fired. The half-inch-wide ball probably entered somewhere under the fourth rib; it hardly mattered, for Morgan saw a tear open in his enemy's shirt and an instant stain of blood just beside his lower spine before he threw the whimpering mutineer to one side and turned to help Colour-Sergeant Whaley.

But this was another old hand who knew his trade. Morgan had seen him stab a sepoy between the shoulder blades just as the Indian had turned to run. It had been a good, clean thrust: the native had arched backwards in agony as the spike struck home, but as Whaley had tried to pull the steel clear, the weapon's socket and locking ring had caught in the native's dhoti and, for a crucial moment, attacker and attacked had been pulling and staggering around one another like a fisherman and an outsize catch. Then another sepoy thought he had a chance and swiped at Whaley, holding a curved knife low, jabbing abruptly. But as Morgan whipped his pistol round to deal with this man, Whaley simply dropped his rifle and jammed bayonet, twisted on the spot and kicked the rebel so powerfully and accurately in the balls that the man bent double and tumbled to the ground.

Whilst the experienced men had been doing well, young Drummer Sweetham had not.

'No, sir, don't shoot.' McGucken had come pounding down the side of the bank just as Morgan was aiming at the last sepoy's midriff. The biggest of all the Indians, he'd side-stepped Whaley and Morgan's private mêlée and beaten the barrel of Sweetham's rifle aside with a tulwar before throwing the young soldier to the ground and flinging himself on top of him. Now the pair of them rolled and kicked in the dirt, boots and slippers akimbo, the Indian with a headlock around the bugler that threatened to squeeze the life out of him. 'A bullet from yon thing will go through both of 'em. Stand clear, sir,' and with that McGucken shoved Morgan out of the way, raised the butt of his rifle over his shoulder, watched the fight for a few seconds and then clubbed the mutineer on the side of the head, the brass butt-plate meeting the man's temple with a dull thud that shattered the skull and sent him sprawling, blood pouring from his nose and ears.

'Fuckin' hell, Colour-Sar'nt . . .' Sweetham climbed unsteadily to his feet, '. . . thank you. I thought I was done for, I did.'

'He makes a habit of that sort of thing,' Morgan panted, standing amongst the twist of human debris. 'He did just the same for me at the Alma.'

McGucken half smiled whilst Sweetham goggled at the man in admiration.

'Well, learn a lesson, Sweetham.' McGucken pulled his smock down and straightened his cap, instantly returning to his stern, paternal role. 'Never let a Pandy get closer than he has to: shoot the fuckers at a safe distance; leave all that close-quarter stuff to the officers.' Again, a slight smile played over McGucken's great, granite face.

In an instant, the top of the nullah was crowned by worried men. Wilkinson's people peered down from the right with cries of, 'You all right, sir?' and, 'Need an 'and, Colour-Sar'nt?' just before Fawcett and the Grenadiers, who, on hearing the shot, had doubled across the open ground, almost sixty of them, anxious for Morgan and Jock McGucken's safety.

'Colour-Sar'nt Whaley,' the Yorkshireman was just finishing the mutineer whose balls he had so badly bruised as Morgan spoke to him, 'get over to Mr Wilkinson, please. I want that covering fire as soon as you like; and thank you for your help down here.'

Whaley, wiping the gore of the mutineer off his bayonet, smiled in response. 'Sir, it's been a real pleasure, it has,' before trotting off to join his officer.

'Now, Alex Fawcett, my bold young bucko,' Morgan's ensign had come scurrying down to join him in the stifling depths of the nullah whilst the rest of the Grenadiers crowded into its sandy, scrubby cover behind him. 'You saw the three guns when we were back up on the ridge. When we come out of this damned ditch and get round those buildings, my guess is that there'll be no more sentries and that as long as Number One's fire is well directed, you should be able to roll the buggers up from their left, but you'll need to have the lads in echelon of platoons, each lot ready to push forward as all three guns fall without any bloody hanging back – got it?'

Christ, I sound like bloody Smith with all this talk of

'hanging back'; it must be infectious. I need to encourage the boy, not brow-beat him.

'Yes, Morgan, the men are already told off into platoons,' said Fawcett, slightly coolly, and indeed, as Morgan watched the men scrambling up the far bank of the streambed, he could see that they had been broken down into four groups of about a dozen men, each sergeant or corporal doing his best to move them forward and keep them in four ranks.

'Right, well, as soon as you hear—' Then they both caught a distant shout, followed by a roll of musketry as Number One Company began their work. 'There it is, get bloody moving,' and Fawcett was away up the sandy slope, drawn sword held in his teeth as he reached at tussocks of grass and boulders, anything to get him to the lip of the nullah and to the front of his men.

The first knot of men hared off after Fawcett, whilst McGucken and Morgan followed the next platoon under the command of Sergeant Ormond. As the troops trotted along, weapons held at the 'trail', parallel to the ground, they moved past the outbuildings and yards that surrounded the temple.

''Ere we go again, sir,' Sergeant Ormond, with whom he had carried the Regimental Colours at the Alma, panted as Morgan loped alongside him. 'Same business, just different stinks. The bleedin' Pandies have been shitein' all over the place; look where yer treading, sir.'

And as they doubled along, Morgan noticed the inevitable detritus of large numbers of ill-disciplined troops – sun-dried coils of excrement, and litters of leaves that the rebels had used to clean themselves, garlanded with clouds of blue-bottles. Ormond was right, the whole place stank most dreadfully, but Morgan's attention was immediately dragged back by another volley off to his left. As he raced to look around the next mud wall, Fawcett sprinted forward with the leading platoon as Number One Company's bullets threw up great clouds of spoil from the sandbags that shielded the enemy's left-hand gun.

'That's a grand bit o' shootin' by Mr Wilkinson's boys, sir,' said McGucken as the lead balls swept the enemy gun crew from their left and rear.

'Aye, and Fawcett's good and close,' said Morgan as the young ensign waved his first dozen men forward, sword knot flapping wildly, every muscle tight for the delicious moment when they would close with their enemies.

'They're not a bad wee pair of pups, sir, are they?' These were rare words from McGucken, who would never have said such a thing to the subalterns' faces, praising them only very occasionally.

'Not bad lads at all,' Morgan replied. 'I just hope that Mr Fawcett doesn't get too close to the next volley, though. I don't want one of the lads catching a ricochet off this stony ground.'

But he needn't have worried, for the men, Fawcett at their head, were already tumbling over the bags and gabions that hid the rebel gun from their view. One or two Grenadiers paused on top of the protective bank to fire their rifles at targets below them that Morgan couldn't see, but most just leapt amongst their foes, their butts and bayonets occasionally flicking into sight above the earth wall as they went about their bloody task.

'Right, Sar'nt Ormond,' Morgan turned to the NCO who was poised with his platoon for the assault on the next gun, 'as soon as Mr Fawcett gives the word.'

'Aye, sir, we're ready.' Sergeant Ormond licked at his parched lips before checking his boys. 'Mek sure your caps are still in place, lads.' Every man ran a searching finger over the copper percussion caps that should have been pressed firmly over the rifles' breech nipples. 'Stand by.'

And then, into the slight cloud of powder smoke that still clung to the front of the gun position, jumped Ensign Fawcett.

With a look of triumph, the young officer turned towards the next platoon, beckoning them forward with urgent sweeps of his sword.

'Oh, no, Mr Fawcett, sir,' muttered McGucken, unheard by the subaltern, 'don't stand out there like balls on a dog. Every damn Pandy in Gwalior can see you.'

Then, even as Sergeant Ormond gathered himself and his men for the rush towards the middle gun of the battery, Morgan saw Fawcett's face burst like a ruptured fruit. One second the boy was shouting, urging them on, full of martial vim, full of the crude joy of war; next, a hole as big as a baby's fist had been ripped beside his nose, his knees buckled and he pitched forward into the ground, quite dead.

They were all thinking the same. The Grenadier Company's last officer to be killed was nineteen-year-old Ensign Parkinson, stabbed to death before Sevastopol when he, just like Alexander Fawcett, had been striving to distinguish himself. Morgan could still remember every word of the note that he had written to the boy's parents, and the memory was made no sweeter by Lance-Corporal Pegg's next words.

'Bloody 'ell, sir, that's another of our young subbies you've got killed.'

That heartless, utterly unfair comment goaded Morgan forward. Without pausing to give any instructions to McGucken, all concern for himself swept aside by self-reproach, Morgan was on his feet, kicking up the dirt as he scrabbled into a sprint.

'Follow me, you lads,' he yelled, gripping the butt of his pistol so hard he feared that he might bend the steel, running so fast past Fawcett's body that he could have no time to see the puddle of blood that was now seeping into the earth below his shattered face. He scarcely noticed the curtain of lead that sang around him as Number One Company fired another perfect volley, and all the time he was thinking, you poor, brave decent lad – why you of all people? Stopping only once, he was soon kneeling, chest heaving, in the embrasure next to the great brass barrel of the second gun. There he paused, more than twenty yards in front of Ormond, Pegg and the rest of the platoon, steadying himself against the metal, which was still hot to the touch, face to face with half a dozen terrified gunners and a pile of wounded and dead, cut down by Wilkinson's covering fire.

The surviving gun numbers were pressed hard against the sandbag wall, cowering from the cracking lead that had already killed and injured so many of their comrades, when Morgan sprang into the embrasure, pistol cocked and menacing.

They look as though they've seen the devil himself, thought Morgan as he crouched, revolver outstretched and, rather to his surprise, remarkably steady. There's more of them than I've got rounds – why don't they just turf me out? But the sepoys stood and gawped at him, brown eyes open wide, lips trembling, hands moving together, dropping weapons and tools, making *namasti*, begging for mercy. But then I suppose I must look pretty, bloody diabolical. Morgan took a minute to survey himself. His trousers were torn at both knees; his smock was filthy from the morning's scrimmages and soaked in sweat; his cap was on the back of his head and fresh torn with shot, whilst both hands were as black as if he had been mining coal. He could only guess at his own expression, but whatever horrid scowl he had adopted, it had clearly shaken the Pandies. Now he signalled with his pistol barrel and all of them sank quickly to their knees.

'Come on, boys, they killed our officer . . .' and through the other side of the embrasure bundled a sweaty, panting Sergeant Ormond followed by an equally torrid Lance-Corporal Pegg and a gang of angry, revenge-filled private soldiers, '. . . destroy the bastards.'

'No, lads,' Morgan gasped, still sucking for air. 'Leave them be – there's no more fight in this lot.'

'But they killed Mr Fawcett, sir,' blurted Lance-Corporal Pegg, who had tumbled down from the top of one of the gabions and was lifting his cocked rifle to his shoulder. 'They're fuckin' Pandies, sir.'

'I can see that for myself, Corp'l Pegg,' replied Morgan as the mutineers began to keen most pathetically at the sight of the advancing Pegg, 'and they can face a court martial: that will decide what happens to them.'

'Bollocks, I'll—' muttered Corporal Pegg, still pacing towards the mutineers, who were huddling together even more tightly, their voices raised high in supplication.

'You'll do exactly as you're told, Corporal Pegg.' Morgan pointed his pistol away from the prisoners and glared at the angry NCO. 'That's what you'll do.'

Pegg hesitated whilst the rest of the platoon watched the little drama. Morgan half expected Sergeant Ormond to weigh in on his side, but no, this was a straight test of character between the two men. If Pegg fires, thought Morgan, all the others will join in and I'll be powerless to stop them. Nobody will even notice another pile of riddled bodies.

Then slowly, Pegg lowered his rifle, not stopping until the tip of the bayonet touched the ground. 'Sir,' said the lad quietly, his face still red with righteous anger, but his eyes unable to hold Morgan's.

'That's better.' Morgan sighed with relief, having won the confrontation. 'Now, Sar'nt Ormond, signal to the next platoon to stay back. I don't want them being hit by whoever shot Mr Fawcett.'

'Didn't stop you draggin' us up 'ere, did it?' muttered Pegg, trying to regain some credibility in front of the others.

Morgan ignored him. 'The rest of you, get the prisoners to tear me a hole in this wall. We'll deal with the last piece a bit more cleverly.'

Each of the three guns in the battery was surrounded by six-foot-high sandbag and gabion walls on three sides, but were open to the rear – just as the Field Artillery manual said they should be. Number One Company had been able to rake the first position comprehensively and disable most of the men in the second bay, but the angle of the third made Morgan worry that many of its crew would still be alive.

'Sar'nt Ormond, cut me half a dozen bits of fuse – about two seconds worth each – and stick them in those gun cartridges yonder.' Morgan pointed to a neat pile of linen bags, each containing about three pounds of propellant powder, which were lined up ready for use by the gun's trail. They peeped out from below a stretch of tarpaulin – the better to resist any stray sparks – once again, just as the manual said it should be done. 'We'll blast the buggers out.'

Sar'nt Ormond busied himself with knife and a coil of fuse, slicing little bits of tarred line against the gunner's measuring board, whilst Morgan spoke to the men.

'Right, six of you, once that hole's clear, we'll all light our fuses and then toss these bloody things into the third gun bay.' He nodded to the next protective wall, about nine paces away from where they were sheltering. 'Leave your weapons and each grab a cartridge.'

Sergeant Ormond dished out improvised bombs into a half-dozen pairs of sweaty hands.

'Corp'l Pegg,' Morgan had decided to allow the NCO to reassert his authority, 'I'll need you to light the fuses; you've got lucifers, ain't you?'

Pegg nodded in reply, obviously pleased that Morgan seemed to have forgiven him.

'Right, let's be at 'em.' Morgan led the way through the breach that the prisoners had torn, pressed his back to the next wall and gathered the men around him, all holding the stumpy bits of fuse together so that Corporal Pegg could light them.

'Get a bit closer, can't you, Fuller?' Pegg had eventually managed to get one of the matches that all NCOs were required to carry – little green chemical tips dipped in candle-wax to resist the damp – to light whilst the bombers crowded round him. Three fuses fizzed immediately, crackling angrily, but the others were less keen to oblige.

'Just chuck the wretched things, lit or not.' Morgan instantly regretted being anywhere near such unpredictable horrors, and all six bags, some spitting, some not, were lofted high over the bank of sandbags, an invisible, native voice yelling in alarm. Even sheltered as they were by the wall, the three, almost simultaneous bangs shook the ground, or so it seemed to Morgan, as a shower of earth and debris pattered down around them.

'Give 'em the bayonet, lads,' bawled Sergeant Ormond as he led the rest of the platoon past the bombers, who were still crouching by the wall, and up and over the basketwork before the enemy had a chance to recover.

By the time that Morgan had gathered his pummelled wits and scrambled after Ormond into the next gun bay, the job was finished. The home-made bombs had shattered not just one of the nine-pounder's wheels, but also most of the dozen or so men who were crowded around it. Some bodies had been eviscerated by the blast and all were blackened – the horrid smell of burnt flesh and spilt bowels hung heavily – whilst any rebels who remained alive were dealt with by the rising and falling steel of Sergeant Ormond's men.

'Not a bad bit of work that, sir.' Colour-Sergeant McGucken poked his head round the rear of the position, whilst Morgan was still trying to take in the scene. 'I've got the rest of the Grenadiers in cover around the other two gun positions, sir; Number One Company have ceased fire and are awaiting your orders – what d'you want them to do?'

'Bring them forward, please, Colour-Sar'nt.' Morgan knew that he had to exploit this success, but the sheer noise and shock of the last few minutes, added to the fatigue of the day, had left him stunned. 'And I'll . . . I'll . . .'

'You'll shake 'em out onto that next wee ridge-line ahead,' McGucken pointed to a steep rise about five hundred paces in front of them, 'from where we should get a good look at the plain in front of Gwalior, won't you, sir?'

'Yes, that's what we'll do. Please see to it, Colour-Sar'nt.' Morgan felt that all the energy had been drained from him. He searched for his water bottle but before he took a deep draught from it he asked, 'Have we any casualties other than Mr Fawcett?'

'Two wounded in the Grenadiers, sir; I don't know about the other company yet – an' we've already collected the ensign's body.' A pair of soldiers crossed themselves sombrely. 'But it looks as though we've got visitors, sir.'

'Fine work, Morgan.' Brigadier-General Smith, his brigade-major, Richard Carmichael, Commandant Kemp and a trumpeter had trotted their horses around the temple and were now right behind the brigade's leading infantry – Morgan's men. 'This battery is key. You've taken it and opened up the whole of this flank into Gwalior; well done. Hark at that.' Morgan could hear a fitful roar of gunfire in the near distance, the other side of the great fortress. 'That's General Rose's troops coming at the place from Morar on the other flank. We've just received a message from him that says that the garrison is running: they've lost their stomach for the fight. I imagine that they've got word of the Rhani's death: you did find her body, didn't you?'

'We did, sir,' replied Morgan quietly.

'Not too quick or easy an exit from this plain of tears, I trust?' interrupted Kemp with a leer.

'Cold as mutton, sir,' answered Morgan, 'killed clean; cut down, then trampled by the Eighth, by the look of her wounds.'

Kemp seemed disappointed.

And I'm damn glad she was, thought Morgan, otherwise

you'd be toying with her just like you did Dunniah, wouldn't you, you mad, cruel man?

'If the mutineers are on the run then, General,' Kemp continued, 'it's even more important that we get into Gwalior pretty sharp and prevent them from saving Damodar. If they can get that little sod onto his mother's throne then the bastards might just recover some of their bottom and—'

But Kemp never finished his discourse, for an artillery ball smacked into the earthen wall no more than a few paces from General Smith's party, hurling sandbags around as if they were cushions, before bouncing and skipping over the heads of Number One Company, who had just started to move out of their positions by the temple.

'Dear Christ, that was close!' Carmichael's utter terror communicated itself to his horse. As he huddled down in the saddle, the animal shivered and bucked.

'Get a grip of that damned creature, can't you, sir?' said Smith with a curl of his lip as he, Kemp and the trumpeter sat studiedly still.

What you really mean, General, my jewel, is, 'Get a grip of yourself,' don't you? thought Morgan as he ran his eye over his brother officer. Carmichael's clean linen and well-scrubbed face stood out starkly amongst the scruffy, dusty men who surrounded him. But even under his tan, he was as pale as milk, as white as the knuckles that held his reins.

'And for God's sake put that fancy contraption away, can't you? What on earth do you intend to do with that against artillery? Save that for when we get up close to brother Pandy.'

Carmichael had pulled his expensive Adams from its holster. Its carefully emblazoned grip had caught Smith's attention some time ago and, judging by the general's tone, annoyed him just as much as it had the officers of the 95th, thought Morgan.

'Take this dispatch for de Salis.' But, as Carmichael struggled to put his pistol away and to grapple with pencil and message pad, Morgan heard a bang and a muffled shout; there was a cloud of powder smoke around Carmichael's waist and he doubled over in the saddle, clearly in great pain. The little group of horses jibbed and shied away from the noise in their midst.

'Why, you've shot yourself, man,' Smith said, more in exasperation than sympathy, as Carmichael, his face contorted and unable to speak, gripped at the two bloody holes in the top of his left thigh, which the revolver ball had torn.

Morgan walked his horse over to Carmichael's and felt in the wounded man's hip pocket for the dressing that regimental orders required. Sure enough, the paper package was there, but not one of the common ones issued to the men; as Morgan tore at the wrappings with his teeth, spilling out the lint that would bind the pad against the wound, he noticed that this one had been bought on Oxford Street.

'There, Carmichael, that'll do for now.' Morgan had deftly passed the bandage round Carmichael's limb without getting the victim to dismount, and knotted the ends tightly. ''Tis a nice, even wound that'll soon mend. Corp'l Pegg, lead Captain Carmichael to the rear. Make sure he goes to our own regimental surgeons, please; they'll look after him.'

'To the rear is it, sir.' Pegg had been taking a lively interest in things from well within cover behind the bank. 'The nag won't need to be led, it won't: Cap'n Carmichael's mount knows its own way to the rear well enough!' There was a ripple of mirth at this from the Grenadiers, who were scattered around and who had not missed a syllable of the officers' conversations, but Morgan could see no look of sympathy or compassion from the men, just indifference for an officer who had used them badly.

So that's the end of your glittering career, Richard bloody Carmichael, he thought. Your body will soon mend but your name will never recover. But even as Morgan watched Carmichael being led away and remembered all the insults, all the snobbery and the way in which he had abused the men over the past few years, he could feel nothing but pity for the man.

'I seem to be getting through my brigade-majors rather faster than I'd expected,' said Smith matter-of-factly.

'Aye, General, but that one's no loss. I had to pull him up by the reins at that little affair we had back on the bridge this morning; all that "fours about" nonsense. Why, if Rissaldar Batuk hadn't gripped those hussars, your erstwhile brigade-major would have led them to Delhi by now. And as for that costermonger's pistol of his, the only time he fired it near the enemy was to shoot himself! Good riddance to the scrub, says I,' growled Kemp.

'Aye, you're probably right,' said Smith, just as another ball whistled close overhead and drove any further talk of Carmichael away, 'but we seem to have taught these badmashes a little too well, Morgan.' Smith was inching his horse forward so that he could scan the higher ground that lay between themselves and Gwalior. 'They've got a concealed battery up there, crafty sods. I'll keep your flanks secure with the hussars.' Then Smith did something of which Morgan had thought him simply incapable: he turned to a huddle of grimy, sweaty men and spoke directly to them: 'But d'you think you could deal with them for me, my old Ninety-Fifth?'

The Grenadiers goggled back with pleasure at being spoken to in such a familiar manner. Then, predictably, from the group to whom he spoke, out stepped Private Matthew McGarry – the freshly flogged, sharp-tongued Matthew McGarry. Morgan's heart sank.

'We will, yer honour. Don't worry your head about it at all. The Owd Nails will do the job.'

'D'you know, I believe you will,' said Smith with, Morgan thought, an almost fond smile flitting about his lips.

'Colour-Sar'nt,' even as Morgan turned, McGucken was

waiting at his elbow for the orders that he knew must follow, 'get the prisoners back to the second gun bay and run that nine-pounder out into a position where we can engage that next battery.' Morgan, his exhaustion suddenly gone, knew how risky manoeuvring the captured gun under the nose of the rebels would be, so the captives could do the job for him. 'Send a runner to Mr Wilkinson and ask him to move his company back to the temple, but to be prepared to advance on my order.' McGucken just nodded his understanding. 'Then find me six lads who know how to handle a bit of ordnance – they'll have to be old hands who were out East.'

Of all the memories that stayed with Morgan into old age of that sun-baked, dust-coated, blood-red rebellion, the next few moments were, for some reason, the most vivid. The prisoners' horrified looks as their own people bounced round-shot amongst them whilst they struggled with the wheels and trail of the heavy gun; his six volunteers who slaved with rammers, shot and cartridge, racing with the Pandies to be the first to load and find the range; but most of all, the fear that had clutched at his bowels but evaporated once he squinted down the long, brass barrel.

'Left . . . left . . . left, steady, Corp'l Pegg.' Morgan remembered how Pegg must have fought with his own sense of self-preservation in order to atone for earlier misdeeds, how the podgy little NCO had struggled to lift and shift the trail of the gun at Morgan's command, fully expecting a rushing iron ball to end the whole matter for him there and then.

He remembered how the men had fretted as he tinkered with the gun's elevation wheel, hoping against hope that his aim was better than the Pandy gunner's, who was certainly staring back at him and cursing his own crew's cack-handedness; how he'd stood clear and jerked the lanyard to fire the piece, trying to look as nonchalant as possible; and how a great cheer had gone up from the men when a metallic clang announced that his very first round had knocked the enemy's barrel clean off its carriage: it killed most of the crew as it spun amongst them like a mighty hammer.

He remembered the brigade commander crowing with delight. 'Ha! Bravo, Morgan. Damn fine shot; now get your lads up and at 'em,' and the lung-bursting run up the half-mile slope with forty parched, sun-bleached crazies panting and yelling beside him. He remembered how the crew of the second gun had fired a mile wide over his head and then run for their lives; and he remembered how he and the men had flung themselves flat on the hot earth, looked down onto the plain below and seen ten thousand or more mutineers streaming away from Gwalior – broken men fleeing the Rhani's broken cause.

ELEVEN

Gwalior

'Well, damn me.' Captain Forbes McGowan and his double company of the 10th Bombay Native Infantry were calling and pointing up into the branches of the trees. 'Come to try your hand at a little crow shooting, Morgan?'

It was almost midnight. Morgan had managed to get a couple of hours' broken sleep up in the gun position that they had taken before the inevitable had happened. His men and the remainder of the 95th had been left in reserve whilst Smith had swept forward with the other regiments of the brigade to the very foot of Gwalior's vast outcrop, the cavalry harassing the mutineers whilst the rest of the infantry mopped up those who couldn't run fast enough. Then, whilst McGucken and the NCOs, dog tired though they were, went through all the checks that battle made necessary, the message had arrived: he and an escort were to make their way to Brigade Headquarters to receive orders. Morgan's tired heart leapt, for he knew exactly what to expect: he was to be sent to help Kemp and his irregulars again.

'McGowan, it's good to see you.' Morgan hadn't seen the man since he was wounded at Rowa, three months or more ago. 'I heard that you'd rejoined, but what's this tomfoolery?'

The 10th were aiming their rifles high and yelling upwards

at the great limbs of the peepul trees below which they stood. Like the rest of the brigade, the sepoys' smocks were filthy and most had wrapped towels around their caps, giving them an especially rakish look. A naik continued the angry, vertical monologue and even Morgan – to whom Hindustani remained a mystery – could tell that he was approaching the end of his patience.

'This looks like capital sport.' Kemp, now officially deputised by Smith to lead a small group up into the bowels of Gwalior's fort, drew his pistol and stared heavenward. 'Come on, Morgan, Pandy often does this: runs till he can run no more, then shins up a tree and lies still, thinking that we're too daft to smoke him. I've seen squirrels do the same.'

Then six or seven sepoys fired at their NCO's word of command, to be rewarded with a crop of bodies falling to the ground with a thump, each set of lungs expelling a mighty wheeze as they hit the earth. But there was still one whimpering above them.

'You've only winged that rogue,' said Kemp as he gripped his horse tightly with his knees, aimed his pistol carefully and sent a ball smacking into the wounded man. There was a pause, then the mutineer fell, narrowly missing Lance-Corporal Pegg, who dismounted with speed and began to harvest the clothes of the dead.

'You told me you were too tired to ride a single furlong, Corp'l Pegg,' mighty had been the moaning back at the gun line when Pegg was detailed by Morgan to accompany him, 'but now you seem to have got your second wind.'

'Aye, sir, Cap'n Carmichael's bit of marksmanship bucked me up a bit, but ah'm shagged out now, sir.' The sepoys looked at Pegg in admiration as the lad frisked each body – finding some valuable on each – in a matter of seconds. 'But not so shagged that I'd miss a chance like this.'

'So it would seem, *Corporal* Pegg.' McGowan was as impressed with Pegg's expertise as his men were. 'I haven't had a chance to thank you for what you did for me at Rowa.'

Pegg, however, was engrossed in his task and hardly listening to the officer.

Then McGowan's eye was drawn towards two more mounted figures whose horses fidgeted in the shadows behind the others. 'Who've you got here, Commandant?' he asked Kemp.

'You know Rissaldar Batuk, I guess, but I'd like to introduce you to the former Sepoy Loleman Dunniah, late of the Honourable John Company's Twelfth Bengal Turncoats.' Kemp sidled his horse over to the native's, grabbed the man by his splinted, bandaged wrist and gave it a twist. Dunniah shrieked, sitting upright in his saddle and throwing his head back in pain. 'Yes, you don't like it when the boot's on the other foot, do you, my lad? You see here, McGowan, a man that I enlisted, a man who ate my salt and whom I treated like a son; a man who spat it all back at me and the Regiment, mutinied and slaughtered my wife, my children and her family in front of each other.'

Morgan watched the cameo, transfixed in his saddle.

'Well, why not run the bastard up from this tree here and now? If he's such a bloody—' But Captain McGowan wasn't allowed to finish.

'Run him up?' Kemp snarled. 'That's too good for the dog. If you'd seen the smile on the wretch's face as he drew a razor across my Neeta's throat then you'd have something altogether more artistic in mind for this jawan – once he's served his purpose.'

Artistic, thought Morgan with a shudder. He'll be wanting to flay the man like that Bombay Gunner the Pandies caught and tied to a tree; I need to keep a bloody long way from you, Mad Dick Kemp.

'And what possible use can a man like that be to you, Commandant,' asked McGowan, 'save as a billet for a lead ball?'

'Well, you'd be surprised. Sepoy Dunniah here is not quite the bazaar badmash that he looks. He was well on the way to promotion in the Twelfth before they turned, and he'd already ingratiated himself with the Rhani . . .' Kemp clasped his hands together theatrically, '. . . God rest the gracious lady's soul. Then he became one of her praetorians with especial responsibility for Prince – or King, as I should now say – Damodar. But, a little gentle persuasion made Dunniah reveal that the young pretender is away on up in yonder fortress in the Pandies' dressing station under the care of the good Mrs Keenan, who also has a few questions to answer for me.'

And I need to keep myself between you, Mary and Sam – always supposing they're both still drawing breath. Morgan's belly was suddenly tight with fear at the thought of Kemp wanting to question Mary.

'Morgan and I have been sent to snatch Damodar; Dunniah will, I'm sure, be a more than willing guide for us, won't you, you devious sod?' said Kemp, giving the Indian's broken arm a gratuitous squeeze.

'Do you know the fort at all well, Commandant?' asked McGowan, staring up at the vast block of sandstone that loured out of the night sky. 'It looks like a whore of a place to get into.'

'Aye, it is, and it's the whoreson inside I'm looking for,' Kemp replied sourly. 'You saw whilst it was still light how the clever bloody Moghuls perched the fort right up there on the top of that rock – well, I ain't been inside since the Forties, but there was only one way to get inside in those days and I don't suppose it's changed. There's a ramp affair cut out of solid rock, which twists and turns its way up to the outer walls on the far side – we can't see it from here – then there's a pair of immense wooden gates at the Hathia Paur – the only entrance – with sentry towers set above, which used to be guarded night and day. Once you're through that, the buildings sprawl all over the plateau – temples, two gaudy little palaces, then the keep proper within, which the Maharajah's troops used to live in, in a series of scruffy barracks, with their own kitchens, stables and the like. Some of the architecture was pretty grand, as far as I can remember; all sorts of elaborate carvings of Hindu gods, elephants and what-not, and some cleverly built *shikharas*. 'Spect all that's been knocked about by our gunfire, though.'

'Why do you suppose that the Pandies haven't chosen to defend the fort this time then, Commandant?' asked McGowan.

'Well, the trouble with Gwalior is that if you think it's a bitch of a place to get into, it's equally difficult to get out of. Once you've locked yourself up inside the gates, all you can do is wait for the siege to start. Modern artillery would leather the place like the old siege elephants and ballistas never could, and the Rhani and Tantya Tope were wise enough birds to know that they would never win against our troops in a slugging match; they had to be able to manoeuvre. That's why she elected to fight well forward and tried to buy herself time to prepare the town and the heights around it for a stubborn defence.'

'Didn't bloody work, though, did it?' asked McGowan with a slight sneer.

'No it didn't, thanks to our nailing the little slut yesterday morning. Then the likes of Brevet Major Morgan here and your jawans following up good and hard. Now all we've got to do is get into the place and find Damodar.'

Kemp made it sound like a formality, thought Morgan.

'Well, have a care as you skirt round the town, sir,' said McGowan. 'There's still plenty of rebels about, and I last saw the Third Europeans heading over to link up with General Rose's troops in the direction that you'll have to take.'

'Third Europeans?' Lance-Corporal Pegg's ears pricked up. 'What, that bloody mob what we saw at Jhansi?'

'I expect so, Corp'l Pegg,' replied McGowan with a smile. 'And if you think they were a mob then, you should see them with a double issue of rum inside of them; I pity any man, woman, child or sheep that gets in their way. I'd give them a wide berth, if I were you.'

'I'm obliged to you, Captain McGowan, but I guess those lads will have a fair idea of where Pandy is and where he isn't.' Kemp gathered his reins. 'Come on, Morgan, and you, Dunniah, you bastard, *jildi-rao*. We'd better find out as much as we can from the Europeans. If we can find one who's sober, that is.' And Kemp trotted off into the town with his little command following, guided by the shouts and rifle fire of the 3rd Europeans, who had their hands full with the horrid business of revenge.

The town below the fortress was lit by flames. As Kemp and Morgan picked their way carefully amongst the shanties and mean mud bungalows, the fires flickered and swayed, causing shadows to race about their path as the wind caught the pyres and sent spark-filled clouds of smoke corkscrewing down the alleys.

'Who comes there?'

A drink-roughened voice challenged the horsemen as they rounded a corner. Its owner, a thickset European in a smoke-stained smock, seemed to stagger slightly as he raised his rifle to an unsteady aim.

'Commandant Kemp, Captain Morgan and three.' Kemp spoke quite clearly and confidently to the sentry as the noise of breaking glass and a female shriek came from a nearby building. 'And who are you, my lad? You can lower your weapon.'

Another high-pitched cry of alarm came from somewhere close at hand.

'Private Joshua Neame, sir, Third Bombay Europeans.' Neame tried to bring his rifle to the shoulder and attempt a salute, but he lost his balance in the process.

'You're drunk, sir. Where is your corporal?' Kemp demanded.

I suppose the commandant has seen more towns sacked than I have, and I guess he knows just how dangerous men like Neame here can be when they've taken drink, thought Morgan, though I can't help but think that interfering with these rogues is damn risky.

'What the fuck's it got to do with you? You're not my officer,' slurred Neame, who must have instantly regretted his boldness, for no sooner had he said it than Kemp was off his horse, knocking the drunken soldier's rifle to the ground and grabbing the offender by the collar.

'It's got everything to do with me, you little turd. Just take me to your NCO unless you want a ball through your skull.' Kemp had pulled his pistol from his belt and was now propelling the unfortunate Private Neame towards the battered buildings with short jabs of its muzzle.

'Hold our horses, Corp'l Pegg; I shall have to go with the commandant.' Morgan, too, had slid from the saddle, but as Kemp bustled a resistant Neame towards the building, a great shriek and the noise of breaking china sent him dashing in front of the pair, pulling his sword from its scabbard as he ran.

'What in God's name are you about, man?' Morgan had barged through a dimly lit doorway into the interior of a hovel that was warm with the smell of too many bodies. An animal-fat candle guttered on a crude shelf inside the little room, where two soldiers were digging at the floor with shovels whilst a corporal held a painfully thin native girl by the hair. He was questioning her in pidgin Hindi, whilst she quailed back at him, blood dribbling down the front of her chin and onto her sari from her nostrils and her torn earlobes.

'Get your hands off that woman at once, Corporal,' Morgan took the scene in quickly: an Indian man lay dead in the corner whilst the three Europeans dug for where they believed he had buried his valuables, 'or I'll—'

'Or you'll bloody what . . . sir?' the corporal asked menacingly, still holding the girl, whilst the two others rose from their digging, drawing their shovels back menacingly.

'I'll . . .' Morgan realised that he'd overreached himself and that the half-drunk soldiers were in a desperately ugly frame of mind. Indian troops might be cowed by a show of confidence, but these men were bent on loot and vengeance. Clearly, they had extracted some information from the owner of the house before they had felled him, then violently stripped the woman of her jewellery, and the three of them would make short work of him if they chose to.

'Or you'll have me to fucking well answer to, you scum.' With a crash from behind Morgan, Commandant Kemp arrived, preceded by a helpless Private Neame, who was flung into the middle of the room, upsetting the corporal and the other soldiers, who were left staring into the muzzle of the big man's pistol. 'How dare you threaten a Queen's officer. Put that bint down, Corporal, and stand to attention when I'm speaking to you.'

The man's sheer force of character dominated the Europeans, thought Morgan. Where he himself had failed to make any impression on them at all, Kemp's whirlwind arrival and fearless confidence had bested them; now they all stood braced unsteadily to attention, as Kemp lowered his pistol.

'That's more like it.' The candle flickered, throwing gigantic shadows on the mud walls. 'Now, what do you lot know of how Pandy's defending the fort? Is the approach guarded at all, can you tell me?'

The soldiers had relaxed now the tension had gone from the confrontation, though the girl still sobbed as she dabbed at her wounds.

'Well, your honour,' the corporal spoke in a thick brogue, 'our officers have ordered us to keep away from the place.

The battle's moving on . . .' Morgan had come to the same conclusion, for the noise of Rose's horse artillery was receding as the pursuit continued to the north-west of Gwalior, '. . . an' we've been told to clear the town o' any rebels an' wait till daylight before any moves are made against the fortress.'

'And this is your idea of clearing rebels, is it, Corporal?' Kemp asked almost conversationally. 'Robbing honest folk and thrashing wee girls?'

'Just fucking Pandies getting their dues, if you asks me, your honour,' the corporal answered.

'Aye, you may have a point,' Kemp replied with a slight grin, 'but tell me anything more you know about the fort.'

'Not much more to say, your honour. There's a bit of smoke a-drifting from it – the guns was firing on it for a while an' probably started some fires – an' we killed a few Pandies carryin' wounded up the approach road with long-range rifle-fire just before last light. Cap'n Broome – our company commander – reckoned they might be some o' the Rhani's bodyguard, judging by their clothes, he did.' Kemp looked at Morgan as the corporal delivered this last piece of intelligence. 'Why are you askin', sir? If you'd be wanting to get into the place, I'd say get yourselves into native clobber; you could pass it off in the dark, so you could.'

Kemp'll love that notion, thought Morgan, remembering how the papers had made so much of Mr Kavanagh's exploits around Lucknow as he fooled the mutineers by disguising himself as one of them. It'll be all right for him – he's already half native – but Pegg and myself trying to look like Brahmins – it'll be the death of us.

'Grand idea, Corporal,' said Kemp, gleefully. 'Strip that corpse, Morgan.'

'An' there's a pile of old clothes here, if you wants them, your honour,' said the corporal, all resentment now gone.

'Aye, good man, thank you.' Kemp had also forgotten the nastiness of just a few minutes ago. He was full of the new stratagem, and even the battered Private Neame now ignored the indignity of being manhandled by strange officers and was nosing around the hole in the floor where the riches were supposed to be buried. 'Carry on then, lads,' said Kemp as he stooped to grab some clothing.

'Carry on, Commandant?' blurted Morgan. 'We can't leave that poor woman here to be . . . well, defamed.'

'What? Oh, you are a sensitive creature, aren't you? Well, if it helps to ease your conscience . . .' clearly, Kemp hadn't the slightest interest in the girl's fate, '. . . I hope you don't mind if I rub a little balm into this officer's guilt-ridden soul, Corporal?'

'Not at all, your honour. Help yourself,' replied the NCO. '—But there's much better quim around, if that's what you're wanting.'

'Bring her with us then, Morgan,' Kemp added. 'She'll help you to make Pegg look less obvious.'

Morgan grabbed the girl by the wrist. At first she resisted, then, when she could see that he meant her no harm, she followed quietly enough. Meanwhile, the shovels started to scrape again at the floor inside the house, whilst Kemp led the way back to the horses and the rest of the party, his whole mind alive, planning the next stage of his quest.

That was an ugly few minutes, that was, thought Morgan. Now those louts are back doing what they do best, and this mad bugger – he looked at Kemp's broad, retreating back and the bundle of clothes in his arms – couldn't be happier. Mary, my love, he looked up at the dark mass of the fortress that loomed above them, I hope this is all going to be worth it and you've stayed true to your salt.

'These bloody stink, they do.' Lance-Corporal Pegg sniffed at his new clothes but, despite the loose robe and the skull cap, he couldn't be anything other than himself. The tanned flesh, brown eyes and wispy beard might just have passed muster in the dark of the night, but his whole stance, the whole set of his shoulders and chin was irrevocably barrack-square. 'And so does she.'

Morgan looked at the man and the snivelling girl, who was sitting on the saddle in front of Pegg, and was reminded more of a bad regimental nativity play rather than a serious ploy to deceive their enemies.

'Hold your tongue, Corp'l Pegg,' whispered Morgan, 'unless you can moan in Hindustani.'

The occasional artillery round still whistled over the fortress from the direction of the retreating rebels and peals of musketry were clearly audible in the distance, but apart from shouts from the town below them and the crackle of fires, all was remarkably quiet. So quiet that Morgan found himself nodding in the saddle once or twice, almost overcome by the uproar of the last day and a half; then he remembered where he was and all lassitude disappeared.

The little group walked their horses as slowly as they could along the steep road that hairpinned its way up towards the fort, the hoofs of their horses scraping the setts and, Morgan was sure, alerting every rebel for miles around. Morgan and Kemp rode at the rear, Pegg and his companion in the middle, whilst Dunniah and Rissaldar Batuk led the cavalcade, the veteran of countless fights and scrapes keeping a pistol discreetly trained on the mutineer.

'Those Europeans did a fair bit of work before they found the grog, from the look of these stiffs,' muttered Kemp to Morgan as the moon caught bundles of cloth and the odd dead bullock and camel that littered the sides of the road.

'Aye. You don't suppose we ought to wait for the main force to assault in daylight tomorrow, do you, Commandant?' Morgan hated to sound hesitant in front of Kemp, but as they drew nearer and nearer to the fort he realised how perilous their task must be and how impulsive Kemp had been in suggesting it.

'No, we need to find Damodar dead or alive just as we did his mother. Once Smith leads his troops in here there'll be chaos, rape and mass bloody murder – exactly the conditions for the rebels to spirit the little sod away. No, we've got to grab hold of him and show the Pandies that their cause is lost, and the best way of doing that is with a small band of men and a great deal of brass neck . . . hush, hark at that.'

They were twenty paces short of the Hathia Paur archway, its gates jammed open by a military cart whose oxen lay dead in their traces, when a subdued challenge came from the stone-faced bastions above it, along with the click of musket hammers being drawn back.

The horsemen came to an instant halt, Rissaldar Batuk replying quietly before looking sharply at Dunniah, who sat silently in his saddle.

'What are they saying, Commandant?' Morgan whispered at the back of the group.

Kemp didn't reply for a while; he sat stock-still waiting for Dunniah to complete the ruse. Eventually, the rebel spoke to the sentries in clear Hindi and Kemp translated quietly for Morgan and Pegg.

'Well, the Rissaldar made the sentries believe that we are all that's left of the Rhani's patrol and told them that she was dead. Then they said that they didn't recognise us – that's when Dunniah spoke up, with Batuk's pistol firmly in his ribs, I'd guess. That seemed to convince them and they're coming down to check us. It appears that what's left of the rebels inside the fort are expecting the Feringhees to attack tomorrow and we'll be a useful addition to their numbers. Quiet now, for here they come.'

Morgan saw three sepoys in the stained uniforms of the Rhani's personal forces come padding through the gate. They were all mature, bearded and turbaned men walking quietly on slippered feet, carrying clean, well-oiled muskets, each sepoy with a short sword and bayonet at his side. The leader had a muttered conversation with Dunniah and the rissaldar before telling the other two men to inch one of the great doors away from the jammed cart, making just enough room for the party to pass in single file.

'Just keep that girl in front of your face, Corp'l Pegg,' said Morgan. 'Don't say a thing if they challenge you, and keep an eye on that bloody Dunniah.'

Pegg nodded, reached around the young woman and urged his horse on, just as the rissaldar walked his charger through the narrow gap, talking all the while to the sentries whilst a sullen Dunniah followed. Pegg and his passenger were next to enter the dark archway that echoed to the horses' hoofs, the sentries paying little attention to either, merely waving them past. It was Morgan's turn next but, just as the sentries were beginning to study him, Kemp decided to distract them with a babble of Hindi.

As Morgan edged his horse forward, he heard a quiet question from the commandant, a reply from the men, a laugh – a laugh that was just a little too loud – from Kemp and then what sounded like a puzzled enquiry from the soldiers. There was a pause, angry, rasping words and then, quite suddenly, the gloominess was split with a flash and the confined space echoed with a deafening bang.

'Ride, man, ride!' yelled Kemp from behind Morgan, barging his horse into his and firing another cacophonous round from his pistol at the sentries. 'They've seen through us.'

Then it was all clattering hoofs on the worn cobbles, the smell of sweat and fear, Morgan slapping at the rump of Pegg's horse in front and a sudden bursting out of the darkness of the archway into the open space of the fort's interior. Just to his front, the remains of a low building smoked gently with a miniature temple rising high and narrow just behind it. As they cantered past, Morgan had time to notice the rich carvings around its lintels before two musket balls sang past them, causing all of the riders to spur on, crouching flat over their horses' manes.

'Right, that's it,' Kemp shouted as a dark bundle of sepoys came spilling out of a barrack block fifty paces beyond the temple, dragging their weapons up into the aim. 'They know something's wrong. No more caution now; let's be at 'em,' and he kicked his heels hard into his mount's flank and pointed his revolver, ready for the next foe.

Morgan pulled out his own pistol, bawled, 'Stay here and guard that bastard Dunniah, Corp'l Pegg; shoot him if he tries to run,' and then spurred Emerald to catch Kemp and Rissaldar Batuk, who were already bearing down on their enemies.

There's only a handful of them, thought Morgan as the sepoys tried to form a defensive line. . . . The three of us should see them off so long as they don't manage a volley. But even as he thought it, he heard a command, and the clutch of men were lit up by sharp, yellow muzzle flashes. Lead balls whirred past him, one of which caught the rissaldar, throwing him from his saddle with a choking moan.

Even if he had wanted to turn and run, it was now too late, for Kemp was already in the middle of the enemy line, kicking left and right at his enemies, leaning down from the saddle, pressing the barrel of his heavy revolver into their faces, shooting, killing and cursing fluently. Some ran for their lives, but an NCO and three other men stood firm, crowding round the commandant, trying to get a clear blow with their bayonets or with the broad blades of their short-swords.

Close as you can . . . As Morgan charged into the mass of struggling bodies, he thought of the advice of the very man whom he was now trying to save when he'd been given the same pistol that he now held outstretched in front of him. . . . *Try to touch the bastards with your barrel before you fire* . . . It seemed an age ago though it was only about four years, just before he'd sailed for the Crimea, when he was still a stranger to violent death. . . . That's close enough, he thought as Emerald barged one of Kemp's attackers onto the ground with her shoulder and he pointed at the back of the neck of another and pulled the trigger. The man had been too busy trying to rip the commandant from the saddle to see Morgan coming. Now the ball hit him at the base of the skull, jerking him forward onto his face below both horses' stamping hoofs.

Kemp was deeply involved with another assailant. As the sepoy had tried a high lunge with his bayonet at the mounted officer, Morgan saw how Kemp had swung his chest back and out of the way like a man half his years. Then he grabbed the sepoy by his forward arm and half dragged him onto his saddle, the musket and bayonet falling away with a clatter. Now Kemp pinioned the man and dashed at his head with the barrel of his pistol, each blow being greeted by a shriek and the crunch of steel meeting bone.

Canny old sod . . . Morgan could only admire the more experienced man's skill, . . . *he knows that he's running short of rounds, so he's saving what he's got.*

Morgan fired at the man on the ground whom Emerald had knocked down, but as Kemp's tussle continued, two more men ran at them, one firing a harmless shot from his musket as he charged. They were easy targets, even in the dark, for the pair ran hesitantly, both obviously scared and uncertain. Morgan's shot hit the man in front in the middle of the chest, half an inch of lead throwing him on his back, the cloud of powder smoke briefly obscuring the moonlit scene. The other saw his chance, though, and scuttled away from the fight as fast as his sandals would let him and as suddenly as the din and clashing of weapons had erupted, there was silence.

'Thank you for that, young Morgan.' Even Kemp's victim

now lay quiet on the cobbles. 'That was a little more exciting than I expected.'

'Well, if you will go charging off on your own, Commandant . . .' said Morgan, but Kemp wasn't listening,

'See if there's anything that can be done for Rissaldar Batuk, will you,' Kemp asked as he swung down from the saddle, 'whilst I deal with this lot?'

Morgan was about to turn his horse to look for their fallen comrade, but he paused and watched his superior. There were four bodies on the ground; Kemp peered at each one, leaving the two who were dead before turning to deal with the two wounded.

First, Kemp's heavy riding boots kicked and thrashed at each victim in turn, lashing at their faces, iron-tipped heels stamping on their balls until the blood splashed about quite freely; only his spurs catching in their clothes inhibited him. The whole performance culminated in Kemp's seizing a lump of shell-torn brick and thumping at both inert men until their features were mush. But, to Morgan, more shocking than the frenzied violence was the litany of hate that Kemp grunted. Each kick, each blow was accompanied either by a storm of Hindi, or broken English where the word 'Neeta' was the only one he could recognise. Then, with both men dead and still, the demon departed. Kemp's furious form became calm, he rubbed his hands with satisfaction, as if he had just bowled a particularly satisfying over, took the reins of his horse and sauntered over to Morgan.

'Right, that's finished . . . and what are you staring at?' asked Kemp with a serene smile. 'The job's got to be done; I'm wasting no more shot on these scum.'

Perhaps, thought Morgan, but you're not meant to enjoy it so much. The last time he'd witnessed a scene anything like the one that had just occurred had been at Inkermann. There, he remembered, the boys had beaten their enemies without hesitation. *But each one of them had been sickened, not grinning at the grossness of it like you are, Commandant.*

After this bestial show, Morgan expected some remorse over the death of the rissaldar, but he was to be disappointed. Kemp's old friend was lying in a smear of blood that had leaked from a ball-torn artery.

'Poor old Batuk; tough jawan he could be. Still, there's no wife to mourn for him – just like the rest of us – Pandy's seen to that.' Kemp pulled the Sutlej medal from the dead man's coat and stuck it in his pocket, rolled the cavalryman on his back and closed both eyes, simply saying, 'Take his *tatt* and pistol, Morgan; put that lass on the horse and check your priming. Now, where's Pegg got to with that fucker Dunniah?' as if such horrors were the most normal thing in the world. Morgan shivered in the warm night, and looked at the dead, bearded face of a man whom he'd come to like and respect deeply, before turning his mount to follow Kemp.

'I won't tell you again.' Kemp pushed the barrel of his pistol firmly into Dunniah's back, making the injured man wince with pain. 'Keep bloody moving.'

With the rissaldar dead, handling the truculent Dunniah had become even more difficult. It soon became obvious to Morgan that Kemp's Hindi was not as good as he boasted and this allowed the captive to delay and prevaricate whilst the three British and the native girl squatted in the shadows of the fort, trying not to draw attention to themselves. Morgan had looked on helplessly as Kemp had questioned their prisoner and indulged in a little, casual twisting of his broken arm before they set off towards the makeshift hospital where Damodar was said to be.

The girl walked at the front of the group alongside Dunniah – Morgan wondered what the poor creature must be making of the whole, mad scheme – with Kemp behind, then Pegg and Morgan leading the horses.

'Look there, Commandant,' said Morgan as they approached a fortified building. 'There's movement just beyond that low wall.' Even in the dark, Morgan could see that sandbag walls had been built at the entrance to the next long, one-storey barracks. Then he realised that the bobbing shape up ahead was a bullock lazily tossing its horns and that behind it was a wagon, peeping out above the wall.

'Aye, I can see it,' said Kemp, before holding a mumbled, unintelligible conversation with Dunniah. 'He says that that's the building that's being used as the Pandies' dressing station and that the doors are always guarded.'

As they got closer, Morgan saw the human detritus of war draped and dumped around the temporary hospital's entrance. Two bullock carts were sprawled across the mouth of the sandbag walls – one was empty with no oxen, whilst the other was full of dead or unconscious men, most in the uniform of John Company. Both animals were still in this cart's traces and around their hoofs were a jumble of wounded, some lying, some sitting, some moaning gently, others deathly quiet. The night prevented Morgan from seeing the details too closely, but they all seemed to be youngish men in a mixture of uniform and native dress, liberally daubed with dried blood.

'Hookum dear?' the universal challenge in stilted English came from the doorway to the barracks from behind another pile of sandbags, the moonlight flashing off steel as the sentry raised his barrel.

'Dunniah Bahadur, woman an' dree,' Dunniah replied. Morgan had seen how the rebels still used English for all military purposes.

The sentry beckoned them forward, recognising Dunniah and stiffening to attention.

Here we go again, thought Morgan. Bloody Pandies as suspicious as you like, and now that the rissaldar's dead, no one to check on what bloody Dunniah's really telling them. And we've got nowhere to run to this time . . .

Morgan looked into the long, low building that they were about to enter. None of the gas mantles seemed to be working and the place was lit by dimly flickering candles.

There's wounded all over the place – it bloody stinks . . . the smell of piss and sweat hung heavily, . . . *and all sorts of rooms and corridors. Can Mary really be somewhere in this hellhole?* Morgan's breathing was suddenly difficult; could it be that after all this time, all this misery, that he was about to see his own Mary again? To add to his worries, a wounded man suddenly started to moan loudly, encouraging others to do the same. *It's like a scene from Hogarth in there, it is.*

But there were more immediate problems to be overcome. Dunniah and Kemp passed by the sentry without remark, but as the native girl came close, the man beckoned her to one side and began an animated conversation, his scrawny head and greasy hair – his topknot was held in a dirty little bag – bobbing and nodding excitedly.

'What's 'e want with 'er, sir?' Pegg whispered, gently fingering a vicious little axe that he'd lifted from a corpse by the main gate.

Morgan answered by just narrowing his eyes, not daring to speak a word of English, nudging Pegg past the sentinel, hoping that he would be too distracted by the blood-soiled attractions of the girl to bother with them. And, up to a point, he was right. Both of them slipped past with hardly a glance from the soldier, but his casual interest in the girl had changed with the tone of his voice, for despite the fact that Morgan couldn't understand a word, he knew that something was wrong. Where the sepoy's questions had initially been light-hearted he was now suspicious of the girl and she was becoming more and more frightened by him. As Pegg and he moved further into the shadowy entrance hall, the sentry grabbed the girl's arm and pressed her against the wall, his enquiries becoming increasingly demanding; she responded by pointing at Kemp with her chin, chirruping wildly and rolling her eyes. But whatever was being discussed was the last thing that troubled the sentry's mind.

Kemp could see what was going on and he had to intervene. No sooner had the girl confirmed the sepoy's suspicions than the commandant moved swiftly and silently, taking the axe from Pegg's belt (without even a by-your-leave) and burying the spiked end of the steel in the rebel's spine. Morgan realised that the last time he had seen such an axe it had been embedded deeply in Thanadur Forgett's body all those months ago in Bombay. Now a similar tool did similar work, for the sentry made nothing more than a gentle soughing noise as the life ebbed out of him. His eyes bugged and his mouth lolled open but, by the time that Kemp lowered him to the floor, there was no more resistance from the man.

Luckily, the collective moaning of the wounded covered the native girl's horrified squeal as the sentry died with his hands still on her. Morgan had some sympathy for the lass; in the last couple of hours her house had been ransacked and her husband killed, she had narrowly avoided rape – but only at the cost of being kidnapped – and she had become involuntarily involved in one of the daftest, most suicidal ventures that he'd ever even thought about. Now complete strangers were slaying her countrymen within inches of her; it couldn't have been the best of days for the girl, he thought.

'Pegg,' Kemp was as calm as if he had just shaken the sentry's hand, rather than stabbed him to death, thought Morgan, 'drag this scum over to the wall yonder . . .' Kemp pointed to an inner part of the corridor where a line of mostly silent wounded lay, '. . . and prop him up with the others so that no one notices.'

'It's *Corporal* Pegg, sir,' replied the non-commissioned officer automatically,

'Yes, quite so. Then you and the girl stay here and don't let anyone in whilst Captain Morgan and I go off to find Damodar and Mrs Keenan.' Kemp paused and flicked a look at Morgan. 'Collect some of the firelocks that are kicking about and if there's any sign of interference, just shoot and keep shooting. Don't let any bugger interfere with the horses.' Kemp glanced at their exhausted mounts, which they had tethered outside in the darkness. 'When we get him we'll be out of here and riding like the devil. Keep the girl with you; use her if you can, but any sign of treachery and take that axe to her.'

He'd hack that poor wee girl down with no remorse at all, thought Morgan as he looked at Kemp, realising that all mercy, all compassion had been driven from him by the horrors of the last few months, and we've only got four horses to get away on so, assuming we find Damodar, Sam and Mary, then Kemp will be looking to ditch someone here, the ruthless sod.

Morgan studied Dunniah, who was cradling his injured arm next to Kemp – all the fight seemed to have gone out of him. Morgan remembered the muscular, rather dashing sepoy whom he had first seen alongside the Rhani in Kotah, then the bold fight that he had put up during the ambush that seemed to be a year ago but was actually only a few weeks. Now he stood forlornly holding his hurts, his eyes lacklustre, absorbed in his own pain, hardly interested in the remains of the rebel dream that lay broken around him. He was in no condition to resist Kemp's growled demands and the pokes that his former commanding officer kept administering to his damaged arm.

'Dunniah seems to be suggesting that Damodar will be under guard in one of these rooms to the right.' Kemp pointed down the half-lit corridor off which an irregular series of rooms and offices seemed to lead. 'I'll take this rogue with me.' Kemp pulled his pistol from its holster and jabbed

Dunniah. 'You take the left side. If you find Damodar just holla, but be ready for a fight.' Morgan saw Kemp quickly reloading the empty chambers of his revolver, and checked his own priming.

It's moments like this that I almost miss Corp'l Pegg, thought Morgan, as he stepped over wounded and dying sepoys to start the search. He's a bloody nuisance most of the time, but he has his uses when life cuts up rough.

Morgan had left Pegg alone with the girl at the sentry point, his eyes wide with lonely fear, his tongue flicking over dried lips, looking more like the pantomime lead than a mutineer.

'You'd best be careful now, sir,' was all that Pegg had managed as he held his rifle pointing rigidly to repel all comers, as Morgan had slid off to start his search of the first room.

The stench was remarkable. There was no light of any sort inside the room and the vinegary smell of sweat and that heavy, sweet reek of rotting flesh and pus hit him like a wall. He could see nothing, but the power of the smell spoke of many people, some of whom moaned softly. But what should he do, he wondered. He could hardly cry out, 'Mary, sweet thing, are you within? Is little Damodar clinging to your skirts?' No, this was no place for Mary and the boys – they would have to be in another room – and, besides, Dunniah was much more likely to know where she was, thought Morgan, with one ear cocked for the commandant's progress in the other rooms.

The next room smelt just as awful, but at least there was a candle burning. Morgan pushed himself over the injured and the dead through the bell-shaped arch of a doorway and looked inside, pistol at the ready. But there was no threat here, nor was there any sign of Damodar, Sam or Mary. Instead, just more suffering men whose ragged clothes and torn bodies spoke of meetings with shot, splinters and bullets.

There was hardly a flicker of interest as he moved on to the next room.

But as he edged back into the corridor, a great, familiar shout came from just across the way: 'No you don't, you rogue!' Followed by two, booming pistol shots in quick succession.

'Commandant, are you all right?' Morgan thrust his head round the doorway opposite to see much the same sort of sight that he'd seen already, except that the wounded who could move inside this room had been roused to pandemonium by Kemp's fire. The officer stood in the centre of the room, framed in gunsmoke.

'Of course I am,' snapped Kemp. 'More than these pair of Pandies are – and what sort of a damn-fool question is that?' Two bodies seemed to have been flung back on the floor at Kemp's feet. 'And why are you whining, Dunniah? I'm like Florence fucking Nightingale to you, I am; should have cut the lights out of you weeks ago.' Dunniah cringed as his mutinous comrades cried out even more shrilly at the sound of English about them. 'Found 'em yet, Morgan?'

'Not yet, Commandant,' Morgan replied as he wondered why Kemp had chosen to kill two men who were already badly wounded, but as he turned back amidst the din to the next room that he was to search on the other side of the corridor, he was met by the snub, black muzzle of a cavalry carbine pointing directly into his face, no more than three feet from him.

The weapon was held steady; Morgan could see the whiteness of the index finger where first pressure had been taken on the trigger, whilst two great chestnut eyes were narrowed in steely determination.

Kemp's right, thought Morgan, his bladder tightening yet again that day. Mary's turned and I'm going to be blown to eternity by the very woman I came to save.

But then her eyes sprang wide open in shocked delight.

Mary Keenan slowly let the weapon drop, smiling with pleasure at the sight of her dog-eared lover.

'And what's taken yous so long, Tony Morgan?' The carbine now hung down at the woman's side; dressed in a filthy sari and a bloodied, make-shift apron, she pushed locks of shining black hair out of her eyes with her other wrist. 'It was four months ago that we saw each other that night in Kotah; couldn't you have be-stirred yourself a bit quicker?'

'Mary, darling girl . . .' Morgan stumbled over a wounded man, any doubts about his lover vanishing immediately.

Ungrateful as she sounds, she's still one of us; how could I ever have thought anything else? Morgan marvelled at the girl's shining hair and peach-soft skin. *Mark you, it's a bloody good job she recognised me, or I'd have measured my length by now.*

But there was no time for Morgan to voice any such thoughts, for Mary had guessed how dangerous the situation was.

'I've got Damodar and our Sam tucked up safe behind me, and no bloody mutineer's going to get their hands on either. How far away are the rest of our lads and how many of you are there Tony, my jewel?'

'It's just a handful of us, Mary. We've come to stop Damodar being put onto Jhansi's throne in place of his mother.'

'Are the rumours true then, Tony? Is the Rhani actually dead?'

Mary took her lover's hand and led him into a much larger chamber in which a trestle had been set up and used as an operating table. Candles gave more light to this room than any other that Morgan had seen since they broke into the fort and it was clear from the gore, the pile of severed limbs that lay to one side and the bundle of filthy bandages, that the surgery had seen much trade.

'Aye, she's dead, God rest the wicked creature—' Morgan started, only to be cut off by Mary.

'No, that's not true. She was a good, brave woman who had no part in the betrayal of the garrison, nor anything to do with the murders of my James, Captain Skene or any of the others. If only the British had listened to what she was trying to tell them, instead of making her turn against them—'

'It's of no matter now, my love.' It was Morgan's turn to interrupt. 'Take me to Damodar. We've got to get him away safely,' and with no more discussion Mary led Morgan to a screened-off section at the very end of the room.

There he found two lads sprawled on cushions in infant sleep that was as oblivious to gunshots as it was to the shouting and mayhem around them. The eight-year-old prince was simply dressed in tunic and tight-legged satin trousers, with clean slippers on his feet. Laid to one side of him was a miniature tulwar, around which was coiled the boy's arm. Next to him was a two-year-old with raven, curly hair and the longest lashes that Morgan had ever seen. He, too, was in remarkably clean native dress, but the pale, translucent skin was in marked contrast to Damodar's.

'Why . . .' stuttered Morgan, '. . . that's Samuel, our beautiful boy.' He reached down and lifted the sleeping child into his arms.

'It is, Tony Morgan,' said Mary delightedly. 'Our very own lad and a damn fine horseman he's had to become over the last few weeks.'

The couple stole the moment. In a filthy, rebel hospital that echoed to the shouts of the outraged wounded, whilst artillery fire still cut the air above the roof, they stood and shared the delight of parenthood.

'Morgan . . . Morgan, where the hell have you got to?' A booming, impatient voice came from the corridor behind them.

'God, that's . . . that's Dick Kemp, ain't it?' said Mary, shocked. 'I thought I saw him riding hard behind us after Kotah.'

'In here, Commandant. I've got Damodar and Mrs Keenan.'

'Capital!' was Kemp's reply as he pushed Dunniah in front of him into the room. The sepoy was so weakened by his injuries that he staggered and fell over one of the wounded, only to be lifted to his feet by Kemp's grabbing him by the hair and tugging him upright. Morgan saw the pain and despair in the Indian's face as he recognised Mary.

'Dunniah . . .' Mary, was clearly shocked by the state of a man who, however much she might have disliked it, had protected not just the young prince but her son as well, '. . . Mother of God, but you're in a desperate state.' She made a move towards him, but was brought up short by the commandant's sneer.

'Ah, Mrs Keenan, what a delight. I'm glad to see you in such fine form.' He dipped his head in *faux* courtesy. 'Please don't worry yourself about your friend here. I can assure you that he's in rude good health, aren't you, you cur,' Kemp shook Dunniah by his topknot, making him shriek with pain, 'and clearly pleased to see you. Anyway, enough of such courtesies. Did I hear you say that you've found the young gentleman, Morgan? Be so kind as to take me to him.'

There was something different about Kemp's voice, thought Morgan. He'd seen him in countless tight corners and scrapes over the past few months – usually the result of the senior man's recklessness and hate-fuelled determination – but there was always an underlying sense of judgement there. Now he seemed to have lost all balance; all that Morgan could see in his eyes was an implacable loathing for everything and everyone around him.

'I will, Commandant.' Morgan passed Sam to Mary, and pulled the screen to one side, waking Damodar in the process. 'He's here, look.' The child sat up and yawned, opening his mouth hugely and screwing up his eyes without any of the inhibitions of adulthood. Then he sat and blinked at the people around him, his lips slightly apart in wonder.

'Yes, you black-hearted bastard, there's your king, there's the only person who can salvage your mutinous cause.' Kemp had pushed Dunniah forward so that he could look once again at the child he knew so well, twisting his hand viciously in the sepoy's hair. 'Well, take one last good look, just like you gave my darling Neeta one last look.' And before Morgan realised what was about to happen, Kemp pulled a knife from his belt and drew its gleaming steel across Dunniah's throat.

Morgan watched as Mary groaned in horror. The sepoy's eyes never left the boy as Kemp's knife flickered over his windpipe, the thin scratch of blood quickly turning into a torrent that soaked the front of the man's dhoti.

'Yes, you scum, take your time.' As Kemp held Dunniah's feeble body erect and the blood leaked out of him, Morgan saw how his knees buckled and his whole frame sagged. 'I'm going to sow your corpse into a pigskin bag, you heathen, and you'll have eternity to ponder what you did to my sweet girl.' Kemp finally let Dunniah crumple onto the floor as death took charge.

Whilst Morgan and Mary stood frozen, watching Dunniah's body twitch and jerk in the rusty puddle that now surrounded him, Kemp strode forward towards the sleepy Damodar, his knife held low and threatening.

He's going to knife the boy as well, thought Morgan, rooted to the spot with horror. That'll kick the heart out of any further uprising – but it can't be right; surely Kemp can't do that to a child.

'And as for you, my lad . . .' the commandant was just paces from the defenceless boy when Mary threw herself in front of him. She clutched Sam, her own child, to her chest and swung to confront Kemp, her face pale with anger.

'Get away from that wee boy, you pig!' Mary stumbled

backwards, her left arm held out protectively, screening Damodar with her body.

'So, now we see you in your true colours, do we, Mrs turncoat Keenan? Get out of my goddamn way or I'll give you the same treatment as that bloody child's going to get.' Kemp brought the knife back slowly, preparing to strike.

There was no time to think. Morgan hurled himself at Kemp, hoping that the stout, older man's reaction would have been slowed by the fatigue and strain of the last few hours: he was wrong. Quick as a cat, the commandant twisted and caught Morgan with a perfect, straight, left jab on the bridge of the nose that sent him sprawling to the floor.

He lay in a torpor of pain and numbness whilst Mary's screams, children's wails and Kemp's angry shouts bludgeoned his consciousness. It felt just like the knockdowns that he had experienced so often in the boxing ring, he thought, yet this time there was no one counting down the seconds. But the urgency to get back on his feet was even stronger, for Mary's yells had ceased abruptly.

Morgan forced himself to stand, clutching at the table for support, wiping a fist across his nose and mouth and, through blurred eyes, realised that his hand was red with blood. Then, as his vision cleared, he grasped why Mary was silent: Kemp had her by the throat. Whilst Damodar shrank in a corner and Sam cried and rolled about the floor, two powerful, lethal hands dug into the woman's neck. Morgan noticed scratches on Kemp's cheeks, but as the officer's fingers tightened so Mary's strength ebbed, her slaps and swipes becoming more and more feeble, her face bright red as she fought for breath.

'You like hitting your betters, don't you, you whoring, traitorous, little Catholic drab?' Kemp muttered as he wrung the life out of the girl.

Get close, stick the muzzle in their face if you can and don't waste a shot. Morgan remembered Kemp's own advice to him as he pulled his heavy revolver from his waistband, thrust it so hard against the commandant's jawbone that it dented the skin . . . and pulled the trigger.

The first shot deafened them all, splashed blood and bits of flesh on the wall opposite and sent Kemp staggering away from Mary. The second thumped into his neck just above his khaki collar, even before the body had time to hit the floor. The third was entirely unnecessary as it smashed into his already dead lungs and there would have been a fourth, a fifth and probably a sixth until all the pistol's chambers were empty – but then Kemp's voice echoed again in Morgan's aching head: . . . *don't waste a shot.*

Mary picked up Sam, put an arm around the terrified Damodar and pushed herself hard against Morgan. They stood there in the candlelight that shone through the powder smoke, ears ringing, looking down at the commandant as his fingers twitched and a spur rasped the stone-flagged floor.

'Bloody 'ell, sir,' a coarse voice disturbed the tableau, 'you all right? Is the commandant badly 'it?'

'I think he's dead, Corp'l Pegg,' replied Morgan quietly as Pegg took in the scene.

'Bloody 'ell, sir . . .' Pegg quickly laid his rifle down and crouched over the corpse, scanning the ragged wound in his head and feeling for a pulse, '. . . 'e is . . . 'e's dead,' a look of disbelief spreading over the corporal's face.

'Yes, I believe so,' answered Morgan, his arm tight around Mary,

'Well, 'e won't be needing this, will 'e?' asked Pegg as he pulled a gold Dublin watch and chain from the dead man's pocket and slipped it into his own.

Glossary

Adjutant: the commanding officer's principal staff officer, usually a captain

Aliwal: British victory in January 1846 during the First Sikh War

Angrez: the English

Ayah: native nurse or nanny

Babu: a clerk or teacher

Badmash: a ne'er-do-well

Bandook: a rifle or musket

Barnshoot: English corruption of the Hindi for the female genitals

Bat: the native language, so for British soldiers to 'sling the bat' suggested some fluency, even if it was only in barrack pidgin

Bat-ponies: baggage animals

Battalion: an infantry unit of seven to eight hundred men

Bhang: hashish

Bint: a girl, used pejoratively by the British

Bishti: a water carrier

Blown for: army expression relating to bugle calls. To be 'blown for' suggests one of the musical signals designed to summon designated groups (e.g., all colour-sergeants) or individuals to receive orders

Boots and Saddles: cavalry trumpet call indicating that troops should prepare to move

Bore: the inside of a weapon's barrel

Brahmin: the highest Hindu class

Brevet: an honorary rank given as a reward that carried extra pay but no authority other than in exceptional circumstances

Bund: an earthen bank

Bus: finished or dead

Caisson: a wheeled, horse-drawn wagon that carried artillery ammunition

Canister: bullets contained in a cloth bag used by artillery at short range against personnel

Carbine: a short musket or rifle carried by artillery and cavalry

Catch a Tartar, to: slang expression to describe a heavy defeat or beating

Charpoy: light, wood-framed bed

Chota-peg: small drink, usually brandy or whiskey

Colours: the pair of flags carried by each infantry battalion

Colt: an American make of revolving pistol

Commandant: the term by which the commanding officer of many of the HEIC's regiments was known. He could equally well be addressed as 'Colonel'

Company: the smallest tactical unit in the British Army, about eighty strong, usually commanded by a captain. In 1857 there were ten companies in a battalion, two of which remained at home as an administrative depot, one of which was styled 'Grenadier' and another 'Light', both titles being superseded in January 1858. At the time of the Mutiny, 'double companies' were often formed, i.e., two companies under the command of one captain

Cornet: cavalry rank equivalent of ensign in the infantry – later changed to second-lieutenant

Crow/red-arse/sprog: all British Army terms of contempt for newcomers or recruits

Daffadar: corporal in an Indian cavalry regiment

Dak: a bungalow or low building

Defilade: to sight weapons in such a way that they can engage a target from front to back

Dhoolie: an animal-drawn stretcher

Durbar: a meeting. In HEIC regiments, a formal durbar was held regularly where only the commandant and the subadar-major were present with the sepoys and junior NCOs, the idea being that any grievances could be aired publicly

Echelon: the arrangement of bodies of troops so that they might attack or manoeuvre in successive waves

Embrasure: narrow slot cut in the wall of an earthwork from which artillery could be fired

Enfield: the .577inch Pattern 1853 Enfield Rifled Musket was the standard rifle of the Queen's regiments during the Mutiny. Issued from early 1857 to the Indian regiments, its greased cartridge was one of the factors behind the start of the Mutiny

Enfilade: fire that sweeps a target from the flank

Ensign: most junior commissioned rank in the infantry, later changed to second-lieutenant

Farrier: specialist cavalryman who dealt with horseshoes and harnesses

Field officers: the mounted officers of an infantry battalion, viz. the commanding officer, the senior and junior major and the adjutant

Firelock: generic term for a small-arm

Full screw: slang for a corporal

Gabion: a basketwork piece of defensive equipment designed to be stood on its end and filled with earth

Gouger: Irish slang for a ne'er-do-well

Guff: Scottish slang for a smell

Havildar: equivalent of sergeant in the HEICs armies

Jawan: a native boy or lad; the word became synonymous with sepoy

Jemadar: most junior officer in the Indian Army

Jildi-rao: get a move on

Jobby: Scottish slang for excrement

John Company: slang for the Honourable East India Company, HEIC

Kila: a fort

Lay of metal: the process by which an artillery piece was aimed by looking over the barrel and adjusting the carriage and elevation wheel

Lost his flint: lost the powers of reason

Mahout: an elephant's driver

Maidan: a plain or exercise area

Mask the guns: when infantry or cavalry move into a position that prevents the artillery from firing without risk to their own troops, they 'mask the guns'

Memsahib: a woman in authority, usually the wife of an officer

Mither: English slang: to pester or annoy

Mohur: gold or cash

Musket: a smooth-bored firearm

Nabob: slang for white grandees serving in India

Naik: equivalent of infantry corporal in the Indian armies

Nails: the old Crimean nickname for the 95th Foot, said to

originate from the admiring comment, 'There may be few of 'em but where you put 'em they stick like nails'
Namskaar . . . kahaang hai . . . ?: Listen . . . where is . . . ?
Nullah: a dried-up river or stream bed

Out East: slang for the Crimea

Peeler: slang for policeman
Piece: technically the barrel of an artillery gun, but often used to mean the entire gun
Presidency: the HEIC governed India via three Presidencies: Bombay, Madras and Bengal, each of which maintained its own army. The bulk of the mutinies occurred in the Bengal Presidency, but there were always concerns about the loyalty of all native troops, with the exception of the Sikhs and the Gurkhas
'Pol: soldiers' abbrevation for Sevastopol
Portfire: the burning fuse by which an artillery piece was caused to fire
Puggaree: turban
Pultan: a regiment
Punkah: reed or grass panels hinged to ceilings and swung as fans

Queen's regiments: those that were in the Crown's service rather than HEIC's

Ramasammy: a meeting or discussion
Redoubt: an earthwork usually armed with guns
Ring: anus
Rook jao-hat jao: pay attention

Sabretache: leather wallet that hung next to a mounted officer's sword; used for carrying messages and documents
Sepoy: Indian infantry private

Shamrock: Irish slang for a prod with a bayonet

Sharney: Scots slang for dirty

Shave: a rumour

Shell: explosive ordnance

Shell jacket: waist-length scarlet coat used for undress duties and campaigning

Shukria: thank you

Solar-topee: cloth-covered, cork sun-helmet

Sowar: Indian cavalry private

Spike: soldiers' slang for a bayonet

Stagging: soldiers' slang for guard duty – probably a corruption of 'staggered duty'

Subadar: a middle ranking, native officer in the Indian armies

Subadar-major: most senior, native officer in the Indian armies

Subaltern, or 'subby': the most junior, commissioned ranks in the army

Sutlej: the river in the Punjab around which most of the fighting revolved in the First Sikh War

Sutler: mobile canteen owner or merchant

Syce: a groom

Tatt: slang for a pony

Tape: soldiers' slang for a chevron or badge of rank; also awarded for long service

Thanadar: a senior police officer

Theek hai, sahib: very good, sir

Tranter: a British make of revolving pistol

Tum lakhri, lakhri tum?: a typical British soldier's reproach to an Indian, translated literally as 'You wood, wood you?' rather than 'You would,' etc. Not surprisingly, most Indians were deeply confused by this refrain

Turkish tinsel: awards from the Ottoman government to British troops involved in the Crimean campaign. Brigadier-General Michael Smith served with Turkish cavalry in that conflict, seeing little action, thus Private Beeston's sneer

Whaler: a ship's boat or the name given to re-mounts, most of which came either from Ireland or from New South Wales

Wing: a tactical unit of half a battalion, four companies strong, usually commanded by a major

Author's Note

Every author likes to think that he has caught the essential attitudes of the characters about whom he is writing. I'm no different and I hope that Morgan, Pegg, McGucken and others express the doubts, horrors and plain ignorance of British troops plunged into the maelstrom of the Indian Mutiny. They knew war – although not civil war – but were bemused by the intricacies of Indian and Anglo-Indian society, especially the mores of the Honourable East India Company and its servants.

The events, and most of the people, are real. I've chosen to take some liberties with the timetable of Morgan's arrival in Bombay and his move up country towards the heart of the Mutiny but, that aside, the battles and skirmishes are as true to life as I can make them.

The language of my characters is slightly different, though. The military slang of the 1850s sounds stilted today, so I've modelled the troops' conversations and attitudes upon those of the men I commanded in the descendant of Morgan's regiment in the twentieth century. I believe that soldiers' needs and aspirations haven't changed much over the years, so my characters talk in the same way as my men did, with a shading of Victorian patois. There is one important difference, though:

contemporary letters and diaries speak with a casual racism that would be unpublishable today. For all the reasons that the reader will understand, I didn't want to reproduce this as faithfully as I might.

Kemp is my own creation – he's only loosely based on the commanding officer of the 12th BNI – but his enemy the Rhani of Jhansi certainly existed. Largely forgotten in Britain, this fighting queen was one of the most colourful and most admired figures of the tragic years of 1857–1859. She caught the imagination not just of her fellow Indians, but also Victorian England, with opinion being divided over her role in the second most bloody massacre of Europeans in the entire Mutiny. Whether you believe that she was essentially innocent (as Mary Keenan does) or damn her eyes as a Jezebel and a mass murderess, like Kemp, is up to you.

One place that the Rhani is not forgotten, though, is modern-day Uttar Pradesh, the area that Lance-Corporal Pegg would have called "Rutter Country'. In Jhansi, Kotah and Gwalior, her statues still dominate the local scenery and, for a handful of rupees, you can buy highly coloured dolls in her likeness. They sit on scarlet chargers, ill-favoured blobs of cloth representing young Damodar tied to her saddle, sharp little curves of steel in either fabric hand. I bought such a doll in Jhansi when I was researching this book; as I packed her away in my suitcase, one of her miniature swords stabbed my finger. A drop of blood fell from my palm and when I looked closely into her beady eyes I swear she was smiling!

Technical language, military pidgin and foreign phrases I have attempted to explain or translate in the glossary. The idiom is, I hope, self-explanatory but anything that isn't clear or is inaccurate is entirely my own fault and flies in the face of advice that I have received.

Historical Note

The Indian Mutiny of 1857–1859 came as a bitter surprise to Queen Victoria's Empire and shook it more fundamentally than any other conflict of her reign. The independence of the HEIC was matched only by its dependence upon Britain (or 'England' as the Victorians might say), and her acquiescence in its expansion. Yet it's a mistake to think that all of Britain's possessions in India rose against their colonial masters. Of the three presidencies into which India was divided by the British, only Bengal turned – and then not all of it. Bombay and Madras, after some shaky moments, remained largely loyal.

So, mutinous Bengal was restored to the Raj mainly by other Indian troops, including Sikhs (whom the British had only recently subdued) and the Gurkhas. The internecine fighting between tribes, castes and religions had more of a feel of a civil war rather than an insurrection against an oppressor. No wonder, then, that Morgan and the 95th found it all so confusing! The relatively small number of Queen's regiments who found themselves in India when the trouble started, or who were sent there to suppress it, were usually profoundly impressed by the skill at arms of their Indian comrades and, indeed, the mutineers.

I suspect that service in the HEIC for a young British officer was considered distinctly second-rate in comparison to the Queen's Service. An HEIC commission cost a fraction of a British one; indeed, an HEIC officer was an employee of a private company and not the Crown – so transfers between the two regimes was impossible. Many Queen's officers sneered at HEIC officers and the troops they commanded, until they experienced their fighting qualities.

But what of the mutineers – or Pandies, as the British preferred? Those who fought at the great pitched battles of Delhi, Lucknow and Cawnpore were easily recognised by the British as products of the same system and, from time to time, bested their teachers. The 95th's foes, though, were rather more mixed. By the time that central Bengal had risen, regiments such as Kemp's 12th BNI were in the minority; irregulars, maharajahs and maharanis' local forces predominated. Whilst their quality was uncertain, the weaponry they used was distinctly exotic, giving a medieval feel to the fighting that dismays McGucken so much.

Post-Mutiny reorganisations saw the disappearance of 'John Company', amalgamations and changes in the Indian regiments with absorption into the British regular Army of such units as the 3rd Bombay Europeans (who became the 109th Foot). The proportion of British regiments in India's garrison was increased, but the 'new' armies weren't to be tested seriously until the Second Afghan War of 1878–1880.

Perhaps the saddest legacy of the Mutiny was the erosion of trust between native and British soldiers that it caused. Some Indian units, such as the Sikhs and the Gurkhas, were exempted but for the majority a friction – most notable, I suspect, amongst the junior ranks – sprang up that hadn't existed before. The mutual respect borne in wars such as those in Persia and China before the Mutiny seems to have disappeared. It's interesting to note, for instance, that British soldiers in India were still being tattooed with images of the well at Cawnpore (down which so many Europeans were thrown) as late as the 1940s.

Morgan, his sons, McGucken and Pegg all go on to witness the reformed Indian Army in action in Afghanistan in 1880. Without stealing any of the thunder of the next novel, the comparisons to today's campaign on the Helmand River are quite remarkable. The battles are fought over almost exactly the same patches of desert, over similar issues and against a political backdrop that is depressingly familiar. As Hegel said, 'Nations and governments have never learnt anything from history.'